MADE MEN 1

NERO

SARAH BRIANNE

YOUNG INK PRESS

Young Ink Press Publication
YoungInkPress.com

Copyright © 2014 by Sarah Brianne
Edited by C&D Editing and Hot Tree Editing
Cover Art by Young Ink Press
Book design by Inkstain Design Studio
Text set in Centaur.
All rights reserved.

This book is a work of fiction. Names, characters, places, and incidents either are products of the author's imagination or are used fictitiously. Any resemblance to actual persons, living or dead, events, or locales is entirely coincidental.

This work of fiction is intended for mature audiences only. All sexually active characters portrayed in this ebook are eighteen years of age or older. Please do not buy if sexual situations, violence, drugs, child abuse, and explicit language offends you.

Connect with Sarah:
AuthorSarahBrianne@gmail.com
www.facebook.com/AuthorSarahBrianne
@AuthorSarahBri

NERO

HIGH SCHOOL DROPOUTS

Elle sat in Spanish, *staring* at the clock. She swore the classroom was a hundred degrees.

With three minutes until lunch, she really missed Christmas break. Not once during the entire break had she gotten this sick feeling. No matter how many times the sensation took over her body, she could never become used to it. It was like an impending doom kind of feeling.

Elle hated school. No, Elle despised school with all her being. The one reason she was surviving Legacy Prep High was because of her only friend in the world, Chloe Masters.

Chloe needed her. Yes, Elle was bullied, but Chloe, now she was tortured. Elle would do anything to keep her safe. She deserved a protector, especially after what had happened.

All the money Elle had saved up working this Christmas break had to go to her high school tuition. Otherwise, she would get kicked out, and that would mean no protection for Chloe. Elle luckily had a scholarship to pay most of her tuition because of her grades, but she had to pay the rest by working at the diner almost every night.

Two minutes until lunch. *I thought when you stared at a clock, it was supposed to make time go slower.*

Elle was dreading lunch. The students hadn't been able to pick on her and Chloe since the last day before break, which meant they were all going to let out their pent-up aggression on them. God help them.

With one minute until lunch, Elle turned her head to see Chloe since the clock was no longer serving her any purpose. Her heart broke a little. Chloe's head was, of course, hung down, and she was wringing her hands in her lap. That was her thing whenever she was nervous.

She pictured her sweet face under her sheet of hair, marred by the deep slashes on her features. One stretched from two inches above her eyebrow down to the hollow in her cheek; the other slash was one inch above and below her lips. Both were on the right side of her face.

Elle shivered at the memory of seeing her for the first time since the new markings and then jumped when the lunch bell rang. She grabbed her satchel and stood.

You can do this. However, the sick feeling was because she really didn't believe she could.

She went to the door and felt Chloe at her back. This was where you could always find Chloe, right behind Elle, for the last three-and-a-half-years. Slowly, Chloe had started inching over every day until she walked just one step directly behind Elle. They had quickly learned that walking side by side meant a bigger target.

She stepped over the line into the hall and headed toward the cafeteria, walking a slow pace. She had a system down for the usual hall breaks; you wanted to take the shortest route to the next class unless there was a huge crowd. A huge crowd meant the ones who picked on them like Cassandra, the school's queen bee. She had learned to never linger because they were always better off in a classroom; the teachers usually stayed in it during hall breaks, waiting for their next class. Lastly, don't look anyone in the eyes. Although, Elle never kept her head down to the floor; that was a bad idea, plus she was never that type of person anyways.

This was the only time the halls were safe for them, though. The cafeteria awaited with far greater dangers for her and Chloe.

Elle reached the lunchroom and looked at her options. Here there were two lines. Line one was different each day, whether it was pizza, turkey, or meatloaf; it was whatever had been decided for the menu at the beginning of each month. Line two was always the same; chicken patty or hamburger and fries every day. However, Elle and Chloe didn't have two options; they had one—whichever line had the less scary people in it. It also meant they usually got stuck in the line that didn't taste the best.

Elle walked toward the back of the shortest line, all of the other students having thought the other option was better. Elle looked over to it, coming to the same conclusion.

Far better, she thought.

Elle saw two figures cut farther up in the line. She and Chloe didn't make a move to call a foul on it, though. It was better not to draw attention.

"You didn't call or text me one time over break. Didn't you miss me?" Cassandra wrapped her arms around Nero's neck.

Nero grabbed her waist. "Sorry, babe. I've been busy."

Nero Caruso. He was the definition of tall, dark, and handsome. He was more muscular than almost all of the other seniors but still slender. Cut is how Elle described that body-type. She could tell he had trimmed his hair over break. She thought it was strange because he'd always had it longer and slicked back for as long as she could remember. Now that it was much shorter, his hair had movement. She liked it better this way. "Does that mean you're too busy for me tonight?" Elle could see Cassandra's breasts rise higher.

In the next instant, Nero caught Elle staring. He held her gaze with his green eyes and then leaned down to whisper something in Cassandra's ear.

"Get a room!" someone yelled in the line.

Cassandra snapped her head back and caught them staring at each other, giving Elle a menacing look. With that, Elle was able to break the eye contact. She felt embarrassed to be caught gawking at them. She had trained herself to never look any of the students in the eye, especially during PDA.

Geez, what is wrong with me today? All Elle needed was to piss Cassandra off. She'd had it out for her since freshman year when a boy Cassandra must have liked complimented Elle on her hair.

4

Cassandra made sure to make Elle the school's target, and the boy had nothing to do with her from that moment on.

The line finally moved along and they were able to grab a tray. Lasagna, green beans, and applesauce were on the menu today. *Honestly, it could be worse.*

Taking a water out of the cooler, she reached the lunch lady, giving her lunch number to her. "1089."

"You can charge the first week only, Elle, then you need to either put money in your account or bring money with you every day." The lunch lady spoke louder than Elle thought necessary. "We are not going through this again this year."

Elle didn't think she could have felt any sicker. "I will." She moved over so Chloe could give her number.

"1072." Elle knew she could have, in fact, gotten sicker at the look on Chloe's frightened face knowing they would have to make it to their table now.

Elle started walking to their usual spot. There were several tables scattering the cafeteria. The studious students used the tables closest to the lines; they weren't picked on, just ignored really. The tables in the back of the cafeteria were used by the popular crowd. Elle and Chloe, on the other hand, had always eaten at the same table for the past three and a half years—the one closest to the door. This table was in-between the two sides but closest to the studious side. Just one table full of nerds separated Chloe and Elle from the popular kids. The robots.

Elle sat with her back to the door; she liked the full view of the cafeteria. Chloe sat opposite of her; she wanted the back of her head to the rest of the world.

"Did you sleep last night?" Elle asked sympathetically. Elle knew Chloe never slept much with the nightmares, but today she looked like she hadn't even slept a full hour last night. She looked pale, almost ghostly. Her black hair was now dull as it attempted to conceal the right side of her face. She noticed the hollows under her stark, gray eyes.

"Not much. I really didn't want to start school back up, I guess." Chloe forced a smile for her friend.

Elle looked at Chloe sympathetically. "Don't worry, Chloe. This will be our last semester of high school. Then, we don't have to see the robots' faces ever again. Besides, maybe forty-five minutes will go quicker than we remember," Elle said, trying to make light of their situation.

"We were gone three weeks, Elle, not three years," Chloe replied lightly.

"Hey, a lot can happen in three weeks. Robots could have asked for a heart over break." They both laughed over that.

"If that was the case, then my whole high school career was one long nightmare and I will wake up right…" Chloe squeezed her eyes shut and opened them a second later, "Now. Well, it looks like no one asked Glenda the Good Witch for help." Elle laughed hard and Chloe couldn't help joining in. Elle was glad when Chloe loosened up.

They both began eating their lunch while Elle carefully looked at the robot's tables. That side was actually pretty diverse. You had a few athlete tables consisting of a full football team table and the rest being a mixture of baseball, softball, basketball and soccer. This left just a few tables.

Her most hated table was the fashionista one, who only bought designer labels and were all mostly cheerleaders. Cassandra was, of course, the head of that table. The table adjoining Cassandra's consisted of the filthy rich, and I mean, filthy. They were all boys with the head being Sebastian, which was Cassandra's twin brother. Elle shivered in fright at not only the sight of him, but the sound of his name.

This brought you to the final table, which Elle really couldn't describe. Three guys had always sat there; one was Nero, who was basically the king of Legacy Prep, and the other two were his crew, as the school liked to call them. The big one was Amo and the smaller one was Vincent; both were seniors, as well. However, Elle noticed a new boy sitting with them.

He must be a freshman. Elle wondered who he was. All she could see was his dirty-blond hair from the back.

She suddenly felt like someone had stepped in her personal space. That was when she realized she had made a huge mistake—she'd dropped her guard.

"I have been looking for you all day. I have a little mess and I needed the waitress to clean up for me." Cassandra took Elle's plate and pushed it off the table. Then the high-pitched screech of her voice started back again. "Go on, clean it up, waitress."

The whole cafeteria grew silent at her words. That word *waitress* made Elle's skin crawl, and yet it might as well be her birth name here as far as they were concerned.

Elle thought about the two options she had. Option one: blatantly ignore it or pretend you didn't hear it; and option two: respond with either a witty response or a few short words. She chose the first then stared at Chloe, wishing she hadn't by her panicked expression.

"Bitch, I know you hear me." Cassandra took Chloe's plate and held it above her head. Chloe quickly tried to move out of the way, but two of Cassandra's fake blonde bimbos moved to stand on either side of her, forcing her to sit back down. "Clean up the mess like a waitress is supposed to do, or the little freak will have her own mess to clean up."

Freak was the only other word that made her skin crawl more than waitress.

Elle felt a washrag hit her face, courtesy of Sebastian. She took a moment to see Chloe wringing her hands. She didn't want this for her.

Okay, this couldn't be worse. Of all days to have the three messiest foods. Elle swallowed her pride and picked up the washrag. Then she really swallowed her pride when she got down to clean the mess up off the floor.

When Elle was done shaming herself, she walked over to Chloe. "Come on, Chloe. Let's go." She held her hand out. She knew Chloe would never take it, but she would get the message to get out of there.

"Sorry, you missed a spot." Cassandra was about to tip the plate over Chloe's head, and as a result, Elle did the only thing she could think of. She pushed the plate harder in the opposite direction, all over Cassandra.

The cafeteria was filled with mixed emotions. Some couldn't help laughing while the others were too in shock of what had just happened to react at all. Elle felt sicker than she had ever been in her whole life. She was seriously about to vomit up the little lunch she hadn't mopped off the floor.

"You fucking bitch!" Cassandra's voice screeched higher than anyone thought imaginable. "You are done."

Elle knew only one option remained now. Run.

Elle grabbed the back of Chloe's shirt. She was in serious shock, but not enough to hinder her from getting the hell out of dodge. Elle ran straight for the door; this was the whole reason they sat at the table closest to it.

Right before she was going to pass through it, though, she noticed Mr. Evans standing in the doorway. Mr. Evans was her first period English teacher and the only English teacher in Legacy Prep who believed you could be creative in English; not to mention he was nice to look at—all the girls had a crush on him since he started teaching here at the beginning of the year.

Shit, she was trapped. Elle stood there, knowing she was a goner. There was no way anyone did that to Cassandra and got away with it.

"Elle, Chloe, go on back to class," Mr. Evans spoke calmly, maybe too calmly, but Elle wasn't about to waste another second of this golden ticket. She had just won the damn lottery.

Elle and Chloe high-tailed it out of the lunchroom. On their way out, Elle heard Mr. Evans calmly speak.

"Ms. Ross, clean up the mess you just made. I can't have other students thinking they can get away with this, now can I? Oh, and when you're done, meet me in the Vice Principal's off..." His voice trailed away.

I am so screwed. No, I am beyond screwed.

When they reached the Spanish classroom and the door came to a close, Elle spoke first.

"I am so sorry, Chloe. It was just a reaction. I didn't want her to spill it on you."

"I know, but what are we going to do? She is going to kill us. You know that." Elle couldn't tell if Chloe was winded by the run or frightened for her life.

Elle sat down and dropped her head on the desk. "I have no clue." She looked back up at Chloe. "Any suggestions?"

"Yeah, we become high school dropouts." Chloe might have sounded sarcastic, yet that couldn't have been closer to the truth.

BIMBO #1

Elle and Chloe were genuinely scared for their life when the bell rang once more to end Spanish class. They were doomed.

The next class she and Chloe had they would be separated. Elle had art class; Chloe had taken it her freshman year; therefore, she couldn't take it with her. So Chloe had health class, and of course, Elle had taken that *her* freshman year. It was a shame their whole lives had changed after they had made their schedules for freshman year.

Elle knew she had to drop Chloe off at her health class first. Unfortunately, it meant double the amount of hallway time for herself. *Great.*

Elle regretfully entered the hallway with Chloe at her back. She picked up maximum speed without drawing too much attention to herself and Chloe. Thankfully, Chloe's class wasn't too far from their Spanish class anyways. Elle was grateful to reach the classroom unscathed.

"Wait at your desk when the bell rings. I will be back to get you. I promise I will be the first one out in the hallway."

Chloe bit her lip. "Um, okay, I won't move from my seat."

"Good, I will see you in a little bit." Elle hoped she sounded strong for Chloe.

"Be careful, Elle."

That sincere, sweet voice made it hard for Elle to turn her back on her best friend and head to class. Although, now Elle had to worry about getting herself safely to class since she knew Cassandra would be waiting for her.

She picked up her feet and hurried as fast as she could.

Elle took a seat. She usually sat in the back of the classroom, but she needed to be close to the door. She was glad, if she was separated from Chloe, it was art class. This was an easy course and wouldn't require partners. She remembered Chloe had said her own class had been small and they had never been paired up. "Partners" was the worst thing a girl at the bottom of the food chain could hear.

Elle sank in her seat when Cassandra's blonde bimbos strutted through the door. *Of freaking course.*

When they took their seats at the other side of the classroom, they stared Elle down. *I am completely screwed.*

They whispered something to each other and one of them picked up their phones to send a text. *Nope, now I am completely screwed.*

Elle knew they'd texted Cassandra exactly where to find her. She thought about texting Chloe that she might be dead soon, but she knew Chloe would worry and leave her desk when the bell rang.

At least when Cassandra came for her, Chloe would be safe where she was, and by the time she decided to leave, most of the students would have gone home.

Right before class started, Nero walked in and took a seat at the popular table, which consisted of Cassandra's bimbos and a few athletes. They each only cared about one thing, status. Status meant their whole life to them. Elle thought, if she had a dollar for every time she heard the word *status*, she would be able to pay for her tuition ten times over.

Elle looked around the room. She was the only person to sit by herself at a table, completely aware of where she stood at Legacy Prep. Even the nerds knew they couldn't talk to Elle. They wouldn't even dare to look at her. Elle never blamed them, either. *It's a dog-eat-dog world in here.*

As soon as class began, the teacher wanted them to go ahead and start their first project. It was easy; all they had to do was make a poster that best showed their individual personality, using any materials they desired.

Elle stared at her blank white poster, wondering exactly who she was. Well, *she* knew who she was, but these walls made it hard for her to be herself. No, she just *couldn't* be herself here.

She was strawberry-blonde, her hair reaching the top of her breasts, and had big blue eyes. She had a slight tan to her skin, which contrasted her hair and eye color. She liked that, being different and having character; unlike the other kids her age who strove to all look the same. She believed she looked younger than the other girls her age, although maybe it was the lack of makeup and fancy clothes. She couldn't quite tell. Regardless, her looks did not define *who* she was.

She opened her bag and took out a sheet of paper. She thought she should draw the poster out first to try to come up with some ideas.

After several attempts, it became hard for Elle to concentrate. The bimbos were laughing so damn loud she thought they were going to go into heat any second. The hottest athletes, not to mention the king of Legacy Prep, surrounded them.

Elle looked at the clock. It wasn't too much longer before school let out. She zoned out, a lot on her mind.

Cassandra was going to kill her, She couldn't protect Chloe at the moment. She was supposed to close at the diner tonight, and she had to find time to do her five-hundred-word essay Mr. Evans assigned about who you love the most. *Yeah, if I even live till then.*

Elle felt a pat on her back, snapping her back to the present. "I hope you make it to see the freak on time. It would be a shame if something were to happen." That was Bimbo Number One, the one closest to Cassandra.

Then, the next thing she knew, all Elle could hear was the squirting of paint all over her. *No, not my big, comfortable white sweater!*

The whole class couldn't help laughing at her torture. That was honestly what hurt Elle the most; not one person would ever rescue her, all they would do was laugh.

"You can thank me later, waitress. I know you've needed a reason to visit Goodwill."

Elle had dealt with enough for the day, and Chloe wasn't there to get hurt by her repercussions. If she was going to die today, at least she was going down with a fight.

Brrring.

Chloe. Elle grabbed her bag and ran out of the classroom unbelievably fast, her retaliation instantly forgotten. Chloe needed her.

That was when it dawned on her. '*I hope you make it to see the freak on time.*' She finally understood—the only way to hurt her was to hurt Chloe.

Oh, shit! I'm coming, Chloe. Elle ran fast down the hallway; she didn't jog or walk fast, she ran. At that point, it didn't matter if she drew attention to herself.

When Elle ran into Chloe's classroom, she came to a halt. She couldn't believe her eyes. Her heart actually skipped a beat.

"Chloe, are you okay?"

FIGHT FIRE WITH FIRE

Elle had walked in to see Mr. Evans talking to Chloe, her elbows on her desk and hands concealing her face.

Chloe looked up. "Yes, I'm fine, El—" Her eyes grew wider. "Are you okay? What happened?" Chloe stood and walked over toward her.

Elle's eyes wandered over to Mr. Evans. "Um, I accidentally spilled paint on myself in art. What are you all talking about?"

Mr. Evans walked over to them. "I was just passing by and saw Chloe in here by herself, so I was making sure everything was okay. Usually, the kids are practically one foot out the door before the last bell even rings."

"Yeah, I know what you mean. She's my ride, and I just told her we would meet up in here."

"How come you met up here and not in your art class? The art class is all the way at the front of the school by the outside door." Elle thought Mr. Evan's face didn't look confused in the least.

"I guess we didn't think about it like that." Elle started walking out of the classroom. "I'll see you in the morning, Mr. Evans. Come on, Chloe; I need to get ready for work." Elle hoped he would let it go.

Chloe joined Elle and they both headed out into the hallway.

"Elle, if you ever need to talk, you know where to find me." Elle turned around at Mr. Evan's voice. "Try and be more careful in art. Next time, it might not be paint that spills."

Nope, he couldn't let it go. At that, Elle kept walking. "Have a good night, Mr. Evans."

They walked through the school, and when they reached the outside, Elle and Chloe felt like a weight had been lifted, like they were almost free.

"So, who spilled the paint? And dang, all over your outfit. That one was my favorite on you."

Elle looked down at her body. *Damn, she even got my favorite pair of faded jeans.* "One of Cassandra's sidekicks."

"Which one? Her?" She nodded toward Nero, who was standing beside his Cadillac with Bimbo Number Two.

Elle could hear them speaking. "Nero, would you mind giving me a ride home? I rode with Cassandra this morning." She leaned against his car, giving him a sweet smile.

"No problem, babe." Nero's eyes traveled from her eyes to her chest. "Leo, let's go!"

Elle had seen a young boy running over to his car. He was honestly a miniature version of Nero, especially before he had cut his hair. The only difference between them was the kid had dirty-blond hair. Elle realized he was the new one who had sat at Nero's table.

"Backseat, Leo." Elle thought Leo made the cutest face at his remark before they all climbed in the car, slamming doors and bringing Elle back.

"No, the other one." Elle shook her head. *I really need to snap out of it.*

Elle and Chloe got into Chloe's BMW. Unlike the other kids' cars, which were all various Mercedes, Porsches, and Lamborghinis galore; it was classy. Not too expensive, not too flashy. Granted, Chloe would never have picked something like that out for herself, but her politician father had given her no choice.

When the doors were shut, Chloe spoke, her face full of concern. "Elle, is something wrong? You're acting weird today."

"I'm fine, Chloe. I guess I'm just getting tired of this same shit every day."

"Listen, Elle, you don't have to stay. You're free to go. If your parents found out how you're treated here, they wouldn't let you come ba—"

Elle's eyes drilled into Chloe's. "I am not leaving you, Chloe. I've told you this a thousand times."

"Well, we have survived this long by not getting into it with them. I am not like you, Elle." Chloe looked down at her steering wheel.

Elle stared at Chloe, knowing exactly what she was asking of her. "All right, Chloe. I won't fight back. I promise."

With that, Chloe pushed the button to start her car. "Fighting back doesn't solve anything, Elle. You know that."

Elle nodded and smiled at Chloe. *No, I used to think that.* Today, however, revelation had come over Elle. You had to fight fire with fire.

Elle walked into her front door, waving to Chloe as she closed it then rested her head against it.

"Everything okay, sweetie?"

Elle jumped up. "Oh, hey, Mom. Yeah, everything is great; just tired is all." Elle scanned the living room. "Is Dad in the kitchen?"

"No, um, he's in bed sleeping."

"Has he not gotten up all day?" Elle started to worry.

"No, sweetie, he just laid down for a nap." Elle's mom gave her a smile. Even she didn't buy her own words.

"All right. I'll be in my room doing my homework before I head to work."

Elle walked through her house, but when she passed her parents' bedroom, she stopped and wondered if she should go in to check on her father. *Maybe later. I'm already depressed as it is.*

Elle went into her room and turned on her computer.

Who do I love the most? She contemplated about her essay. Evans' English class was by far her favorite; she wanted to be a writer someday. She honestly knew the answer. Yet, she felt a little betrayed at the moment by her father - the person she loved the most.

Regardless of how little her father talks, he would always wish her a good first day of school, and this would have been the last time. She decided to put her feelings aside for the sake of her grade. She got about halfway done before she looked at the clock and realized she needed to get ready for work.

She dressed in her uniform, which she hated probably more than life itself. She was convinced it was twenty years old since the red had turned into more of a burned-out orange. *At least, I'm pretty sure it used to be red.*

Elle threw on her pea coat, her best Goodwill buy to date.

When she was finally ready for work, she walked out of her bedroom and headed toward the kitchen.

"Hey, Josh. How was the first day back?" Elle couldn't help forgetting about all her problems when she saw her eight-year-old brother's face.

"Fine, I guess." Josh shrugged. "How about yours, Elle-bell?"

Elle looked hard at Josh. Other than his blond hair, she felt as if she might have been looking in a mirror because of his expression. "Fine, I guess." She decided she would need to talk to him soon; find out how school really was going. "That smells good, Mom. Save me some for later?"

"Of course, sweetie. Oh, your dad is in the living room." Elle's mom gave her a real smile this time.

Elle walked into the living room where she waited for her dad to say something, but he never did.

She went for the door, but before she opened it, she said, "School was great, Dad."

She was honestly disheartened. Not only had he not wished her a good last first day, as was his tradition, but now he hadn't even asked how it had gone.

Brushing off the hurt feelings, Elle walked outside. The cold air against her skin made her happy. The smell was always crisp and clean. There was just something about the sound of hearing her boots crunching in the snow that lifted her spirits instantaneously.

Elle walked to the bus stop, and from there the bus would take her downtown. When she boarded the bus, she took a window seat, looking out at the passing scenery. She really did love Kansas City, Missouri. It was her home; however, the past few years had made her feel like she didn't belong anymore.

Maybe I do need to leave with Chloe.

Her stop came up and she exited the bus, heading down the few blocks it took to get to the diner from there. While walking, Elle didn't mind the noise and action; she liked watching the passersby going out for the night.

However, it wasn't long before Elle's attention was drawn by two men standing outside of the Kansas City Casino Hotel, which was right next door to the diner. One had bags under his eyes; Elle thought he must have been on something. He kept looking over his shoulder, like someone could be coming for him any second. The other one was sternly speaking to him. She couldn't hear what he was saying, but Elle knew he was trying to get him under control.

When Elle passed in front of them, she heard the cool one say,

"The big boss gave you a job. You don't have a fucking choice." The thick, Italian accent made it difficult to hear with the city noise.

Elle kept walking. She didn't care about whatever it was; it was none of her freaking business.

She entered the diner and hung her coat up on the rack. It was an old diner in need of a serious upgrade. The downtown buildings were all old, although some had kept the same flare they had possessed many years ago. *Like this dress I'm forced to wear.*

Elle didn't mind work. She got to meet people she would have never met under regular circumstances, especially with the casino hotel next door. The tips were never bad, either. She did make enough to pay the rest of her tuition at school.

Once she'd clocked in, Elle started waiting her tables. Monday was always a slow night because everyone was mostly too tired from the weekend. This made work pass slowly for her, forcing her to hear her own thoughts. Yet, after today, she didn't want to think.

She was one of the two employees on the schedule to close tonight; consequently, she hoped it would pick up soon, since otherwise she would lose her mind.

As the time passed on, Elle was never freed from her thoughts, though. The diner only ever had a few people in and out the whole night. Thirty minutes before closing, she started to clean up to get ready for the morning. In no time, she was done and only had the trash left to take out. Therefore, she went to put on her coat and grab her purse.

Afterward, picking up the trash bag, she went into the kitchen and called out, "I'll see you tomorrow, Steve. Have a good night." Steve was the diner's cook.

"Later, Elle." He kept at cleaning his stove.

Elle went out the back door to throw away the trash, planning on leaving from the alley between the diner and the Casino Hotel. She locked the back door and threw the trash into the dumpster. Elle had turned around to start her walk to the bus stop when she heard voices entering the alleyway.

"Please, please, don't kill me."

"Shut him the fuck up before I blow his brains out right here."

Elle ran to hide behind the dumpster. She knew she did not want to come face to face with that voice.

She could hear some footsteps come closer. "All clear, boss."

As they all entered the area behind the diner, Elle couldn't help peeping from behind the dumpster. It was pitch black from where she was, yet she was able to see four men thanks to the light from the diner. One was dressed in an expensive suit, his dark hair combed back. He was an older man. Under normal circumstances, she believed he would be super-sexy and handsome, but right now, he scared the piss out of her. He was definitely the one in charge.

Before I blow his brains out. Yep, that was him.

She noticed the man being held with his mouth shut was the crazed guy from earlier, who had been standing outside the casino hotel. A younger man was holding him, looking almost as scary as the one in charge. She believed him to be twenty years old, though he could possibly be scarier than the *boss*.

"Go get the car, Sal, and be quick about it." Elle could feel nothing other than chills when she heard his voice. *Damn, that man is scary.*

"Sure thing, boss." The third man wasn't as frightening as the others. He might have been if the two Hannibal Lecters weren't standing there, however.

The man ran out of the alley as fast as he could.

A minute passed, and Elle could tell the poor man knew his fate. He possibly looked more scared than Elle was at the moment. His instincts started kicking in and he tried to fight off the one holding him, biting the hand covering his mouth. The man dropped his hand before he thought he would lose it, giving the man free reign to scream.

Before he could let a cry for help escape, the one called Boss pulled a gun from the inside of his suit jacket. With that, Elle couldn't look anymore. She knew what was going to come next.

Bang.

One was all it took.

Elle started to hyperventilate, covering her mouth before they could hear. She knew if she didn't stay quiet, she would be next.

A car skidded up, and she heard the doors open and bodies being shuffled in. Before the doors were even shut, the car skidded right back out.

Elle kept her mouth covered as tears started to well in her eyes. She needed to get out of there in case anyone came back to clean up the mess. *You can do this.*

When she peeked out from behind the dumpster once more, no one was in sight. At that point, Elle couldn't let herself think anymore; she needed to let her body take over. She jumped out from behind the dumpster and did the only thing she could do—run the hell away.

Sal stopped the car outside of his boss's home. *Thank fucking God I'm home.* The piss smell of the dead body was getting to him.

"Sal, go back to the Casino and get rid of the tapes and make sure his piss is cleaned out of my car." It hadn't been the smartest thing to kill that dumb-fuck in the alley right where he worked, knowing people would hear the gunshot and they didn't have time to clean up the blood, but he told himself, he hadn't had a choice.

"Okay, boss, I'll call you when it's done."

"Lucca, get rid of this piece of shit and don't come home with that blood on your fucking shirt. Whatever slut you got at home tonight don't need to be turned on by that shit. Capiche?" He was mad at his son. He shouldn't have let his fucking hand get bit. He had risked everything the boss had worked for his whole life.

His son gave him a quick nod. The boss could tell he was disappointed in himself. The only reason he knew was because he wore the exact same face the boss made when he fucked up. His son was growing more and more like him every day. He knew he was sure as hell just as scary as him; it was just the lack of experience.

He got out of the town car and went up to his house. He needed a fucking drink after that mess. He picked up the bottle, poured the brown liquid into his glass and then went to his cigar box and pulled one out. Sitting down behind his huge desk in his big leather chair, he started to settle. There was nothing like whiskey in one hand and a cigar in the other to calm his nerves.

An hour passed, and his thoughts became less gruesome. He led a hard life running the family and this city; however, he wouldn't have it any other way. He belonged at the top, and everybody else knew it, too.

A knock came at his door, ruining his alone time.

Sighing, he let out a harsh, "Come in."

"Boss, I ain't got good news." He was holding a laptop in his hand.

He pinched the bridge of his nose and handed Sal his glass. "Fill the glass to how bad the news fucking is."

Sal went over to the alcohol station where he quickly poured the glass half-full. After a second, he decided to say fuck it and filled the glass to the rim.

"Fuck, Sal, bring me the damn glass and tell me the bad news already." The boss understood, whatever it was, it was nothing he wanted to hear in this lifetime.

"Good news for you, you get a fucking front-row seat, boss." He opened the laptop and pressed a button on the keyboard.

He knew exactly what he was watching, a surveillance of the alleyway. Luckily for him, it also showed behind the diner next to his casino.

The first few seconds showed nothing. It was almost as if Sal hadn't pressed play yet. Then a young girl came out from the back of the diner with a trash bag, walking over and then throwing it in the dumpster. A second later, he saw her run behind the dumpster and into the darkness. He could no longer make her out.

"Fuck."

"Oh, wait, boss, it gets better." The boss didn't like his fucking tone.

He saw the whole murder play out. Nothing changed from his mind; he knew what the fuck had happened. He downed the shot glass. He knew exactly what was going to come once the town car sped away, and damned if the girl didn't run out from behind the dumpster exactly how he'd played it out in his mind. Then she was gone.

Sal slammed the laptop closed.

"Who is she?" He knew Sal better have some fucking answers.

"Elle Buchanan. She works at the diner next door. We do have another problem, though, Bo—"

"Fuck, Sal, how much worse could this shit get?" He was over it. He knew the girl would die, so what the fuck was the problem?

"She's a senior at Legacy Prep High, boss. She's still seventeen for the next month. I know you're against whacking kids, but she's practically an adul—"

"What the fuck did you just say?" He didn't like what had just come out of Sal's fucking mouth. This family was built on rules, and not even he liked to break the family rules. Furthermore, out of all these rules, this was one he would *never* break.

"Sorry, boss, I shouldn't have said it. I just want to protect the family." Sal started to get nervous; you never disrespected the boss.

He stood from his chair and looked Sal in the eye. Flexing his jaw, he said, "I fucking say how to protect this family, capiche?"

Sal swallowed then nodded. "Capiche. So, how are we going to handle this?"

He walked over to pour himself another drink. "Leave the laptop. I'll destroy the tape and handle this myself."

Sal left the room at that. His boss had said he would handle it, and he knew he would.

Taking the full glass with him, he sat behind his desk again. He had an idea. Not only could he take care of the girl, he could see where an upcoming soldier's loyalties lay.

He pulled out his cell phone, and within two short rings, he heard a girl's squeal come over the line.

"Yes?"

"Tell the girl to scram. I have a job for you, son." With that, he ended the call.

The girl's squeal helped solidify his notion that his son could get the job done. He would find out what exactly the girl had seen and if she needed to be taken care of on her eighteenth birthday.

As a knock came to his door for the second time tonight, his son, unlike Sal, didn't wait for his approval to come in. The boss studied Nero as he walked into the room. His dark hair was wet and he smelled of sex. For the first time tonight, the boss actually smiled.

He's just the one for the job.

REAL DEAL WHACKING AND ALL

lle understood the crazed man. She was turning into a crazed person herself. She ran to the bus stop as fast as her legs could take her, and when she was on the bus, she stared at everyone around her, wondering if one of them was going to kill her right there. When she got off, she ran as fast as her legs could take her again until she reached her front door.

Her hands were shaking so badly she barely managed to get the door unlocked. It took a few tries before the key made it into the slot. Jerking the door free, she slammed it and deadlocked it. Afterward, she stood, staring out of the peephole for five minutes. She could feel in her bones that someone was going to come for her.

"What are you do—"

Elle jumped and screamed so loudly she practically pissed herself. "Jesus, Dad, you scared me half to death."

"Why are you staring out the door? Was someone following you?" Elle could feel her dad start to worry.

"No, of course not. I thought I saw...a big dog or something." Elle looked through the peephole again. *Okay, this is the last time.*

"Well, whatever it is, it isn't going to claw through the door."

Elle forced a laugh. "Yeah, you're right." *Okay, this is really the last time.* She peeped through the hole.

"Uh, Elle, I was about to heat me up some of your mom's dinner; why don't you come eat with me? I know you don't eat the diner's food." He was right, but seeing a man murdered had really made her lose her appetite. *For the rest of my life.*

"No, thanks, I'm really not hungry. I don't feel too well, Dad." She really wanted to go to her bedroom.

"Elle, please?" The look on her dad's face made it to where she couldn't refuse.

"Okay, Dad. Want me to roll you in?" Elle smiled as big as she could. When her dad nodded, she grabbed the handlebars of his wheelchair and rolled him through the living room and into the kitchen where she put him at the table.

"Here, let me make you a plate." She went to the fridge and pulled out the leftovers, making him a plate of fried chicken and mashed potatoes. She heated it up in the microwave and then set it in front of him with a fork.

"I'm sorry about today, Elle. Last night was miserable for me. I couldn't take it anymore, so I took some of my pain pills. I've been out of it all day." He sat, picking at his food.

"It's okay, Dad. I know this whole thing has been hard on you these last few years." Elle really did understand. Losing the ability to walk is something she would never have been able to deal with.

"It's no excuse to be drugged out of my mind. I promise I will try to be better." He looked her in the eyes. He needed her to believe him this time.

Every few months, he would get like this. The aches and mental pain would break him down, make him swallow those pills.

"I know you will, Dad." Elle touched his hand. She really did want to believe him.

Her dad picked up the chicken leg and took a big bite. *Oh, gosh.*

"You sure you're not hungry, Elle? You look like you haven't eaten in days." He wiped his mouth on the back of his hand.

I think I'm going to hurl.

"I'm not very hungry. I think I'm becoming a vegetarian." Elle got up from the table; she had to get out of there. "Night, Dad."

"Goodnight, Elle-bell."

If Elle wasn't about to throw up at what she had seen that night, she would have been happy. She loved her father more than anyone and hated when he decided to become someone else, even if it was just a day. *It used to be months.*

When Elle finally made it to her room, she threw off her uniform and got into her pajamas. She lay down on the bed, staring at the ceiling.

What the hell just happened? Elle had no clue what to do.

Call the cops? She knew no amount of cops could save her from that man. She would have to go into Witness Protection, and he would still probably find her.

Skip town? Then that meant no protection for Chloe.

Nope. Tell my parents? She knew that just brought her back to her parents calling the cops or skipping town.

So, clearly, my only option is pretending it didn't happen. Well, at least until he finds me. Who is he?

She needed to find out who he was so she could at least see him coming. Elle decided to replay what had happened that night. It was hard for her to do since the only thing she could remember was the sound of the gun going off.

Then a word started to stick out in her mind—Boss. She remembered the least-scary man had called him boss. *Boss?* Then another memory struck her mind. *The big boss gave you a job. You don't have a fucking choice.* The crazed man had been scared for his life. He had known his fate hours before. A grown man had been scared to death of him. *The big boss, job, no choice.*

Holy shit, I just watched someone get whacked!

Elle had heard the rumors and stories ever since she had been born in Kansas City about it being one of the mob capitals of the United States. She thought the stuff was for the movies, though; that they really were just rumors.

She forced her eyes shut and pictured the boss. She saw an older, dark-haired, handsome man wearing a suit.

Oh, God, they even wear suits.

Elle knew she had just met the mob boss of Kansas City; that he was the real deal, whacking and all.

I am so fucked.

Elle sat in English the next morning, barely listening to Mr. Evans when he addressed the class. With everything that had happened last night, she had forgotten to finish her essay. The whole morning had actually been a blur; she couldn't even quite remember how the hell she'd ended up here.

"Elle, Elle, Elle?" Elle looked up at Mr. Evans.

"Uh-huh?" Elle was lost today as well.

"Do you have your essay to turn into me?"

Elle felt everyone staring at her. She was sure this would just add to her bullying.

"My essay? No, sorry." Elle watched Mr. Evans walk on to the next student.

When Mr. Evans walked up to the front of the classroom, she noticed an empty seat where Cassandra had sat yesterday. She looked around the room, wondering if she'd decided to move.

Hmm, no Cassandra?

She took that as a blessing since she had never missed a school day. Not ever. If a girl like her missed a day, she felt as if she had missed a year of her life. Cassandra had to be in everyone's business, thus missing a day meant missing something potentially good.

Elle still felt like eyes were watching her. She looked around the room again; she couldn't find anyone sticking out, though. It wasn't like she was a particular point of interest, especially when Mr. Evans had laid out a strict no-bullying policy in his classroom.

Elle heard the bell ring and looked at the clock.

Gosh, next class already?

She and Chloe packed up their things and started heading for the door.

"Elle, can I speak to you for a second?"

Elle looked at Chloe and hoped she understood to stay put.

She walked over to Mr. Evans' desk. "Yes?"

"You don't strike me as the type to fail at turning in assignments."

"I think I caught a stomach bug last night. I actually did the first half of the assignment before work, and by the time I got home, I was too sick to finish. I apologize." Elle hoped he believed her. It was honestly the truth, minus the bloody details.

"That's okay. I wasn't actually going to grade them. It was just meant to see where each student actually stood in English. I will take it that you are at least average, since you hope to write as a profession." By his statement, Elle could tell he believed she was telling the truth. He was too good at sifting through truths and lies.

Well, ninety-nine percent of teenagers do lie about why they don't have their homework.

"Thank you, Mr. Evans. I appreciate it." Elle thought he really was a nice guy. No teacher had done what he had done for her and Chloe.

At the thought of Chloe, Elle looked back to see if she was there. She wasn't. *Dang, why would she do that?*

It was time for Elle to leave. She headed for the door.

"Don't let it happen again, Elle." Elle didn't care about his parting words. She went out the door and went straight for Pre-Cal.

Her butt better have made it to class.

Rushing too fast, Elle felt someone run into her. She had been so worried about Chloe she had forgotten to check who was in the hall to ruin her day.

As Elle felt arms around her waist, steadying her, she had to look up to see who was about to blame her for hitting them. *Nero. Great, of all people.*

"Sorry, I didn't mean—"

"Why are you apologizing?" Not once had he ever acknowledged her for her whole high school career, let alone spoken a word to her. What's more, right then his arms were still holding her waist. She also realized, up close, his voice was deep. She didn't like being this close to him; she tried to back up, but he wouldn't let her go.

"Tell me why you apologized, and I'll let you go."

She looked up at him, afraid he might hurt her at first, but his face showed no maliciousness. He merely looked genuinely curious. She really didn't know what to say; partly because she didn't know why she had apologized, and the other part of her was thrown off at his handsome face and deep voice.

"I-I don't know why I said sorry. It was instinct, I guess." She spoke to his chest; she couldn't look at him this close and speak directly to him.

She felt his arms drop after a few seconds and swore that, before he let her go, his hands made a bigger, deeper impression. She looked up at him again. He had really green eyes. She had never seen natural green eyes before.

"Do me a favor and don't apologize to anyone who doesn't deserve an apology. Got it?" He demanded an answer from her.

She didn't like demands. "Don't I deserve an apology, then?"

Nero smiled and took a step toward her. "I'm *not* sorry."

Elle stared at Nero.

Is this real?

She hadn't realized the bell had gone off and no one was roaming the halls. By the time she did, she began to feel uncomfortable. She didn't like the way Nero was making her feel.

"I better get to class." Elle needed to make sure Chloe had made it there okay.

She walked away quickly, far too uncomfortable. Moreover, she felt Nero watching her, making her even more self-conscious.

"Watch where you're walking next time." She didn't have to turn around to see he was smiling.

She reached Pre-Cal and was relieved to find Chloe. *She is not going to believe that Nero freaking Caruso talked to me.*

DON'T LIE TO ME

Elle decided to wait until lunch to tell Chloe what had occurred in the halls since anyone could listen in on them in the classroom. Plus, they would have something to talk about over lunch.

Elle found that, without Cassandra, no one paid any attention to them. It was like they were invisible. Some might think nothing could be worse than being invisible, but Elle and Chloe certainly liked being un-noticed. It was like they were on vacation. Hell, Elle would give anything to be Casper the friendly ghost and trade in her being-bullied days. Anyone who had never been bullied could never understand what she and Chloe went through five days a week.

Before Elle knew it, it was five minutes until lunch. She hadn't even thought about the murder once since the hallway break when Nero had run into her. She wondered what that meant, but then quickly pushed it out of her mind.

I should be in an asylum, yet I have never been happier. She thanked God for whatever the reason Cassandra not being there was.

The lunch bell rang and Elle and Chloe headed for the door. When they reached the hallway, Chloe spoke.

"This is the best day of my life!" For the first time in years, Elle saw Chloe smile at school, not to mention in the hallway.

"I know. Best freaking day ever. I wonder why Cassandra isn't here."

"Who cares? I never thought one person was the sole reason for high school being such a nightmare for us." Elle loved seeing Chloe like this.

"Yeah, me either." They walked in the cafeteria and looked at their choices. They still picked the line that was less intimidating, not wanting to push their luck. *Chicken patty day it is.*

They grabbed their lunches and sat at their usual table, and then Elle leaned over the table and said, "I have to tell you what happened when you left me this morning. By the way, what the hell? Why did you do that?"

"Because Mr. Evans said he needed to speak with you, not me. I knew it was about you not turning in your essay. He wasn't going to talk about it in front of me, you know that." Chloe picked up a fry and tossed it in her mouth. "Oh, and why didn't you turn in your essay? It was the first assignment of the semester."

"I was sick. Listen, I have to tell you something. You're not going to believe who talked to me and didn't want me dea—"

"You were sick? Really, that's the excuse you're giving me? I hope you didn't use that on him."

"Uh, yes, I was sick. That's the truth and he believed me. Why can't you?"

"Probably because not once have you *not* turned in an assignment, and you get sick all the time. You practically stay sick. There isn't anything that goes around that you don't catch."

Elle stared at Chloe. She was right; she was always getting sick. Her friend wouldn't take the sick card. However, Elle couldn't tell her that she had seen a man get whacked last night. She could never tell anyone she had seen what happened. Elle had watched the movies— the less you knew, the better. They couldn't hurt you for information you didn't know.

"Well, this was a different kind of sick." Elle hoped Chloe would take it. She wanted to move on to something she *could* tell her.

Elle looked over at Nero's table. He wasn't there.

Hmm, he's always right there.

"Hey, babe, can I sit here?" Elle turned her head and saw Nero standing there, holding a tray.

Did he just really ask that, and did he just really call me 'babe'?

"Are you serious? Sit *here*?" Elle pointed to the chair beside her.

"Yes, I was talking directly to you, wasn't I?" Nero was definitely a smartass.

Elle looked at Chloe, whose mouth hung open. Elle knew right away she didn't want anyone around her; Chloe didn't like new people.

Besides, the moment 'babe' had come out of his mouth, she had solidified her decision. *I don't care if it is a handsome mouth.*

"No, you clearly weren't because my name isn't 'babe'. I bet you don't even know my name. So, no, you cannot sit here, Nero." That was the first time she had ever spoken his name, although at least she knew it. Elle was sure he didn't know hers.

She could tell Nero was shocked by her answer. *He must think he can call a girl 'babe' and get what he wants.*

"All right, babe. I'll eventually be sitting right there. I can wait." With that, Nero walked off. Elle didn't even have time to think of a remark back.

He just said what? As Elle saw him go back to his usual table, she noticed almost everyone was staring at her, mostly the girls.

Elle glanced back at Chloe, whose mouth was still hanging open. Once she was finally able to swallow the food in her mouth, she let the questioning begin. "Don't you think I deserved a little warning?"

"Jesus, Chloe, I tried to tell you twice, but you kept interrupting me. I said you weren't going to believe who talked to me."

"Well, tell me already!" She thought Chloe was going to shake her if she didn't spill.

"When you left me, I went in the hall and he bumped into me. I tried to tell him sorry, but he told me to not apologize for something I didn't do. He actually talked to me and wasn't mean." Elle suddenly felt a little bad for talking to him like that, but then she thought better of it. *I mean, what if he is trying to pull a prank on me or something?*

"I can't believe it. Nero is... nice?"

"No way. He is..." She looked over at him. He was perfect, at least on the outside. However, he had never talked to her a day in her life. She was positive he had slept with half the girls at school; therefore, he didn't lack for companionship, which only left two options. He either wanted to sleep with Elle or do something horribly mean to her.

Either way, he isn't going to fool me. "He wants something, but I'm not going to find out what it is. I know exactly who Nero Caruso is, and 'nice' is the last word I would use to describe him."

"Yeah, but aren't you just a little curious?" Chloe raised her right eyebrow. It was missing a patch of hair from her scar. Elle noticed her black hair was swept behind her ear. "I know I am." She hadn't seen her this happy in a long time. She hated the fact that Cassandra would be back tomorrow to ruin it. Chloe deserved to be happy.

"No, I'm not." Elle didn't even notice she was lying to herself at that moment.

When Elle and Chloe finished their lunch and went to Spanish, Elle still couldn't believe the audacity of Nero.

'All right, babe. I'll eventually be sitting right there. I can wait.'

Who in the hell does he think he is? Oh, right, the king of Legacy Prep. Elle didn't care if he was king of the world, she could feel he had an ulterior motive.

I mean, why now? Why does he want to talk to me now?

Before Elle knew it, it was time for the last class of the day. Elle walked Chloe to her class, continuing to keep up her speed in the halls, yet she worried much less today.

"Stay here and wait for me. We're not going to try to be bold just because Cassandra isn't here. Clearly she's the ringleader, but you know just as much as I do she is not the only one who likes to ruin our lives." Elle gave Chloe a serious face. She wanted to make sure she got the full picture.

"I know. I'll wait right here." Elle felt satisfied Chloe didn't want to risk anything, either.

"All right, catch you later." Elle started her walk to the other side of the school.

When she reached her classroom, she sat at the table she had been at yesterday. She was still going to leave as soon as the bell rang. Elle didn't trust anyone in this school besides Chloe.

As Elle felt someone sit down beside her, she turned and saw Nero sitting at the table with her.

"What are you doing?"

Nero smiled. "I'm sitting. I've decided I'm not going to be nice and ask your permission."

Elle looked around the room, noticing Cassandra's bimbos looked pissed. Everyone else's faces looked completely confused.

I'm just as confused. "I don't think that's a good idea. Your status is dropping every second you sit there." Elle made sure she had her best sarcastic tone on.

Nero laughed. "You think I give a shit what these people think?"

Elle looked at him; like, really looked at him. He was much taller than her, but when they were sitting down, she didn't have to look up to see his face. He had dark skin and was cleanly shaven, but she could tell he could grow a beard like any older man. Something about his eyes intrigued her; it was like they were emeralds.

"No, clearly you don't."

As soon as Elle went up to the back of the class to pick up her poster, Nero followed right behind her. He found his first and headed back to the table. Elle grabbed her blank poster and headed back as well. She laid the poster on the table and took her seat.

"How come yours doesn't have anything on it?"

"Because I haven't decided what to put on it." Elle actually still hadn't decided what to do with the darned thing.

"You do know you're just supposed to throw shit on it you like, right?"

"Yes, I know that." Elle stared at her poster and bit her lip. *Who am I?*

"You're thinking too hard about this. What makes you happy?"

Elle looked at Nero. She could tell he was confused as to why she didn't know what to put on her poster. She swore he looked almost concerned.

What makes me happy? She had never thought of it like that. A lot of things in her life made her upset; however, she knew what always made her happy; it was how she stayed sane.

Elle opened her satchel, then grabbed some lined paper out and a pen.

She looked at Nero, and for the first time, she gave him a smile. "Thanks."

Nero threw his arm behind her chair. "No problem, babe."

And then he ruins it. "Don't call me that. You should go back." Elle nodded toward the table he had sat at yesterday. The two girls had been putting daggers into her skin the entire time. "I think they miss you calling them 'babe', anyways."

"Yeah, you would know. I saw you watching me yesterday."

"I don't kno—"

Nero grabbed the back of her head and made her look at him. "Don't lie to me. Not now, not ever." His deep tone became serious and his eyes demanded an answer.

Elle could only nod, her mouth starting to turn dry. She wasn't scared of him. *But I probably should be.*

"Good. Now, this is where I'm going to sit whether you have a problem with it or not. I understand if you don't want me to sit with you at lunch, for now, but don't tell me to move again."

After a second, she retorted, "Fine." Elle tried to make it seem as if she allowed him to sit there, but she knew she hadn't won that one by the way he was smiling. *Arrogant asshole.*

Shutting out the boy next to her, Elle was finally able to begin filling the paper with her words. She had always loved to write; it helped her escape everything that troubled her, and Elle had a lot of troubles.

Every now and then, she could sense Nero staring at her. She thought it was a strange feeling to have a boy look at her the way he did. She couldn't describe the sensation because she had never had it before. No boy had ever looked at her or paid her any attention in high school. Now, within one day, Nero was talking to her and choosing to sit beside her. She didn't know how to feel about it.

Her emotions had been all over the place the last couple of days. As a result, Elle kept doing what she was doing—writing.

"Can I use your pen a second?" Nero held out his hand.

"Yeah, sure." She gave him the pen and saw him outline something on his poster, although she couldn't make anything out.

"You know, in the supply closet there are much better writing pens. The words will stand out better with a nicer pen."

Elle could see Nero might be a while with her pen, so she got up and headed for the closet in the back of the class, which had several shelves; Elle had no idea where the pens would be.

"Here." Elle felt Nero's body lightly at her back as he reached over her and grabbed something out of one of the top bins, bringing a pen down and handing it to her. Elle gave him a half smile and started to walk out of the closet, but something had been bothering her; she needed to know something from him because, right then, it didn't make any sense why he was talking to her.

She decided to turn around and ask him, looking right up at his face. "Why now? Not one time have you ever spoken to me, and now you're acting like we just met or something."

"You really want to know?"

Elle swallowed hard. She probably didn't; however, she needed to. She nodded and looked down at his chest.

"All right." He shut the closet door then took a step toward her.

"W-what are you d-doing?" With every word she spoke, she took a step back. Nero took one more step toward her until her back hit the door and she was pinned.

"Yesterday, I saw you staring at me and Cassandra, and later, I caught you again in the parking lot with Stephanie." He took a step closer, closing the small gap she had placed between them. "Usually, people feel too uncomfortable. They won't even look in my direction." As Nero leaned down, Elle thought he was going to kiss her for a second; instead, his mouth came close to her ear. "But you couldn't pull your eyes away." His words made her ear warm, causing the rest of her flesh to become heated.

He grabbed her chin to make her finally look in his eyes. "There is something dying to come out…" His finger traveled down her neck and stopped right above the swell of her breasts. "And I want to be the one who brings it out, Elle." Hearing her name brought her out of the trance he had put over her.

He knows my name?

He moved his hand beside her waist and turned the doorknob, backing up to give her room to come forward so the door could be opened. Elle scooted free, her body no longer warmed by his. She didn't understand why she instantly regretted moving away, though.

When he opened the door all the way so she could exit the closet, Elle grew embarrassed with all the stares she was getting. She was sure Cassandra's sidekicks were thinking of a thousand ways for her to die by the looks on their faces.

She headed back to her table, but before she could sit, the bell rang. *Time to go, thank God.*

Elle picked up her bag and darted out the door, flying out so fast she never saw the look on Nero's face. He was completely dumbfounded.

Elle ran down the halls without being aware if she was running to Chloe or away from Nero.

Definitely to Chloe. Elle thought a second more. *Yep, Chloe!*

She reached Chloe's classroom, anxious to get out of there. "You ready?"

"Yeah, you okay?" Chloe looked concerned.

"Uh, yes, why wouldn't I be? Okay, let's go!" Elle almost grabbed Chloe's hand, stopping herself before she made contact. Chloe brought her hand up to her chest and looked down to the floor.

"I'm sorry, Chlo-"

"It's okay. Let's go." Chloe walked past Elle and started heading for the doors.

Elle watched Chloe walk right past her. *Shit.*

Every now and again, Elle would forget about Chloe's past and problems, right until she was about an inch away from touching her, and then the memories would all come back. Elle knew they not only showed up for Elle, but for Chloe, as well.

They reached the parking lot and Elle thought she had déjà vu. *Times two, apparently.*

The two bimbos were leaning against Nero's car. A sick feeling grew in Elle's stomach while she walked as fast as she could to Chloe's car, passing Chloe and reaching her car first. She rested her hand on the door handle, desperate to get in the car.

She looked up, only seeing Nero's back as he talked to the girls. The girls' faces she could see, however, and she really wished she couldn't.

When Chloe unlocked the doors, Elle threw herself in, keeping her face straight forward. There was no way she was turning her head. Elle's sick feeling started to move up ever so slightly from her stomach.

Chloe turned the car on and started to back up. She turned the wheel and headed out of the parking lot, forcing Elle to look at something she didn't want to see—a pair of legs in high heels entering Nero's Cadillac. Elle knew by the shoes the one going home with Nero tonight was Bimbo Number One.

Elle touched her chest; the feeling had found its mark.

PROTECT THE FAMILY

Elle had to regretfully go to work that night. If she wanted to stay and protect Chloe, she had to keep working. She figured if she quit working the night of the murder, well, then she might as well call the boss herself and tell him she had witnessed the whole ordeal.

All night, Elle viewed the diner and carefully looked at everyone's faces. She needed to be sure one of the three men weren't in the diner waiting for her. Subsequently, every time someone walked in, she looked at their faces. She did it over and over and over.

She took the coffee pot over to one of her tables to fill up the cups of the two men there. Elle had seen them before many times in the diner.

As she was filling up the blond one's cup, he asked, "Did you hear about someone getting shot behind the diner last night?"

This actually wasn't the first time she had been asked; it was like the fiftieth time. Apparently, it was a thing for you to go to a place where a possible murder had taken place. Everyone wanted to know what had happened. It reminded Elle of high school. *I don't think I'll ever get away from it.*

Elle kept to the same story she had told everyone, including the cops. They, of course, had asked her a few questions since she'd closed the diner the night before.

"Yes, I found out when I got into work today."

She saw the man take a sip from his coffee as she went to fill up the other man's cup.

The brown-haired one asked her, "I hope you weren't here last night while it happened?" His face showed he was asking a question, not that he was concerned. Elle started to get small chills on her arms, but she made sure to stay cool.

"I was working last night, actually. I closed the diner for the night. The cops told me I must have just missed the whole thing." Elle made sure she said cops. *Now they know I didn't open my mouth.*

The two men looked at each other for a split second, confirming what Elle had feared. *They work for the boss.*

He smiled. "You are one lucky girl. That would have been horrible to see something like that at your age."

The luckiest. Elle smiled back. "Yeah, I'm pretty sure I would have lost my marbles seeing something like that. Do you need anything else?"

The only reason Elle could keep calm was because they had no idea she had witnessed the whole thing. *Clearly, they don't have a problem with killing; otherwise, I would have been dead already.*

"No, thanks." They both stood up before one of them threw a couple of bills down on the table. "You be careful out there."

Elle smiled and nodded then watched them walk out the door, letting her finally breathe again. *Thank God.*

Elle believed she was in the clear. *For now, anyway.*

He could hear the sound of his phone buzzing on his wooden desk. He picked it up without having to look at the caller ID.

"She's smart. Came into work like nothing happened, claiming she must have missed the whole thing. Cops spoke to her already. She made it seem like they got nothing from her."

"Yeah, Sal called about an hour ago. She played dumb to the cops. You're my consigliere, Vinny; what do you think?" He took a cigar out of his box then snapped the lid closed.

"I'm advising you to figure this shit out on your own. It will be good for you. Just keep me updated."

"Okay, I've got it handled for now." With that, he ended the call and lit his cigar. His consigliere was right; she was fucking smart. He knew she wasn't opening her mouth in the near future. The only thing he didn't know was if she had actually seen him and his crew do it or just heard what had occurred. That, he needed to find out. She might not be saying shit now, but you never knew if a person would down the road. Besides, if his enemies found out he had left a witness alive, it could bring down his whole operation, everything he had done to be the one calling the shots.

Elle had simply been in the wrong place at the wrong time. *That I know all too well.*

He pushed the bad memory back. He couldn't feel sorry for the girl. His son had been there, as well as Sal; he had to protect them both. He had made an oath long ago to protect the family.

He leaned back in his expensive, leather chair, taking a hit of his cigar. Exhaling, he watched the smoke fill the room.

It was time to check in and see if any progress had been made.

Nero lay in bed, looking up at the ceiling. Something had been bothering him ever since Elle had run out on him in art class. No girl had ever run away from him, and they sure as hell wouldn't after what he had pulled on her in the closet. *Any other girl would have begged me to fuck them right there.*

Playing with Elle had built tension inside of him. He needed to get it out, and when Stephanie and Stacy had been waiting for him at his car, he had known exactly how. He had chosen Stacy because she had been exactly what he needed; nothing was off-limits with her. At least, that had been what he'd thought he needed, but his dick was still hard. For the first time in years, Nero was sexually frustrated. *Fuck, would she hurry?*

Nero's phone rang. "Yeah?"

"Tell me how it went."

Nero got out of the bed and opened the door leading to his balcony. Walking out, he shut the doors.

"Well, she showed up to school. I gotta say, I was kind of shocked she actually did. Should have known, though, she wouldn't let her friend go to school without her. First class, she was a little out of it. Looked mostly tired but snapped back pretty fast."

"Did you talk to her?"

"You don't seem surprised." Nero must have missed something.

"I had Vinny and Enzo check in on her at the diner. She had enough balls to go to work, acting like she was already gone before it happened. When the cops asked her about the murder, she pretended it was the first she'd heard of it."

"So, I assume this was a test. How did I do...boss?" Nero made sure his father got his meaning.

"Don't take it personally, son. Answer the question."

"Yes, I talked to her. It's going to take time for her to trust me, though. She doesn't exactly have reason to trust anyone in school. As you can see, she's not your typical high school girl."

"Yeah, I'm seeing that, especially after years of seeing the girls you and your brother bring home. Why can't either of you bring a girl like that home?"

"Probably because we'd have to work too hard to get in their panties."

"Well, you have one month to get into them and find out what she saw. Oh, and I don't want to see another girl walk through my front doors unless it's Elle. Mistake number one already. A piece of advice, father to son, she ain't the cheating type. You're done fucking around. Consider yourself married off till the job is done." All Nero could hear after that was a tone saying his dad had said his peace.

Nero squeezed the phone. *Done fucking around. That's a joke.*

He opened the door and lay back down on the bed, considering what his dad had said about Elle. *'She had enough balls to go to work.'*

Elle had fooled the cops and everyone else besides the family.

Nero smiled. *Elle, I am going to have fun with you.*

Nero heard the bathroom door open right on cue. Stacy came out, showered and dressed. She headed for the door. "See you tomorrow, Nero."

"Did I give you permission to leave?" Nero grabbed her hand.

Stacy beamed and jumped on top of him.

No, he was not quite done with her tonight; he had only grown harder at the thought of Elle. Nero was sure he would fuck Stacy until the thought of Elle disappeared. Little did Nero know, however, it was sleep that would come first.

Elle lay in bed, exhausted. Work had been mentally draining, worrying about who was going to walk through the doors next. Then she had to come home and do homework on top of that.

To top it all off, the thought of Nero going home with another girl was really messing with her brain. *Why do I even care about him?*

She didn't understand why guys were attracted to girls like Cassandra. *Oh, yeah, right.*

Elle knew she was nothing like them. She didn't have money, didn't buy fancy clothes, and didn't throw herself at boys. *I'm just a waitress.*

It really bugged Elle to not be able to shake him from her thoughts because, clearly, he only wanted to get laid and girls meant nothing else to him. Moreover, Elle would never picture herself with a guy like Nero.

Honestly, Elle had never pictured herself with anyone. She had never liked anyone enough. Elle was definitely a virgin—hell, she had never even been kissed before. *I am definitely not his type, and he isn't mine.*

Elle had decided long ago, no matter what changed, she wouldn't be with anyone at Legacy Prep High because not one of them gave a shit about her. All the times she had been bullied, all the laughs and stares— she blamed them as much as the ones causing the actual pain.

Elle spent the night begging for sleep to come and rescue her from her thoughts, but not even sleep gave her a reprieve from Nero.

When *Elle walked into English* class the next morning, she came to a halt, causing Chloe to bump right into her. Elle slowly started walking to her seat, unable to believe it. She stopped at the seat in front of hers, staring down at a gloating Nero. She really wanted to wipe that smirk off his face.

"Good morning, Elle." Elle could hear how shocked Chloe was at hearing her name come out of his mouth.

Completely ignore him, Elle decided.

She took her seat, and of course, all she could see in front of her was Nero. She had spent the whole night trying to forget him, and now he'd graced her with an upfront view of himself.

She turned her head to look at Chloe, unable to look at him anymore; even the back of his head was handsome. She didn't even want to get started on the back muscles she saw under his white button-up shirt.

It wasn't long before Elle couldn't even look at Chloe, either; she had a big smirk on her face.

Attempting to ignore them both, all Elle could smell was Nero's cologne; it was the scent of pure man. The smell of him brought her back to yesterday in the art supply closet. She got chills at the memory of his finger running down her skin. *Stop!*

Elle swore this was the longest class of her life. She needed to get away from him.

She jumped out of her seat when the bell rang and threw on her bag. She would wait for Chloe in the hall. The problem was, Nero was prepared for her running away today. He grabbed her arm.

"Could you please stop doing that?"

Elle looked down at his warm hand, holding her back. "Doing what?" She gave him the same smile he had been giving her before.

"Running from me."

Elle laughed. "I am not run—"

Nero squeezed her hand ever so slightly. "Remember what I said yesterday, Elle."

Elle looked him in the eyes. *Damn, he really must not like liars.*

"I just wanted to walk you to class."

"Nope, sorry." She jerked her arm away from his grasp and ran straight out of there.

Waiting in the hallway, she hoped Chloe would appear before him and was thrilled when she did. Elle wasted no time in walking to their next class. She got there quickly and they took their seats.

Once she was settled, Elle couldn't help feeling Chloe's eyes on her. She looked over at her best friend to see she was smiling from ear to ear.

"Stop it! I swear, if you don't stop looking at me that way, I'm going to find a new best friend." Elle covered her face with her hands. It was hard not to smile with Chloe.

"Hmm, like Nero?" Chloe was way too happy for Elle's liking.

Elle sunk down in her desk. She really wanted to dislike Nero, but everything was telling her to like him.

"Elle, I don't know why you're trying so hard to dislike him. He clearly likes you."

"Are you joking right now?" Elle was serious.

"Uh, no."

"I dislike him because he didn't give a shit about me all the times I was pushed around and hit. Or how about all those times I was called waitress, all the mental abuse I took, no *we* took. Then, just two days ago, he called you a freak in English—I know it was him." That had been on our first day back from Christmas break in English class. Mr. Evans had asked us to introduce ourselves, and when Chloe had finished, a whisper of "freak" had echoed around the room, coming from Nero's general direction. "Now, for some odd reason, he wants to be friends? No, screw that." Elle was done thinking about him; she wasn't wasting any more thoughts on him.

"Listen, Elle; all I can tell you is when I see him look at you, I know he likes you. Maybe you should give him a chance. I think you're fighting your feelings because of me."

"Chloe, it doesn't matter." Elle didn't want to talk about this.

"It does matter. I want you to be happy, Elle. Don't do this because of my fears. I don't think Nero would do anything to hurt you, or me for that matter. I could get used to Nero, for you, of course." Chloe looked down at her hands.

Elle smiled. She loved her best friend. Chloe meant everything to her. It would take a lot for Chloe to trust Nero, though.

He is going to have to prove himself big time.

The day went on and Elle realized Cassandra still wasn't back in school. She and Chloe were able to have one more day of peace, and they enjoyed every second of it. The only bad thing about it was they were sure, when she got back tomorrow, it would be Hell.

Elle and Chloe went to the cafeteria when the bell rang and got in line to eat chicken patties, again. They sat down and Elle scanned the room. She knew she was looking for Nero but didn't want to admit it. When she finally spotted him, he was at his table.

Elle looked back down at her food and began to eat, but then saw Sebastian out of the corner of her eye, heading her way. She had no time to warn Chloe. *This is going to be bad.*

She paid him no attention when he stood, looking down at her. "Have you heard why Cassandra isn't here?"

Elle kept her eyes glued to Chloe.

"Well, she was suspended. Do you know why?" Elle could feel him losing his temper with each passing second. She wasn't going to look at him, though. He honestly scared the shit out of her.

Sebastian slammed his hands down on the table. "I am talking to you, waitress!"

While the whole cafeteria went silent at his outburst, Elle could see Chloe was absolutely terrified; she had practically jumped ten feet. As Elle finally looked up at him, she thought he resembled a complete psychopath.

"Now, do you know why?"

Elle said nothing, only looked at his crazed face. There was never a point in saying a word to Sebastian; it only made things worse. *And yes, it's been worse than this.*

"Do you?" That was it; he snapped. Elle could see him jump toward her. He wanted to put his hands on her and make her answer. Elle shut her eyes, waiting for it to come.

"I better not see you lay your fucking hands on Elle, ever. I don't want to see you talking to her or even looking in her direction, and that goes for Chloe, too. Because, if you do, I will make damn sure everyone in this school will be calling you the freak. Do you understand me?"

Elle was no longer scared of Sebastian with one glance at Nero. His voice was too calm, his face too composed, but his green eyes promised his words were true.

Sebastian was shocked. He knew not to question him, though. He only nodded. That, however, didn't stop him from giving Elle a look that said he would get her next time, when Nero wasn't around. She knew he would, too. *That, I have no doubt of.*

When Nero was satisfied he understood, he finally let him go. Then Nero looked around the cafeteria, making sure everyone was paying attention.

"Their names are Elle and Chloe, and you will call them by their names."

Elle had not been expecting that, and by the expression on Chloe's face, she hadn't been, either. She couldn't believe he had not only told Sebastian to fuck off, but the whole school, as well. All these years, she had gone with not one person standing up for her, and here Nero had stood up to the whole school.

Elle watched Nero come over to her. "You okay?"

She hoped her face didn't look as dumb as she thought. *It does. I know it does.* "Um, yeah, I'm fine." She looked over at Chloe to make sure she was good. She didn't look terrified anymore; she looked a little dazed. Elle was certain she looked the same.

Nero grinned. "Do you think I could sit here now?"

Elle knew he deserved some consolation for what he had done. Still, she felt that this wasn't going to change anything. She didn't believe his intentions were good and knew a guy like Nero would never like her. Elle figured she could let him sit with her, though. *It's not like he will keep sitting here, anyway.*

She glanced at Chloe to make sure she was okay with it. She knew she wasn't thrilled, yet she would deal.

Elle looked up at Nero and smiled. "Sure, why not?"

"Good." Nero looked up across the cafeteria and motioned a 'come here'. Elle saw Nero's crew get up from their table and come toward them. *Oh, shit.*

She immediately got up and stood beside Chloe. "What are you doing?" She could feel Chloe getting nervous.

"Uh, I'm sitting here, and they sit where I sit."

"No, I said *you* can sit here. I didn't say they could."

"What's the big deal?" Elle saw it dawn on him the moment he asked. He could figure it out by the way she was standing in front of Chloe.

"They can't sit here, Nero."

Elle watched Nero hold up his hand, stopping his crew.

"Ba-Elle, listen; letting them sit here will make sure no one will ever say or do anything to you and Chloe again. They won't hurt you. I promise." He made sure to hold her eyes, letting her know he was telling the truth. "They won't touch Chloe, either. I give you my word."

Elle looked at Chloe. She knew she was running out of room to protect her friend in this Hell. This semester had started out terribly, and it was only the first week. Elle knew she needed help, and if anyone in this school could protect Chloe, it was Nero and his crew. *Sorry, Chloe.*

Elle sat down beside Chloe. "You better not be lying to me, Nero."

Elle knew he had heard her; he nodded, not only for her, but for his crew to come over.

Elle whispered to Chloe, "It's going to be okay. I haven't let anyone in here hurt you, have I?" And she hadn't. Elle did whatever it took to make sure no one laid a finger on her. Yes, that meant Elle got the short end of the stick in here, but Chloe got the shortest end of the shittiest stick outside of here.

Elle gave Chloe a smile when she finally answered, shaking her head no.

Elle could see the signal Nero gave the young blond one to sit beside Chloe. That tugged at her heart a little. He was a good choice because he was practically a kid and had never had any part in their bullying.

Nero took his seat on the other side of Elle and draped his arm on the back of her chair as Amo and Vincent took the other two remaining seats across from them.

"This is my little brother, Leo." Leo flashed his shiny, white teeth.

Jesus, he is a miniature Nero.

"Leo, this is Chloe." He nodded toward Chloe.

"Hey, Chloe." Leo held his hand out.

Elle quickly took his hand. "Sorry, she's germaphobic. I'm Elle."

Elle watched the four guys stare at her and Chloe. The situation was already awkward, and that had just made it a lot more so.

"That's freaking genius, Nero. Why haven't we thought of that after all the gross hands we've had to shake?" Leo laughed at his own joke, the guys all joining in, and Elle couldn't help herself from laughing with them. Even Chloe chuckled.

Elle automatically liked Leo. It was something you couldn't help; he was completely adorable with his long, dirty-blond hair and deep-blue eyes. He knew how to handle himself even at a young age, and Elle knew he had gotten it from his older brother.

Surprisingly, Elle thought lunch was going well. Nero, Amo, and Vincent talked mostly to themselves the whole time while Elle asked Leo questions about how he liked high school so far. Leo, being easy to talk to, had Chloe chiming in, as well. It was a nice lunch. They'd never had any company besides themselves. They, of course, never minded it, but it was a nice change. It was time to head back to class before they knew it.

Elle and Chloe got up first to take their trays to the trash, but Nero stopped Elle. He grabbed her tray and took it from her while Amo came up and grabbed Chloe's tray. Chloe, however, didn't let it go; she kept her hands on the tray, holding it tight. Amo held on tighter and slowly pulled it closer to him, freeing it from her hands.

"I-I can throw away my own trash." Chloe kept her eyes down to the floor; no way she would look a big guy like Amo in the face.

Elle tried hard not to laugh at little Chloe fighting for her tray against Amo.

"Yeah, so what's your point?" Amo was asking a rhetorical question because he knew Chloe wasn't going to be able to answer it. He went to the trash can with Nero and tossed it in.

"Catch you later, girls." Elle and Chloe smiled at Leo as he went off to his class. *He is way too cute.*

"What class are you in?" Nero asked Elle.

"Spanish, why?"

"Because we're gonna walk you to class." Amo started walking out front and Nero took Elle's arm to start walking. Chloe walked right behind Elle like she did as usual. Nero stopped and turned around. "What are you doing, Chloe?"

"Um, walking?"

"Why the hell are you walking on Elle's ass?"

"This is how I always walk." Chloe's face was confused as to why it mattered.

"Jesus Christ." Nero ran his hand through his hair while Amo and Vincent shook their heads. "Chloe, walk beside Elle."

When Chloe took a hesitant step forward and stood next to Elle, Elle gave her a reassuring smile and nodded for her to start. It took a minute for her to comfortably walk beside Elle because it was hard for her to look at something other than Elle's back.

It even felt slightly awkward for Elle. She had grown used to Chloe being right at her back. It was also hard for her to let go and trust Nero on his word. Yet, here she was, walking beside her best friend on her right and Nero on her left while Amo and Vincent rounded out the front and back.

She tried not to notice the stares she was getting down the halls; not that she could blame them. They had started the day out as invisible, and now they were walking with the king and his court.

They reached the classroom and Chloe practically ran inside. Amo and Vincent leaned against some lockers close by. Elle was going to go in her classroom; however, Nero grabbed her arm, dragging her back.

"What is it with you running away from me?" He tugged her close to him and held on to her waist.

She tried to free herself, but honestly, it was useless. "Stop it. People are staring at us." The constant attention from everyone was seriously making her blush.

"So, let them. I didn't get a thank you, you know?"

"Well, you're not going to get one now." He still was not budging on letting her go, even just a little.

Nero smiled. "That was not the right answer. Now you're not going to like how you'll be thanking me."

Elle laughed. "Oh, really? And how's that?"

"I'll need a kiss as a thank you." He grabbed her chin to position her face.

"No, no, no. I am not kissing you. You're crazy to think I would kiss you in front of everyone." She felt her face grow even redder. *No way is my first kiss going to be here, with him.*

"I can wait then. I'll get my kiss by the end of the day. Oh, and stay here. We'll be back to pick you up, so don't even think about leaving without us. Your ass better be right here, understand?"

"Excuse me?" Elle's body returned to normal. *He can't tell me what to do.*

Nero squeezed her tighter. "You don't want to defy me, Elle. Remember, you owe me a thank you." He let her go.

Elle was astounded as she stormed into her classroom. *Who does he think he is?*

She thought he was unbelievable. No way was his mouth coming anywhere near hers. *'I'll need a kiss as a thank you.' Ha! As if!*

Elle suddenly realized she had made a deal with the devil.

LIKE A DISNEY MOVIE

lle had lost all concentration at school with everything going on. Her life felt like the twilight zone to her now. Plus, she still had no idea how to handle the whole murder thing. She needed to find out about this boss and see if she could get in the clear.

Then there was Cassandra.

'Well, she was suspended. Do you know why?' Elle knew why. It was all because of her in the lunchroom. Cassandra was going to pay her back, and it wasn't going to be pretty. Forget the boss killing her, Cassandra was going to make sure she was six-feet under the moment her feet stepped back into school.

Elle cringed at an old memory from freshman year.

Cassandra and her two blonde friends stood over her in the locker room. "We heard what happened to your father. Good thing he paid your tuition before the school year started."

"What do you mean?"

"Well, how the hell is he supposed to make enough money in a wheelchair? I know he lost his job. Such a shame that your first year will be your last year at Legacy Prep High."

Their sadistic laughs ran through her ears. She wasn't going to listen to her talk about her father that way, though. "Yeah, and it's such a shame you feel the need to stuff your bra. Can't you at least stuff them evenly?" Elle knew she had gotten her with that one.

She started to walk off, done with the conversation, when Elle felt Cassandra jump her from behind, making her hit her head on a bench. Cassandra quickly sat on top of her back.

Elle pushed back the throbbing pain in her head. She had to get up.

Elle tried to push off the ground.

"Help me hold her down!"

The other two girls joined in and pinned her arms to the ground.

"Chloe, give them to me," Cassandra called.

She saw a girl appear from behind a set of lockers through a veil of blood that was draining down her forehead and into her eyes. She remembered seeing her the first day of school and thinking she was gorgeous with her black hair that had a slight wave at the ends and her unusual eyes. She had never thought it was possible for someone to have gray eyes. She stood out among the other girls in her class because she was very short and already had a womanly figure for her age. Elle could tell the girl was uncomfortable, that she hadn't agreed to what was going on.

"Chloe, give them to me."

Chloe pulled a pair of scissors out from behind her back.

"You don't want to be like her, do you?" Cassandra asked.

Chloe shook her head, holding the scissors out, and Cassandra snatched them away.

"Now, bitch, think again next time you turn your back on me." Cassandra grabbed Elle's ponytail and began cutting it off. Elle could only cry with each snip. There was no one around to help her, and she was helpless with three girls holding her down.

When Cassandra was done, she waved Elle's now-chopped-off ponytail in front of her face. "A girl like you doesn't need long, pretty hair like this anyway."

Cassandra finally got off Elle and so did her friends before they started walking out of the locker room. Elle continued to cry as she sat up and scrunched her legs in front of her, holding them tightly.

Elle looked up and saw the pretty girl standing there; her eyes were glossy like she was on the verge of tears. She whispered, "Sorry," before she ran out of the locker room behind Cassandra.

Elle learned a valuable lesson that day as she cried, bloody and alone in the locker room. She learned to never drop your guard.

The bell brought Elle out of her dark memory. *The past is the past and lesson learned.*

She decided she was going to walk Chloe to her class as usual and Nero was just going to have to get over it. Elle and Chloe got up to head to their next classes, but Elle stepped into the hallway only to be dragged sideways.

"What did I tell you?"

"You told me, but I decided not to listen." As Elle gave him a smirk and took a step toward Chloe's next classroom, Nero grabbed her hand and locked his fingers between hers.

"Do you honestly think I should let you walk Chloe to class and then let you walk all the way by yourself to Art? I'm sure Sebastian is dying to get his hands on you, alone. But how about when they get smart and realize you don't give a shit what they do to you and they go for Chloe? Cassandra is only suspended, but she will be back, Elle. And until then, Sebastian will do her dirty work and so will Stephanie and Stacy."

"Yeah, you would know about Cassandra and Stephanie; you all are so close. Oh, wait, I forgot Stacy, too."

His saying their names had brought the memories back of him being with all three over the past few days.

"That is a separate conversation we can talk about later. Right now, I'm asking you, do you want to get Chloe hurt? Because you know I'm right."

Elle knew he was right, although that didn't mean she liked the truth.

She looked over at Chloe. "He's right, Elle."

Elle let out a sigh. "Fine, let's go."

Elle tried to walk forward, but Nero kept her still. "We're going to do things my way now. Amo is in health class with Chloe, so he is going to take her to class and bring her back to you in Art. Got it?"

"No freaking way." Elle started shaking her head violently back and forth.

"This isn't a discussion anymore, Elle. Chloe, is he in your class?"

"Um, yes." Chloe looked down at the floor.

"Good. Now, Amo will take you to and from class for now." Nero looked at Elle's pissed face. "Only for the last class of the day, and he will sit beside you in class. Are you okay with that?"

"No, she's not." Elle watched Chloe closely. *She better say no.*

When Chloe looked up at her, she knew what she was going to say.

"Y-Yeah." Chloe quickly looked back down at the ground and started wringing her hands.

"All right. Go on, Chloe. You'll be safe with Amo."

Nero gave Elle's hand a little squeeze. She had forgotten he was holding her hand; however, she hated his guts right now and didn't want him touching her. She tried to pull her hand away, but he held it close. She heard Vincent laugh and stopped trying to free her hand.

"Come on, Chloe." Amo started walking and Chloe fell in behind him. She looked afraid, but Elle didn't know if it was because she was afraid to look Elle in the face, or from having to go along with the biggest guy in the whole school. Elle saw his stature in front of Chloe's tiny body. *Probably both.*

Elle looked Nero in the eyes. "I hope you're happy."

Nero smiled. "Not yet, but I will be when I get my kiss later."

"You're seriously stupid if you think I'm going—"

"Now, Elle, what did I tell you about lying?"

Elle rolled her eyes.

"Come on; let's go."

Elle was surprised when he went in the same direction as Chloe and Amo, considering their class was in the opposite direction. They kept a few feet behind them. Elle could see them the whole time as it wasn't hard pointing out Amo from the small hallway filled with other students. Everyone parted like the red sea for him to get through. She assumed that was why he had walked in front of them earlier.

Elle tried not to smile. She didn't want Nero to know she appreciated him letting her follow Chloe to make sure she was safe. *I still don't like him.*

She tried to free her hand from his again, but he pulled her to walk closer to him. She heard Vincent's laugh again and turned her head to scowl at him. He kept laughing.

Elle watched Amo open the classroom door. Chloe stood there, waiting for him to go in first. She saw him mouth the word go when she clearly wasn't going to head in. Chloe stomped in and Amo walked in behind her, shaking his head as he shut the door.

She's safe. Elle didn't want to admit she was probably safer with Amo than she ever had been with her.

"Can we go to class now, or do you want to miss it by staring at the door all day?" When Elle kept staring at the door, he grabbed her chin to look at him. "Elle, she'll be fine, I promise."

Elle nodded and they both walked hand in hand to art class.

"Thank you for letting me watch her go to class." She didn't want to say thank you, but she had to for that.

A smile touched Nero's lips. "Oh, now you thank me. So now I know to do nice things for Chloe, not you. Have you both always been inseparable?"

Elle thought about the memory she'd had just a little bit ago. "No, we met here."

"Really? What made you so close that quickly? Because I remember you both freshman year, and back then, you were always standing in front of Chloe."

Elle shrugged and kept her eyes forward. "I guess we could relate to each other."

She could feel Nero's eyes look at her and knew he was trying to get something from her face; as a result, she made sure to reveal nothing.

They were about halfway to class when Elle really noticed what was going on. It became surreal to her that she was walking down the hallway, her hand locked in Nero's while all the students could only stare. She heard them whispering, and most of the girls were throwing her dirty looks. Elle decided not to care. It wasn't as if they could possibly torture her more than she already had been. She thought she should at least enjoy the moment of a boy holding her hand for the first time.

Nero's hand felt nice in hers, like it was a perfect fit. *At least what I think is perfect.*

His hand was strong. It wasn't too soft or too rough. Her fingertips rested on his knuckles, which felt big and bony. *He probably cracks his fingers too much.*

She slightly moved her fingertips and could feel a scrape on his middle knuckle, thinking he seemed like the type that would punch walls.

They reached their art class and Nero nodded his goodbye to Vincent, who had followed them the whole way there, walking a few steps behind.

Elle decided to pose the same question. "Have you three always been inseparable?" Elle asked as they took their seats.

Nero laughed. "Yeah, pretty much. Our fathers are all friends, so we were basically forced to like each other when we were young. Now we're one big family."

"Aww, that's actually really cute and ador—"

"Shh... No, it's not, Elle." He was looking around the room for someone that could have heard.

Elle couldn't help laughing. "That's so adorable your fathers are friends—" As Nero tried to cover her mouth to get her to quiet down, she kept giggling and moved her face out of the way, grabbing his hands so she could finish. "And so are all their sons. It's cute, like a Disney movie." She laughed hysterically at that last bit, bringing tears to her eyes.

"You've done it now." He stood up and took her hand, making her stand and walk with him to the back of the classroom toward the art supply closet.

Her laugh still filled the air. "What are you doing?" she barely managed to get out.

"Getting my thank you," he gritted out.

Elle immediately stopped laughing. *Shit.*

WALK BESIDE THE BEAST

Nero *forced Elle inside the* closet. She seriously regretted teasing him now. As he shut the door, it was no longer funny.

Nero pushed her against the wall.

"I'm—I'm sorry. I won't joke about how cute it is again." She thought Nero looked at her like a wolf and she was his prey. He grabbed a piece of her hair and spun it around his finger. "I mean, it definitely isn't cute. Nope, it's manly that all the fathers and sons are all best friends." Elle was more and more nervous with each word she spoke. She knew she wasn't making it better.

"You're not helping yourself out here, Elle." He placed his hand under her ear, his fingers grasping her hair with his palm resting on the side of her neck, positioning her for the taking.

Elle didn't know what to do. She blurted out something she hoped would save her. "Don't. I've never been kissed before."

Nero looked at her a second and saw she wasn't lying. He rubbed his thumb back and forth across her jawline. "All right. Well, for the first time only, I'll just take a small kiss."

Elle's heart stopped beating. "Here?"

Nero nodded and leaned his face down, his mouth an inch from hers. "Here."

Her stomach filled with butterflies. Elle could only close her eyes as his lips touched hers. He didn't force it; he'd said it perfectly, just a small kiss. It was just a brief second of his lips closing over her bottom lip, and then it was gone.

When Elle opened her eyes, the fluttering in her stomach didn't stop. He looked hungrier than before, but he pulled away. Elle knew she better leave before the wolf changed his mind about a small kiss. Without a word or sound, she scooted out the door, keeping her head down. Elle was too embarrassed to look at anyone who might have noticed her and Nero going in the closet. She took her seat, staring at the table, her mind a jumbled mess.

She saw her poster appear on the table before her, and then Nero took his seat beside her. She definitely couldn't look at him after that, so she quickly pulled out some paper and started writing, spending most of her time at the task. It was hard to concentrate after what had happened, yet she really was too embarrassed to even look at him.

She would peer out of the corner of her eyes every now and then when she knew he wasn't paying any attention to her. The next time, when her eyes glanced out, she noticed his knuckles. She had felt the scrapes but hadn't realized how inflamed they were. They were all bright red. Before she put much thought into it, the bell rang. Instinct kicked in, and she stood up to retrieve Chloe.

Nero took her hand. "No, Amo is bringing her to you, and we'll all walk out together."

Elle watched the students leave before her, feeling odd; she was always the first one out. "Please, let me go get her."

"Elle, look at me." Elle looked down at Nero after she realized he wasn't going to let her go if she didn't. "Do you trust me?"

Elle looked at Nero hard. For some reason, she knew, when he made a promise, he would keep it. He was just that type of guy. She couldn't explain it.

Elle quietly said, "Yes."

"Okay, well, sit then." Elle didn't want to sit; she wanted to wait outside the door for Chloe. Nero sighed and pulled her down on his lap. "You should really start listening to me."

She tried to get up, however, one arm rested behind her back, holding her hip, and the other arm rested on her lap, his hand gripping her leg. When she struggled, he only held tighter, his hand moving farther up her leg.

"Relax, Elle. They will be here in a minute."

She didn't want to feel stupid, so she quit struggling and just sunk into his lap. She felt calm after a minute. For the first time, she felt almost safe within these walls.

The moment Elle saw Amo in the distance, she jumped off Nero's lap. She waited by the door where Vincent had arrived a minute earlier for Amo to reach them. When Amo stopped in front of her, Chloe emerged from behind him.

"Nero, we need to talk. Chloe will not get off my ass. I told her," Amo looked right at Chloe in the eyes, "to walk beside me, but she refuses to even say a word to me."

"T-that's how I walk!" Chloe blurted.

Elle started laughing; it was too hard not to.

"Oh, now you can talk because Elle's around." Elle only laughed harder. "I blame you!" He pointed at Elle.

"Me? What did I do?"

"You taught her to walk like that."

Elle took a step forward, going toe to toe with Amo. *Yes, he is big. And yes, he is scary, but he knows nothing.*

"No, I didn't teach her shit. She learned to walk behind me when everyone started bullying us."

"We never bullied you."

"No, but you all sure as hell didn't stop it. Come on, Chloe; we're leaving."

"All right, calm down." Nero grabbed her hand, stopping her again. *That is really pissing me off.*

"You're right. We're just as guilty. All three of us are sorry, and we are trying to make it up from now on. But you and Chloe need to help us out here. Chloe, listen to Amo and try to talk to him every now and then."

"And…" Amo got out.

"And get off Amo's ass. Walk beside him from now on. It's safer there, anyway. Someone could grab you from behind him if they wanted."

Chloe swallowed and nodded.

"Yeah, like she'll have much room to walk beside the beast." Elle stuck out her tongue.

Amo was about to say something, but Nero held up his hand. Instead, Amo started the walk to the school's front doors. Nero tugged Elle to walk beside him and Chloe fell in behind with Vincent following them all.

"Chloe, beside."

Chloe moved out from behind Elle with her head down while Amo shook his head in front of them. *He is really rubbing me the wrong way.*

When Chloe finally looked up, she gave her a sympathetic smile, but Elle thought it was nice to finally walk beside her friend again.

As they reached outside the doors, the cold air whipped her face and Nero pulled her closer. She did love the cold, but she also liked the warmth of Nero.

Elle noticed Sebastian staring at them before he entered his car. She also noticed his black eye, which is when it clicked for her. *Nero doesn't punch walls, just faces.*

They reached Chloe's BMW and Amo was the first to notice something wasn't right.

"Someone slashed her fucking tires."

Nero ran his hands through his hair, pushing back the dark strands from his face. "All right. Elle and Chloe, I'll take you both home."

"It's okay. I've gotten flat tires before. I can drive on them for a few miles to the dealership."

"Oh, God, is she serious?" Elle was shocked it had come from Vincent.

"Chloe, you are not driving on flat tires, and not with Elle. I'll take you home. Your dad can take care of the car, right?"

"I-I can drive it. That was the whole point of buying the tires." Elle felt for Chloe. She definitely wasn't going to tell her dad. It wasn't like he was going to give a shit, anyway.

"Jesus Christ, I gotta get out of here. I'll take Leo home for you. Good luck with these crazies." Amo walked off and yelled for Leo to come on.

"Chloe, you're either going home with me and Elle, or Vincent will take you home."

Vincent gave Chloe a wicked smile. Although he was the shortest of the three, Amo and Nero were freakishly tall. Additionally, Vincent was the pretty boy of their group; he was perfectly tall and had the perfect body type. *Well, if you were into the whole perfect thing.*

His light-blond hair and baby-blue eyes, paired with his pretty face, had all the girls vying for his attention.

"I'll go with you and Elle."

"I thought so. Later, man." They went their separate ways, with Elle and Chloe going with Nero and Vincent heading toward his own car.

Nero held onto Elle's hand as he opened the back door for Chloe to get in. She slid in and shut her door, and he then opened the passenger side door for Elle to get in. Elle climbed into Nero's Cadillac, thinking about how practically all the other girls in the school had climbed into this seat, as well. She hated thinking about it; it made her sick. She knew, no matter what, she wasn't going to be like one of those girls, though.

Nero didn't have to be told the way to go to Chloe's house; he knew exactly where she lived without asking. The whole city knew. He pulled up to her house, swinging in the cul-de-sac and stopping the car right in front of the picture-perfect, big white house.

Chloe opened the door. "I'll text you later, Elle."

Elle turned her head over the seat and smiled. "Okay. Bye, Chloe."

Chloe got out of the car and shut the door then turned around and waved goodbye to her friend. Elle waved back and mouthed "good luck" to her before Nero drove off.

When they reached the long, paved road, realization hit Elle as she told him where she lived. She was now alone, with Nero, in his car.

Wonderful.

I'M NOT A RAT

Elle, *finally being alone with* Nero in a confined space, really studied him. His battered hand held the steering wheel not too tightly. He was calm, looking like he was almost at peace. She could tell he was thinking, that maybe he drove to think. He looked like he loved being behind the wheel. His eyes, that looked like they belonged to an animal, were pinned to the road ahead of him. Why had she thought of him like a wolf earlier? *Maybe that's because of the color.*

His black hair was just slightly in his face. She could tell he was still getting used to his shorter hair by the way he would push his hair straight back to smooth it down. She liked when he did that because he only did it when he was feeling something. *Because he acts like he has no emotions.*

His tan contrasted with his white shirt, making him look possibly tanner than he was. He always wore a light-colored, up shirt, but he never buttoned it all the way up; consequently, you could always see a hint of his chest. He wore dark trousers, as well, always in dark gray, navy, or black. This actually was typical for a prep school; every student dressed to impress. However, Nero's look was very dull compared to the other male students who dressed rather flamboyantly. They would have finished it off with a hideously-colored jacket and made it a full suit.

Nero's smile drew her out of her thoughts. "What are you thinking about?"

"Trying to figure out what you're thinking."

"Oh, so that's why you haven't pulled your eyes away from me."

Elle moved her eyes to the road. She was embarrassed he had caught her gawking.

"I was thinking about what you said earlier. About how we never did anything to stop them from hurting you."

Elle kept her eyes on the road, not saying anything. The thing was, there wasn't anything to say.

"I don't know why we didn't. I thought only the girls were doing it, to be honest. I didn't know that Sebastian was, too." Elle saw his hand grip the steering wheel, his knuckles turning white from the pressure.

She turned her head to look out the passenger window. She didn't want her face to show anything.

Nero took his injured right hand off the steering wheel and grasped Elle's hand. "He has done something to you before, hasn't he?"

Elle looked down at his hand in hers and observed his knuckles. She touched the scrape that lay on his middle knuckle and ran her fingertip along each red and swollen area, weaving in and out of all four knuckles. "I saw Sebastian's face in the parking lot. You should really put some ice on this."

Elle's silence answered his question.

"Then he and I are even now." She kept the pace of running her finger along his knuckles as his hand lay in her lap.

"You're not going to tell me what he did, are you?" He pulled his eyes off the road for a second to look at her.

"No, I'm not."

"Why not?"

Elle thought about those two words. '*Why not?*' After these last years, she had never told a soul about what happened to her in school, and had never revealed to anyone about what had happened to Chloe. Then, just two nights before, she had seen someone murdered and had instantly been certain she was never going to tell anyone in her life. So, why not? Elle felt like maybe she was wired that way—to keep secrets, to keep her mouth shut. She was always like that. It was in her DNA. She pictured the boss in her mind and that brought her to exactly why she would never tell.

"Because I'm not a rat."

As Nero looked at her at that last word, she looked back at him and felt like he was almost smiling on the inside; his eyes, at least, looked like he was.

"All right, I can respect that."

The car ride was nice. She was very comfortable there, holding his hand. They didn't have to force conversation; they both liked the silence at times.

When they were about halfway to her house, he asked her, "Can I take you out sometime?"

"Like on a date?" Elle hadn't been expecting that.

Nero laughed. "Yeah, like on a date."

Elle didn't know how to respond.

"Let me guess, you've never been on a date before?"

"Uh, no, I haven't. I work, you know, so I don't know if I can."

Nero removed his hand from hers. "Give me your phone."

"Why?"

When Nero gave her a look to not question him, she reached in her bag and then handed him her phone. It was perfect timing because he had stopped at a stop sign.

"What the hell kinda phone is this? It has fucking buttons."

"You mean a keyboard, yes."

"Yeah, I can see that." He punched in some buttons and she heard his phone ring. "All right, add that number in your phone."

She took her phone back and started saving his contact. "Okay, A-S-S-H-O-L-E. Got it." She smiled really big, proud of her quip.

"Very funny. Text me your schedule later so I can decide when we can go out."

"We're not going on a date."

"And why is that?"

"Because you've dated every girl in school since this semester started." Sure, she might have been exaggerating, but only a little. He *had* practically dated every girl in school, and three within the last

SARAH BRIANNE

week. The three that made her life a living hell every day.

"I don't date them, Elle."

"Like that makes it better!" Elle crossed her arms. *He is literally an asshole.*

His voice became dark. "Elle, did I ask to fuck you?"

Elle became uncomfortable, refusing to answer him.

"No, I asked to take you out on a date. Something that I haven't asked any girl before."

Elle turned her head toward him. She knew he wasn't lying. Nero wasn't the type to take a girl out on a date; he was the type to take them to his bed. She still wasn't going to respond to him, however.

"I'm done with those girls. I know you don't believe me, and that's fine, but I'm telling you anyways."

"It's still a no."

"You know, that's really hard for me to believe when you've been holding my hand for practically the whole car ride."

Elle didn't care, she wasn't holding it now.

He pulled up to her curb and jumped out before she could even put her hand on the door handle. He opened her door and she stood up from the car while he blocked her with his body, his hand holding the door so she couldn't move.

"What are you doing now?"

"I need another thank you."

She put her hands on his chest to protest, but before she could say anything, his lips planted on hers.

This kiss was different than the one before. This time, he was greedy and tried to take more, but Elle wouldn't open her mouth. He grabbed the back of her head to position her face higher, hoping she would slightly open. She didn't. His tongue outlined her bottom lip right before he pulled away.

She noticed her hands had continued resting on his chest when she was brought back to reality. She wasn't quite sure if she'd even kissed him back. She was actually pretty sure he had done all the work. The butterflies from earlier had returned the moment his lips had been on hers, and they were still there.

"I'll pick you up tomorrow morning for school."

"What?" Her mind was still jumbled after the kiss.

"Chloe can't pick you up tomorrow with her car in the shop. I doubt whoever drives her to school tomorrow will want to come out of their way to pick you up."

Yeah, they weren't. "So, I can catch the bus."

"Really, Elle? The bus?"

"Yes, I ride it practically every day to the diner downtown."

Nero's face looked shocked almost. "You ride the fucking bus that goes downtown, at night?"

"Yeah. So?"

"Do you realize how unsafe that is for a seventeen-year-old girl?"

"Do you realize I don't have a choice?"

"Well, now you do. What time do you work tonight?"

"No, you are not taking me to work. I've survived this long riding the bus."

"Jesus, Elle, I am taking you to work." Nero's eyes started to get that scary look again.

"No, you are not!" When she pushed at his chest to get him to move, he didn't even budge. Instead, Nero thrust his body closer to her, pinning her body to his. He took her chin in his hand to make sure she saw his face. His look became hungry again, as though the wolf had returned.

"That shit has the opposite effect on me, Elle, so be careful the next time your temper comes out." Nero took a deep breath in and out. "Go to work on your bus. Enjoy it, though, because it won't last much longer."

Elle tried to open her mouth to speak, but he wouldn't let a word come out.

"I will be here tomorrow morning to drive you to school. If your ass gets on the bus, there will be repercussions. I dare you to ride the bus tomorrow because, either way, I'll win." His grin was almost deadly.

"Just because you think you're the big bad wolf, I should do as you say? Well, it doesn't work that way with me."

Nero blinked a few times. He clearly looked confused. "The big bad wolf?"

"Yes, that's what you remind me of—a wolf," Elle said it matter-of-factly.

Nero shook his head. "Elle, lay off the movies a little."

"No. Can I go now?"

Nero smiled. "Sure, if you give me a kiss goodbye."

"So, if I kiss you, I can go?"

Nero smiled wider. "Yep."

"Promise?"

When Nero nodded, Elle rose up on her toes. She put her mouth close to his. Right when she went in, she moved her face slightly and gave him a peck on the cheek. Elle returned to her heels, laughing.

"That doesn't count."

Elle, still laughing, said, "Yes it does. You said I could leave if I kiss you. It's your fault you didn't say where. You promised." She knew she had him. He had promised.

"You're right. I keep my promises, Elle. Just remember that." Nero removed his hand from the car door to let her pass. "Don't forget to text me your schedule. Actually, let's make it a picture of your schedule," he said, smiling.

Elle had really had enough. She walked past him, holding up her hand and pointing at it with the other. "Actually, go rub some dirt on it."

Nero laughed, shutting the door to lean on his car. "Seven-thirty, Elle. I'll be right here." Nero leaned there, watching Elle run up to her house.

There was an upside to her running from him. The view was great.

THE BIG BAD WOLF
WANTED A TASTE

When *Elle was finally able* to shut the door, closing Nero out, she let out her breath.

"Elle, who is the cute boy? You didn't tell me you had a boyfriend."

Elle turned around, becoming embarrassed at seeing her mother looking out the window.

"He's not my boyfriend."

"Oh, sweetie, you can tell me. He is handsome. You should bring him over for dinner."

Elle rubbed her temples. "Mom, he is not my boyfriend. He just gave me a ride home."

"Why didn't Chloe give you a ride home?" Elle's father asked

She hadn't seen him when she'd first come in.

Elle thought quickly. "Her car wouldn't start." She was good at the lies now.

"Your mother's right; bring him over for dinner. I'd like to meet him." Her father rolled off into the kitchen.

This day is getting better and better. From behind her mother, Elle saw Josh appear, who was also looking out the window.

"What's his name?" Josh asked quizzically.

"Uh, Nero." She didn't know why he wanted to know.

Josh started running around the living room, yelling, "Elle and Nero, sitting in a tree, K-I-S-S-I-N-G. First comes—"

Elle started walking to her bedroom the moment he started singing. She slammed the door, shutting him out. *Better and better.*

She jumped on her bed, deciding to rest a second before she had to get ready for work.

She picked up her phone, staring at it, deciding to call Chloe. After a few rings, Chloe answered. "Hey," she quietly said.

"Did you tell your dad?"

"No. No point. I told Lana and she said her husband will take care of it for me."

Lana was her housekeeper and had been for years. She was practically Chloe's only parent. Chloe could tell her things she needed and Lana would help her out.

"That's good."

"Lana will be driving me till I get my car back, so…" Chloe didn't want to say it.

"That's okay. Nero said he would give me a ride tomorrow morning, and I always have the bus."

"Oh, really? Tell me how the car ride home was." Chloe's voice hinted at a smile.

"Fine."

"Just fine?"

"Yep. Fine, Chloe."

"He kissed you, didn't he?"

Silence met her answer.

"Oh, he totally did! Tell me, how was your first kiss?"

"Well, it technically wasn't my first."

"Oh, my gosh, what?"

"He kissed me earlier, in Art, in the supply closet."

"That is so freaking sweet."

"Yeah, yeah, yeah. Listen, Chloe, if you get to school before me, I can't help you."

"I know. I can figure out something, I guess. I'll be there at the exact time we always are." Elle hated that Chloe had returned to her usual non-happy voice, but she'd had to tell her.

"All right. I'll try to be there at the same time, but we know Nero is late practically every morning."

"I know."

Elle felt terrible. She was going to have to figure something out.

"I'll see you tomorrow, then."

"Bye."

Elle hung up the phone. She couldn't say bye.

Her wheels started turning in her head about how she could solve this problem. She decided to think while she got dressed for work.

While she was thinking, something Nero had said earlier crossed her mind. *'Do you realize how unsafe that is for a seventeen-year-old girl?'* She wondered how in the hell he knew she was seventeen. Actually, most of the seniors were already eighteen, besides her and Chloe. *So, how would he know?*

Nero started to feel confined at home, especially in his room. The job his father had given him had started to wear on his mind. This was his first job, the job that was going to adopt him into the family. Yes, his blood might biologically be a part of the family, but his blood didn't bleed *with* the family. *At least, not until the job is done.*

He had always been aware, ever since he had been young, he was going to follow in his father and brother's footsteps. He was going to bleed and die beside the family. *No matter what it takes.*

He wondered why Elle had been the one behind the garbage can that night. Any other girl would have been easier for him to crack—hell, the job would have already been done if she was like all the other girls he had been with. But not Elle. He couldn't even get her fucking mouth to open to stick his tongue down her throat, let alone tell her secrets. She had sat in his car and even protected a piece of shit like Sebastian, therefore getting her to tell him what had happened wouldn't be easy.

The thought of Sebastian pissed him off. He couldn't get the image out of his head of him lunging for Elle. *She just sat there and closed her eyes.*

He'd had to get Sebastian, to get his hands on him. As a result, he and his crew had made sure to get him alone. They worked out a plan to offer him some weed once they dropped the girls in Spanish class. They gave Sebastian a total bullshit peace offering to say he was sorry, that the heat of the moment had gotten to him. The heat of the moment had gotten to him all right.

He punched the shit out of him behind the school. *Little bitch took one punch and was cold turkey.* That didn't stop Nero and his crew. They each landed a kick on his helpless body.

Nero smiled. Elle hadn't seen the nice bruises he was sure Sebastian had under his clothes.

Again, with the thought of Elle, he grew hard. His body was out of whack. Typically, some girl would be in his bed to remedy his situation, but after his father banned him from girls other than Elle, he couldn't risk it. Kissing her had definitely set him off. The little nothing of a kiss in the closet had even set him off.

Usually, that would have been a joke of a kiss, but something about it had made him want more. Subsequently, when he had arrived at her house, he had kissed her again, harder. She hadn't even kissed him back, which made it that much worse. No girl had ever not kissed him back. He knew he was a good kisser—well, he used to be really sure of it.

When she had pushed him, it had been everything he could do

not to set her ass in his backseat and do as he pleased, certain he could get her to comply.

He grinned at what she'd called him earlier, *'the big bad wolf.'* Elle was right; he was the big bad wolf. He knew it worked perfectly to describe him because, every time he looked at Elle, he saw a cute, helpless animal.

He liked Elle's size; she was a good match for him. She wasn't tall but wasn't short. Her ass and boobs were the same in proportion, both a little bit more than a handful, and he liked that. But her hair and eyes were his favorite things about her.

Her darker-blonde hair had a hint of pink in it, and it had a nice wave to it throughout without being curly. Her eyes were huge and blue like the ocean. That was why she was this cute animal to him, because every time he looked into her big blue eyes, the big bad wolf wanted a taste. *More than a taste.*

When it dawned on Nero that he was on the verge of going insane, he made a phone call.

He spoke the second he heard grease flying. "Is Elle working?"

"Elle isn't here right now. She clocks in about an hour from now. Want me to leave a message?"

He knew what was going to come next. "No, I said Mel." He couldn't risk the guy who'd answered the phone telling her about someone calling for her.

"No Mel that I know of that works here."

"Sorry, wrong number." He clicked the phone off and got up out of bed, grabbing his keys off the nightstand. A job needed to be done.

DEATH WISH

Nero parked his car a little way back from the house. He turned off his engine, cutting the lights, complete darkness surrounding him. He only had to wait about five minutes until the front door opened and his target emerged. *Right on time.*

As she was walking down the sidewalk, he noticed what she was wearing. Her dark-grey coat covered a dark-orange dress. He had never seen her in a dress before. He noticed her long, lean legs and wondered why she only ever wore jeans. He knew the dress was a uniform, but it was totally working for him. He made a note to himself to see her in it up-close sometime before the job was done.

When she turned the corner, putting his car at her back, he turned the car on. He waited until she was almost out of eyesight before he put the car in drive, staying far enough behind until she made it to the bus stop. He then put his car back in park while she sat on the bench.

When an older guy came and sat on the bench beside her, something grew in his stomach. Nero watched the two talk, not understanding why she was being so friendly to a complete stranger. He knew they didn't know each other by the way she shook his hand and introduced herself.

Nero watched the man very closely until the bus rolled up and they entered. On the drive downtown, he stayed on the bus's bumper the entire time. He could see through the bus at stop lights. The guy had sat directly behind Elle. Nero didn't like it one bit. *There are fucking twenty other seats.*

Each second he saw her on the bus, the more he felt like pulling it over and throwing her in his car. He was a guy and knew exactly what the older man behind her was thinking—hell, he wanted to pull the bus over just to kill the guy.

When the next stop came, he saw Elle get up and turn around to say bye to the man. *What the fuck! She is asking to get killed.*

Nero wondered where Elle thought she lived. *The city is run by the fucking mafia.* He knew not only that, but she had seen someone murdered on these streets just days ago. *She has no idea that the big boss of the Caruso family was the one who did it, either.*

That was when Nero knew Elle had a death wish. She threw herself in front of Chloe every time at school; she worked in a diner at night downtown, and she rode the bus to get there.

When she got off the bus and the doors closed with the guy still inside, he started to ease himself back into sanity. He stayed behind her the few blocks she had to walk to get to the diner. When she made it inside, he parked his car again. Nero ran his hands through his hair and closed his eyes. He was gaining a headache after watching Elle be careless for her safety.

He observed her for a bit through the big diner windows, pouring coffee and taking orders. The diner was full with mostly men, most of them having come from the Casino hotel. He knew because he had watched them walk from one door down to the diner. After quite a bit of time had passed, he grew sick of watching the men's faces as she came to the table. *I can't watch this anymore.*

Nero turned off his car and got out, locking the doors. If he watched Elle another second, he was going to walk in there and watch her pour him coffee for the rest of the night. Instead of walking in the diner like he wanted to, he went to the Casino's hotel doors. He needed to be put out of his misery and get this job over with.

When he opened the doors and walked inside, the smell of smoke enveloped him and the different tones of slot machines greeted his ears. For some reason, Nero loved the smell and the loud noises. He saw peace in it. It was his second home.

He walked through the casino, going up the escalators where he turned around, looking at the view. The people laughing and having a good time, the different lights, and the cast of smoke that filled the air made him smile. He could see his future as the escalators brought him higher, and that made Nero exceptionally happy.

He walked off the escalators, bringing him to a security check for the hotel rooms. The guard waved him forward, letting Nero pass the people waiting to show them their room keys.

Getting on the elevator, he hit the top floor, holding down a series of buttons until it flashed. It made it possible for Nero to ride the elevator without a stop for people to come on. He was glad for that feature; otherwise, it would take all night to reach the top floor.

After the smooth ride of the elevator, Nero watched the door open. He walked down the long hallway, playing out what to say in his mind. When he came to the guarded door, he stopped.

"He wasn't expecting you tonight."

"I wasn't expecting to come down here."

"All right. One second." Nero watched the guy whisper into his earpiece for a brief moment.

"He said you can go in." The big guy opened the door and moved out of the way.

"I'd hope so," Nero replied as he walked through the door.

When the door was slammed shut, Nero looked around the big, dark yet bright room. Hardly any lights were on, but all the TV screens in there filled it with light. The people looking at the screens didn't once turn their heads to see who had entered.

Nero walked to the other side of the room, coming to a chair beside another door. He took a seat, knowing from experience it could take a while.

Nero pulled out his cell. He had a few texts, but not the one he wanted. He scrolled through his contacts, stopping at Elle's name. He hit the text button, bringing him to a new conversation, typing the words, **You at work yet?**

Four minutes passed and he got a reply that made him grin. **Maybe.**

Nero pulled up the keyboard, this time typing, **Schedule?**

Elle looked at her phone under the bar, and read the text message she had just received before putting it back in her apron. She walked through the swinging doors, bringing her to the kitchen. She went to the wall holding the OSHA binder and a long piece of paper. She stared at the words that titled the top. "Biweekly work schedule." Her eyes traveled down the paper, looking at the two-week sentence.

'Let's make it a picture of your schedule.' She didn't know if giving him her schedule was a good idea. If she did, well, then she couldn't lie to him, using work as an excuse to get out of doing something with him.

Elle stared at the paper a little longer, coming to a conclusion and a solution.

She pulled her phone out of her apron and snapped a picture of her schedule. Going to her recent texts, she knew exactly what to say.

Nero felt his phone vibrate in his hand. Turning it over, he read the words, **How about a trade?**

Nero was intrigued. **What do you want?**

A minute later he read, **If you want the schedule, then we will** need to be at school early before Chloe gets there.

Nero liked that Elle cared for her friend so much. It showed him she was loyal. However, her loyalty didn't change the fact he didn't like that idea. Nero had never been a morning person. He was already going to have to get up early as it was to pick Elle up for school. No way was he waking up *that* early. He decided to counter.

Elle felt her phone vibrate in her apron while she poured coffee to one of her tables. She was going to make good tip money tonight; the diner had been full practically the whole night. She went to the counter and pulled out her phone, not understanding why everything had to be so difficult when it concerned Nero as she read his message. **I'll tell Amo to be there early. He can watch her.**

Elle didn't know why this was a discussion. She was the one with the schedule. **No schedule then**. She hit the word send.

Elle had refilled the coffee cups to the brim when her next message came back. **Then no one there to look after Chloe.**

Elle cursed his name. She should have thought about him using Chloe's safety against her.

Elle decided to text Chloe first. **Amo will be at school before you get there. Stay with him till I get there, okay?**

Elle took an order from one of her usual customers. She always liked when he came by. He would tell her funny jokes and make sure she was tipped well.

When she put his order in, she read her message from Chloe. **Please, no, Elle. I'll be fine.**

Elle thought realistically for a second. *No, she wasn't going to be fine.*

She sent Chloe another message. **Cassandra could be back tomorrow. Amo will meet you at your parking spot, all right? You know it's the best thing.**

After Elle dropped an order at a table, she went to the back again, laughing at Chloe's reply. **UGHH FINE!!**

Elle decided to go back to the kitchen and take another picture of the schedule. She would let Nero win the battle, *again.* But from now on, she decided things were going to change. She was going to win the damn war.

Nero thought he was going to doze off in the oversized leather chair before Elle texted back. He knew he had her when he had texted her that no one would be there to watch Chloe; thus, he didn't understand why it would take so long to reply. *She already lost.*

When his phone finally vibrated, he looked at her reply. **So, Amo will be there?**

Nero knew he had won again. **Yeah, bright and early. You have my word.**

A minute later, he read her reply. **Tell him to meet Chloe at her parking spot then.**

A moment later, the text was followed by a picture message.

He clicked it open to enlarge the image. The picture ended up turning out to be better than he had thought; he could use this to his advantage.

When he went through the one-week schedule, Elle's name definitely stood out. *Dammit, she works every fucking night practically.*

Nero thought about what he had gone through that evening. He figured if he didn't get this job done, he was going to turn himself gray at an early age.

When the door opened at last and a familiar face walked out, Nero heard him say, "He's ready for you now."

Nero decided to hit send on the message he had made before the door had opened. **Deal.**

As he rose from the chair, Nero responded, "Thanks, Sal."

HOW TO WILLINGLY LOVE
A CARUSO IN A MONTH

The boss heard Sal say, "He's been out there waiting for a while now, boss." The meeting had just come pretty much to a close.

"He can wait. Why do you think he's here, boys?"

"I saw her. She ain't the usual. She's the kind you marry then fuck." He stared at his son, standing in the corner as he put a cigarette to his lips and lit the end with his metal lighter.

The lighter had actually been a gift from the boss the day his son had become the underboss. He thought that every man shouldn't have just any ninety-nine cent lighter you could pick up at a gas station as you checked out. No, this lighter had been handed down over generations. He had used that very lighter for years. The only thing was, he wished his son lit cigars, not cigarettes. *There's a lot I wish he did differently.*

"So, you've been following her?"

"Not exactly," his son said as he exhaled and smoke filled the room.

The smell made the boss want to reach for one of his cigars, but he didn't like to mix that shit with his good stuff. "So, what exactly were you doing?"

"I watched her for a bit." He took another hit off his cigarette.

"What for?" He knew why, but he wanted his answer.

"I had to make sure things were going in the right direction."

"Are they?"

"How about we ask him?" He nodded his head toward the door.

His son was right; not only was he a little suspicious on whether Nero could get the job done, but his own brother was, too.

"Sal, bring him in."

He watched Sal open the door and head off to take care of some things. Nero came in and shut the door behind him. Unlike his older brother, he took a seat in one of the chairs.

"How was school today, son?" By the look on Nero's face, he knew he understood what he meant.

"Promising. I got her to come around."

"Really? How's that?" He studied his son. He would make sure everything that came from his mouth was the whole fucking truth.

"I gained her trust. She's not exactly the most popular girl in school, so I made them lay off her and her friend a little. Then I got lucky and one of them slashed her friend's tires, the same friend who takes her to and from school. Took her home. Taking her to school.

Going to make that a permanent thing."

"That's good. Do you have any proof you have her trust? Not that I don't believe you, Son, but she's smarter than you think." He did believe Nero was telling the truth; he just knew a girl like Elle could pull the wool over his eyes.

"Yeah, she gave me her work schedule. Told her I needed it to see when we could go out sometime." Nero handed over his phone with the picture already up on the screen. Boss Caruso looked it over.

He heard the flip of the lighter open, then it firing, his older son moving on to another cigarette. He watched him flip the lighter shut. His son had learned every Zippo trick out there. *He's gonna break the fucking thing soon.* The only reason he didn't take it back was because he knew his son would get it repaired if need be.

He took out a cigar. He didn't care about the smells mixing at this point. He pulled out his own lighter and lit the end.

Inhaling the wonderful taste, he moved on, "So, what is it you really wanted to tell me?"

He watched Nero run his hands through his hair. "I don't think she will ever tell. She keeps a lot of shit hidden. Been beat up real bad a couple of times, but would never tell who it was. I asked her if a certain person did something to her, and she protected him. He's a real piece of shit, too, so there's no reason for her not to tell. I asked her why and she told me she wasn't a rat."

He exhaled after a long hit. "She said that she wasn't a rat, specifically?" When he watched his son nod, he flexed his jaw. He would move on for now. "Who is her friend?" *Elle might tell her over anyone.*

To his surprise, his other son answered the question and Nero looked just as shocked. "Chloe Masters." He watched his son emerge from the corner and squeeze Nero's shoulder. "You're welcome, brother. I figured she might have given you something good for taking her home. I hope you can save her by her eighteenth birthday. You don't mind sharing, do you? Don't worry; you can have her first. Virgins aren't my thing. I prefer a little experience."

Nero stood, looking his brother in the face. "I don't think either of us are her type."

"Let's hope she learns how to willingly love a Caruso in a month. You know, for her sake." He inhaled his cigarette, letting the end turn bright red.

"Yeah, Lucca, let's hope that ends up being me. You know, for her sake." Nero left the room, slamming the door shut behind him.

Boss Caruso squeezed the bridge of his nose. "Chloe Masters, huh?"

Lucca finally took a seat in front of him. "That's the one."

"Shit, we were all getting along so well." The relationship they had with Chloe's father was crucial to his business. It had taken a while to get him on his payroll, and it hadn't been easy.

"Yeah, one big, happy family." Lucca put his cigarette out in the ashtray and got up to head for the door.

"Keep following her, son."

He had known the second he saw that one-week schedule, Elle was one step in front of Nero. He owned the Casino Hotel; therefore, he knew schedules were typically more than a week in advance.

"I planned on it, boss." Lucca left the room without a sound. Boss Caruso wasn't even sure the door had closed.

He thought about what Nero had said as he brought the cigar to his mouth. *'She told me she wasn't a rat.'* His gut had been right; she had done more than just hear what happened in that alleyway, and he was going to do whatever it took to find out exactly what she had seen. He exhaled in an attempt to get rid of the horrible cigarette smell permeating the room. *I've seen a lot of men turn rat.*

Nero walked out of the room, fuming on the inside. He only hoped he didn't give himself away. When he made it to the elevator, he decided to text Elle again.

Need a ride home?

While the elevator traveled down, he made sure to keep his calm. He had to keep in mind that this whole place had cameras everywhere.

When he exited the elevator, he started his journey back to his car, passing the security guards, going down the escalator and walking out of the casino. He had walked into the casino earlier with a different feeling than he had when he walked out.

When the city noise greeted him, he turned his head to look at the diner next door. It took everything he had in him not to walk in there and take a seat at one of her tables, especially seeing how packed it was now with men. He took a deep breath in and smoothed his hair down before he walked back to his car.

He unlocked the doors and slid in, glad the windows were tinted. At night, it was impossible to see in.

He punched the steering wheel with his already-battered hand, drawing blood from his knuckles for the second time today.

You're welcome, brother.

Nero wanted to fight his brother like they usually had when they didn't agree. But this time, he couldn't. It was job related and you didn't just get in a fight with the underboss unless you're prepared to get your hand chopped off. Not even if you're brothers. The family was built upon one thing, respect.

He knew his brother wouldn't touch Elle in that way, but he still didn't like the words that spat from his mouth about her.

That's not why I'm even fucking mad, is what he told himself. *They don't fucking think I can do it.*

He hated the fact they were going behind his back. Once you give someone the job, then it was their job alone. There was no bullshit. This was Nero's first job, and he didn't want any help.

I can do this on my own.

Nero watched Elle through the diner windows. He saw her laughing while she filled up cups at a table full of men. He gripped the steering wheel, having had enough. He was going to walk in there.

He got out of his car and saw Elle go to the bar. She looked down and started smiling. He had stopped walking immediately. The smile stopped him in his tracks. The smile she had on her face was one he hadn't seen before. He felt his phone vibrate.

Bite me, he read.

He pulled up the keyboard. **I'd love to, when I take you home.**

He stayed put, watching her just a little longer.

She went back to the bar and smiled that same smile that made his chest a little weaker. He wasn't sure what it was.

His phone vibrated again.

I'm sure you would, wolf. I can make it home to grandma on my own.

Nero texted back, **You watch way too many movies. What's your favorite movie, anyway?**

Nero smiled as he got back in the car. Elle's smile had calmed him down. Now that he knew what her real smile looked like, the ones she was giving her customers couldn't even compare.

I don't have one. I like too many. You? he read when his phone vibrated again.

Nero and Elle texted each other throughout her shift, getting to know one another. Nero surprisingly enjoyed it; watching her smile behind the bar when she thought no one was looking at her, while secretly texting.

He wasn't into texting girls. Really never gave a shit what they had to say. High school girls only wanted to gossip and he only wanted to fuck them. Elle was different; she only answered his questions and asked her own of him. He told himself that this was a good thing for the job; she had to get to know him to completely trust him.

He watched her end her shift and put on her coat. He was relieved she was finally getting out of there. She walked the few blocks to the bus stop and got on while Nero followed right behind her the entire time. She exited the bus and he turned his headlights off, trailing her until she made it to her house.

When she got in, Nero rubbed his eyes. The night had been rough on him. He didn't think he could watch her go to and from work again. The city was dangerous and Nero really knew exactly how dangerous it could be. He had no idea how she was still in one piece, or sane for that matter, for as long as she had been working there. He was going to have to come up with something. And by seeing her schedule, he needed to do it soon; otherwise, his sanity was going to be the one lost, *for good.*

He picked up his phone, rolling through his contacts before he hit call. It rang three times before it was answered.

"What do you need now, Nero?"

Nero laughed. "You didn't let the two little girls get to you, did you?"

"Nope, not at all."

Nero could hear something in the background. Smiling, he asked, "Is that anyone I know?"

"Nope, she goes to public school. I'd rather not have all your sloppy seconds."

Nero started thinking. "Public school, huh?"

"Yeah, and they come without sticks up their asses."

"Does she come with friends?" Nero knew he was going to go crazy if he didn't find someone to get rid of his blue balls.

"A lot of them. That's the best part about public school."

"Well, let's set something up." Nero looked at Elle's house.

"Immediately."

A deep laugh came over the phone. "Sounds like one little girl is getting to you."

"Well, that's actually why I called. Amo, I have a job for you."

THE ENJOYMENT OF
TERRORIZING LITTLE KIDS

lle woke the next morning exhausted. Her body wasn't used to going to school and working. She knew it would take until the end of the week to do so. She got out of bed and went through her usual morning routine.

She looked at her small collection of clothes and couldn't decide what to wear. *I really gotta go shopping, soon.*

She decided to grab one of her favorite t-shirts—Goodwill was always good for awesome t-shirts, whether they were funny, strange, or band shirts. This one was white and sported her favorite band. She picked dark, tight jeans; brown booties; and an old, brown leather jacket. The jacket was another piece from thrift shopping that had become one of her staples.

She was happy with her outfit. She had never believed the price tag determined how good an outfit could look. However, without fancy labels sewed in her clothes, everyone at school had free reign to pick on her.

She moved on to brush her hair, the wavy mass softened by the bristles and making it shine. She threw on her usual light makeup; powder, mascara, and her pink lip balm. Satisfied with the way she looked, she grabbed her satchel and headed out her bedroom door.

She walked through her house and checked the time. Nero was supposed to be there in five minutes. She wasn't sure if she would still ride with him; she would make up her mind when she walked out the front door.

When she made it to her kitchen, her family was already seated at the table, eating breakfast. She grabbed a biscuit and started smothering grape jelly in between.

"Good morning, sweetie," her mother said.

Elle smiled. "Morning, Mom." She walked over to her brother and ruffled his hair. "Hey, kiddo."

"Hey," Josh said, picking at his food.

"He doesn't want to go to school today," her father broke in.

"Why don't you want to go to school today?" Elle looked at her brother.

"I just don't want to ride the bus." He picked at his food a little more.

"I know, kiddo. I hated riding the school bus, too. Want me to walk with you to the bus stop?"

"Yeah, I guess." He put his fork down.

"All right, go get your stuff." Elle took a bite of her biscuit.

"That boy taking you to school today?" her dad asked.

"I don't know yet." Elle took another bite.

"Well, let your mother know what day you're off this week, and she will cook a dinner so you can invite him over." Elle looked at her father. He didn't look very pleased by the way he was shoveling food.

"Dad, it's not like that with us."

Elle's dad stopped shoving food in his mouth. "Do it."

Elle nodded and took another bite of her biscuit before setting it down. Josh was ready, wearing his backpack. Elle checked the time, seven-thirty.

She and Josh headed out the house, and she held Josh's hand as they walked down the driveway. Nero wasn't there, so she took that as a sign to take the bus. She would drop Josh off at his school bus stop first since it was on the way. They started walking down the street.

"Is there a reason why you don't want to ride the bus anymore?"

Josh didn't say anything.

"Fifth-grader, huh?"

"How'd you know?" Josh looked up at her finally.

"Because I've been picked on, too."

"What did you do?"

Elle thought for a second and decided to tell him the truth. "Nothing."

"That's what I do, and they haven't stopped." Elle's heart started to break. She didn't want her brother to go through what she had.

When they were about halfway to Josh's stop, a car Elle

recognized drove past them and then parked on the curb in front of them. Nero stepped out of the car and leaned on it, crossing his arms. Elle could see Nero looked even unhappier than he usually did. *Great, just what I needed.*

"Hey, isn't that your boyfr—" Elle covered his mouth.

Nero's face started to become less pissed. "I still heard him."

When Elle and Josh caught up to Nero, she felt his eyes look her up and down. She noticed his face didn't look pissed at all anymore.

Elle became self-conscious and grabbed her jacket tighter around her. "Josh, this is my *friend*, Nero. Nero, this is my brother, Josh."

"Hey, little man." Nero held out his fist. Elle noticed it looked worse than the day before.

Josh smiled and fist bumped him. "Hey, Nero. Cool name!"

"Thanks, it's Italian. Is there a reason why you're walking toward the bus stop, Elle?"

Elle decided to not tell the whole truth. "Yes, I told Josh I would drop him off at the bus stop." Elle lowered her voice. "I think a fifth-grader is giving him some trouble."

"And you think you going with him is going to solve his problem?"

"Maybe I can talk to the kid and—"

"Jesus, Elle, that will only make it worse. Here, come on." Nero nodded his head toward the bus stop, and Elle and Josh started walking again with Nero walking beside Elle the rest of the way to the stop.

When they were a few feet away, Nero stopped. "All right, Elle, you wait here."

Elle decided not to argue. *I'm not the popular one. He would know.*

Elle ruffled Josh's hair. "All right, kiddo, I'll see you later."

"Bye, Elle-bell." Josh hugged her waist before he and Nero headed toward the bus.

When they got there, Elle could tell exactly who the kids were that had been picking on Josh. They were already picking on another poor, little kid. However, as soon as they noticed Nero and Josh, every kid stared. Elle knew why, too; Elle, herself, had been a little terrified when she saw Nero for the first time, and that had been years ago.

When the school bus pulled up, Josh and Nero bumped fists again and Josh jumped on the bus. Nero walked over to the older bullies. The little kid was able to run free when Nero reached them. She knew Nero was talking to them but wasn't able to hear what he was saying. By the looks on the kids' faces, Elle knew it wasn't things you should probably say to a kid. Under different circumstances, Elle might have cared by the way they ran like their lives depended on it once he was done, but she was getting sick of all the bullying. Moreover, she certainly wasn't going to tolerate it when it concerned her little brother.

Nero started walking back toward her with a smug look on his face. *He might have enjoyed that too much.*

Then Elle pictured Josh's upset face. *Nah.*

When he reached Elle, he grabbed her hand to start the walk back to his car. Elle let him do it without resisting. *He did just help Josh.*

"Hmm, I wonder what kind of thank you I should get for that."

That's what the smug face was for. "The enjoyment of terrorizing little kids?"

"No, that was just a bonus." He pulled her body in a little closer. "I'll think of something."

Elle laughed. "I have no doubt."

"Good, Elle-bell." Nero said the last part sarcastically.

"Oh, gosh. Don't you start that."

"What? I think it's cute, like a Disney movie or some shit like that." He wasn't done being sarcastic. She thought she might have deserved that, though.

"Yeah, from an eight-year-old boy."

She and Nero walked to the car peacefully. She almost didn't want it to end. She liked walking her street in the cold beside him.

Nero held onto her hand and went to the passenger door. Elle was expecting him to open it for her; instead, he pushed her up against the car.

"So, I'm going to pretend your ass was going to come back and meet me in your driveway."

"I was just going to help Jo—"

As Nero moved and pinned her body against his, she looked up at him, thanking God this wasn't happening in front of her house. She noticed his face looked tired, like he had hardly gotten any sleep the night before, and she was clearly making him cranky.

"What have I told you about lying to me, Elle?" His face was just inches from hers. She figured he was super cranky; however, she didn't know why he was taking it out on her.

"I believe you told me not to lie to you. Not now, not ever." She didn't like his attitude at all. *It's his fault he can't sleep.*

"So, why did you just try to lie to me?"

Elle really didn't know why other than it honestly was a reflex at this point.

Nero grabbed her hair, moving her head higher. "Why did you just lie to me?"

Elle had definitely had enough. "You don't have to be so grouchy in the morning. Go to bed earlier if you're so damn tired."

Elle saw something break in Nero's eyes. What she had just said to him had clearly sent him over the edge. She realized she probably shouldn't have said that when his lips slammed down on hers. This time, the butterfly feeling came back stronger. She didn't think it was possible, but Nero was much hungrier than the last time he'd kissed her.

Elle forgot all about his attitude and placed her hands on his chest. The way he was kissing her made her start to kiss back this time.

Nero grabbed her hip with his free hand, pulling her even closer to his body. Elle could feel his bulge grow on the lower part of her belly, making her realize what was going on. She tried to push his chest away and Nero bit her lip. *Ouch.* He then sucked it in his mouth to take the pain away, making Elle forget how turned on Nero was getting. He had started to do things to her with the way he was licking her lips, trying to enter. He pulled her hair a little harder with no success.

Elle heard him grit out the word "open" on her lips. She didn't like when he pulled away to talk, her own desire making her mind crumble. She opened her mouth.

The feeling of his tongue entering her mouth was one Elle didn't think she'd like, but when their tongues met, Elle wondered why she had fought it so hard. His tongue managed to get hers to release from her mouth, giving him the opportunity Nero had been waiting for. He sucked her tongue into his mouth, making Elle rise to the tip of her toes and dig her nails into his chest. She involuntarily let a moan escape from her lips.

The moan made Nero do the opposite of what Elle had thought he would do. He pulled his lips from hers, making her return to her feet. He then rested his forehead on hers as they breathed heavily. Elle could still feel his bulge before he pulled his hips slightly away, yet Elle was aware it had only grown bigger.

After a few seconds, Elle caught her breath and realized what had happened between them.

"You bit me!" She touched her lip to see if there was any blood. There wasn't, but her lip felt a little swollen.

Nero laughed. "Technically, you asked me to. Remember?"

"I was being sarcastic." Elle licked her lip to see if she tasted blood, feeling it start to pulsate.

Nero got the hungry look in his eye again. She thought he was going to give her another rough kiss, but this time, he tenderly kissed her bottom lip, letting his tongue swipe over the part that felt like it was burning.

He raised his head up. "Better?"

Elle didn't think a guy like Nero could be that sweet, yet the way he had done that had caused her heart to sink to her stomach, joining the butterflies that still filled it.

Elle's ability to form words had fled her at that point, and as a result, she just nodded her head.

Nero grinned. "Good." He finally released his body from hers, giving her room to move so he could open her door. "We're gonna be late."

Elle slid in the car, her mind starting to return. *Very slowly, apparently.*

He opened his door and got in. "By the way, don't think I forgot you tried to lie to me again."

Her mind fully returned. "So, how long is it gonna take for me to turn into a wolf, so I can run the hell away from you?"

I WANT A FUCKING HUG

Nero *got a good laugh* out of that one. She had never heard him laugh like that before. His mood had greatly improved. *Yeah, because he finally got to stick his tongue down my throat.*

"Just don't lie to me again. I'm not going to put up with it the next time."

Elle knew she should really start cutting down the lies. "Fine, I won't lie to you anymore."

Nero looked at her, and when he was satisfied with her answer, he started the car. Once he was on the road, Elle decided to ask the question that had been bothering her all last night.

"How did you know I'm seventeen?" She kept her eyes on Nero.

"All the seniors are either seventeen or eighteen. I just went with the one that popped in my head first. Lucky guess." She watched Nero not move his eyes from the road. She knew Nero had only had two options. *There was a fifty-fifty shot.*

"How old are you?"

"Turned eighteen in August."

"Feel any different?" Elle was curious if she would feel like an adult, even though she felt like an adult already.

"Other than the fact I can buy cigarettes and get charged as an adult, nope."

Elle laughed hard. She'd figured that was about how it would feel.

Nero looked at Elle and she quit laughing as he grabbed her hand. Looking at his hand woven in hers, she noticed again it actually looked much worse than yesterday.

"Was there another face that needed punching?"

Nero smiled. "Nope."

"Nero, you can't lie to me if I can't lie to you." She was going to make sure everything was going to be fair between them.

Nero looked at Elle. "I'm not lying. I didn't punch anyone."

Elle knew he wasn't lying. *Liars don't look you in the eye when they lie.*

"Will you do me a favor and quit punching people and things?"

He squeezed her hand. "I don't make promises I can't keep, Elle."

"Well, will you do me a favor and *try* to quit punching people and things?"

Nero took her hand and placed a kiss on the back. "For you, I will." He kept her hand on his side, putting it in his lap. She thought about snatching it back, but the look he gave her made her reconsider.

She relaxed in his car for the rest of the way to school. She wished she didn't have to go, content with staying in his car, but she needed to be there for Chloe.

They pulled up into the parking lot and Elle scanned her eyes across the lot for her friend. When she didn't see her, Elle started to get anxious to get out of the car.

She figured Nero had caught on. "Elle, I told Amo to go ahead and take her to class. She will be right there when we get there." He held her hand a little tighter. "Together."

Elle decided to calm her nerves. "Okay." *I'm sure she's fine with Amo.*

Nero finally let her hand go and she exited the car, grabbing her bag. She decided to trust Nero, and instead of running to her classroom, she stood by the car. As Nero reached her, he took her hand and they both started walking in the building together. Elle did walk faster than she thought Nero would like, but she didn't care—she just wanted to see Chloe.

When they got close to the classroom, Elle noticed Amo leaning against the lockers. He looked even rougher than Nero did this morning.

After she finally reached the door, she poked her head inside. Relief flooded over her when she saw Chloe right in her seat at the back of the class. She could tell Chloe might have been a little pissy, but she would take that.

Grateful, she did something she was sure she would regret later, yet she was too happy Chloe was safe. *I may finally have someone else I can trust with her.*

Elle hugged Amo's side, then she leaned up as high as she could and kissed him on the cheek, barely making it. "Thanks."

Elle ran off into the classroom to go be with her best friend. She couldn't be happier.

Nero couldn't be more pissed. He didn't understand how Amo could get a fucking thank you without asking. How he could get a kiss without asking. *How come she never throws herself at me for a hug? I want a fucking hug.*

He decided to keep his cool, though.

"Did she just do what I just think she did?" Amo asked, pointing in the direction Elle had run away from Nero, *again.*

"Yep, she did."

Amo held up his hands. "Hey, man, I didn't do anything."

Nero grabbed Amo's shoulder. "It's fine, man. Someone looks like shit today. Rough night?"

"Try rough fucking morning." Amo lowered his voice. "That girl is fucking nuts. I can't babysit her anymore. Tell Vince to do it; he'll like watching her."

"That's exactly why he can't watch her. Elle ain't going to trust him with her." Hell, Nero wouldn't trust his sister with Vincent. In five seconds, he could have any girl drop to her knees.

"Well, I don't know what to tell you. She practically screamed when I almost touched her, and it wasn't the kind of scream I made Christa do last night."

Nero knew this job wasn't going to be easy. The girls were possibly tighter than him and his crew.

"Listen, you know our job. We want in, don't we?"

Amo nodded. "Okay. Fine."

Nero decided to change the subject. "Christa, huh?"

"Yep, and Christa has a shit ton of friends waiting to meet some prep school guys tomorrow."

"Good. You, me, and Vince deserve a reward after these two." Nero had to get laid.

The way Elle's mouth felt only made it worse. He hadn't planned to kiss her like that; however, the only other thing he wanted to do was choke her for telling him to go to bed earlier. The only reason he had stayed up the whole night was because all he could think about was a way to get her to stop riding the bus. *And fucking her brains out.* Then, when she moaned in his mouth, he had to stop because, if she made another sound, he was sure to take her on the hood of his car.

"Yes, we do, man. Oh, that reminds me, when I met Chloe this morning, her car was still there. I figured her dad would have picked it up."

"Yeah, me, too. Maybe he was too busy running the city." He didn't know why else he would leave a BMW.

"Or maybe he doesn't like dealing with her crazy ass just as much as me."

"Elle, I can't deal with him. He's crazy!" Chloe tried to keep her voice down, but Elle knew she was about to lose it.

"Shh, I know, but you are here in one piece, untouched, right?" Elle was making sure no one had tried to give them any trouble.

"Barely! He tried to push me to walk beside him. All he had to do was tell me to."

Elle laughed. "Chloe, you gotta start to get used to walking beside us. It's okay as long as we're with them. This is a good thing we got going now. I'm not as worried anymore. Are you?"

Elle knew she wasn't by the way she looked. She definitely had gotten more than an hour of sleep.

After a minute, Chloe finally answered, "No, I'm not that scared when they are around."

"See, Chloe. They can get us to survive the rest of the semester. Then, when we're out, we won't need them anymore." She knew they would finally be free, and it was going to just be her and Chloe.

Chloe sighed. "Whatever. Fine."

"Want to go shopping tomorrow? I got Friday off. I think we deserve it." Her closet seriously needed some help and she deserved a girl's night.

"We sure do, surrounded by those three idiots."

WHAT'S UP HIS BUTT?

lle watched Nero walk into the classroom. Whatever he and Amo had been talking about had made him pissed. *Geez, I thought he was pissed earlier.*

This time, Nero was fuming. Elle thought she should probably be a little scared. When he started to take his seat right in front of her, he gave her the look of death. *Okay, now I am a little scared.*

She had no clue what had gone on between them in the hall, but something told her she probably didn't want to know.

After Mr. Evans assigned everyone *Beowulf,* they started going around the classroom, reading a scene aloud by playing popcorn. Elle honestly wasn't paying attention; she was too preoccupied thinking about what Nero was so pissed about.

Nero's look of death brought a memory to her mind.

Elle and Chloe left their science class a bit after the final school bell rang, waiting to let the crowd die down. Elle had noticed Chloe had started walking a step behind her, but still halfway at her side. Every day since they had started to become friends, she felt her edge over more and more at her back. Elle understood why—hell, even her head stayed down to the point where she needed to use Elle to guide her anyway.

Elle didn't mind being her guide. She knew it was hard for Chloe to show her new markings. Elle would have been the same way. The cuts still looked red and nasty, but they were healing better every day. Elle just wished her mind would begin to heal.

As Elle walked down the hallway, she saw Sebastian and a senior doing something fishy. Sebastian handed over the money while the senior handed over a small bag. Elle figured they thought they were being sneaky doing it in the back hall when all the teachers had checked their minds out for the day an hour ago.

When the deal was done, Sebastian looked around as the senior left with his money. Elle quickly turned her head, afraid Sebastian might have seen her. She guessed he hadn't when he didn't come after her.

She was closer to the doors when she had to take a sharp turn to get out of the halls and reach the front. When she took the turn, she felt a huge whack on her face. She swore she heard her nose break from the hit. Elle was whacked so hard she fell back on her ass. Reaching for her nose, she could feel the blood rush down her face, soaking her shirt.

Elle looked up and saw Chloe frozen in place and Sebastian standing over her with a huge-ass biology book in his hands. Elle was terrified by the look on Sebastian's face.

"You need to fucking keep your eyes to yourself, bitch."

"I wasn't going to say anything. I don't care what you do." Her hands and arms were now saturated in blood.

"What the fuck did you just say to me? You don't care what I do?" Sebastian reared the book back in his hands as Elle covered her head. She felt a smash on her forearm and prayed it wasn't broken, either, because of the sound she'd heard.

"Keep your fucking mouth shut, the both of you."

Elle looked up. She was sick to her stomach that he would go for Chloe. Exactly as she'd feared, he reared the book back again, this time toward Chloe.

"Noooo!" Elle moved to grab his leg and was happy when she didn't hear the book connect.

"Don't you tell me no." Sebastian raised the book back a third time.

Elle managed to get her arms up to cover her again when he smashed her same arm. By the sound, she knew it was as good as broken from the second impact.

Sebastian finally left, satisfied with what had taken place. Elle didn't even care about her arm when she looked up at Chloe's crying face. The tears were illuminated red on the right side as they slid down her slashes. It was worth it to her. . .

"Elle, it's your turn. Elle." Elle was brought back by the sound of her name coming from Mr. Evans.

"My turn?" She was starting to become embarrassed when she saw everyone staring at her, especially when Nero turned around.

"Yes, Chloe popcorned you." Elle couldn't believe someone had picked Chloe. *They probably wanted to hear her stumble.*

Elle was grateful when Chloe moved over and put her finger at where to start reading. Elle began reading immediately, not wanting to make a bigger scene. When she popcorned Nero, she decided to follow along this time because she was afraid of the same thing happening again. The class actually flew by for the remaining time now that Elle had decided to get into the story.

The bell rang and Nero actually walked out of the classroom. For some reason, she'd thought he would wait for her. Elle and Chloe packed up their things and walked out to see Nero, Amo, and Vincent leaning up against the lockers, talking. Elle walked over toward them, feeling Chloe following behind.

As soon as Elle got there, their conversation came to an end. Nero nodded his head at Amo and he started walking. Nero was still mad, and he wasn't trying to act friendly. Elle decided not to care, and subsequently she went to follow Amo.

Chloe walked beside her. Although she was still somewhat awkward, she was getting the hang of it. Elle also thought Nero would walk beside her, but he didn't do that, either. She turned her head back and saw he was walking beside Vincent today.

Elle was starting to get mad at herself. She didn't know why she cared so much, but she did. She had actually been getting used to him walking with her and holding her hand. *I don't miss holding his damn hand.* Elle decided to get that out of her mind.

"What's up his butt?" she heard Chloe whisper.

"I don't know. He was fine before I walked into English. The moment he walked in, though, he flipped a switch and turned into a different person." Elle kept it at a whisper, as well. The halls were noisy enough to block out anything they said. Besides, they were walking a few feet in front of him while they walked a few feet behind Amo.

"He's probably bipolar, Elle. You saw the look in his eyes yesterday with Sebastian." She was probably right. Whatever Nero had, however, he needed to be on medication for his problems.

"I bet you're right," Elle whispered back. "He has to have something wrong with him. No one is that perfect and good-looking without having a screw loose."

Nero heard Vincent laugh and asked, "What happened?"

Nero kept his eyes on Elle in front of him.

"Nothing."

A moment later, he watched Elle turn around. *That's fucking right.* He figured she would be confused as to why he wasn't walking beside her, holding her hand. He didn't want to fucking hold her hand right now; he had barely been able to contain himself from punching Amo in the face earlier. He had gone for it, then he grabbed his shoulder instead.

He had been prepared to fight one of his best friends over a stupid girl, and it hadn't even been Amo's fault. *Although, he didn't give two shits about moving. No, instead, he let her hug and kiss him.*

"Really? Because, by the look of her face, I think there might be a problem." Vincent was still smiling. Nero thought he was enjoying the show.

"She did something I really fucking wish she didn't." Nero thought he would confide a little in Vincent, who was the ultimate woman killer. Vincent not only slept with girls their age, but girls much older than them. Nero was almost sure he'd even slept with some girl's hot mother.

"Just talk to her about it. Girls love that shit. Tell her it really hurt you, and that she needs to say sorry by sucking your dick. That's what I would do."

Nero shook his head at his friend. The guy was crazy. There was no way Nero would talk to her first. She needed to figure out what she had done on her own. Nero wasn't going to give Elle the satisfaction of knowing it had hurt him.

"No, man, I'll enjoy watching her crawl back to me."

Nero made his mind up. *She will crawl, and she won't fucking do it again.*

Nero looked over at Vincent when he spoke. "A piece of advice: that girl will never crawl to anyone. You'll be lucky to get that girl on her knees, period."

"If I'm lucky enough to get her on her knees, why would you say she needs to say sorry by sucking me off?" Nero kept his eyes on Elle. The girls were whispering. He figured Elle was talking about him. *About how much she misses me already.*

Vincent's laugh drew Nero's attention. "I said if it was me, man."

Now Nero's head was filled with the image of Elle sucking Vincent's dick, which only made him even more furious. He was glad they'd finally reached the girls' classroom; he couldn't look at Elle any longer. Walking behind her was torture; it was hard not to look at her ass, thinking about giving in and talking to her just so he could kiss her again and grab it.

Nero watched Amo wait by the door while Chloe walked in the classroom right before Elle turned again, looking him in the eye. Nero stared back like he didn't give a shit, then he watched Elle stomp into the room.

Nero looked at his crew, who were laughing and shaking their heads. Nero was on the verge of giving them a lesson or two. He ran his hands through his hair.

"Let's go." *This is going to be one long-ass day.*

Elle went to her seat, not believing the way Nero was acting toward her. *He can't even tell me bye!*

Once they were settled, Chloe asked her the question Elle had been waiting for. "You okay? You're, like, zoning out now." Elle knew Chloe always worried.

"Yeah, I'm fine, Chloe. I'm just a little tired from work."

Chloe nodded and their class began, bringing Elle back to her memory from earlier. She had been forced to get her nose reset and her arm had indeed been broken. That was another day she had learned a valuable lesson. *Don't look anyone in the eyes.*

Unfortunately, Elle wasn't the only one who had learned a lesson. From that day forward, Chloe had started completely walking behind her. Elle welcomed her there. She was glad to become Chloe's armor.

Calculus flew by and Elle hoped Nero's mood was no longer sour. Something in her even wondered if she *would* find them in the hall waiting for her.

When she exited her classroom, she didn't know whether she was grateful to find them there or unhappy. She looked at Nero's still-pissed-off face and came to a conclusion. *Very unhappy.*

This hall break went the same as the last. Nero continued to walk behind her, next to Vincent, when he was more than capable of holding her hand. That was what was driving her mad. Her hand itched to be held by his, whether she wanted to admit it or not.

They were close to the Spanish door, and still, Nero refused to talk to her. *He's acting like a child.*

Elle really hated the whole silent treatment thing.

She watched Amo do as he usually did; stand beside the door. She knew he hadn't opened it because that would force her to go in and not talk to Nero.

Chloe walked in the classroom, and Elle's feet told her to walk in, as well, but her mind told her otherwise. Elle decided to turn around instead and face Nero.

"What is your problem?" She looked straight at his green, scary eyes, wishing she hadn't said it.

She saw Vincent smile and walk toward Amo, leaving her to deal with Nero alone.

Nero calmly asked, "What do you think my problem is, Elle?" She didn't like his calm voice because it didn't match the way she knew he felt.

"I don't know what your problem is, that's why I'm freaking asking." She tried to mimic his calm voice.

Nero was quick. He grabbed her arms and scooted her away farther from the others' ears, placing her against the lockers. *What is it with him and shoving me against things?*

Nero lowered his head to speak in her ear, keeping his hands on her arms to lock her in place. "My problem is simple, Elle. I have a problem with you having no trouble saying thank you to someone else. I have a problem with you wrapping your arms around someone else. And I have a big fucking problem with you not minding kissing someone else. Not one fucking time have you done any of those things to me without my asking, or just doing it because *you* want to, not because *I* want you to."

Elle listened to every word Nero said to her. She had never considered he was mad at her, much less that he could be mad at her for that. She hadn't even thought about what she was doing to Amo; she had simply been elated Chloe was safe and sound.

Nero looked at her face for her reply, but she didn't know what to say. She had been caught off-guard.

"I-I wasn't even thinking. I was happy that he brought Chloe there safely."

"Why do you think he did that, Elle?" His eyes were becoming even more furious.

Elle knew, but things were different between them. "I know, Nero, but I don't like Amo." She turned her head away; she couldn't look at his eyes for this. "It's not easy for me to do those things when I've never done them to someone I like."

She heard Nero exhale before he grabbed her chin to look at

him. "I don't want to see you ever touch another guy again. You can kiss and hug your father and brother, but if I find out you've touched another guy—I don't give a shit who it is—they won't live to let it happen again."

Elle swallowed hard and nodded her head. She believed him. She couldn't believe she was going to say it. "I'm sorry."

She thought Nero was waiting for something, yet then he kissed her. It was a hard kiss, and she let their tongues meet for a brief second before he pulled away.

"I'm still pissed, but we're going to be late for class." He let her go, and she pulled away, going into the classroom. She blushed and ran in the room when she saw Amo and Vincent smiling. This time, Amo held the door open for her.

A PAGE FROM CHLOE'S BOOK

The lunch bell rang and Elle and Chloe walked out of their Spanish class. Elle was happy to see Nero's face and eyes had calmed down. She walked over to him as Amo started walking toward the cafeteria. Elle reluctantly began walking behind him when Nero didn't act like he was going to move. *I guess he is still pissed.*

After a few steps toward the cafeteria, Elle felt Nero's hand grab hers. She looked over at him and smiled, and then, on her own, she decided to walk closer beside him. She really had missed holding his hand.

When they reached the lunchroom, Amo stopped to wait for them. Once they were in one, big group, Nero spoke.

"So, what do you girls want to eat?"

Elle dropped her hand from Nero's when Chloe and her eyes met. They didn't know how to respond.

"It's either pizza or the same line that's always been here of chicken patties and hamburgers." Elle and Chloe both turned their heads to stare at Nero. They had never gotten to pick on taste.

"I don't care," Elle got out.

"Yeah, uh, me either." Chloe looked at the floor.

"Jesus, pick already. I'm fucking starving." Amo, on the other hand, was still grouchy and tired.

Elle looked at the two lines. Hardly anyone was in the chicken and hamburger line. "Chicken patties sound fine."

"Who the hell doesn't choose pizza?" Vincent obviously wasn't happy with their choice.

"Elle, do you like pizza?" She looked at Nero, remembering what he had told her about lying. She had already made him mad once today, and she'd learned she didn't like it when he was mad at her.

Elle silently said, "Yes."

"Chloe, do you eat pizza?" Amo asked that time.

Chloe looked over at Elle, and Elle hoped she understood to tell the truth. She nodded.

"So, why the hell can't I have pizza?" Vincent clearly wanted some pizza.

"Elle, why did you pick that line?" She looked up at Nero and bit her lip. She really didn't want to lie to him. Therefore, the only thing she could possibly do was evade the question, and by the looks of their three faces, they weren't going to let her off.

She decided not to look at their eyes. "We always pick the line that doesn't have anyone in it."

"And what happens if the lines are about the same?" She really wished Nero would quit asking her questions.

She felt all their eyes on her, waiting for her answer, except Chloe's. She was looking at the ground, wringing her hands. She didn't want them to know anymore than Elle did.

"Hey, guys, what's up?" Leo had found them and joined in, giving her hope she might not have to answer.

"Shut up, Leo. Answer the fucking question, Elle." Elle was shocked Amo had been the one to say that. *All hope is lost.*

Elle decided to take a page from Chloe's book—she looked at the floor. "If the lines are even, then we pick the line that has the least scary people in it."

"Jesus Christ." Elle heard Nero say.

"For fuck's sake," Amo chimed in.

"Motherfuckers," Vincent added.

"Does that mean they don't want piz—"

"Shut up, Leo!" Nero, Amo, and Vincent all said it at the same time, making Elle and Chloe jump.

"From now on, you fucking eat what you want to. Do you both understand?" Elle nodded her head at Nero. Chloe still didn't reply.

"Chloe, if you want fucking pizza, you eat fucking pizza, got it?" Amo yelled at her. Chloe didn't waste any time to nod in understanding.

Elle was ready to move on, so she decided to scurry away to the pizza line, no matter how badly her instincts screamed to go in the other line. Chloe wasted no time following her.

As Elle hurried away, she thought she heard Vincent say, "Let's fucking kill 'em."

Leo ended up being the first one to join them. They were all the way in the back of the line since they were talking while everyone else had gotten in. When the three guys finally joined them, they didn't look very pleased. *I don't know why they even asked me what I wanted to eat if pizza was clearly the only option.*

"No way I'm waiting this fucking long. You know they run out of pizza. Let's cut," Amo said.

By the looks of the guys' faces, they were ready to cut. Elle didn't feel comfortable about it. "No, that's wrong. We're not cutting." She looked at Nero to make sure he understood.

"Sorry, sweetheart. After what you just told me, I frankly don't give a shit about right and wrong." Vincent passed them and yelled "move" to the person ahead of them. She watched Amo join in, making everyone part the line.

Elle was shoved by Nero to move forward, giving Elle and Chloe no option other than to cut the line. Elle was shocked Nero was making her do this; she didn't feel right about cutting in front of people.

When they reached the trays, the guys stopped and grabbed one. Amo handed his to Chloe and Vincent handed his to her. Elle reached and grabbed it, swearing Vincent's face made her do it.

Now that she and Chloe had a tray, Elle walked through the line, figuring she might as well enjoy it. Once next week started, she was going to be lucky to eat without lunch money. The cost of lunch had gone up to a ridiculous price, but no one at a prep school would dare complain.

Elle got out of the line first, charging it to her account. She waited for Chloe to come out of the line. By the way the boys had probably pissed everyone off, she decided not to go until one of them had checked out. Nero checked out first and started walking back to the table with Elle following behind.

Once they were seated, Elle was caught off-guard when Nero pulled her in for a kiss on the cheek. She still wasn't used to him, and she definitely wasn't used to it when she was around Chloe.

Elle was glad when Leo sat again at the empty seat next to Chloe. She could tell Chloe eased a bit when he did. Elle looked around and saw that all the boys had bought an extra piece of pizza. *That's why they never have any left.*

Elle smiled when she picked up her pepperoni pizza and saw Chloe doing the same. For once, she actually liked what she had gotten for lunch.

"When was the last time you ate pizza at school?"

Nero couldn't just let me enjoy it, could he? She was really starting to hate the whole honesty thing. "Since middle school."

"I had it freshman year." Elle looked over at Chloe. *That didn't help, Chloe.*

While the guys were becoming agitated by her answers, she didn't understand why they would ask these questions when they knew they wouldn't like the outcome.

She figured Leo sensed everyone was on edge since he tried to change the conversation. However, the thing he asked was possibly the worst thing he could, making it only worse.

"Chloe, how did you get those scars?" She knew Leo was young and didn't know how she got them but figured everyone else had already heard about it.

She waited for the guys to say shut up, because this really would be the right time to do it, but they didn't. They clearly wanted to hear it, too.

Elle looked at Chloe, who was staring at her plate. She really hated that Leo had asked that.

Elle decided to get the story over with. "She was in a car accident."

"Oh, dang. When?" Leo became intrigued.

Elle put down her pizza. "When we were freshmen."

"That suck—"

Elle grabbed her head. She heard a buzzing noise and started blinking, trying to focus on what had just happened. She had seen something fly out of the corner of her eye a moment ago, and whatever it had been had really started to sting her head. As the buzzing started to cease, all Elle could hear was laughter.

Elle felt Nero and the rest of the guys stand up, then she heard Nero's voice. "Who the fuck just did that?"

While the room became eerily silent, Elle grew scared. The guys were already pissed off; she didn't want them to get hurt because of her.

Elle managed to get the word "don't" out while she pulled her hand from her head, trying to grab Nero's. That was when she saw the blood on her hand.

Nero immediately noticed it, as well, distracting him from his questioning.

"Shit, Nero. She needs to get out of here," Vincent spoke.

Elle still felt Nero fuming as he tried to get her to stand.

"Yeah, let's get them out of here, and we can deal with the fucker outside of school," she heard Amo quietly speak.

Nero helped Elle up, grabbing her around her waist as she stood. "It's going to be okay, baby," he murmured.

Elle tried to nod her head, relieved he hadn't started a fight. Vincent had come around to help walk her out of the cafeteria and Elle let them lead her out. When they reached the door and exited, Nero bent down and picked her up, holding her in his arms.

She tried to search for Chloe, afraid she might have been too shocked to come. "Chloe."

"Shh, Amo's got her."

Elle calmed down and relaxed into his arms. She fought the feeling to close her eyes, no matter how much she wanted to, as her head rested on his chest.

As Nero passed the victory wall that was filled with sports memorabilia and encased in glass, she wondered where he was taking her. She heard a metal door open and a ceiling that felt like a thousand feet high greeted her. She didn't understand why he was taking her in the gym.

He walked to the other end and she had a feeling of where he was taking her. She didn't exactly have the greatest memories of that place, either.

"Vince, bring me the first aid kit."

I WILL ENJOY
WATCHING YOU SCREAM

Nero sat *Elle down on* one of the benches. She knew he was taking her in the locker room.

She heard the door open again and saw Vincent set a white box down on the bench beside her before leaving without saying a word. She had a feeling he might have been just as pissed as Nero.

Nero went to the sink and wet a bunch of paper towels. He then walked back over and handed her one to wash her hand before he lowered himself in front of her, going to his haunches. Elle could only stare up at Nero as he pressed the towels to her head. His face was calm while his emerald eyes looked like they were on fire. She had gotten used to the calm exterior while his eyes showed his true feelings. *He is so beautiful.*

"I don't think you'll need stitches," Nero said, opening the first aid kit.

Elle tried to lighten the mood with a laugh. "Well, that's a first." She regretted it the moment the words left her mouth.

"Elle, this isn't funny." Nero stopped what he was doing to look at her. "I can't let them do this to you anymore. It's hard enough to hear that you pick what to eat based on who the fuck scares you less."

"I know, Nero, but please." She took his hand and touched his battered knuckles. "You promised me you would try."

She watched Nero take a deep breath before he went back into the box and pulled out a white tube, squeezing the ointment on the tip of his finger. He reached up and rubbed it on her head.

Elle made a face when it started stinging.

"Oh, yeah, this might sting," he said.

Elle smiled, finally able to calm him down a bit. "Thanks for letting me know beforehand."

Nero actually smiled back. "No problem."

He grabbed a Band-Aid from the kit and opened it.

"Do I want to know how you know your way around a first aid kit?" *I probably don't.*

He placed the Band-Aid on her head then and leaned his head down. Elle felt his lips brush her skin just above it.

"Nope."

I figured.

Nero stood and took Elle's hand to help her up. When she was standing, he swept her hair off her forehead. She saw Nero look closer.

"How'd you get that scar?" Nero touched the high end of her forehead off to the side. A faint scar remained there that almost went into her hairline.

She didn't like where this was going. She looked away from him, unable to answer him this time.

Nero grabbed Elle's face. "How did you get that fucking scar?"

"I-I can't tell you." Elle could never tell him how she had received it. She didn't want him to find out Chloe had been a part of it in this very room. She couldn't risk lying to him and making him mad at her, either.

Elle became frightened at what he did next.

"God dammit, Elle!" Nero picked up the first aid kit and threw it at a wall filled with lockers. The kit broke in half and everything came flying out. Nero then pushed back his hair and shut his eyes.

She realized he had hit the breaking point. She was about to witness all Hell breaking loose.

He started walking for the door and Elle ran after him. She was afraid he would end up doing something terrible. *What if he got expelled? Then he'll leave me.*

Elle picked up her feet and reached out her hand to grab him. "Nero, please. Please, stop."

Nero stopped when Elle's hand touched his. She walked into him as he stood there, wrapping her arms around his neck.

"Don't leave me," she whispered, placing her head in the crook of his neck.

Nero backed her up two steps, putting her back against a wall of lockers, placing his hands on the lockers beside her.

Elle mumbled into Nero's neck. "If you start a fight, you'll get suspended or worse, expelled."

Nero gritted out, "Baby, I can't let them get away with this." She felt Nero go completely still, though he remained on the verge of walking out.

"Nero, I don't want to be alone again." Elle squeezed him tighter and tried to push her face into his neck deeper.

Nero harshly said each word. "Then make me stay."

Elle removed her head from his neck and looked up at him, knowing what he was asking. She had found out what it was like being close to him and him not touching her. Elle didn't want to find out what it would be like not seeing him; as a result, she would give in and give him what he wanted.

"Take off your jacket." His still-harsh voice started to make her nervous. Nero hadn't moved an inch; he was like ice.

Elle reluctantly started taking off her jacket, though he didn't give her any space to do so with his arms still braced on the lockers and his body against hers. She could feel his eyes over her body as she shrugged it off. When the jacket hit the floor, Elle's heart started beating out of her chest. She had no idea what to do; she just knew he wanted her to do something to him for a change.

Elle decided to do what she had been dying to do from the first time they were in the art supply closet alone. She had always kept her eyes mostly to his chest for several reasons. One, she couldn't look him in his eyes most times. Two, her eye-level was at his chest. Lastly, she enjoyed looking at it under his white dress shirts.

Elle raised her hands to his shirt and went for the highest button he had fastened on the top middle of his chest. She shakily unbuttoned it, revealing more of his chest. Moving her hands down, she managed to release another button, exposing his whole chest and the top of his abdomen.

Elle thought her heart was going to explode looking at his perfectly-toned chest. The tanned skin begged her to touch it, so she slowly placed her hands on his taut muscles. She leaned in and lightly placed a kiss in the middle as she parted his shirt wide by moving her hands across his chest. She loved the feel of his skin under her hands, warm and smooth. She kissed his chest again and again, determined to make him stay.

This time, when Elle kissed his chest, she let her tongue lick the skin. Nero tasted better than she had imagined. Enjoying the taste, she raised higher, kissing and licking him up toward his neck. She felt his rage turn into desire with every passing second as she ran her hands up his chest then behind his neck and into his hair.

She had been itching to run her hands through his dark mass, jealous every time he did so. She pulled his head down closer to her so she could get to his neck without straining her legs. She paid the same attention to his neck as she had to his chest, but she hadn't broken Nero yet.

She greedily sucked his skin into her mouth and bit down. Elle smiled against his skin when a rough noise escaped his mouth. *I hope it left a mark.*

It did.

When Nero still refused to move, she lapped at her bite mark, proud it was going to be there for a while.

Elle felt Nero finally drop his hands from the locker. He put a hand in her hair and pulled while his other went to the lower part of her back. She looked up at him and saw his eyes were hungry; however, they were no longer hungry for blood.

Elle was ready for his kiss this time. She wanted it just as much as he did. She wanted the taste of his mouth; therefore, when his tongue entered hers, she sucked on it, trying to mimic what he had done to hers earlier.

Nero grabbed Elle's ass in his hands, squeezing it and lifting her higher. She felt his hardness through her jeans against her mound. Earlier, it had frightened her, but now, she was driven by pure lust. Nero was making her feel things she had never felt before, and Elle was sure it should scare her.

Nero had moved his hands up her back under her shirt. She didn't think they could feel any better than they did when she held them. *Oh, but they definitely do.*

Nero returned Elle's favor from earlier, kissing her down her chin to her neck. He licked the skin, making Elle let out a whimper from the sensitivity, giving her goose bumps.

Elle started to breathe heavily; his touch was driving her crazy. He sucked her neck into his mouth, making Elle grip his hair, pulling him into her neck. Elle released a moan as he sucked another part into his mouth. Nero moved his hands to her abdomen at the sound, causing a trail of fire on her skin.

When Nero's hand rose higher, the spell she had been put under started wearing off. She managed to get out "Nero," and she was certain it sounded like a moan, so she pulled his hair back.

Nero switched to the other side of her neck, licking and sucking, giving the same care to the opposite side. Elle felt herself melt once more before his hands started going higher again, making her skin burn. He was getting too close to her bra. Even being in pure ecstasy, Elle wasn't ready for that step.

She tried again. "Nero." She steadied her voice. "Please." She thanked God it sounded less like a moan this time.

Elle could feel how bad he wanted to just lift his hands a little higher; consequently, she dropped her hands to his arms. "I can't."

As Nero rested his head in her neck, letting his breathing calm, Elle was able to slow her breath, as well. The cold air of the locker room made her shiver from the still-exposed skin of her belly. She knew he was probably continuing to debate feeling her boobs.

Elle let out a deep breath as his hands slowly traveled back down her stomach. She might have regretted it a little bit, but she knew he was taking his time to make her regret it. *Well, it worked.*

She did miss Nero's face in her neck as he stood straight up. He looked in her eyes, and she wondered if she made a good decision starting something like that with a guy like Nero. She knew he was like a wolf. The man was definitely an animal, and he looked at her only as food. Yet that excited a small part of Elle, and that was what scared her the most.

Nero returned to his original position by bracing his hands on the lockers. *Really, did that just not happen?*

"Put your jacket back on." Elle didn't know what to think when he said that, but she had made up her mind that she would do as he asked if it meant he wouldn't get in a fight because of her. Not to mention, she didn't want to test him when he was a second away from ripping her clothes off.

Elle slid down the lockers with what little room Nero had given her, keeping her eyes on his body, making sure he wasn't going to pounce while she felt for her jacket on the ground. She felt Nero's gaze too intently and looked up at his eyes, watching her crouched down at his feet. A shiver went down her spine. She had a feeling he'd had that planned.

Elle touched her jacket and took it in her hands, wishing she could look away, but he held her eyes like he dared her to move them. There was no way Elle would take that dare. She slowly rose up from the ground, her own sexual desire growing between her thighs.

She swallowed as she stared into his lustful eyes. For once, she knew exactly what he was thinking, the image he was playing through his mind. She had to get her jacket back on somehow in the confined space.

Her breasts met his still-exposed chest through her thin bra and t-shirt as she pulled her jacket up her back. The moment it was on, Elle backed up as far as she could, wishing somehow she could melt into the lockers.

"Now button my shirt." His voice still sounded rough. Elle was afraid, when this was over, he would beat the shit out of someone to blow off some steam.

Elle decided to regretfully and politely ask, "When I do, are you going to storm out of here and murder some—"

"Baby." His gruff voice sounded through her ear as he closed what little space she had left. "You really don't want to try me right now."

Elle squeezed her legs together. *What is he doing to me?*

As she picked up her hands and went to button the lowest one she had undone, Elle decided to lean in one last time for a taste. She was going to give him a reason to be at school tomorrow. She sweetly placed a kiss on the part of his chest she was about to conceal, then she buttoned it.

Nero clearly isn't the sweet kind of guy. Subsequently, this time, she ran her tongue up the small gap of chest about to be covered before she buttoned the final button.

Elle smiled back up at him, satisfied, but she really shouldn't have. *Oh, shit.*

Nero grabbed Elle and flipped her around, shoving the front of her body into the lockers, ensuring the side of her face that wasn't hurt was the one pressed up against them. Elle felt the whole front of Nero's body flat against her backside. She could feel through her jeans that he was harder than a rock on her ass. His hands were on her abdomen again, but this time, they were above her thin shirt. Elle thought her legs would fall off if she squeezed them together any tighter.

Nero spoke in her ear. "I will find out who hurt you today, and I will fucking enjoy them screaming in pain. I will find out every single thing anyone and everyone has done to you, and I will enjoy watching them all scream in pain."

Nero moved his hands up her shirt and grasped each breast, making Elle arch back into him. "Then I will enjoy watching you scream as I fuck you because, baby, I will pop that cherry very soon." Nero must have read her mind as he gave another tight squeeze to her breasts. "I give you my word that my dick will be the first and only to slide in and out of your tight, wet pussy, and you will be the one crawling and begging for me to take it."

Elle couldn't believe the words that had come from his mouth, but her body was betraying her by enjoying every harsh word. She had no response and remained unable to think of one when he flipped her body back around to conquer her mouth one last time. Her mouth had betrayed her, as well, by letting him suck her tongue in his mouth. Nero grabbed her hand once he was finished making his point. *Yeah, by completely violating me!*

Nero walked her out of the locker room. When the gymnasium greeted her once again, she felt confused, used, and needy. Her damned body was turned up to a thousand degrees after that last event.

When she saw Amo, Vincent, Leo, and Chloe on the bleachers, her body decided to add complete embarrassment to that list.

She glanced over at Nero, saw his smug, gorgeous face, and felt she was playing into his very-skilled hands. He had her right where he wanted her, and she knew it. *'You will be the one crawling and begging for me.'*

With what had taken place in the locker room, she had already gotten on the ground to start that crawling and begging. She had taken it there because she'd realized she didn't want to lose Nero just yet.

She liked it when he held her hand. She liked it when he paid her attention. She liked looking at him and talking to him. Most of all, she felt she and Chloe were just a bit safer in this hell hole with him.

If getting on the ground is what keeps those good things in my life, then fine. But I will not crawl, I absolutely will not beg.

Stupid wolf!

PERFECT. LET'S ALL BREAK NECKS

Stupid girl, you have no idea what you just did. Now that Nero had seen a flash of the true Elle, he was going to make sure she would come out and play. He didn't think a girl could be so innocent and sexy at the same time.

The way Elle had been incredibly eager to please him and greedy to have him had made it almost impossible for him not to take her. The only reason he had fought himself was because he planned to have her for good. He didn't know if it was because she was about to die by the hand of his father, or if it was because he had found out the extremes of her torture. It could have been the moment he saw the blood on her hand, or the proud look in her eyes after she licked him.

Nero smiled to himself as he walked across the gym. When he had told her to make him stay, he honestly had thought she'd merely kiss him. Instead, Elle had taken it to the next level by unbuttoning his shirt. That was when he had known she really wanted him.

Then he thought he would see the extent of how much she wanted to please him by telling her to pick up her jacket. When she had slid down the lockers, his dick had never been harder in his life. Furthermore, when he had seen her eyes that were aware exactly of what he was picturing—her sucking his dick—his dick somehow had become harder. He'd had her right there on the ground, and still he hadn't taken her. *Yeah, and my dick regrets it.*

So, he'd thought the least she could do was button his shirt back. Nero had to get something out of the whole thing if he was walking out with blue balls, and that was how he had decided to show her what her future held. *She just* had *to lick it and give me the proudest fucking look.*

The feel of her tits and ass in his hands had been exactly how he had thought they'd be. *A little more than a handful of perfection.* After that, all Nero had to do was hold them after he ripped her clothes off.

When Nero and Elle walked closer to the bleachers, he let her run to Chloe's side. He was somehow not shocked that Chloe ended up looking worse than Elle after the whole thing, reminding him of what had happened during lunch. His hate began to outweigh his sexual needs again.

A moment later, Amo, Vincent and Leo walked over.

"Please tell me we can kill every motherfucker in that lunchroom now." He had known Vincent was ready for a fight.

"I want the piece of shit who threw the carton of milk. Where did it come from?"

Nero didn't think someone would try to pull a stunt like that with his crew there. Although Nero knew that the person had hit their intended target, it could have hit any one of them. He was blaming himself; he had been paying attention to what Elle was talking about. *I should have seen it coming.*

They all three shook their heads.

"All right, we need to ask around and make people talk." Nero smoothed his hair down. "For some fucking reason, Elle won't tell me what else they've done to her. That's at least the second scar she will have on her head, and there's no telling what kind of shit won't leave a mark. I don't care who has touched her, whether it's dicks or bitches. We will do exactly what they did to her. I want every fucking detail."

Amo finally spoke up. "That sounds fair, man." Nero knew Amo was on the verge of murder just as much as he was. *Good, I want Amo to snap some fucking necks.*

"Yeah, way too fucking fair," Vincent agreed.

Perfect, let's all break necks. "Then we've got three fucking rounds of payback."

Nero looked over at Elle sitting beside Chloe, whispering. He knew she was trying to comfort her. Nero was drawn to Elle by the way she protected Chloe. *I just wish it didn't mean becoming the target.*

"She all right?" Amo asked him.

"Unfortunately, she takes hits too well." He didn't like how she could make a joke out of what had happened. *She was probably happy it ended up hitting her.*

Nero wasn't okay with that.

"She's some tough shit." Vincent's voice sounded proud.

"Yeah, I think the question is, will *she* be all right." Nero noticed Chloe didn't look quite as well.

Amo was definitely looking forward to the destruction about to come. "Let's fucking find out."

When Elle saw Chloe's face, she ran to her side and sat down next to her on the bleachers.

"You okay, Chloe?"

Chloe's face was a blank stare toward the floor. You would think there was nothing inside of her, but Elle knew she was fighting back her demons. Her hair was a curtain on the right side of her face; it killed Elle.

Chloe had actually been starting to become slightly comfortable. Elle noticed she had slept, eaten, and showed her face more in the passing days. *Now it's all gone to Hell.*

When Chloe gave no response, Elle tried again.

"I'm fine. Just a little bump is all. You know, it wasn't the worst thing that could happen to me. There's a good thing in all this; they can't get close to us clearly with these monsters." Elle pointed to the guys talking a few feet away. "So, now they have to throw things at us. A milk carton, huh? That is totally cliché. I can't believe the robots thought they'd take us down with that." Elle knew Chloe appreciated a good joke.

When Chloe's eyes glanced over at Elle, she knew she could break through.

"It could have been worse, you know?"

"How?" Chloe whispered back.

Elle smiled. She had gotten her to talk. "Well, the worst thing that could have happened from the whole thing was the milk carton could have busted. Chocolate milk is a bitch to get out."

When Chloe attempted a smile, Elle relaxed.

"So, what do you think they're going to do when they find out who threw it?" Elle looked up at the four guys staring at them.

"Something tells me I'd rather not know." Chloe lowered her voice even more, not wanting them to know they were talking about them. "I thought Nero might have been crazy, but did you see Vincent? He has a multiple personality disorder that's way worse than being bipolar."

Elle kept her voice down, as well. *I definitely don't want them to hear.* "I noticed that, too. He went from Brad Pitt to Rambo in two seconds."

When Chloe let out a chuckle, Elle couldn't help giggling with her.

Elle saw the boys walk over.

"Oh, crap, did they hear us?" Chloe asked nervously.

Elle looked at their pissed-the-hell-off faces. "Quick, act like you're still upset."

Elle saw Chloe's head snap back down as the boys closed the gap.

Vincent sat down beside her and wrapped his arm around Elle's shoulders. "How do you feel, sweetheart?"

Elle looked at Vincent's baby-blue eyes. He was back to being Brad Pitt again. "Good. I kicked that chocolate milk's ass, right?"

"Yeah, straight to the ground." Vincent laughed.

Elle and Leo laughed with him and even Chloe let a laugh escape, but Nero and Amo didn't think the joke was funny.

Vincent took the chance to ask Chloe, "And how are you, sweetheart?"

"I-I'm fine." Elle couldn't guess if she was still trying to play along that she was upset or couldn't handle Vincent's flirting.

"Would you two happen to have a feeling of who might have thrown it?" Elle wondered why Vincent was asking all the questions. When she looked at his pretty boy face, she found out why. He was trying to use his good looks and charms on them to find out what they wanted.

"Nope. Do you, Chloe?" Elle turned to Chloe, hoping she wouldn't dare open her mouth, either.

"Me, either." Chloe shook her head.

Vincent gave a smile. "How about, maybe I should start to ask someone?"

"Maybe a lunch lady saw. I'd start there." Elle smiled back.

"I say we start with Sebastian," Amo said.

"That the psycho from yesterday?" Leo asked.

"That's him. Let's get the girls back to class." Nero sounded like the boys wouldn't be heading back to class.

Elle reluctantly stood. She didn't want to go to Spanish since she couldn't keep an eye on him there.

Nero gave her a look to go on and start walking, but Elle needed them all to understand something.

"Listen, I'm going to say this, and I really hope you all listen. That was the first time since I started coming here they were too scared to show their faces. Usually, they stand right in my face and do whatever they're going to do while the teachers look the other way.

"I'm not rich, and my family doesn't have power; that's why they get away with it, and that's fine. But you can't go around hurting the kids whose parents would come in here and blow a gasket, threatening to pull their kid out.

"Legacy Prep only wants one thing, and that's money. If I leave because of bullying, then they get to keep my scholarship money, and that is a hell of a lot more than my paycheck and tips I give them for the rest." Elle hoped she drove her point home.

"We're just going to talk to them, sweetheart," Vincent said, standing up.

Let me make it clearer.

"Let me paint a picture for you guys. If you three go and start a bunch of fights, then you get kicked out of school. That leaves Chloe and me stuck here alone with all the people you just pissed off. So, you all think about that when you go to talk to them."

"That isn't going to fucking happen," Amo said, crossing his arms.

When Elle went to open her mouth again, Nero shut her up. "Elle. Class. Now."

As Elle stomped off, ready to wring all their necks, she heard Chloe getting up to run beside her. Nero caught up to her, attempting to hold her hand, but she wasn't in the mood. Unfortunately, Nero couldn't have cared less, and as such, she was forced to hold his hand back to class.

When they reached her classroom, Elle had some parting words.

"None of you better do anything stupid." Then she walked off without even telling Nero goodbye.

"*Does she know who she's* talking to?" Amo asked when Elle slammed the classroom door.

"Oh, yes, she does, and that's the problem." After what he had done with her in the locker room, she was very aware of the kind of man he was.

Nero saw the guys all shake their heads. *We're all going to be lucky to come out of this sane.*

Looking over to Leo, Nero spoke. "Go on to class. Ask around. Let me know if you find anything out."

"All right, catch you guys later." Leo walked off.

Nero and his crew were going to miss the last part of class again to have some alone time with Sebastian once more.

Vincent started walking toward the back of the school. "Three guesses where the bitch is, and the first two don't count."

I BET YOU CAN'T EVEN AIM YOUR PISS IN THE TOILET

Nero *followed Vincent out the* back school doors; they were hardly used and only there in case of an emergency. Walking out, they headed along the school building, following the smell. When they reached the rich-boy douchebags smoking pot, it was everything Nero could do not to beat the shit out of Sebastian right then and there.

"Get the fuck out of here." Nero wanted to make it clear they didn't want to finish their weed, but mostly, he enjoyed watching them run.

When Sebastian tried to make a run for it, too, Nero pushed him hard, making him fall backwards. "I don't think so."

"Hey, I didn't do anything." Sebastian held up his hands.

Nero squatted down beside him. "Nothing? Really? So, you didn't happen to fucking throw the milk at Elle's face?"

"No-no, of course not. You think I could really throw something across the cafeteria and not miss?"

Nero watched Sebastian practically shed a few tears. "Yeah, you're probably right. I bet you can't even aim your piss in the toilet."

Sebastian tried to smile and laugh. "Yeah, I can't even do that."

"I guess you didn't happen to see who did, then?"

Sebastian violently shook his head.

Nero looked up at Amo and Vincent standing above them. "What do you think? You think he's telling us the truth?"

Vincent smiled. "Maybe we should help him remember."

Sebastian was practically crying now. "No. I-I don't know anything, I swe—"

"All right, calm down." He needed Sebastian to get his next message. "Now, I'm going to give you one last chance. You tell us right now everything you have done to Elle and Chloe, and I will make sure I won't let Amo kill you."

Nero watched Sebastian look up toward Amo. Amo didn't have to make himself look scary. *He's already scary as fuck.*

Sebastian thought about his next words. "I haven't fucking touched them."

Nero grabbed Sebastian's face over his mouth, squeezing as hard as he could without popping his fucking head off. "If I find out you're fucking lying to me, I promise, you will be unrecognizable by the time I get done with you. Understand?"

Sebastian nodded as hard as he could and Nero shoved his face down, making his head meet the concrete floor. Sebastian finally let his tears run.

"Now you can get the fuck out of here."

Nero watched Sebastian get up and scramble off. *Yeah, just like a little bitch.* He really couldn't do much more to Sebastian no matter how much he wanted to smash the liar's face in. Elle was right; they had to be smart about what they did on school grounds. However, outside of these walls was going to be a completely different story.

Nero stood back up and noticed his crew didn't look very pleased. Hell, Nero wasn't pleased that he couldn't hurt Sebastian the way he would like.

"We find someone to talk and tell us everything. Then, we get him outside of school." Nero needed them to focus. *Like Elle said, look at the bigger picture.*

"Fine." Vincent wasn't happy about his choice, but he wasn't the one calling the shots.

Amo started walking away. "I'm going back to class."

Nero had known Amo wasn't going to approve. When Amo wanted to hurt someone, he didn't care if they were innocent or guilty; he would kill and not give a shit. Nero knew this because he normally would act the same way, but this time, it was different. He had to take Elle into consideration, and he wanted this handled properly.

Nero watched Amo walk away and out of sight. He leaned his back up against the school and squeezed the bridge of his nose. He was starting to really regret his decision.

Vincent leaned against the wall beside him. "He'll come around. You know how Amo gets when he wants to kill something."

"Yeah, which is making me want to change my mind."

"As much as I want to chop Sebastian's fucking dick off, you're right. It'll be much more fun hurting him after we know what he's done." Vincent said exactly how he felt, and it helped Nero accept his decision.

He relaxed his muscles. "It will be, won't it?"

Vincent smiled. "It will, but I don't know if it will be as much fun as what you and Elle did in the girls' locker room. I'm guessing you took complete advantage of the situation?"

Nero had taken advantage of Elle being hit in the head. *I deserve something from it if I can't kill someone.*

Nero looked over at Vincent and saw him look at his neck. Nero smiled, remembering how hard Elle had bitten him. He would have never guessed Elle would be the rough type. The bite had caused him to give in and play with her.

"Of course I did. She got me good, didn't she?" He hadn't looked at it yet, although he could feel he had a nice mark on him.

Vincent laughed. "She did. Damn, please tell me you took my advice."

"Oh, I got her on her knees, but I want her crawling."

"Oh, God, you didn't. Nero, it's the polite thing to do; girl gets on her knees and you give her something to do." Vincent started shaking his head at him.

Nero smiled at him. "Just think about how much more fun it

will be after she's been down there a while."

"Man, you're fucking lucky I know you actually like her; otherwise, I'd show her the hospitable thing to do. Wait, you like her, right? Because we do have a good thing going with the other girls at school."

Nero didn't even have to think. "Touch her, and I'll chop your fucking dick off."

"So, that means I can at least think about her suck—"

Elle couldn't wait for Spanish class to end. She was too anxious to see if the guys would actually be there because, if they weren't, well, she and Chloe would no longer be able to continue at Legacy Prep.

When the bell rang, Elle wasn't anxious anymore to get up and see if they were out there. *I know they couldn't help themselves.* She thought about how pissed their faces were in the gym. *There's no way they couldn't.*

Elle reluctantly got to her feet and headed for the door. When she looked out into the hall, there they were, leaning against the lockers. *Well, what do you know?*

Elle noticed Vincent was kind of hobbled over, holding his stomach, and his face looked like he might be sick. She became worried and started walking up to him.

"Vincent, are you okay?" Elle walked closer to him, passing Nero.

Vincent held up his hand. "I-I'm fine."

Elle stopped walking toward him; however, she didn't think he sounded very good, either. As a result, she took another step and held up her hand to check to make sure.

Vincent waved his hand in front of her. "No, don't come any closer. I'm fine."

What is wrong with him? Elle didn't know what had happened to him.

Nero grabbed her waist, pulling her toward him. "He said he's fine."

Elle looked up at him, and Nero took the opportunity to claim her lips. He gave her a quick, firm kiss, making her forget about... *Wait, what was I talking about?*

"All right, Amo. You can take Chloe to class," Nero said, nodding toward Amo.

Elle had been taken off guard by his kiss, but she was quickly brought back by his words.

"What? No. We need to all walk together." Elle couldn't let Chloe walk with only Amo after what had happened with all of them sitting at the table.

"Come on, Chloe." Amo motioned for Chloe to start walking, everyone acting like they hadn't even heard a word she had just said.

Elle pushed at Nero's chest for him to say something when Chloe looked down at the floor and slowly started walking. Nero just squeezed her hips tighter without saying a word as they watched them walk to health class. Elle tried to squirm out of his grasp as he held her around her waist with one arm. *One arm? Really?*

Nero lifted his other hand and grabbed her hair, pulling it down. "You need to stop questioning me. I'm the one with the dick, and the sooner you realize that, the easier this will be. Trust me, baby, you'll start to like it that way." Nero dropped his hand from her hair.

"Come on."

Nero took her hand and led her in the same direction as Amo and Chloe had gone. *I do not understand him sometimes.* They followed them at the same distance as they had the day before. Elle saw Chloe was still walking at his back. *Old habits die hard.*

When Amo stopped and turned around, Elle saw his scary-ass face say something really low to Chloe. Moreover, whatever he had said to her made her quickly move to stand beside him.

Elle and Nero laughed at the two, and Elle could hear Vincent attempt a laugh, but a sound of pain escaped instead. Elle turned her head to look back at Vincent and saw he was walking farther back than he usually did. When she looked him in the eyes, he swiftly turned his head in another direction. *What is going on today?*

Elle turned her head back to watch Chloe safely walk to the classroom. When they were a couple feet from the door, Chloe tried to run. She had her hand on the doorknob when even Elle could hear Amo loudly scream, "Chloe."

Elle tried to run to Chloe, but Nero held her hand tightly, making her stay in place. Elle had to remember the words Nero had just spoken to her—*'I'm the one with the dick.'*

Elle reluctantly stood there and watched as Chloe dropped her hand from the doorknob. Amo closed the distance and grabbed the door handle himself, opening the door for her. Chloe kept her eyes down as she slowly walked into the classroom like she was defeated with Amo following her in then slamming the door.

Nero started walking again, pulling her hand to head to their class.

"Does Amo know we're following him?" Elle couldn't tell.

Nero shrugged. "I haven't told him we are, but he might know on his own. Don't get used to this, though; she needs to learn not to depend on you."

Elle smiled up at Nero before she laid her head on his arm. She liked when Nero could actually be sweet. *Well, try to be sweet.*

Elle noticed Vincent could hardly keep up and had fallen way behind. She decided to ask Nero what had happened to him.

"Why is Vincent acting so weird? He won't even look at me."

Elle could have sworn she saw Nero smile before it vanished. "I don't know."

Elle tried again. "Do you know what happened to him? It looks like he got hurt or something."

"I think he just got a little winded."

Elle decided to give up. *There's no telling what they got into.*

After Nero walked Elle into their classroom, she took her seat while Nero went to get their posters in the back of the class. Elle started pulling out some blank paper and a pen from her bag when she noticed Nero hadn't come back with their posters. She looked up and saw he was practically sandwiched between the two bimbos.

Elle's heart started to ache. This ache was the type that felt like her heart was splitting in two. She could only watch as Nero went through the posters on the back table with the two girls on either side of him, their bodies rubbing up against his while they talked to each other. Elle couldn't hear what they were saying, though.

She had to look down before her heart ripped in two. *I can't watch.*

She picked up her pen and quickly started writing. Nero joined her a few seconds later with their posters. She didn't pull her face away from her papers to look at him; she didn't want to see his face. *Which is probably smiling from ear to ear right now.*

She also didn't want the bimbos to see they had hurt her; therefore, she never picked her eyes up from writing the entire class period. It was hard for Elle to concentrate and write words fluidly without Nero noticing she was attempting to ignore him. She later realized she didn't want Nero to see she was hurt, either.

She didn't even know if she had a right to be upset since she hadn't seen Nero respond to them. *Yeah, but he didn't try to stop them, either.* She couldn't stop picturing them pressing their boobs into his arm. *I have a fucking right to be upset.*

Nero had tried a few times to gain her attention by flirting with her throughout the class period. However, Elle never gave in and kept her attention on her writing. When the final school bell rang, Elle leisurely put her papers back into her bag.

Nero didn't talk until the classroom had cleared out. "Is there a problem?"

"Nope." Elle sat there, playing with the zipper on her satchel. She knew better than to get up this time.

Nero had practically burned a hole in her face. "You sure about that?"

"Yep."

Elle and Nero sat there in silence. She had nothing to say to him. She thought it was a joke to have believed Nero could be satisfied with one woman.

He used to go through three a day. Elle sadly wished she was exaggerating.

'I don't want to see you ever touch another guy again.' When Nero had spoken those words to her earlier, she had believed it as Nero taking them being together seriously. She hadn't realized he didn't think the touching thing was a two-way street.

Elle stood and went to the door when Amo and Chloe reached the classroom. "Is Lana picking you up?"

"Yeah, she's out front waiting for me," Chloe said, trying to smile.

Elle knew Lana wouldn't be able to take her home, but it never hurt to ask. Elle gave Chloe a reassuring smile and then started walking for the doors. She didn't even wait for Amo to start walking out in front; she wanted to get out of there and away from Nero as soon as possible.

She walked out the doors by herself with everyone else a ways behind her. She waited in the student pick-up area to watch Chloe get into Lana's car. A minute later, Chloe had caught up to her, and whispered "bye" as she headed for the car. Elle knew that Chloe noticed she was upset at something, yet Elle made sure to smile at her to let her know she wasn't upset with her. She would text her later to make sure she understood. Elle wasn't even upset at Nero or the bimbos; she was upset at herself for thinking she and Nero might work.

After Elle watched Chloe close the door, she started walking toward the next bus stop.

Nero yelled, "Where are you going?" He and the guys were

waiting about ten feet away from her while she had watched Chloe get in the car.

Elle kept walking.

Nero shouted again, "Elle?"

She kept walking.

Then Elle felt Nero snatch her arm. "Where the hell do you think you're going?"

She tried to jerk her arm away, but like it usually was when he had a hold of her, it was useless. *I am sick and tired of this shit!*

"Let me go! I'm going to ride the bus!"

"No, you're not, Elle. You're riding with me." Nero pulled her in the opposite direction.

Elle did not appreciate him telling her what to do anymore. *He doesn't tell me what to do and who I can't touch.*

"No, I'm fucking not!" Elle hit Nero's arm as hard as she could and jerked her arm away. She wasn't stupid, though. As soon as her arm was free, she started running.

Elle hoped she had the element of surprise on her side as she ran as fast as she could. She didn't look back to see if Nero was coming after her. *I'm not that dumb, either.* Unfortunately, though, Elle was that dumb to think she could outrun Nero.

Nero grabbed Elle from behind, and Elle started hitting and kicking him to let her go.

Nero's voice sounded cold. "Elle, stop it now."

She didn't care how scary he sounded; she wasn't going to stop. The emotion of seeing the girls rub all over Nero had driven her body crazy.

Nero swung her body around to face him and held her arms tightly to keep her still. He kept his same, icy composure when he said, "Now, tell me what the fuck is wrong with you."

"Fuck you!"

THE TWO SIDES OF ELLE

When *the words came out,* Elle saw Nero's eyes snap. He swiftly bent over and threw her over his shoulder before spinning around and walking toward the student parking lot.

Being higher up in the air, she realized she hadn't gotten very far before Nero had caught her.

"Let me down!" Elle tried hitting at his back and attempting to kick her feet, but she really didn't want to fall face-first on concrete.

Nero, without a word, spanked her ass every time she hit at his back. *What the hell? He can't do that.*

She smacked his back with each word. "Let. Me. Go."

Slap, slap, slap.

Elle looked around the school grounds. "Does no one care? He is forcing me to his car!" Elle watched. No one frankly gave a shit what was going on, though.

Nero mocked her, "They all look the other way, remember?"

Sadly, Elle had been telling the truth; they couldn't have cared less about her.

When Nero had finally passed Amo and Vincent, laughing hysterically, they started walking behind them. She had to look at their faces as they were practically in tears.

"Vincent, are you going to let him do this to me?"

Vincent responded too quickly for her liking. "Yes, I am."

"I would ask the beast, but I already know his answer." Elle started to become furious at them all. No one was going to come to her rescue.

As a result, Elle would try another tactic. "Please, let me down."

"I will if you tell me what your problem is."

Elle really didn't want Nero packing her the rest of the way, and at least this way, when she told him, Nero couldn't see her face and how upset she was.

Elle took a deep breath in. "I saw the blonde bimbos rubbing their boobs all over you, Nero. And they practically went into heat. No, actually, I take that back; they were in heat."

"Blonde bimbos? Who are they?" Vincent asked, laughing even harder now.

"Cassandra's two little sidekicks." Elle hated how Nero had slept with them when they had treated her so terribly.

Vincent smiled wickedly. "Oh, you mean Stacy and Stephanie."

"Oh, God! Is there any girl you guys don't sleep with?" Now she knew they all passed girls around.

Amo defended himself. "Hey, I've never fucked them, so don't accuse me."

Elle knew exactly why he hadn't. *I know it isn't because he is a good boy.*

"Yeah, because they're afraid of you. Trust me; I'd be terrified to see what you're packing, too." Elle felt her body shake from Nero's laughter.

"No, doll, they're not afraid of me; I just prefer to fuck girls I don't have to see again."

Elle dropped her mouth at what Amo had said. She'd figured Amo was the worst of the three, but she hadn't realized by how much. Elle wanted to get off the subject. She knew they all slept around, and she just wanted to get down. *I told him what was wrong.*

"Put me down. You said you would let me go."

"Well, that was before I knew why you were mad," Nero said.

Huh? "What does that mean?"

"Means you'll run."

Elle had been going to. *Shit!* Elle screamed and smacked his back as hard as she could. She wanted him to at least feel some pain.

Slap.

"Ugh!" Elle rolled her eyes and gave up. *We're already almost there anyway.*

When Nero reached the car, he unlocked his doors and opened the passenger door before putting her in. Elle heard the sound of the lock again and watched Nero lean against her passenger door as he talked to Amo and Vincent.

Elle weighed her options. *Clearly, running doesn't work, screaming for my life doesn't work, and telling him why I'm upset, again, doesn't work.* She was out of options.

No matter what, Nero was driving her home. She didn't want Nero to completely win, so she looked around the car. When she looked at the backseat, Elle knew exactly what to do.

She climbed into the backseat, smiling at herself. She knew why Nero wanted her in his car. *Because he is going to sweet-talk his way out of this and hold my hand, making me give in.*

Elle knew that, after what had occurred in the locker room, she would most likely give in because that was exactly what she had done. *Not this time.*

Nero slid into the driver's seat and Elle enjoyed the look on his face when he realized she wasn't there. She enjoyed it even more when he looked in the rearview mirror and she was there smiling at him.

Like I said, fuck you! Elle had learned to say that kind of stuff in her head.

Elle heard Nero take a deep breath and watched him run his hands through his hair. She was kind of shocked when he didn't say anything and started the car.

He put the car in reverse, pulled out of his spot, and then drove off the lot.

Elle sunk into the backseat of Nero's car and slammed her eyes shut. She leaned her head against the window, the glass feeling cold against her head. Elle thought about today's events. She didn't know how she had gone from being whacked with a milk carton to Nero hotly slamming her against the lockers and all the way to being practically kidnapped by him because she was upset girls had been touching him. She had gone through so many emotions today, and now they were starting to wear on her.

A part of her was still needy, wanting Nero to finish what he had started, while the other part of her wanted to cry. She wanted to cry for herself being picked on by having things thrown at her and being publically humiliated. Then she wanted to cry because something inside of her had really started to like Nero, and Elle ultimately knew it would never work between them.

She started to feel crushed by her emotions as a tear slipped down her cheek. She quickly wiped it away, wishing her problems would wipe away just as easily. The whole car ride, she suffered from her thoughts, and the ride to her house was quite a bit of distance.

Elle opened her eyes as the car pulled over; she wasn't in front of her house like she'd expected, but they were close. She didn't know why Nero would stop. However, Nero got out of the car, and a moment later, Elle watched the backseat door open on the other side. He slid in and positioned his body toward her as he draped his arm over the backseat.

"Baby, come here." Nero's voice sounded like he was commanding her. The part still needy and the sliver inside of her that liked Nero wanted to do as he asked, yet Elle wanted to fight the feeling.

She laid her head back on the window and shut her eyes with her thoughts.

"Now," his voice rang through her head, his command much stronger.

Elle picked her head back up and looked at Nero's body, opened for her. The two sides of Elle were fighting against each other, and when one finally won out, she scooted her body toward him. She didn't know why she had given in, but Elle hadn't realized yet that more than half of her wanted Nero and it would never be much of a fight.

When Elle's hips touched his leg, Nero's arms circled and pulled her into his body. Her head was no longer resting on the window but on Nero's chest. The hand that had been on the backseat now was in her hair as he soothed her head, and the other went under her jacket to do the same to her back.

Elle eased into him and let him soothe her. She figured he had seen her cry and that was why he was doing this. No one had ever taken care of her all those nights she had cried silently in her bed. Only Chloe knew her torture, and she had much worse to cry about.

She didn't know how much time had passed as she lay in his arms. Elle had closed her eyes and thought she might have dozed off until Nero's voice broke the silence of the car.

"It wasn't what it looked like. Yes, maybe from their point of view, but I promise, I didn't want it to happen." Nero spun a piece of her hair and continued, "I'm sorry you had to see it, and I am asking you to trust me. I don't want anyone else, and I'm not going to have anyone else, Elle."

Elle wanted the sound of his warm voice to continue, however she had to have the conversation with him. "How am I supposed to believe you, Nero?" *You always have and, most likely, always will be a player.*

Nero contemplated his answer before he spoke. "If you were any other girl, Elle, I would have fucked you in the girl's locker room today. Trust me; you would have let me, and you sure as hell would have enjoyed it. Instead, I didn't because then you would be like all the other girls I've been with," he paused a brief second, "completely meaningless." Nero grabbed her hair, and Elle finally looked up at him. "I told you not to touch, and now I'm telling you I won't touch. I give you my word, Elle."

When Elle watched him speak, a feeling would always come over her that he was telling the truth. *I can't believe I'm going to trust him.* Her mind was still not onboard with her body.

"Promise?" She needed him to say it.

Nero smiled down at her. "I promise, baby."

Elle smiled back right before he kissed her. She welcomed him in her mouth, letting him set the speed. He caressed her lips, taking care to learn every inch of them until his tongue ventured inside to do the same.

Unlike the last time she had worked to please, she wanted him to please her. Nero didn't seem to mind as he pulled her on his lap, making her straddle him. Her hands went to his hair so she could remember the feeling of it running through her hands. Elle should have known he would when he squeezed her ass in his hands again.

Nero deepened the kiss, forcing her tongue out so he could draw it into his mouth, and once again, she loved the feeling. She really wished she would have done it sooner.

Nero moved down to kissing her neck, nipping and licking better than he had before. *Yeah, because he has to make it up to me.* Elle would definitely make him, too.

Nero went lower and kissed her collarbone as his hands travelled up the front of her body over her clothes. They held her sides, right under her breasts, and Elle's breath caught in her throat as his mouth moved lower, sucking the top of her right breast into his mouth. Her t-shirt normally came above them, but Nero had pulled it down, showing the tip of her thin bra.

Elle swore her breasts had started to swell by the feel of his mouth on her. As she pushed his head closer, afraid he would stop, Nero lifted his hands higher and started rubbing her nipples with the pad of his thumbs, quickly rubbing them into a peak. She couldn't concentrate, once again under Nero's control.

Her nipples began to ache from the hardness and her breasts started to become too sensitive under her bra. When Elle felt Nero's fingertips go under her bra, over her left breast, she quickly grabbed his hand, hoping he wouldn't pull it down. Elle let out a moan when Nero bit her breast in response, paying her back for what she had done to him earlier.

Nero tried to pull it down again as he laved away the sting, but Elle squeezed her hand over his.

"Baby, please, just let me have a taste." Nero talked while he kissed her skin.

Elle whimpered "no" in his ear. She wanted him to. *Like, really want him to.* But Elle had a feeling Nero wouldn't stop at a taste. She knew a guy like Nero devoured the whole thing. Elle would like being devoured by him, yet it wasn't the right time or place for her.

Nero threw his head back on the seat and she watched him try to collect himself while she tried to do the same. Nero had dropped his hand and Elle couldn't help smiling. No matter how bad Nero wanted her—and she knew how much he did because he had grown hard underneath her—he would never force himself on her. If she ultimately didn't want to do it, Nero wouldn't make her.

Elle gave him a quick kiss. "Thank you."

Nero gritted out, "No problem."

She began to try to maneuver off his lap and felt his hardness grind underneath her.

Nero quickly grabbed her hips, and held her in place. "Careful, or I'll throw being a gentleman out the fucking window and watch your tits bounce in my face."

Elle stopped breathing, becoming nervous for what he might do next.

Still holding onto her hips, he moved her off his lap and set her down beside him. Elle felt relieved and almost disappointed at the same time.

Nero finally let Elle go and ran his hands through his hair. "Not since I was a boy have I felt a girl's boobs through their shirt."

Elle tried hard not to laugh. *Poor Nero.* She was proud of herself to be clearly the only girl to make Nero wait.

Elle leaned up and gave him another kiss on the cheek. "I'm sorry." She knew she didn't look very sorry by the way she was smiling.

"You are going to make this up to me." Nero's voice was in a commanding tone once again.

Elle really didn't like where this was headed as she stared back at him, waiting to hear what he wanted. *What now?*

"I am driving you to work tonight."

"But—"

Nero put his hand over her mouth, shutting her up. "And from now on." When Elle's eyes tried to say otherwise, he continued, "I'm not asking; I'm telling." He removed his hand from her mouth and stole a kiss from her.

Why not? It was the least she could do for him for being a gentleman. Hell, she would get a free ride out of it, and if she didn't like it, she would figure out a way to get out of it. It was a win-win.

Since Elle had decided to give in and let him take her, she had another idea to go ahead and get something else over with that was going to be painful.

"Nero, do you want to meet my parents?"

YOU WOULDN'T LET ME
HAVE MY WAY WITH YOU

*E*lle *squeezed Nero's hand as* she walked up her driveway. *Should I be doing this? Is this really a good idea?*

Elle figured today was going to be as good of a day as any. If she did as her father asked—Nero coming over for dinner—it could possibly be much worse. Dinners were long and stressful; however, with her having to go to work tonight, this was going to be a Band-Aid and she was going to rip it right off. She figured Nero was going to have to turn back around to pick her up anyway.

Elle put her hand on the door. *My parents are going to be pissed I didn't warn them.*

She thought it was going to be really funny if this whole thing backfired and Nero walked in on something—the something being anything. *Like what if Dad took his meds again? Or Josh wrecked the house?*

Elle held onto the door handle, thinking about if she should get Nero to turn his ass back around. *Fuck it!* Elle turned the door handle.

When Elle came into the house, she saw her whole family looking out the front window.

"Mom, Dad?"

"Hey, Nero!" Josh came from the curtain and ran toward her and Nero.

Nero held out his fist. "What's up, little man? How was the bus ride today?"

Josh bumped his fist. "Great, thanks for taking me to the bus stop today."

Nero smiled. "Anytime."

Elle smiled to herself as she watched Josh run off into his bedroom. When she could no longer see her little brother, Elle turned to her parents.

Well, here goes nothing. "Mom, Dad, this is my friend, Nero."

Elle's mom came over and hugged him. "Elle has never brought a friend home besides Chloe, and such a handsome one at that."

Elle was slightly embarrassed by her mother, but she had to agree; Nero looked sexy as hell.

From where she had bitten him, he had a nasty hickey on his neck—thankfully, Nero had found a tie in his car. He had buttoned his shirt all the way up and put on the black tie, covering his hickey as long as he didn't turn his neck too far to the side. She hated covering up such a beautiful masterpiece, but looking at Nero all dressed up made him look even more scary, yet sexy at the same time.

Nero kissed her mother's cheek. "Nice to meet you, Mrs. Buchanan."

Elle's mom noticed her head, moving toward her to examine it. "Oh, sweetie, did you walk into a wall again?"

Elle quickly laughed. "Yeah."

Nero looked at her for a moment then walked over to her father sitting in his wheelchair and held out his hand. "Nice to meet you, too, sir."

Elle thought time stood still while waiting for her father to shake his hand. "Nero…?"

"Caruso."

"Good to meet you, too, Nero. Sit down," her father said, turning his wheelchair toward the couch.

Nero took a seat on the couch and Elle sat down beside him. Her mother sat in the armchair facing the couch, as well.

Elle could tell her mom was dying to talk to Nero. She had always asked Elle to bring over some friends and wondered how she was doing in school. Elle thought she probably should have warned Nero by the look on her mother's face.

"So, Nero, you go to Legacy Prep with Elle?" her mother asked.

"Yeah, I'm a senior there, as well."

Elle's mom smiled wider. "So, tell me, is Elle the most popular girl in school? She tells me about—"

Elle started laughing. "Now, Mom."

"Elle, let your mom finish." Nero started smiling and wrapped his arm behind Elle on the couch. "Elle tells you what again?"

I have made a huge mistake.

Elle's mother's smile returned. "She tells me about all her wonderful friends and how much she loves Legacy Prep. After her father's accident, we weren't sure if she was going to be able to stay, but Elle begged us to keep letting her go there. She said she just loves it there so much."

Elle glanced down at the floor. *Oh, God, this is worse than I could have imagined.*

"Yeah, well, she is the most popular girl in school. Everyone just loves her. I had a hard time getting her to talk to me."

Her mother started laughing.

Elle managed to laugh with her mom while she looked over at Nero. He was enjoying this too much.

"So, are you going to stay for dinner, Nero?" Elle's mother asked.

"No, I work tonight, Mom. Nero is going to give me a ride."

"Oh, okay, sweetie. Yes, my Elle of course gets straight As. That pays for some of her tuition. She works at Magical Cupcakes to pay the rest." Her mother was beaming.

Oh, shit. Oh, shit. Oh, shit.

Nero's face jerked up. "Where?"

"You know, Magical Cupcakes. It opened a few years ago in the suburbs. That's where Elle works, of course."

Elle looked over at Nero, silently pleading. "Yeah, Nero, I told you that's where I work. Remember?"

Nero stared back at her for a few seconds then he turned back to her mother. "Oh, yeah. Sorry, I forgot."

"Honey, why don't you and Elle go make some snacks. I'm sure they are hungry after school." Elle's dad hadn't pulled his eyes away from Nero.

"Right. Come on, sweetie. Let the boys talk." Her mom stood up, smiling from ear to ear, and started walking to the kitchen.

Elle looked over at Nero, hoping he understood not to talk too much. *Oh, and good luck.*

Elle stood and followed behind her mother. She was thankful Nero hadn't been fazed by the obvious lies she had been telling her parents over the years.

Going into the kitchen, her mother pulled out some deli meat while Elle went to grab the bread, knowing her mom was going to make sandwiches.

"He is so nice and handsome, sweetie. I like him."

Elle laughed at her mother. She couldn't be happier that Elle had invited him over. Her mother had begged her for years to bring friends to the house. Yes, Chloe would come over, but her mother always wanted to meet the other kids she said she was friends with.

"Yeah, the nicest."

Nero watched as Elle stood to leave the room. He had to be honest; he had been dying to meet Elle's parents. He wanted to meet the bastards who let Elle continue to go to school where she was bullied.

But, damn if her mother wasn't the nicest woman on Earth. She was just too kind and dumb, believing every lie Elle had spun. Her mom was clearly the completely oblivious type, one of the people who thought there was no such thing as violence.

Then her father was in a wheelchair. *What the fuck?* At first, Nero was willing to forgive him like he was with her mother, but looking at his glaring eyes now, he didn't give a shit if the man could no longer walk or not. Nero was starting to get a pretty good idea how bad Elle might have been hurt in the past, and the man staring back at him should have been well fucking aware something wasn't right at school for her.

Nero stared back at him. He had been raised by much scarier men than him. Elle's dad was a little bunny rabbit compared to his father. *Does he actually think he can scare me?*

Her dad kept his eyes pinned to Nero. "I'm guessing Elle didn't tell you I was in a wheelchair, did she?"

Nero didn't move his eyes. "No, she didn't."

"Figured. There's a lot that girl doesn't tell."

Well, why don't you fucking make her? "Yeah, I'm gathering that."

"Your last name's Caruso. It sounds familiar to me. Would I know your parents?" Elle's father asked.

No way in Hell. "I don't think so. My mother passed away when I was younger, and my dad pretty much keeps to himself now."

"I'm sorry to hear that." His passive tone showed he wasn't really. "What does your father do?"

Nero had been waiting for that question the moment he'd said his last name. "He owns a casino hotel downtown."

"Really? I doubt he can keep to himself owning a casino hotel."

Nero shrugged. "He has great managers."

"I bet he does. Do you plan to work for your father or are you going to college?"

Nero had a feeling Mr. Buchanan knew his answer. "I'm going to work for my father."

Nero watched Elle's father smile and ease up. "Elle is going off to college. She hasn't decided yet, but she can pick anywhere she wants to go pretty much."

Nero smiled back. "That's good. Elle should go to college."

Nero could tell Mr. Buchanan hadn't been prepared for his answer. Then his smile returned. "Hmm, for some reason Elle didn't apply to the university here."

I fucking wonder why? "Well, there's still half a year left to apply. You never know, something could change her mind."

Nero saw his face grow pissed, about to say something, when he heard Elle and her mother enter the living room. Nero kept his smile, glad his message had been clear to Elle's father.

He looked at Elle's mother as she held out a glass of water. She looked like the older version of Elle, the only difference being she had laugh lines and was slightly plump, making Nero happy Elle would age well.

Nero took the glass of water. "Thank you, Mrs. Buchanan."

Elle's mom smiled and took her seat. "You're welcome. I hope water is okay."

"It's great, thanks."

He looked over at Elle when she didn't sit down. She was holding a plate of sandwiches and her own glass of water.

"Come on, Nero. Let's eat in my room."

Nero couldn't wait to get Elle alone and talk to her about all the lies she had told her parents. *No wonder she can't help but lie to me—she's living two fucking different lives.*

Elle's eyes rolled. "With the door open."

He looked over at Elle's father's face, which was fuming.

Nero stood up, smiling. *Elle isn't going anywhere.*

Elle handed over the plate of sandwiches to Nero so she could open her bedroom door. Opening it, she walked in with Nero right behind her then closed the door. *Crap.* She re-opened the door, leaving it halfway open.

She turned around and saw Nero standing there with his hands full. "You can sit on my bed."

"You sure about that?" Nero asked sarcastically.

Elle pushed the door a little more closed. "Yep."

She walked to her bed and sat at the top with her back propped on her pillows, up against her headboard. Nero walked over to the other side and did the same. She watched him as he got comfortable and set the plate between them.

Nero took a big drink of his water and held out his hand. "Remote."

Elle looked around her room for her remote control. She had an old box TV that faced her bed. She grabbed it off her nightstand from under some old magazines. She was thankful her room wasn't too messy. Although, she had a bunch of knickknacks and random stuff in her room from over the years since she always had a terrible time throwing stuff away.

Elle handed Nero the remote, curious as to why he demanded it the second he sat down.

Nero clicked on the TV, and a few seconds later, a picture came in focus. Elle shut her eyes and started rubbing her head when she realized what channel it was on. *This just gets better and better.*

Nero looked over at Elle. "Really, Elle? The Disney Channel?"

"The Little Mermaid came on last night." Elle couldn't ever pass up a classic; it didn't matter if she even owned the DVD.

Nero shook his head and changed the channel to an old sitcom. He turned the TV up loud and grabbed a sandwich. "Magical Cupcakes, huh?"

That's why he wanted the remote. Elle realized she wasn't going to be able to watch one of her favorite reruns; as a result, she picked up a sandwich herself and turned toward Nero.

"Yeah, didn't you know I worked there?" Elle said in her own sarcastic tone.

"Yeah, that uniform hanging on the back of your door is almost identical to the pink t-shirts and jeans they wear." Nero took another bite of his sandwich. It was almost gone by the huge bites he was taking. "Is there fucking anything you haven't lied to your parents about?"

"Uh, yes." *Yes!*

"Like the fact you have a friend other than Chloe, and that you love school so much?"

"I'm telling her what she likes to hear. What she wants to hear, Nero." Elle wanted her mom to be happy, and making up stories kept her mom happy.

Nero got out of bed, finishing his sandwich, and started looking around her room, snooping. He clearly found exactly what he was looking for and grabbed the big book off a shelf filled with movies, books, stuffed animals, and everything else you could think of. He came back and sat down on the bed, flipping it open carefully and studying each picture.

She had started filling the book up when she was a young girl, putting in pictures of her at various places and doing different things.

She'd had a good childhood. Her parents had been great, school had been great, and everything had, indeed, been great. Right until her father had gotten a big promotion at the factory and wanted the best for Elle. They had pulled her from public school and enrolled her in Prep School for her freshman year.

Her parents had wanted this for her badly, and Elle had always been able to make friends, therefore she hadn't wanted to let her parents down. It was just unfortunate that her father's accident had occurred right after her freshman year had begun.

Elle swallowed when the next page Nero turned to would end up being far different than the ones he had seen before. He turned the page and Elle noticed his face change. There was about a year difference between this page and the last. The first thing you would notice was her hair was short. Then you'd see she had lost some weight.

The thing Elle noticed the most was Chloe in the picture. She hadn't looked at the photo album in a while, just realizing exactly how brutal Chloe's scars looked in the beginning. Her mother would constantly snap pictures of her and Chloe, whether they were watching a movie or doing a school project.

"Funny how your hair was one length your whole life, but the first picture I see with Chloe was one where your hair is chopped off."

Elle could only stare at Nero. There was nothing she could say. Nero wasn't dumb, and she wasn't going to lie to him, so it was better not to say a word.

She watched him keep flipping the pages right after he stared at the picture for an eternity. She knew he was studying it, looking at every inch of the photo before he would move on. She was just thankful that some injuries over the years were hidden under her clothes.

Elle was glad to see Nero finally close the book in his hands. He then stared at the closed book for a while before he finally lifted his head to look at her.

This time, when Nero looked at her, Elle knew it was different. It was almost as if he was looking at her in a whole new light. She stared back into his green eyes, waiting for what he was going to do next.

"Is there even a fucking point in asking you?" She knew Nero was trying to stay calm.

Elle said nothing; instead, she slowly took the book out of his hands and got up to return it to the bookshelf where it belonged.

After she had, she took her place again on her bed. She watched the TV screen, letting the show unfold.

After Nero hadn't moved for a while, she knew he was trying to calm himself down, being in her parents' house. However, there was nothing Elle could tell him to make him feel better; not the truth, anyway.

Elle felt Nero's hand reach out for her arm and turned to look at him. He started pulling her toward him, so she scooted over. She could at least give him that. He wrapped his arm around her and Elle laid her head on him.

"You do know I'm going to find out," Nero said with confidence, certain it was a sure thing.

"I know you will." Elle did know, too. When a guy like Nero wanted something, he wasn't going to stop until he had it.

They watched shows until it was time for Elle to get up and get ready for work. She had felt Nero slowly start to calm down and ease into the bed and her as the time passed. Elle would laugh at the funny parts and she saw Nero even smile at one. *A little smile counts.*

"I gotta go get ready." Elle was waiting for Nero to move his arm to let her go. He didn't of course, making Elle laugh. "Nero, I need to get dressed."

After she said that, he quickly moved his arm. Elle looked at him weird. *Okay,* now *you move your arm?*

Elle got up out of bed, grabbed her uniform off the door then went out to the bathroom to get changed, dressing quickly and throwing her hair up in a messy bun.

She returned to her room and saw Nero sitting at the end of her bed. When she came in, she stopped at the look on his face. His eyes went over every inch of her body before a smile touched his lips. His hand came up and waved her to come closer.

Elle didn't want to walk toward him, yet her feet started walking anyway. She didn't know how Nero did that to her. She stopped in front of him.

"You look pretty hot in that uniform." Nero's face looked pleased.

Elle chuckled and reached for Nero's tie, straightening it. "Not as hot as you do in this tie."

"Oh, so you're actually attracted to me? I didn't know."

"Well, duh. How could I not be?" Nero was every girl's dream.

"Probably because you wouldn't let me have my way with you in the car, and on top of that, you introduced me to your parents as your *friend*." Nero made sure he sounded extra sarcastic with the word 'friend'.

Elle tried hard not to laugh, miserably failing. After the giggle fit, Nero looked as if his ego needed some stroking.

"Nero, do you know how handsome you are?"

"Nope, but you can tell me."

Elle knew Nero was perfectly aware of exactly how handsome he was, but regardless, she would tell him. "You are the handsomest guy I have ever seen, and I am very attracted to you. But I have a feeling you know that."

Nero grabbed her around her waist. "So, I'm just a friend?"

Elle looked into his eyes. "I don't know, are you?"

"No, baby, I'm not."

AN ITCH THAT NEEDS
TO BE SCRATCHED

Leaning back in his oversized chair, he told the person waiting behind the door, "Come in."

He watched as the doorknob turned and his oldest son walked in. Boss Caruso took in his son's appearance. *For fuck's sake.*

"Please tell me why you think it's okay to wear that?"

In their line of business, your wardrobe was limited. Everything was Italian-made and business attire. *You wear an expensive suit, shoes, and a watch. End of fucking story.* They were judged and respected by what they wore, and that was how they kept control of the city. However, his son had his own attire of dark jeans and a black t-shirt.

"Nice to see you, too, boss," he said as he pulled a pack of cigarettes out of his pocket.

"You know I don't like that fucking smell in here."

Not saying a word, he flipped his lighter open and lit the end of the stick, inhaling the smoke for a long hit and then blowing the smoke out and filling the whole room. Lucca never had to reply, his actions saying his own words for him. He walked to his father's desk and took a seat, pulling an ashtray toward him.

Boss Caruso continued to watch his son, waiting to see if he was ever going to say what he needed to say and leave him be. He had been here at the Casino Hotel and had to deal with people all day. As a result, he really wanted to leave so he could go to his home office and smoke his cigar and drink in peace, but his son looked like something had been weighing on his mind.

When he had waited long enough for his son to talk, he gave up. "I'm guessing this is about the girl."

Lucca flicked his ashes in the tray. "Nero met the parents today."

He finally understood his son's displeasure. "That means one of two things."

"Yeah, he has her. She likes him enough to meet the family, but then Nero could actually start liking her. It's tough to sign a girl's death certificate when you've met her family."

He stared at his son, taking everything in. "So, is he playing her or does he love her?"

Lucca took a long puff before he answered. "I guess I'm going to have to find out."

He nodded to his son while Lucca put out his cigarette. "Next time I see you, you better be in a fucking suit for once."

He watched as Lucca got up to leave and headed for the door then turned the doorknob and went through, but before he could shut it, Boss Caruso had some final words.

"You do know *the family* comes before *family*, even if it's your own brother."

He expected his son to not say anything; however, Lucca gave him his own final words. "Yeah, you taught me that with Mom, remember?"

The slamming of the door echoed in his head. He got up and walked over to his bar then picked up and held the crystal glass in his hand right before it shattered. For him, it was something he would never forget. He poured a new drink and his bloody hand picked up the sparkling glass filled with whiskey. *This will help.*

Nero stood on his bedroom balcony, looking out. He had dropped Elle off and was now waiting on Stacy and Stephanie to get there. *I have an itch that needs to be scratched.*

He figured no one was going to be home tonight, thus he'd texted the girls to come right up. He didn't wait that long before he heard his bedroom door open and high heels walking across his floor. Turning around, he smiled at the two slutty-looking girls walking to meet him on his balcony. *A big fucking itch.*

When they reached him, they stood on either side of him, hugging and pressing their bodies against his.

"Nero, I missed you," Stephanie said.

"Well, I missed you more," Stacy said over her.

Nero laughed. "How about, whoever makes me come the fastest missed me the most?"

The two girls laughed in agreement and grabbed for Nero's clothes. They were only able to un-tuck his shirt and undo one button before they heard the bedroom door open.

"Nero, you didn't tell us we were going to have a party!" The girls were practically jumping in joy when they saw Vincent and Amo walk in and join them on the balcony.

Stacy grabbed Vincent while Stephanie grabbed Amo.

"Do we finally get to fuck you?" Stephanie asked, wrapping her arms around Amo.

Amo responded by backing her up against the concrete railing and Vincent mimicked him by doing the same thing to Stacy. Nero walked to the balcony door and slid it closed, closing them all off from the bedroom.

Amo and Vincent took a handful of their hair, each yanking it down until they screamed in pain.

Nero walked toward them, standing in-between their now-crying screams. He let the sound soak in his ears, finding it peaceful. Nero then held up his hand, making Amo and Vincent stop.

He grabbed both girls, pulling them to his side as he wrapped his arms around their shoulders. Their crying was much softer now, and Nero could feel them trembling.

He took a deep breath, soaking it in for just a moment longer. "I know you two whores love to talk, right?" He heard Stacy cry a little louder. "Well, I need one of you to tell me everything you or anyone else has done to Elle."

"W-what? W-we don't know a-anything." Nero looked at Stephanie as she talked then looked over at Stacy and saw she agreed.

Ultimately, Nero knew these girls were followers; they weren't the ones to really instigate Elle's torture—the hurt kind of torture, anyway. *They clearly never did give a shit, though.*

"How about you just give me the name of the worst one. Then I'll leave you two alone so you can get back to sucking dick." Nero wanted the true source, the one who, without a doubt, had hurt Elle and put her in all those casts and covered her in bruises and scars. That way, he could make the person sing about every little thing that had happened to Elle, and the little piece of conscience he had left wouldn't get in the way. Because Elle was going to eventually find out if he hurt anyone, and he didn't want that to be someone who hadn't done that much damage to her.

Nero looked back and forth between the crying girls, their dark, skanky makeup running down their faces. When they clearly weren't going to talk, Nero nodded for several seconds before he grabbed his own pile of fake hair in both hands. He shoved their torso over the railing, letting their faces meet the two-story drop. The cries that now filled the air were ones he really enjoyed. *Yeah, but all good things must come to an end.*

"Give me a fucking name!" He shoved their heads farther down, making their feet slightly come off the ground.

The screams were torturous before Stacy tried to get a word

out of her mouth. She tried again, finally gaining enough strength. "Ch-Chloe!"

Amo stepped closer. "What the fuck did she just say?"

Nero pulled the girls up, tossing Stephanie to the side. He held Stacy in place in front of him. "What did you say?"

Through sobbing, she managed to get out, "T-talk to Chloe."

Nero let Stacy go.

"Vincent, make them aware of what happens when they talk."

He ran his hands through his hair, trying to get it to smooth down. He heard the balcony door open and the cries start to disappear. He and Amo stood there, looking out into the distance. They waited for Vincent to return before anything was said.

"What the fuck did she mean by that?" Vincent asked, returning.

Nero waited to hear what Amo would say first.

"Chloe would know who all has hurt Elle. Maybe she's saying to ask Chloe who has hurt them."

Nero thought about Amo's words, but something didn't feel right to him. He didn't understand how the pieces fit yet, however. They were all there, but it was a matter of putting it together.

He pictured the photo book of Elle's, remembering how badly he had wanted to shake her and make her tell him everything. How badly he had wanted to paralyze the rest of her father's body after seeing Elle's nose broken and a cast over her arm. *All the fucking black eyes.* Nero knew that was just what was visible to him. There could have been several under her clothing, not to mention all the times it healed before a picture had been taken.

He decided enough was enough. The next person he questioned, he was going to get some real fucking answers. *No matter what.*

Nero looked at Amo to make sure he knew how far he would go if need be. "Well, then, we talk to Chloe."

CAN YOU PASS THE SUGAR?

Elle *had a big crowd* again at the diner tonight. She was thankful; it would help keep her mind off Nero. The way he and her father had looked at each other when they'd left had her confused as to what they had talked about. Whatever it was, she probably didn't want to know. The ride over had been nice and she had to admit she liked it. She could definitely deal with him driving her to and from work.

Elle looked at the door to see who walked in, still on the lookout to make sure the boss and whoever worked for him didn't walk through. Every time that door opened, her heart raced until she realized they had no relation to the murder. When Nero walked in, her heart calmed. W*ait, what is he doing here?*

Elle could only stare as Nero walked to a booth in the corner. He took a seat with his back up against the wall, giving him a full view of the diner. He had brought a bag with him. She had no idea what he had planned.

Elle walked over to his table. "What are you doing here?"

Nero smiled wide. "I'm starving."

She didn't like where this was going, although she knew better than to question Nero when he was set on something. She was at work and needed to treat him as a customer; consequently, Elle reluctantly took out her notepad and pen.

"What can I get you?"

"Surprise me."

Elle put the pad and pen back in her apron and smiled. "Would you like me to pick your drink, as well?"

Nero leaned back in his seat. "No, I'll take a coffee."

Elle realized he was clearly just getting comfortable. *The perfect night for the perfect day.*

Elle went to the window and asked for the special then she went and grabbed a plate, holding a mug in one hand and taking the coffee pot in the other. She returned to Nero's table and set the plate and cup in front of him, looking at him right before she poured the dark liquid into the mug. Elle could read his face and knew he had been waiting for this moment.

Returning her eyes to the mug, mostly because watching him look at her that way had started to heat her body, she managed to successfully pour the coffee. Nero's hand covered hers for her to stop pouring, making Elle look at him again. She didn't know how something like pouring coffee for Nero could turn sexual.

"Can you pass the sugar?" Nero's free hand pointed to the

packets of sugar at the other end of the table.

Elle looked at the ceramic box holding the packets. She knew he could very well get them and it would be easier for him to, but for some reason, Elle leaned over the table, having to go to her toes to reach them. She could feel Nero's eyes all over her body, exciting her. She figured that feeling was the reason she wanted to please Nero.

Elle slowly slid the sugar across the table until it lay in front of him.

Nero's thumb rubbed the top of her hand. "Thank you." Then he finally released her hand, letting Elle look away from his eyes that had held her prisoner, as well.

She licked her now-dry lips before she left the table without a word. Elle felt his eyes all over her body again as she walked away. She tried to get her thoughts and body under control as she waited on her other tables. By the time she managed to do so, Nero's order came up in the window.

Taking the hot plate, she headed for his table and set the plate of food in front of him. His expression now was sour, unlike the one he'd had on when Elle poured him coffee. *What got into him?*

Elle left the table when Nero gave no response, continuing to work despite Nero distracting her. His eyes hadn't left her while she waited on her tables and he ate.

When she picked up his dirty dishes, he looked pissed. She had even re-filled his coffee with a smile, trying to get him to lighten up, but he hadn't. Elle had no clue what was pissing Nero off so badly.

Eventually, Nero pulled out his laptop from his bag along with some schoolwork. *I guess he is staying till I get off.* That made Elle nervous.

Nero was a complete wild card to her, and he was at her work. What he did in here would affect her, and this job was how Elle continued to go to school.

When the diner started to die down and her shift was almost over, only Nero and a table full of four guys remained. Elle picked up the coffee pot to refill their cups, going to the full table and filling up their cups first.

"Can I get you all anything else?" Elle spoke as she filled a cup.

"No thanks, babe." the good-looking one of the group responded. Elle figured they were in college by their university attire.

Elle smiled and walked away once all the cups were filled.

"Elle," she heard her name called from the corner of the room.

Elle turned around and headed for the corner where Nero was sitting. Nero's face was now beyond pissed.

"Sit."

Elle looked around. "I can't."

"Now."

Elle looked back at Nero and felt like she only had one option, and that was to sit. She sat down in front of him, tired of his constant glares.

"What is the matter with you?"

Nero kept his voice calm and low so no one could hear their conversation. "I don't like you pouring coffee and serving food to all these fucking men. The only coffee I want you pouring is mine."

Huh? Elle was taken off-guard by his response. First, she realized she liked his possessiveness, and then she realized the extent of his possessiveness.

"Nero, it's not like I enjoy it."

"Do you think I enjoyed sitting here the whole night, having to see a bunch of old men stare at your tits and ass?" Elle tried to speak but couldn't get one syllable out. "Then listen to douchebags call you 'babe'?" Nero's voice started losing its calmness.

"Hmm, I wonder who that reminds me of," Elle said sarcastically.

"My fucking point. Tell them to fuck off next time." Nero was fuming now.

Elle was pretty sure Nero was about to do something very stupid, so she leaned forward and took his hand from the table. Taking a deep breath, Elle said, "Nero, this is where I work, so I can continue to go to school, and unfortunately, I pay most of it with the tips alone. That means putting up with the looks, stares, and babes. I can't just tell them to fuck off; I could lose my job."

Nero ran his hands through his hair and flexed his jaw. When he nodded for her to get back to work, Elle stood and started to walk off.

"Are you forgetting something?" Nero pointed to his coffee cup.

Elle went back to the side of his table and decided to place her breasts expertly in front of his face as she refilled his coffee. The lust that had shown on his face before returned, and Elle smiled again. She didn't know why she wanted Nero happy, or why that part inside of her wanted to please him, but Elle admitted she enjoyed doing so.

Elle scurried away, laughing when Nero tried to reach out and grab her. She saw the smile on his face, discerning he was finally in a better mood. She went ahead and started to clean up for the night; she was closing, of course. She asked the cook to throw away the trash this time. *Lesson learned.*

About ten minutes before closing, the table with the college students was still there joking around. They weren't being rowdy or anything, but you could just hear them talking and cutting up with each other. They didn't look like they had any plans to leave soon.

Elle went over to their table and took away some of their dirty dishes. "We close in about ten minutes."

The good-looking one smiled at her. "We were just about to head out." Then he quickly moved his elbow and a fork fell to the ground. "Sorry, babe."

Elle's heart started racing. She quickly looked over at Nero, silently pleading for him not to do anything. When the guy didn't make a move to pick it up and the other guys stared at her in anticipation, Elle had to pick it up.

She quickly squatted down to hurry up and retrieve the fork. When she stood up and grabbed for the rest of the dishes, she noticed their displeased faces. They had clearly wanted her to bend over and get it. *No way in Hell.*

Elle tried to force a smile as she walked away. She prayed Nero wouldn't do anything and just leave it be as she went behind the counter and pretended to be busy so she could see if anything were to happen. She could tell Nero was on the verge of going crazy. She hoped he had listened to her earlier.

When the college guys walked out of the diner, Elle stood

frozen as she waited to see if Nero would follow after them. When he didn't, Elle relaxed.

Elle went to the now-unoccupied table and grabbed the tip off the table as well as the little dishes left. Dropping them off at the dishwasher, she headed for Nero's table, unable to meet his gaze.

"How much?"

Elle kept her eyes on the table. "Ten for the meal."

Nero stood and pulled out a silver money clip full of cash and handed her a hundred-dollar bill. "Keep the rest."

Elle looked at Nero finally and started shaking her head. "I'm not taking your money, Ne—" Nero swiftly grabbed her and had her sitting on the edge of the table. *How in the hell?*

He parted Elle's legs with his body and pressed himself up against her. His face came close to hers as he harshly spoke. "You are lucky I'm just asking you to take my money after fucking watching that. I am desperately trying to restrain myself right now." Nero took the folded hundred-dollar bill and touched her chin with it before slowly sliding it down her neck to her chest and under her dress.

Elle's chest started to rise and fall heavier than it ever had before. Nero had blocked her legs, making it impossible to squeeze them together. She could feel the wetness start to soak her panties when Nero's hands went to her bare thighs under her uniform, pushing it up. He greedily kissed her as he stroked her sensitive thighs, sending chills up her back.

Nero's hands went to the inside of her middle thighs when he said, "Now, you're going to send me the rest of your work schedule in return for not shoving my foot up his ass. I'm not stupid, Elle. I know there was more." Nero moved his hands higher up her thighs. "I can go back there and find it for myself and still have enough time to catch him if you don't."

His hands were now mere centimeters away from her mound. She was sure he could feel the heat and dampness coming from her.

She nodded, half of her hoping he wouldn't go any farther and the other half hoping to find out what it would feel like to be touched there for the first time.

Nero slowly slid his hands back down her thighs and returned her to her feet. "Now, hurry up. I would like to get the fuck out of here."

Elle didn't know how she got her legs to hold her up, much less walk to the back kitchen. She tried to shake off what had happened between her and Nero as she quickly took out her phone and sent Nero the first picture she had taken yesterday, showing her whole schedule. Elle figured there was no harm in giving it to him. She had already planned to keep riding with him to work now.

She walked farther back into the kitchen to tell the cook she was leaving. "See you this weekend, Steve."

He didn't even look up from the dishes. "Bye, Elle."

Elle walked back through the swinging doors and went to the cash register, putting in ten dollars' worth in tips instead of breaking the hundred. Elle smiled. She didn't want to take Nero's money. *But I did work for it all night.* She turned some lights off and grabbed her coat before walking to Nero, who was waiting by the door.

Her smile never disappeared when Nero drove her home. As

they reached her house, Nero parked at the next house down, making Elle curious as to why he had done it. When he spent a long time kissing her goodbye, Elle realized why, remembering her family looking out the window earlier.

She lay in her bed that night, still unable to stop smiling. Being with Nero made her happy in her life once again. She had forgotten the feeling.

That night was the first in years Elle fell asleep with a smile on her face.

THANKS FOR KILLING OUR FUCKING DREAMS

Elle sat in Spanish, looking at the clock. *My, how things can change.* This time, Elle didn't mind the ticking when she usually wished somehow time would freeze so the ticking would stop. This was a monumental moment in her life.

She had been terrified of lunch time ever since...

Brrring.

"Can I solve this problem?" she asked her teacher. Elle decided to finish her algebra problem as everyone else ran out of the classroom to go to lunch. It's not like she was in a hurry to sit all by herself at lunch anyway.

"Go ahead. Shut the door on your way out."

Elle didn't have time to even nod before the teacher ran off into the teachers' lounge.

Elle finished her problem and went out to head to lunch, sure to close the door behind her. Her classroom was all the way in the back of the school.

As she started heading down the hallway, she began hearing laughter from a crowd. Elle kept walking to get out of the back hallway and into the main one. When she did, she came right into a group of people. She already knew who the girls were, but she hadn't met the guys yet.

"That's who I was telling you about, Sebastian." Cassandra pointed toward Elle.

Elle saw a guy walk forward who looked almost identical to Cassandra. The only reason they didn't was because they were of opposite sex.

"So, you're the little bitch who disrespected my sister?"

Elle tried to pass him. She knew exactly where this was going.

"Oh, no, you don't. We're going to take a little walk." Sebastian hooked his arm in hers and headed back down the back hallway.

"Get off me." Elle tried not to move with Sebastian and then began fighting him.

Another guy hooked her other arm and both of them started pulling her down the hallway.

Elle desperately tried to fight them, kicking and screaming. Tears started to fill her eyes and a powerful feeling came over her that what was about to happen to her would change her forever.

Elle was now being pulled through the back school door. She saw the girls following behind her through her tears while she heard their laughter over her screams. . .

Elle shook her head. *It doesn't matter anymore.* She had already cried too many nights because of that day, and the memory was too bad to bring up. *I don't want to ruin a good day.*

Elle was having a good day, too. Nero had picked her up again, another house down of course, and Amo had brought Chloe safe and sound to English this morning. Now she was going to have a great lunch, no matter what anyone decided to throw at her.

When the bell rang, Elle got up smiling.

Chloe smiled at her. "Someone's happy."

Elle laughed. "Yeah, you don't look too unhappy yourself." She had told Chloe last night why she had been upset yesterday. Chloe actually stood up for Nero, agreeing with what he told her in the car. Needless to say, Chloe enjoyed having three big shields to stand in front of her.

Elle stopped in the doorway, looking at the guys leaning against the lockers. "Yeah, I guess they aren't so bad."

Chloe stopped beside her. "You're right." Chloe paused. "Well, besides the beast."

They both started giggling, unable to hold it in.

Nero walked toward Elle, smiling. "What are you all laughing about?"

They both looked at each other. "Nothing."

"Yeah, right, nothing. Clearly they were talking about us," Amo said, crossing his arms in front of his chest.

Elle smirked. "Nope, just you." Elle started laughing again at the look on his face, making Chloe laugh with her.

Nero took Elle's hand, laughing as well. "Come on, girls; leave him alone."

Elle let Nero push her and Chloe along, still laughing at Amo's face. She saw Vincent pat him on the back before she turned away. She knew Amo just wasn't used to girls talking to him that way.

Apparently he doesn't talk with girls when he could be doing something else with them. Elle figured that was why bugging him made it that much better.

As they walked into the cafeteria, stopping to talk in a circle, Elle had déjà vu all over again.

"What do you want to eat?" Nero asked, looking at her.

Elle was about to turn around and look at the line, but Vincent's voice stopped her.

"The question was, what do you want, not the opposite of what they are fucking eating."

Elle looked at Chloe, smiling. "Tacos?" She couldn't believe a day would come where she could actually pick what she wanted to eat at school.

Chloe smiled back. "Tacos."

"Jesus Christ, probably never had tacos, either." Amo stomped forward, going to the line.

Amo was right, but Elle wasn't about to tell them that.

They went through the line, this time not cutting—besides Leo. Technically, he cut to join them, though. Elle figured Nero had told them not to cut by how unhappy Amo and Vincent looked.

After they went through the line, Elle headed to their table but saw that it was already occupied. *What? We have always sat here.*

"Come on, Elle; we've moved." Nero pushed her forward, keeping her going until the only empty table she saw was the one in the back corner, deep in robot territory.

"You two sit here." Nero pointed to the two seats that faced the rest of the cafeteria.

Elle and Chloe sat down while the boys took their seats. Elle couldn't see the rest of the cafeteria because their bodies blocked her view. She felt awkward.

"Why did we move? This isn't our table."

Nero picked up his taco and took a bite. "Now it is."

"We have sat at that table since freshman year." Elle needed to be close to the door so she could escape if need be.

"No one cares, sweetheart." Vincent picked up his taco and took a bite.

Elle stared at the boys, chowing down on their tacos. *Why would they move us?* Elle looked behind her. *It's just walls.* Elle looked in front of her. *They're blocking my view.* Elle leaned up to see over Vincent's head and saw that the whole football team was sitting at the surrounding tables.

Realization hit Elle that only a tank or a sniper could reach her from now on. Elle quickly kissed Nero's cheek, finding it incredibly sweet he would do something like that for her. When he smiled at her, Elle's heart started to ache. She was really starting to care for Nero and wondered if she was going to regret that someday.

Elle decided to finally start eating. After a few bites, she turned to Chloe. "Can we still go shopping tonight, or is your car not fixed yet?"

"Lana told me it should be done after school, so we are going," Chloe said happily. "The towing company was supposed to pick it up this morning. If it can't be fixed in time, then she's going to get me a loaner."

Thank God!

"Good. Do you want to sleep over tonight?"

"Yep, we need to catch up on some movies."

Elle heard Nero mumble under his breath, "Oh, Lord." She then kicked him under the table.

"I have to know. Do girls really have pillow fights at slumber parties?" Vincent flashed his smile.

Elle rolled her eyes. *Typical.*

"Yeah, I wondered that, too." Leo said.

"Are you all serious?" Elle looked at their faces. They looked serious.

"I wanna know," Amo chimed in.

Nero turned and looked at her. "Do you?"

Elle pushed at his shoulder. "No, we don't. We wear green face masks, paint each other's toenails, and watch old movies." She looked around at their disappointed faces.

Vincent threw down the rest of his taco. "Wow, Elle, thanks for killing our fucking dreams."

Nero watched Elle's ass as she followed Chloe into Spanish class. *Hey, I can't help it.*

He had pulled Elle aside earlier, telling her he had wanted to take her on a date tonight since this was the only night she had off this week. She told him she desperately needed new clothes and some girl time. Nero smiled. *I'm getting to her.*

He couldn't complain to her because he had asked Amo to hook him up with a girl tonight. However, yesterday he had decided no other girl was going to satisfy him. His dick craved Elle. *It will have her, too.*

"I don't understand why Chloe's father hasn't fixed her car yet. She said Lana was going to, and that's who's been picking her up and dropping her off," Amo spoke when the door came to a close.

"Yeah, I don't know. It doesn't seem right, but maybe the man is just too busy. Lana clearly is the help, and you know people like that force their kids to be raised by their workers. I'll ask Elle about it sometime, but you know she doesn't give up shit." Nero knew Elle wasn't going to tell him, yet if he asked strategically, maybe he could find out something.

"Well, we know if she doesn't say shit, then that isn't good." Amo continued after a moment, "My dad knows I set us three up tonight."

Nero ran his hands through his hair. "Shit."

Amo laughed. "Yeah, I figured you might have changed your mind."

"Doesn't matter. Now I have to go." Nero would go. Amo's dad would tell his father if he didn't go, and since they were in public school and no relation to Elle, it would be uncharacteristic for him not to. *Hell, it will look good that I go.*

"The girls wanna go to Poison," Amo said.

"Fuck me." Nero hated that place. It was an expensive-ass lounge for teens. Nero never needed to go to a lounge to get laid and waste all his money in the process. He figured the girls wanted to go since they had most likely never been. Now Nero was going to not only have to pay for him, but her, and he wasn't even going to get laid by the end of it.

Vincent shrugged. "I heard Cassandra is planning to be there tonight, so it might not be that bad."

Nero smiled. "At least I'll get something out of the night." He would pay double what the night would cost him to get a hold of Cassandra. He hadn't seen her since she'd tried to fuck with Elle in the cafeteria. "Just give me the shy one out of the group, but I'm sure you two won't mind."

Vincent spoke quickly, "Fuck no, man. I'll be able to swoop in and have two to play with."

"Not if I swoop in first," Amo replied.

Nero shook his head as he walked away. *Tonight might not be so bad.* He could get even with Cassandra, and keep making his father think Elle was just a job. Nero smiled, thinking it was all working out.

What could possibly go wrong?

YOU'VE GOT THIS ALL WRONG, MOTHERFUCKER

Elle flipped through the rack of clothes. *The Goodwill gods are not looking out for me today.* They had scoured every thrift store, and all Elle had been able to find was more t-shirts. She had only been able to find three she liked, and they were a little iffy with all the holes they had accumulated. Elle was looking for something different, but of course, those staple pieces only came along every so often.

Going through the racks, Elle thought about what Nero had asked her on the drive home. He had asked her if she was planning to drive with Chloe again once her car was fixed. She had told him she hadn't made her mind up for his sake. She liked riding with Nero, but she would be there for Chloe before him. That wasn't what bugged Elle, though.

He had then proceeded to ask her why Chloe's car had still been parked at the school until this morning. That brought up a whole can of worms Elle would never talk about. She had been thankful when he dropped the conversation pretty quickly, yet now she was thinking it might have given him some information he had wanted to know.

Elle moved to another rack, this time smiling at remembering when Nero had parked a house down. She had been able to see he was a little upset still that he wasn't going to take her on a date yet; as a result, she had promised him, the next time she was off, she was all his. That was when it dawned on Elle.

They were becoming pretty serious. Yes, it might have only been a few days between them, but Elle had seen since freshman year that Nero was never around only one girl. She had watched the way he treated girls, and he didn't treat her the same as them. *Well, maybe in the beginning he did.*

Elle couldn't describe the feeling. She didn't even attempt to understand it, but something in her said it was right. It only grew stronger every second they spent together alone as well as when Nero kissed or touched her when no one was looking.

"What about this?" She saw Chloe hold something up a few racks down. The emerald green color struck her.

"I love that." Elle walked over and took the garment from Chloe then headed to the dressing room.

She threw off her shirt and put it on. Elle looked at herself in the mirror, loving her reflection. It was a tight, V-neck sweater that was almost meant as a dress. It hugged all her curves and the color looked fantastic next to her hair and skin coloring. Elle knew it would match perfectly with her black leggings at home.

Elle opened the door so Chloe could see the outfit.

"Oh, my gosh, you have to get that. I would wear that. Well, if it was black."

Elle laughed at her friend. Chloe only wore one color and that was black. She could barely remember Chloe in bright and cheery clothes so long ago. Honestly, Chloe looked good in anything. Her clothes might be black, but they were expensive. Her father forced her to dress in the nicest ones, and even though he didn't approve of the color that much, he at least didn't force her to wear a different one, like pink.

Elle shook her head at the thought of Chloe wearing the color pink.

"Thank God. I was beginning to think I wouldn't find anything. At least this will replace my white sweater Bimbo Number One destroyed." Elle had loved that sweater, but this one was definitely going to make up for it.

"Me, too. Maybe the person who donated that brought more. We better hurry up and look through the rest of the racks. It's late and they close soon."

Elle nodded and turned around to head back in the dressing room. She heard Chloe laughing behind her, making her stop to look at her before she closed the door.

"What is so funny?" Elle inquired.

"I was just thinking about what Nero's face is going to look like when he sees you in that."

Nero listened to the obnoxiously-loud music playing. It was very dark with almost-neon lighting all around. They sat at an uncomfortable, high table as they ordered some drinks and appetizers.

Nero looked around the full table. Amo and Vincent looked like they were at home, sitting beside two public school girls who were wearing glitzy, tight dresses. Unfortunately, the girl beside him was dressed the same way and there was not a shy one out of the group.

Nero hadn't even caught their names when they'd introduced themselves. Before Elle, he would have had all their names in one second and their dresses off the next. Looking at Amo and Vincent, he could tell they clearly liked that Nero was out of the game.

Nero's eyes had wandered the whole night, looking for Cassandra. *I find her, get what I want, and then I'm out of this fucking place.*

He could sense the girl he was with was getting a little wounded that Nero wasn't paying her any attention, especially with his friends all hands-on and frisky in front of them. At first, he did feel a little bad, but then, when she started to get a little hands-on and frisky herself, he didn't care that he was rude, pushing her hands off him. This girl was far from Elle, and that was who both of his heads wanted.

Nero turned his attention to the dance floor. That part of the lounge was crazy, and he had no intention of going near it. Everyone was barely two inches apart, dancing on top of each other. *Get a bunch of horny teenagers together and you get an orgy.*

As Nero saw a fake blonde appear on the dance floor, he turned toward Amo and Vincent and waved his head toward the mass of dancers. Nero stood with Amo and Vincent, them telling the girls to wait there.

Nero kept his eyes on the back of the fake-ass blonde hair. *I fucking got you.*

He and his crew pushed through the teenagers, who desperately needed to get laid already, until he finally reached the girl. Nero spun her around, and his control started to shake.

"Ugh, today is not my day, is it?" Elle said as she finished up with the last rack.

"I cannot believe we only found one thing." Chloe was now sitting on the floor.

Elle looked over at her friend, who was exhausted from trying to help her find clothes. "I know. Let's pay and get the hell out of here. I'm starving."

"Thank God. My stomach has been growling for the last hour," Chloe confessed.

Elle and Chloe walked to the checkout and handed over the green sweater.

"It'll be three dollars," the older woman said from behind

the counter.

God, I love Goodwill. Elle handed over the three dollars, and the woman handed her a grocery bag with her sweater inside. She and Chloe then headed for the door.

Dinng.

Elle pulled out her phone as they headed toward Chloe's BMW. Her phone displayed there was a new text message from *Asshole,* making Elle smile.

"Who was that?" Chloe asked once they were seated in her car.

Elle knew she was asking because only Chloe usually texted her.

"Nero. Let me see what he said."

Elle went to her messages and read, **Meet me at Poison, urgent.** Elle stared at the words, confused.

"Well?"

She looked over at Chloe. "He said to meet him at Poison and that it was urgent."

Chloe stared back at Elle, just as confused. "Well, we did always wonder what it looked like inside."

"Yeah, but I don't have enough money to get inside that place." Elle didn't know what could be so urgent. Her stomach started to roll in nervousness.

"You don't; I do." Chloe smiled.

"I-I—"

Chloe stopped her. "Elle, he said it was urgent. Do you want to go or not?"

Elle's feeling took over her body. "Let's go."

When Nero looked at her face, he was immediately disappointed it wasn't Cassandra. Nero let the girl go and turned to his friends.

"Fuck! I can't stay here any longer." His control was finally gone.

Amo laughed. "It must be hard seeing every sad sack in here is going to go home and get laid when you haven't even got Elle's top off yet." He had to speak loudly for Nero to hear him.

"Fuck you." Nero went to walk off, but saw Vincent frozen in place, staring. Nero followed his eyes to two girls dancing together.

"Who is that? I need to fucking meet her," Vincent said with his mouth practically hanging open.

Nero knew which girl out of the two he was talking about instantly. The girl was wearing a black dress that was loose at the top but tight over her ass. The material barely covered it, showing her long legs. He was sure if she bent over slightly, her whole ass would hang out. She was long and lean, the narrow type, and even though she wasn't Nero's type because of the small curves—*I prefer something I can grab on to*—he was even entranced by her dancing.

It was pretty dark in here, though the sudden flashes of neon every so often could sometimes light up the person's face; however, the guys hadn't seen either of the girls' faces yet.

Nero noticed the guys around them salivating to dance with the girls. They tried to join in, but the girls kept pushing them away, making them all the more desirable. A flash quickly illuminated the girls.

"Wait, I think I know them." Vincent squinted his eyes.

Nero looked at them harder. The other girl in the purple baby-doll dress looked familiar to him, as well.

The girls danced around until they faced them. Another flash lit up their bodies.

"Holy shit, that's my fucking sister!" Vincent remarked.

Nero recognized the girl in the purple dress was Vincent's sister the moment he said it. Adalyn had become Vincent's stepsister when his mother had married her dad when Vincent had been a toddler. They had grown up together and hadn't realized they weren't related by blood until they could understand the concept. Adalyn might technically be Vincent's stepsister, however to him, she was his sister.

"Yeah, but who's the one I need in my fucking bed?" Amo was infatuated with the girl dancing, as well.

Vincent stared at the girl shaking her ass as she pushed her light-brown hair back. "Lake, my fucking sister's best friend."

"Damn, have you been keeping her all to yourself?" Amo couldn't pull his eyes away.

Unfortunately, neither could Vincent. "No, man. I've known her since preschool, so don't fucking think about it."

Nero laughed, his anger now gone. Vincent was clearly caught off-guard by her. Vincent had evidently never thought about Lake that way, but right then, he was seeing her in a new light. *Literally, neon light.* Nero watched as Vincent's face started to become pissed and torn at the same time.

"Shit, man, just think about all the years you've missed out on that one," Amo said.

Nero was trying to cease his laughter.

"They are dead," Vincent declared, his nose practically flaring.

Nero figured it was probably hard seeing them this way, especially his sister.

While he looked back at the two girls dancing, two guys came up and started to grab them. *Oh, shit.*

"No, *they* are fucking dead!" Vincent started pushing through the crowd with Nero and Amo following him.

Nero knew this was not going to turn out well for the two guys, as well as Vincent's sister and her best friend.

Nero smiled as they came closer. *Tonight is looking up.* Nero had always looked forward to a good fight.

"Vincent?" Adalyn yelled as she pushed the guy off her.

"Huh?" Lake shoved the guy as she turned to see.

The two girls quickly started walking toward them.

Vincent yelled at them, "What the fuck are you both doing here?"

"They are with us." Two guys pulled them back behind them.

Nero noticed they weren't the ones who had been trying to dance with them.

"Okay then, who the fuck are you two?" Vincent asked, pointing to the two who had been trying to dry-hump his sister and her friend.

The two guys reached out and grabbed the girls back.

The one who held Vincent's sister spoke. "We're the ones who are going to fuck them by the end of the night. So find your own."

"Hey, get off me!" Lake hit at the guy holding her by her ass.

"You really shouldn't have said that," Adalyn said to the guy pinned to her waist.

Vincent started rolling up his sleeves. "You've got this all wrong, motherfucker. That's my sister you're holding there, and unfortunately, it will be the last girl you'll be able to hold."

The guy groping Lake started to laugh in his face. "This bitch isn't your sister." He looked down at Lake. "Looks like your mine."

Vincent flexed his jaw at the two guys who had been groping the girls on the dance floor. "These fuckers are mine; you two get the little shits who brought them here."

Nero and Amo started rolling up their sleeves, grinning, looking at the two trying to grab the girls back into their possession.

Nero grabbed Vincent's shoulder. "Man, I thought you'd never ask."

Amo snickered. "You guys can thank me later for bringing you here."

OUT OF THE POISON'S DOOR

Elle and Chloe walked into the dark lounge. Elle hoped Chloe would be okay surrounded by so many people. She looked over at her and saw she tried to make herself as small as possible so people couldn't bump into her.

"We should go bac—"

"Fight! Fight! Fight!" the chanting sounded over her voice.

"Shit, Nero!" Elle started running toward the crowd with Chloe right behind her. Elle's mind couldn't think as she pushed through the crowd for them to pass, her body only reacting.

Elle and Chloe finally reached the front of the crowd, their mouths dropping open at what they were witnessing.

Nero was toying with a helpless guy, letting him get close to take a shot, but then he would strike out, punching him in the face. The guy was too slow and dumb to stop him.

Elle moved her eyes to Amo when he reached out and took a guy in a chokehold, his feet dangling high off the ground. What really drew Elle's attention was Vincent. He was fighting off two guys, making them end up hitting each other when Vincent would move out of the way. The one to recover first came back at Vincent, kneeing him in the groin and making him fall to his knees. Vincent recovered quickly, taking the guy's head in his hand and kneeing him right in the face, making him completely fall to the ground. Vincent laughed as he walked toward the other guy, now begging. Still laughing, he picked him up by his shirt, making him stand.

Vincent cocked his fist back. "You piece of shit." Punch in the face. "Motherfucker." Another punch in the face. The guy toppled over to the ground, and Vincent put his shoe over his hand flat on the ground. "Don't ever touch my sister again." Vincent picked his foot up then smashed his hand, making the poor guy scream in pain.

As two girls winced inside the circle, Elle figured one of them must be his sister.

Elle returned her eyes to the three guys now laughing at the destruction they had caused. Elle then looked at the four unmoving on the floor. They were a bloody mess.

Elle looked up and took a step forward. "Nero?"

She watched the three guys cease their laughing and look toward her.

Nero looked at her like she was crazy. "Elle, what the hell are you doing here?"

Elle thought he acted like he definitely didn't ask her to be here.

"You texted me to come here." When he still looked confused, she repeated his text, "Meet me at Poison, urgent?"

Nero shook his head, still confused. "I didn't text you."

Elle saw three girls appear in glittery, tight dresses. They each wrapped their arms around Nero, Amo, and Vincent.

"That was so fucking hot," the one holding Nero around his waist said.

Elle stepped forward. "Who are you?"

Nero, stunned, went to push her off and tried to speak, but she beat him to it.

"His date. And who the hell are you, bitch?" The girl spoke and looked just like Cassandra.

Elle backed up before the tears started to well in her eyes. She pushed through the crowd even though she heard Nero yelling her name. She ran as fast as she could through the people, starting to suffocate. She felt the shattering of her heart take place. Finally, she reached the doors taking her outside and greeted the cool air. Stopping to turn around, Chloe was right there, thankfully. She returned to her escape, going for Chloe's car.

"Elle, stop!" Nero's voice commanded again.

Elle stopped in place. *I'm done doing what you say, and I'm fucking done running from you!*

Elle quickly spun around and saw that Nero had stopped in his tracks along with Chloe, Amo, and Vincent, waiting to see what took place.

Elle picked up her feet faster and faster, heading right toward

Nero. She could see the *oh, shit* written all over his face.

Elle hit as hard as she could on Nero's chest, repeatedly making him back up a step with each hit. "Fuck you, fuck you, fuck you! fuck you!"

Nero grabbed her arms, stopping her. "Elle, it wasn't what it looked like. I promise."

Elle laughed mockingly through the tears that ran down her face. "Oh, it wasn't what it looked like? Just like how yesterday it wasn't what it looked like when you were sandwiched between two other fake blondes? You fucking promised me yesterday!"

Nero brought her closer to him. "I need you to trust me."

Elle looked up into his emerald eyes. "I am sick of all your bullshit promises, and the 'I give you my word.'" Elle's shattering heart finally crumbled. "I will never *ever* trust you again, Nero."

She watched Nero's determined eyes. "Elle, listen—"

Elle spat in his face. "No! I'm done listening to you. I'm done doing what you ask. Don't fucking talk to me again." Elle's voice rose louder. "Just leave me the fuck alone!" Elle snatched her arms back as the inside of her started picking up the broken pieces, attempting to place them back together.

Nero had been bad news from the start, and Elle had known it. *Nero is not worth this.*

She backed up and looked toward Chloe. "Let's go."

She watched Chloe's face turn into one she had never seen before. Chloe walked up to Amo and kicked him right in his shin.

Amo grabbed his shin. "Ow! What the fuck did I do?"

"You should be ashamed of yourself. And you, too." She pointed to Vincent as he backed up a few steps. "I know you put him up to this."

Chloe turned around and stomped off toward Elle. When she passed Nero, she stopped. "I have nothing to say to you. You know what you just lost."

Chloe finally kept walking to Elle, who was stunned at Chloe's behavior and happy her friend had stood up for her.

Elle silently thanked God this had happened sooner rather than later as she walked toward Chloe's car. She questioned what her sanity could have been if she had spent a long time with Nero.

Opening her door and getting in, she slammed it. Shutting her eyes, she replayed his words. *I promise, baby.* Her tears started falling again.

Elle wiped them away when Chloe got in the car. She didn't speak, just drove to Elle's house.

Chloe parked her car in Elle's driveway, and then they slowly got out of the car, going in her home and to her bedroom. Elle sat on her bed with her head in her hands.

"Do you want me to leave?" Chloe whispered to her as she sat down beside her.

Elle shook her head and looked up. "No, stay."

"Okay, I can go make some popcorn and ice cream and we can watch your favorite movie, *The Little Mermaid.*"

Elle chuckled through her new tears; her friend could always cheer her up.

"I'll be right back," Chloe said, getting up.

Elle watched her walk out the door then scrunched herself up in a ball. No matter how much she tried, the pieces kept falling. There wasn't enough glue in the world to keep her shattered heart together.

Nero stood there, watching Elle get in the car. *Fuck!*

He had no idea how he was going to fix this colossal fuck-up. Elle had dealt with enough, and that had been the last straw for her. The look on her crying face had killed him. He didn't even know where to start on telling her the truth.

'You know what you just lost.' Chloe's words had struck him. He did know, and that was what killed him the most.

Nero didn't even understand why she was here. *I didn't text her.* Nero pulled out his cell phone from his pocket and went to his messages. Sure enough, Elle's exact words from earlier displayed on his screen. Nero knew no one had taken it from his pocket. *How in the hell did that happen?*

"We need to get out of here before the cops show!" Adalyn said as she and Lake came out of Poison's doors.

"What the hell were you all here for?" Vincent asked, storming toward them.

Adalyn and Lake pulled their dresses down and pulled their tops up to cover their cleavage. "Why the hell do you think?"

Vincent's face started to contort.

Lake stepped in, confessing, "I begged her to come dancing with me. It's my fault. The only way we could get in was going with those guys. We didn't do anything with them, though."

Vincent took a deep breath. "Good. You can't date boys until you graduate. I don't care if it's only a few months away. I won't say anything, but I better not catch you two again."

Nero watched the two both nod, even though it took Lake hitting Adalyn's arm before she did.

Vincent held out his keys. "Go get in the car. I'm taking you both home."

Adalyn snatched the keys and they both started running.

Vincent yelled, watching Adalyn hold her dress down as she ran, "You're burning those fucking dresses when we get home!"

Lake tried to pull her dress down at Vincent's comment.

Vincent changed his mind. "Actually, give them to me. I want to get rid of them."

Nero would have laughed under different circumstances; Vincent was clearly just as shaken up as he was right now.

Vincent walked toward him. "My fucking retinas are burned from watching my sister's ass in there."

Amo was able to laugh, though. "Yeah, right, you were too busy watching Lake's ass to notice it was even your sister with her."

Vincent was about to say something, but then thought otherwise, looking at Nero. "I'm sorry about Elle, man."

"Yeah, I feel bad. I set this whole thing up, then Elle and Vincent's sister happened," Amo added.

Nero ran his hands through his hair. "Oh, yeah, we owe you a thanks, right?"

"Thanks a fucking lot," Vincent got out.

They started to hear sirens coming closer. "Let's get out of here. Amo, you're going to fucking owe me for this."

"All right, man, I understand."

They all started walking to their own cars.

As Nero walked toward his Cadillac, he thought of Elle's last words. *Just leave me the fuck alone!* He opened his car door, getting in. *Not in a million years, baby.*

Nero spun out of there right before the cops arrived. He didn't know how he would win her back yet; all he knew was he wasn't going to stop until Elle was his. *For good.*

THE HORROR IN THE MIRROR

Elle spent the whole weekend in her bed, trying not to cry. *Yeah, unsuccessfully.* The only time she left her bedroom was to go to work, which she couldn't get out of. She hated leaving the house to do so, though.

The love of watching the city pass through her bus window and as she walked to work was now gone. Elle had felt like a mushy mess; her eyes were stained red, her hair was unkempt, and her clothes were mismatched. She had actually thanked God for her uniform this weekend.

Elle went through varied emotions. She went from happy that it was over so soon between them to sadness it was over and all the way to straight-up ax murderer that he had done this to her, and everything else in between.

Elle promised herself she was going to get over him by Monday.

There is no way Nero is seeing me like this.

Elle was determined Nero wasn't going to think he had gotten the best of her. She was going to move on, and he was going to see it Monday morning.

When Monday morning rolled around and Elle's alarm clock went off, she thought of a new way to destroy it when school was finally over. She woke up groggy. *More like I feel like shit.*

Turning on the bathroom light, she saw the horror in the mirror. She didn't exactly know if this was even fixable. She wished Chloe was there to help. *Wait, Chloe can help.*

Elle ran back to her bedroom and hit Chloe's number. It rang several times. Elle knew it was pretty early and thought she should hang up, but then it was answered.

"Hello?"

Chloe sounded wide awake to her. She knew she'd hardly slept, but damn it was early.

"Chloe, I need your help. I look like shit."

Chloe's voice sounded almost cheerful. "Be right there. Bye."

Chloe was definitely the one for the job. She had to look like a million dollars a lot of the time, due to her dad's work. She had to go to many occasions with her parents and look like the part of the perfect, beautiful daughter. Unfortunately, with her scars, her father made sure she looked like two million dollars, so it would distract from the slashes down her face.

Elle knew if any other girl had Chloe's markings, they wouldn't pull it off, but since Chloe was beyond gorgeous naturally, she made them look beautiful. *Chloe can pull anything off.*

Elle brushed her teeth and washed her face before Chloe got there. When she did arrive, she immediately got to work. Elle kept her hands locked in her lap and didn't move while Chloe was working on her. She thought Chloe would wear gloves before she even started working. She didn't, and Chloe made sure to use all the tools.

"Okay, what are you going to wear?" Chloe asked as she put away her hair tools.

Elle shrugged. "I don't know. Just a t-shirt and jeans, I guess."

"I did not do your makeup and fix your matted hair for a t-shirt and jeans." Chloe walked into Elle's closet and came out. "Where is the green sweater?"

Elle looked at the floor. "I don't want to wear that."

"Why not?" Chloe asked, sitting on her bed.

Elle knew it was stupid, but the only reason she had liked it instantly was because it had reminded her of Nero's eyes; as such, she didn't want to wear it. Elle didn't want to tell Chloe that, though; therefore, she simply shrugged.

"Elle, do you want to make him regret ever cheating on you and shove it in his freaking face?"

Elle thought for a second. *Yes, I fucking do.*

Elle got up and went into her closet, shutting the door. She dressed in the small space, putting on her black leggings and getting the sweater down from the top shelf. Then she put on some high, black boots.

She came out and Chloe's mouth went into a smile. "He is going to cry himself to sleep tonight."

Nero leaned up against his car in the student parking lot. Amo and Vincent had joined him a few minutes earlier. His car was just a few feet away from Chloe's parking spot. Nero knew he and his crew were still going to have to provide some protection; if anyone got wind of him and Elle breaking up, she would be done for.

Nero rubbed his eyes. He hadn't gotten much sleep the past few nights. He wanted to believe it was going to be easy winning her back, but honestly, Nero had no idea where to start. He had no women expertise outside of the bedroom.

He had spent the weekend following Elle to and from work, *again.* Moreover, Nero found it even more miserable than the first time he had done it. Watching her so close and not talking to her was torture. Then not going into the diner while she worked was the worst kind of torture.

He had noticed she didn't look like herself and was clearly in pain. He figured that was why he didn't talk to her or pop up in the diner; he didn't want to cause her more damage. *She's had enough of that.*

"How are you, man?" Vincent asked, breaking through his thoughts.

"Fine," Nero answered quickly, not wanting them to think he was torn up over a girl.

"And how's she?" Amo asked.

"She looked pretty rough last night," Nero confessed.

Vincent laughed. "You're going to have to come up with

something good, man. Thank God, I'm not you."

"Yeah, I know. Listen, we need to be on them. I think Cassandra comes back today." Nero knew he wasn't going to be able to get too close without making up with Elle yet, but he needed to get as close as he could.

Amo and Vincent nodded. They waited for about five minutes until Chloe's BMW appeared and pulled in her spot.

Nero watched as the passenger's door opened and a pair of black boots hit the ground. When the door was closed shut, he blinked his eyes several times before he realized it wasn't going to change anything. *Holy hell.*

Nero felt an intense amount of emotions as he watched Elle's ass sashay across the parking lot in that outfit. Firstly, he wanted to fuck her. Secondly, he wanted her to dress like that more often. Lastly, he wanted to know why she looked perfectly fine.

When only Elle's back was visible, his first emotion returned harder. *It's been a fucking while, okay?*

Nero noticed his friends gawking. "Hey, fuckers, move your eyes to someone else."

"Damn, Nero, you were right. Elle is just so heartbroken." Amo couldn't hold in his laughter.

Nero leaned up from the car and ran his hands through his hair. He turned back to them and saw Vincent closing his eyes, whispering something.

"What the hell are you doing?"

Vincent whispered something else before he opened his eyes. "I was just thanking God for leggings."

Elle and Chloe went through the chicken patty line. *Picking what we want is now over.* Elle knew it had been good while it lasted, and honestly, she didn't even know if she was going to be able to eat today. She had completely forgotten about lunch money, not like she would have paid the ridiculous price for it anyways.

Elle and Chloe moved up the line. She had been on the lookout the whole morning, and Chloe had started walking behind her again. She did notice that the three assholes had been following them all day, though. *I don't need to be followed!*

Elle and Chloe grabbed a tray full of fries and a chicken sandwich and then went to give the lady their number. Elle held her breath, wondering if she was going to get away with it. When she did, she couldn't believe it. Elle figured the only reason she had was because the lunch lady in the other line was much meaner. *So, I guess I'm stuck eating chicken patties for the rest of the semester.*

Elle walked toward her and Chloe's original table, but found it full. "Shit."

She looked around and saw the only table that was unoccupied was the table in the corner that they had sat at Friday. Elle turned and walked toward that table. As she did, she noticed Nero, Amo, Vincent, and Leo sat at the table closest to it. *Of course they are.* The other surrounding tables were still filled with the football team.

Elle took the seat facing the lunchroom again, and Chloe took the one in front of her, just like she always had before. *I guess some things can never change.*

Elle gave Chloe a reassuring smile. Chloe hadn't been prepared to go back to their old ways. Elle had watched her as she had blossomed back into her old self. It had been the happiest Elle had seen her since she had met her the first day of high school.

Elle picked up her sandwich to take a bite when she noticed the lunch lady from the other line was heading her way.

"Uh, Chloe, why is she coming toward us?"

Elle watched Chloe swing her head around and then quietly speak, "Should we be afraid right now?"

"I don't—"

Elle gasped as the lunch lady snatched her sandwich out of her hand and put it back on the tray. "I told you last week, Elle, you need to pay for your lunches. No more charges." Elle heard her mumble under her breath, "This isn't a damn charity," as she walked away.

Elle and Chloe's mouths hung open as she then walked right up to the trashcan and threw away her tray. She knew this school had really gone to the next level when they'd rather throw away food than feed a hungry child.

"Can she do that?" Chloe asked, turning back around.

"She just did," Elle said, wanting to disappear.

Chloe pushed her tray away. "You can have mine. I'm not that hungry."

"No, Chloe. I don't want it. It wasn't what I wanted anyways."

Chloe wrung her hands in her lap. "Yeah, me either."

"Did that just happen?" Nero heard Leo ask.

"Fuck this school. Why do we even go here?" Amo added.

Vincent looked at Nero. "That was the most fucked-up thing I have ever seen. Something needs to be done about that."

Nero was trying to calm himself. *Yeah, by thinking of a thousand ways to murder that old-ass bitch.* He would deal with that later.

Ho took a deep breath. "Vincent, I need you to do me a favor."

Vincent smiled. "Strangle the life out of her?"

That sounded nice. "Maybe later. I need you to go buy Elle another lunch, and don't get the chicken sandwich. I know they didn't want that shit." Nero stopped and looked back at their table. "Get them both new lunches."

Vincent sounded surprised. "Why me?"

"Because Elle won't take it from me, and she will think I paid if Leo gave it to her." Nero paused, not wanting the next words to come out of his mouth. "And for some reason, she likes you the most between us."

Vincent looked over at the lunch lady who had thrown Elle's tray away. "I'll be happy to."

THE FIVE STAGES
OF HEARTBREAK

lle picked her head up from the table as she felt something being set on top of the wood.

"What is this?" Elle looked at the tray being set before her filled with chicken strips, mashed potatoes, and corn. She also saw Vincent set a tray in front of Chloe, as well.

"Lunch." Vincent then set down a water bottle in front of her.

Elle pushed the tray toward him. "Take it back."

Vincent let out a breath and pulled a seat underneath him as he sat down. "Listen, sweetheart, I know you don't want to take it because of what happened with you and Ne—"

"This has nothing to do with that. I don't want it," Elle retorted as she pushed the tray closer to him.

Vincent put his hand on the tray and pushed it back to her. He looked straight at her as he spoke. "It has everything to do with that, but what you need to understand is I care about you, too. So, you're going to fucking eat it and enjoy it. And I will be walking you both to class until you and Nero figure this shit out," Vincent turned to look at Chloe, "because I'm sick of watching you walk behind Elle. Walk fucking beside her."

Elle watched Chloe's eyes grow big. Elle attempted to protest, but Vincent was a little too crazy to tell no. She did like Vincent and could handle him being around her. *But there is nothing to work out between me and Nero.*

When Vincent was satisfied, he took Chloe's old plate from the middle of the table and threw it in the trashcan closest to the lunch lady as he stared her down.

"Oh, my God. I think he may need to be admitted," Chloe whispered.

Elle's eyes went back to Chloe. "He is a psychopath, for sure, but he is the nicest one out of the three."

"Sorry, Elle, but he isn't. Nero is." Chloe stated it like it was a fact.

Elle opened her mouth. "No, he isn't!"

Chloe picked up a chicken strip and took a bite. "He is, too. You're just in the denial stage."

Elle reluctantly picked up her own strip, thinking it looked too tasty, and took a bite. "The denial stage?"

"Yeah. The five stages of heartbreak."

Elle rolled her eyes at her best friend. *There's no such thing.*

She and Chloe had a good lunch, regardless of what had happened. When it was time to head to class, Vincent came back over to walk them. One look at Vincent's face and she let him; bringing Hannibal Lecter out wasn't on her to-do list for the day.

Vincent walked beside Elle and Elle walked beside Chloe. She had to admit it was pretty weird because Vincent had walked behind Chloe before while Nero used to walk beside her. She turned her head and saw Nero and Amo walking a few feet back. *Ugh!*

Elle was going to have to get over that because, unfortunately, they could walk wherever they pleased.

Turning her head back around, Cassandra appeared before her. Elle came to an immediate stop. *Oh, shit.*

Elle had seen she was back at English class and wasn't eager to see what she would do to her for getting her suspended.

"Long time, no see, waitress," Cassandra's high-pitched voice rang in her ears.

Vincent slung his arm around Elle's shoulders. "I figured you would have found out that Nero told everyone not to call Elle that anymore. I guess no one gives a shit about you when you're gone."

Cassandra's mouth gaped open then quickly shut as she took a step forward. "I heard. I just didn't believe it. I missed four days of school—thanks to you—and *you* somehow think you're the queen?" Cassandra looked Elle up and down, laughing hysterically. "You're wearing the sweater my mom tossed into the Goodwill bin last month. You're a trashy, little waitress, and that's all you'll ever be."

As Elle looked at the deranged face on Cassandra as she laughed, she wanted to run and get the stupid sweater off her body.

"And you're just a slutty, little whore who is jealous that your tits weren't able to fill the sweater out." Vincent laughed in her face. "I thought it looked familiar, but I guess I'm only used to seeing you without clothes and on your knees."

Elle couldn't believe her ears and was shocked beyond belief while Cassandra looked like she had just been punched in the face.

Vincent pulled Elle to move along as he threw his final blow. "Come on, Elle. Don't worry; no one will recognize the slut's sweater on you. We're all used to seeing her naked and swallowing."

Elle moved with Vincent, still stunned. She looked at Chloe, shaking her head and wondering if it was real, too.

"I think that might have been a little harsh." Cassandra had never been treated like that in her life. She despised Cassandra, but Elle didn't wish her own life upon her.

"Sweetheart, I frankly don't give a shit."

Elle couldn't move a bone in her body as the tears slid down her cheek. She had watched the face of the beautiful girl named Chloe kick her in the ribs. Elle had nothing left anymore, becoming numb and paralyzed by the second person in the group to beat her.

Elle had begged at first—pleaded—but it all had still led her to the continuation of the beating. So, Elle had given up, thinking maybe lying there broken would be enough to get them to stop.

The laughing still punctured her ears along with the jokes. Those had hurt just as bad as the various shoes kicked at her face and body.

"Let's get out of here," she heard one of them say. "The bitch got the message. Good job, Chloe."

Elle couldn't help staring up into the gray eyes, trying to deliver her message. When Elle could no longer see her, she had known Chloe had understood.

Elle lay there, wondering how long it would take for death to come and rescue her from her nightmare. She closed her eyes, feeling the warm, red liquid start to coat her body. She knew it was coming soon. Soon, she would be free...

Elle heard the rapping of the door enter her dream. "Sweetie, don't you work tonight?"

Elle tried to open her eyes, blinking back the wetness that had formed in her sleep.

The sound returned. "Elle?"

Elle finally saw her bedroom door before her and was able to remember where she was at. "Yeah. Sorry, Mom. I fell asleep."

"Okay, sweetie. I was just checking."

Elle rubbed her eyes as she heard her mom walk away. She barely remembered how she had ended up here. Finally waking up enough, she remembered the whole day. *If only I could forget.*

When Elle had returned home from school, she had been mentally exhausted and gone straight for her bed. She'd curled up into a ball, not being able to help thinking about the day.

Nero had given her space, never walking too close to her and staying far behind. He hadn't sat next to her at English, lunch, or even Art. He'd sat at another table that had some football team members. *At least he didn't sit with the bimbos right in my face.*

Elle admitted it had been hard seeing him again. She had grown used to being around him in the short time they'd had. For some reason she didn't know, he had grown on her.

Now Elle had to deal with Vincent. He wasn't bad. *Okay, he is terrible, but there's worse.* Elle was glad he had been there when Cassandra had found her; otherwise, she wasn't sure what would have happened to her. He had taken her to and from classes with no one giving her any trouble. That, she was thankful for. Furthermore, even though she would rather not see Vincent because of Nero, she would deal with it because he'd made sure she and Chloe were safe.

Elle rolled over, looking at the time. She needed to start getting ready for work. Tonight she had the late shift and was the one to close again.

Elle yawned, wishing she could stay in bed just a little longer. About to rise, she glanced at her bookshelf and noticed something that didn't look right.

Elle studied the bookshelf that was jam-packed and full of different things, yet to Elle, she knew something was missing from it. Elle looked at the space that used to hold her photo album. It was gone.

Elle rose up and went to the shelf, wondering if it had been moved. She went through the whole thing. *Not here.* Elle looked around her room. *Nothing.*

Elle distinctively remembered Nero putting it back on the shelf. *Nero!*

Nero couldn't believe he was going to suffer through another night of watching Elle go to work as she boarded the bus. *Why the fuck can't I talk to her?*

Nero had no idea how to win her back. He'd thought he would find some way during school, but no opportunities had been presented.

Nero followed the bus to the stop Elle got off at. As she departed, a sick feeling in his gut appeared. He had noticed a guy wearing a dark hoodie had kept a few paces behind her.

Nero kept his eyes glued to Elle as he went to park his car, his gut feeling too strong. When he got out of the car, a bus passed in front of him, blocking his view. His instincts started screaming at him to run to Elle, but he had to wait for the bus to move out of the way for him to go. When the bus sped on, he looked for Elle.

Where the fuck did she go?

Nero ran across the street, looking for her or the guy in the hoodie, yet he couldn't see either of them. *Shit.*

As he noticed an alleyway just a few steps ahead of where he had seen Elle standing last, he began running as fast as he could, making a sharp left. Nero's heart stopped along with the world around him.

Elle was pushed into an alleyway.

Before she could scream, her mouth was covered. Elle kicked and hit at the person, holding her from behind. *The boss came for me.*

Elle knew she probably wasn't going to get out of this alive, but she was going to do whatever it took to possibly survive.

Shutting her eyes, she bit at the hand over her mouth, just how she had seen the man who had been murdered do. *Fuck, he died.*

Elle bit harder when the guy didn't remove his hand. She felt her body being thrown into a brick wall, and then she heard the sound of her skull hitting the brick. Elle slid down the wall, slowly feeling herself lose consciousness.

"Shit, I didn't..." she heard a deep voice say as he held her face in his hands.

Elle tried to fight the feeling of darkness, but her lids became too heavy for her to hold. *Stay awake!* Elle held her eyes open a moment longer to see the face of a man she had seen at the diner. It was the college guy who had dropped the fork. *Why would he...?*

Elle's eyes fell closed as her mind slowed down, trying to shut off. She felt a commotion going on beside her and heard the sound of flesh hitting flesh. Elle attempted to say a name as darkness fell upon her.

THE CLOCK IS TICKING

Nero sat in the chair beside his bed, trying to steady his hands. His eyes never moved from Elle as she lay there, unmoving. He kept telling himself she was going to be all right; he just wished he could believe the doctor's words.

He had called the doctor his family used—legally and illegally—to come to the house as fast as possible. He'd told Nero she would be fine, and that she just suffered from a concussion. Nero wondered how many more times her head could take a hit before serious damage was done. *God only knows how many times she's been hit in the head.*

Nero ran his hands through his hair as he got up to stand over her. He had never seen anything more beautiful in his life. He ran his fingers across her tan skin on her cheek, feeling the softness. She looked peaceful to him, and he would have thought she was actually at peace if she didn't have a bandage on her head.

Nero had been waiting for Elle to be in his bed, and here she was, in one of his old t-shirts she had been changed in to. The feeling wasn't what he had hoped, though.

Nero looked at his now-fucked-up hand. He had beaten the guy to a bloody pulp and left him there to live or die. *I really don't give a shit.*

The past few days had confused Nero. One thing had happened after another where it concerned Elle, and he knew he had been missing something. Moreover, he had only grown further confused when the douchebag who had hurt Elle looked sorry for what had happened.

Nero took a deep breath as he reluctantly left his bedroom. He headed down the stairs and went through his house, going up to the door he was seeking. Nero turned the handle of the office door and went inside.

"I was wondering when you would finally figure it out. I hope you're not too mad, brother."

Nero walked toward the edge of the big desk holding Lucca's feet.

"Mad that you slashed Chloe's tires? No. Mad that you paid guys to make me jealous? No. Mad that you hacked my phone and texted Elle so she could catch me with another girl? No."

Lucca put out his cigarette. "Technically, Sal hacked your phone; I just told him to."

Nero flexed his jaw. His brother's nonchalant attitude was getting the best of him. He thought about Elle lying upstairs and that was when he hit his breaking point.

Nero reached out and slammed the back of the leaning chair down as hard as he could, making Lucca fall with it. Nero's feet were then swept out from under him as Lucca grabbed his ankles, making him join him on the ground.

"Motherfucker, he could have killed her!" Nero moved on top of Lucca, trying to hold him down.

Lucca laughed in his ear as he maneuvered Nero off him. "Yeah, but he didn't. The moment I saw her, I knew you'd like her. So, I had to see how much you actually cared. I just didn't know she would have you whipped so quickly."

Nero elbowed Lucca in the gut to get the upper hand. "Why did you do all this to fucking prove that I liked her?"

Lucca quickly got Nero on his back and tightly held his neck. "Careful, brother. This has to do with the family, and I'm your underboss. We're not fighting over some girl. This one saw me, Sal, and Dad murder a man. And anyone else who fought me over a job wouldn't live with both of his hands."

Nero did know that was the truth. He was breaking a lot of rules right now just because Lucca was his brother. Nero relaxed under Lucca's hand at the realization, done fighting, and Lucca let go of Nero's neck as he stood.

"The clock is ticking, Nero. You need to find out if she saw any of our faces. If she did, then you gotta figure out a way to keep Dad from killing her. She needs to trust you, and you need to move things along at a quicker pace."

As Lucca put out his hand to help him up, Nero took it. "And you paying the broke college fucker to kidnap her was supposed to do all that?"

Lucca smiled at his brother. "She was dragged into an alley and you rescued her. Sounds like some great fucking makeup sex to me."

Nero ran his hands through his hair, pulling back the mass from his eyes. Lucca had placed Elle right where Nero had wanted her.

"What do you get out of all this?"

Lucca picked up his chair from the ground and sat back down in it. "Nothing, besides my brother's happiness."

Nero snickered. "Yeah, right."

Lucca shrugged. "Okay, I might gain something out of this. Just remember what I'm doing for you and Elle."

Nero walked toward the door. He knew Lucca was trying to help him not get Elle murdered by their father. *It's just a shitty way to do it.*

Nero turned the door handle to leave.

Lucca smiled through his voice. "You're welcome."

Nero slammed the door on his way out. He knew exactly what his brother meant by 'you're welcome'—Nero had been waiting for Elle to end up in his bed for what seemed like a year now.

As Elle's mind started to flicker back to life, she didn't remember her bed feeling so big and warm.

She sunk into the bed, loving the feeling. Elle's mind flickered again. Her head felt heavy and sore; she didn't even want to attempt to move it. *Why does my head hurt so badly?*

It all came flooding back; she remembered being pulled into an alley. *Or was that a dream?* Her head screamed at her, and the taste of salt entered her mind as the memory of biting the man's hand returned.

Elle opened her eyes, and the image before her was one she had never seen before. Anxiety filled her body as she remembered being thrown into a wall. *Where am I? Does the boss have me?*

She felt the bed sink in beside her and strong arms envelope her. Elle remembered the scent, bringing good memories back to her and making her nudge in closer.

"I've got you, baby," a voice cooed to her, one she knew and made her feel safe.

Elle loved the smell that started to surround her along with the deep voice that murmured sweetly in her ear. *How do I know...?*

Elle's mind fully awakened as her eyes shot open. Her face was pressed into Nero's chest, her body being held by his. She pushed at his chest, trying to get some distance.

"Get off me."

"Easy, Elle. You hit your head." Nero rose up on his right elbow, not letting her go. His other hand was on her waist, but he let her lie back to give her some room.

Elle looked around the huge bedroom. It was mostly white with big, dark-brown furniture. She saw a leather armchair beside the bed that looked like someone had just gotten up from it. Her focus then shifted to the glass door, a balcony on the other side. The room was masculine yet beautiful.

"Where am I?"

Nero laughed. "My bedroom."

Elle thought about how in the world she'd ended up there. The face of the college student appeared in her mind with the sound of flesh hitting flesh.

Elle looked up at Nero. "How did you get there so quickly?"

Nero took a minute to respond, not wanting to admit the answer. "I've been trying to find a way to talk to you since Friday. For some reason, I ended up just following you."

Elle stared into Nero's eyes. *He's been following me?*

She didn't know how to feel about it, yet she could tell it had taken a toll on him. He looked like he hadn't slept in a few days.

Elle shut her eyes for a moment, trying to grasp how she'd ended up here in this glorious bed, wearing…"What the hell am I wearing?"

Nero smiled, flashing his teeth. "One of my t-shirts."

Elle hit at Nero's arm repeatedly. "You changed my clothes!"

Nero grabbed Elle's wrists, holding them above her head as his body rolled on top of hers. "No, my sister did, but I can easily fix that."

Elle's heart started to pound and the butterflies she hadn't had in days filled her belly. *No!*

"Get the hell off me, Nero. I don't want your skanky germs all over me."

Nero grinned as he bent his head to her neck. "You don't mean that."

Yes I do. "Yes I do!"

Nero parted her legs underneath him and pressed his clothed, hard dick at her opening.

"Do you want me to stop, baby?" Nero placed a kiss on her neck.

Elle's breathe caught in her throat. *No.* "Yes," she slowly got out.

Nero still kept his body above her. "What did I tell you about lying?" He flicked his tongue out and licked her skin. "Do you want me to stop?"

Elle's wetness started to seep through her panties. Nero's hardness was just a fabric away.

Elle whispered her confession, "No, but you hurt me. I don't look or act like all the girls you screw around with, and I don't want to be. I will never be enough for you, Nero." The fact hurt worse than anything she could have imagined. Elle was the complete opposite of the girls he was used to, and it made her feel like Nero wasn't even attracted to her.

Nero leaned up so she could see his face. "I wasn't going to go, and I had planned on letting Amo and Vincent fight over the third girl." He made sure his eyes told her what he meant. "I heard Cassandra was going to be there. She wasn't, though. And I was about to leave when Vincent found his sister."

Elle stared at Nero to see if he spoke the truth. She let out a breath, not sure if she should really believe him. Her body might not need the explanation, not caring why he had gone, but her heart and mind needed to understand.

Nero started kissing and sucking at a small piece of her neck, his hands running down her arms.

"I didn't mean to hurt you, baby. I admit I made the date, but that was before I finally realized I wanted you."

Elle's heart started picking up the broken pieces, placing them back together. She grabbed Nero's hair, unable to stop her body from touching him.

Nero moved his hands down her body to the tops of her bare legs. "I fucking love the way you look. Your strawberry-blonde hair and big, blue eyes." Nero ran one hand up the back of her leg, under the oversized shirt, going over her tiny, boy-short panties. "I love your ass." Then he went up her belly to grab her breasts over her thin bra. "And these."

It was hard for Elle to concentrate on his words. She was just glad she'd decided to wear underwear that covered more than her others today. Because she couldn't fight Nero; his hands felt too good over her body.

As Elle arched into him, her body screaming for more, Nero groaned into her neck and his hand that hadn't moved from her thigh went to her pussy, holding it through the barely-there material.

Nero's voice turned harsh. "I won't fuck you tonight because I know you're nothing like the girls I've been with, but you're going to let me play."

Elle held her breath, becoming nervous, not knowing what 'play' meant to Nero. She had never experienced anything sexual in her life. She guessed Nero felt her nerves when he kissed her hard on her lips. Her memory of how he tasted wasn't as good as the real thing, either. She hungrily kissed him back, trying to make up for the kisses they'd lost.

She felt Nero's hand start to rub her through her panties, his whole hand cupping her, grinding across her back and forth. Elle pressed herself harder into his hand, her arousal rising higher as her wetness seeped through her folds.

Nero put his lips by her ear. "You are so fucking wet for me, baby. Have you ever come before?"

Another rush of moisture escaped her as she listened to his words. She didn't want to answer.

Nero kept his rhythm on her pussy, but then moved his other hand under her bra to grope the sensitive flesh he had been waiting to hold.

"Have you?" His whisper was now gone.

Elle shook her head, not able to deny Nero his answer.

Her chest rose when he rubbed her nipples into tiny peaks. His fingers felt rough over her delicate skin, making it almost unbearable.

"Good. The first time you come will be in my hand, and the second time will be with my dick in your pussy." Nero thrust his tongue in her mouth as his thumb found her clit.

The way he was skillfully stroking her nub had her eyes rolling to the back of her head. The pleasure Elle felt rocked her body and her hips began to thrust uncontrollably, wanting more and more.

Elle grabbed Nero for support as she teetered on the edge, her lack of experience not letting her last long. Her head fell back in a moan. She was close.

She felt Nero's control shake above her, wanting his own release, but he continued to only pleasure her.

Elle started to feel the shuddering, and this time, Nero covered her lips as she moaned into his mouth. She squeezed her thighs together as the jolts went off within her, making it even more powerful because Nero's hand continued its rhythm.

Elle lay there limp as her body went through the aftershocks. Shortly after, her heart started to calm along with the butterflies. She noticed Nero had to take a minute, as well.

Nero moved his weight off her, rolling on his back and then pulling her to his chest.

He spoke through his breath. "Baby, you're more than enough for me."

Elle laughed. "Promise?"

Nero kissed her forehead under her bandage. "Promise."

She felt her heart start to glue itself back together. Elle gave up in fighting Nero. Her whole instinct and being told her to trust him. He had seen to it that her pleasure came before his, and she figured that had to be pretty hard for him.

"Thank you."

Nero lightly tugged her hair and pulled it back so she would look at him. "I'm not going to let you stay a virgin forever. I know you want my dick just as bad as I want your pussy, baby, and that's why it isn't going to last much longer."

Elle smiled at his determination. "We will see."

She knew it was going to last for a while. She was going to make Nero work for that after what he made her feel. *I don't care if he just gave me... Holy shit! I just had my first orgasm.*

Elle shoved her face in Nero's chest, not wanting him to see her expression.

"Elle?" Nero tried to get her to look at him.

She covered her face with her hands when Nero got her head up. It didn't take long for him to remove her hands. She tried not to show she was blushing.

Nero laughed, finally understanding. "There's nothing to be embarrassed about with having your first orgasm. If it helps, that was fucking hot as Hell."

Elle opened her eyes. "Like that helps."

"You're going to have a lot more, Elle, so you might as well get used to it." Nero made it a fact.

Ugh! Elle rolled her eyes at Nero, and he just laughed at her. Nero was convinced of them being together sexually, as well, and looking at the face that never gave up, Elle wondered how long she would last.

Elle's head started to sting a little, reminding her how she'd ended up here in the first place. She could still hear the sound in her ear before she had passed out.

Elle grabbed Nero's hand to look at it. She could tell he didn't want her to see it, but Elle studied his hand anyway. It had been healing the last time she had looked at it, but now the whole hand was seriously messed-up. Every knuckle was inflamed and bloody looking. She had no idea how they weren't broken.

"What did you do with him?"

Nero didn't sugarcoat it. "I beat the shit out of him and left him there."

Elle thought that should have scared her or resonated with her; instead, she brought his hand to her lips and placed kisses over each knuckle.

"You should get someone to look at this, Nero."

"It'll be fine. I'll go disinfect it and wrap it up later."

Elle looked up at him, pleading "Can you please quit fighting now? Trying not to doesn't work for you."

Nero waited a moment to answer. "Yes, for you, I will."

I've heard that before. "That's what you said last time."

Nero shrugged. "I mean it this time."

Elle heard Nero's phone ding.

"Chloe's here."

What?! "She is?"

"Yeah, so are Amo and Vincent."

NOT EVEN A MORSEL LEFT

Elle went down the huge wrought-iron staircase into the foyer. Nero had given her tiny shorts and said they were his sister's. *They don't look any different than my underwear, but at least I'm a little bit more clothed.*

Nero had called Chloe from Elle's cell, telling her what happened and that Elle was going to sleep over at his house for the night. When he'd asked her to cover for Elle and say she was spending the night at Chloe's, she had insisted on seeing Elle to make sure she was all right. The only thing Elle didn't know was why Amo and Vincent had decided to show up.

Elle finally got to the bottom of the staircase where Chloe was waiting. She instantly knew Chloe must have been at an important dinner by the way she was dressed. She wore a black, long-sleeved, Peplum dress with black tights and heels. Her outfit was meant to be business attire, but Chloe's curves made it look like she was dressed to go on a hot date.

"You didn't leave until it was over, did you?" Elle was worried. She didn't want Chloe to get in trouble.

Chloe silently shook her head.

Elle saw that Chloe was a little rattled at what had happened to her. She'd figured that would happen.

She tried to smile for her friend. "I'm okay. Thankfully, Nero was there, and that's all that matters." Elle wished she could properly comfort her friend by giving her a hug, or anything, but she never could, having to use only her words.

Chloe nodded.

Elle whispered. "Do you think Mom will believe I'm spending the night over at your house?" Elle was going to have to think of a reason why because, after three-and-a-half years, Elle had never spent the night over there. She had almost spent the night at Chloe's once right after they had become friends, but unfortunately, it hadn't lasted very long until Elle left, asking Chloe to come with her.

Chloe finally spoke. "I-I don't know."

Elle didn't, either. "What about if I told her we have a project due tomorrow?"

Chloe tried to ease up. "It might work."

"Come in here a second," Nero yelled from the other room.

Elle didn't know why Nero needed to yell. *Why couldn't he come and tell me?* Then she remembered he was Italian. *Oh, yeah, right.*

Elle and Chloe followed the voice, leaving the foyer and going into a huge room that was the living room and kitchen combined. The space was ginormous. She wanted to see what the outside looked like because she was pretty sure it was a small mansion.

As Elle walked towards Nero, only seeing the back of him, she also noticed Vincent, Amo, and Leo beside him. *Great.*

She saw Nero turn to look at her and behind him one tall-legged, golden blonde appeared. She was stunning and looked like a young Victoria's Secret model, even in a floral, modest dress. Elle had remembered seeing her at school, but she had never spoken to upperclassmen or even met any of them. The kids in her grade were already bad enough.

Elle watched her walk towards her and then the girl gave her a hug.

"You must be Elle. It's nice to meet you." Her voice sounded sweet, which was the opposite of what she thought it would sound like.

"This is my sister, Maria." Nero laughed, looking at her stunned face.

Elle lightly hugged her back. "Nice to meet you, too."

Maria pulled away and went to hug Chloe, but Chloe took a step back.

Elle tried to laugh it off. "This is Chloe. She's a little bit of a germaphobe."

"Oh, sorry. I'm a hugger, and I haven't learned yet that everyone else isn't. Nice to meet you, Chloe."

Chloe tried to smile. "You, too."

Elle quickly asked, "How many are there of you guys?" Elle wanted to know if she should prepare herself for another Caruso sibling.

Maria laughed. "There's one more, Lucca. He's the oldest. Then you just have me, Nero, and then Leo. Oh, and Dad, but that's all of us that live here anyway."

Elle knew Maria was older than Nero, but she also knew it couldn't be by much, *and another brother?* Elle admitted she wasn't very anxious to meet the oldest brother. She had a feeling, if the two youngest boys were heartbreakers, she didn't want to see the oldest.

"That's a lot of Caruso's."

"You did know Nero was Italian, right?" Maria pulled Elle over to the couch and waved for Chloe to come, as well.

Elle was taken off-guard by her. "Um, yeah, he mentioned it."

After she sat down on the couch next to Maria, Chloe sat down on the other side of her.

Maria whispered to her and Chloe, "I haven't talked to anyone besides my family since last semester. I just have to get through this week then classes start back again."

Elle and Chloe both started to laugh. Now Elle understood the poor girl; she was surrounded by guys and had been dying for female companionship.

"They won't let you leave?"

"I go to college, and they still treat me like I'm thirteen years old."

Elle knew at one look why they treated her like that. *She's the definition of a bombshell.* She just wondered what their parents looked like to create three knockout children—the fourth one remained to be seen.

"Do you go to the University here?"

"Yep. I didn't have an option to apply anywhere else." Maria shook her head.

"What are you going for?" Elle asked her.

"Business." Maria looked over at Chloe. "I love your outfit."

Chloe raised her eyebrows. "Thank you."

Elle knew Chloe was shocked, not expecting or used to getting compliments from anyone. Elle started to like Maria. All the pretty girls at school were mean to her and Chloe, and none of them were even close to being as pretty as Maria. She felt bad for her, though; clearly they had gone to the next level in over-protecting.

"Maybe I can talk Nero into us three going shopping?"

Maria's face lit up. "Yes! I am dying to go shopping! That would be so much fun."

Elle smiled, knowing how well they were all going to get along.

They spent some time talking and laughing about movies, clothes, and makeup while the boys talked about God knew what. Nero had ordered some pizzas, insisting she needed to eat something. By the amount of pizzas he'd ordered, however, everyone benefited from her needing to eat.

Once the pizzas arrived, Elle noticed how uncomfortable Chloe was getting in a group and different environment. She saw her eyeing two doors that led into the backyard, and from what she could glimpse, a beautiful garden.

"Do you think Nero would mind if I walked out there?" Chloe whispered to her when everyone got up to go to the table.

Elle shook her head. "No, he shouldn't." Elle smiled at her, knowing she needed some fresh air. "Go on."

Elle and Chloe both stood but went in opposite directions. Elle went to the table where everyone was around the pizza boxes, grabbing a slice, and Chloe walked out the back doors.

Vincent threw his arm around her. "How are you doing, sweetheart?"

Elle laughed at him, remembering him asking that the first time she had gotten hurt. "I'm fine. Just another bump on the head."

"Yeah, I know you are." Vincent laughed, dropping his arm to take a seat at the table.

Elle looked at the only seat left, which was beside Nero. All the other chairs were spaced a little bit out, but this one was really close to Nero's chair.

She took the seat, her leg lying against his. She noticed he didn't look very happy, though; he had obviously heard that it was *just another bump on the head*.

She watched Nero take a slice of pizza out of the box and throw it on a plate. He slid it in front of her. "Eat."

Elle honestly didn't feel hungry, yet Nero's face told her she better eat. She figured she could take a few bites to make him happy.

"Where's Chloe?" Amo asked, looking around.

Elle quickly responded, "She already ate before coming over and had been dying to see the backyard." She turned towards Nero. "I hope that's okay?"

Nero nodded to her as he took a bite.

They all talked around the table, and she watched the boys throw back pizza like it was nothing. Elle had taken her few bites and called it quits; subsequently, she just sipped on her water that Nero had put on the table, waiting for her.

Nero draped his arm over the back of her chair. "Aren't you going to finish that?"

Elle looked at Nero and shook her head. "I'm not that hungry." *You lose your appetite when someone tries to kidnap you.*

"You need to eat." Nero looked like he didn't want to be tested.

Elle looked around the table and noticed no one was paying them any attention. *I really can't eat.*

"I'm not hun—"

Nero's other hand shot out to the high part of her bare thigh. "Finish the pizza."

Elle stared at Nero before she slowly picked up her slice. She had no idea why, other than her body aimed to please him. She always got a tingly feeling under her skin when she did as Nero asked.

Elle took a bite, the feeling of sickness strangely gone, and the taste was now delicious. As she felt Nero start to rub her thigh in agreement, Elle took another bite and licked at the little bit of red sauce left on her lip.

Nero rubbed her thigh higher under the table, and Elle's heart pumped faster. Elle found it erotic as she continued to eat her pizza that no one knew Nero continued to praise her by rubbing her thigh in different motions. After she had eaten every bite and even licked her fingers, Nero gave her a special touch, lightly grazing her femininity.

When not even a morsel was left, Elle came out of her haze.

What the fuck is wrong with me?

I DIDN'T MEAN TO SCARE YOU

Chloe sat under the beautiful white gazebo that sat in the middle of what was possibly a garden with white lights strung around. She thought the backyard was lovelier than the inside, and that was saying a lot.

There was a light snowfall, dusting the backyard. She had never seen anything whiter.

The backyard was huge for Kansas City. She could only imagine what the yard looked like during the spring. She just wished she could see it.

The gazebo had an iron bench, two chairs, and a small table, all close together. Luckily, they hadn't accumulated any snow yet because of the roof. She had chosen to sit on the bench since it was in the middle, overlooking the whole backyard.

She felt a sudden peacefulness here in the backyard. *I would live here if I could.*

Technically, Chloe wanted to live anywhere besides where she did now. That was why she had applied to every college in the country practically. She only had a few months to go and then she would run as far as she could get.

She was happy she'd decided to sneak out here, doing what she had always done. Chloe had always snuck away if she had to go to a function with her father or if important people had come to hers. Chloe was always there for looks. *For a picture-perfect family.* Little did the city know how much of a fraud it was.

Chloe moved her eyes to the house, peering into it, seeing them all sitting around the table, laughing and eating pizza. *I don't belong anywhere.*

She had trouble fitting in. Every time she met a new person, she felt like they only stared at her scars. She had lost all confidence in herself when she had gotten the marks. Before them, she had been outgoing and free. Now, she could barely talk to anyone, merely responding minimally.

The only person I can be myself with is Elle.

Being around Elle, she felt safe, and the old Chloe was able to come out. However, once someone else came around them, she cowered back. Recently, however, she would peek her head out when she was around Nero, Amo, Vincent, Leo, and just now Maria. *A little.* She didn't even understand why she was because honestly, people scared her, and she had good reason as to why.

Chloe continued to watch them. *I don't think they even know I'm gone.* Her heart had been empty for too long, wanting to find a safe place she could belong.

"Hey, darlin'," a deep voice sounded behind her.

Chloe jumped at the sound. A second later, a man appeared on the other side of the rails. He was terrifyingly beautiful and scared the hell out of her, regardless of how handsome he was. She didn't think a man that good-looking should ever exist, nor a man that chilling.

Chloe didn't move a muscle, completely frozen in place.

He kept walking toward the entrance of the gazebo and went up the step. "I didn't mean to scare you."

She had no idea how she hadn't heard him. She didn't even know where he had come from.

She watched him lean up on a pillar, blocking her exit. After every hair had managed to stand up on her body at one look of his eyes, Chloe darted her gaze down to her lap and started fiddling with her hands.

"I'm Nero's brother, Lucca. I would shake your hand, but you wouldn't shake it anyway."

Chloe quickly glanced back up at him before looking down again. *How did he know that?*

Lucca read her eyes. "I overheard that you're apparently germaphobic."

Chloe glanced back up at him again. *Apparently?* He was really starting to freak her out now.

Chloe attempted to decide if she should honestly be afraid and try to run away. *Yes, I should.* However, Lucca was blocking the only exit, and she was not going anywhere near him.

Chloe saw him move; as a result, she regretfully had to look at him again. She held her breath when he put his hand into his pocket to pull something out. When a pack of cigarettes came out, she let out her breath. She continued to watch him pull a cigarette out and then hold it between his lips as he put the pack back in his pocket. Going into his other pocket, he pulled out a lighter. Chloe thought she was going to have a heart attack if he went into his pocket again.

Lucca flipped his lighter open and lit the end, making it burn a bright red as he inhaled.

"You don't mind, do you?"

Chloe slowly shook her head. She wished she could look away from him, but she was too afraid. She could tell he was Nero's brother without a doubt; they both oozed confidence and sex. They looked very similar, as well.

Lucca had the same skin color, but she couldn't quite tell if his hair was black or brown. The same went with his eyes; she couldn't tell if they were blue or green. She would swear they were one color before the string lights picked up the other color, changing her mind all over again. Lucca, however, was a billion times more frightening and a million times more handsome than Nero. She figured it had to do with the age gap, but one thing they were very different about was the way they dressed. Nero only dressed in button-up shirts and slacks while Lucca was wearing a black sweatshirt and dark, loose jeans.

She wasn't used to seeing hair as long as his. It was swept back, yet it touched the back of his neck. He clearly didn't care if it wasn't trimmed and neat, just like his unshaven stubble. Everyone she was around always looked immaculate, making his bad-boy appearance more like 'don't cross me or I will murder your entire family tree.' *I don't think it matters what he wears; he would look like that regardless.*

"Aren't you a little cold out here, darlin'?" His voice also oozed just as much confidence as Nero.

She felt uncomfortable with him calling her that. *If I tell him my name, he'll stop.*

"M-my name is Chloe."

She watched him smile as he took a puff, holding the cigarette between his thumb and index finger. He exhaled. "The mayor's daughter, right?"

Chloe nodded gently. She knew that practically everyone was aware she was the mayor's only child. *Right?*

"You were in that car wreck a few years back. I remember reading about it in the papers. Is that how you tell everyone you got those scars?" Lucca tapped his ashes in the snow without moving his eyes from her.

Chloe swallowed and looked back down at her hands. "That i-is how I got them."

"No, it's not. I know a knife cut when I see one."

Chloe glimpsed back up at him. *How did he know?* "I-I d-don't know what you're t-talking about."

Lucca flicked his cigarette in the yard. "Yeah, you do."

A chill went down her spine at his words, causing her to stand, not able to stay around him any longer and not liking where this was headed.

She walked a step forward, hoping he would move. His muscular frame was blocking the whole entryway. She didn't want to know how many hours he'd spent in the gym; she could see his muscles through his thick, dark sweatshirt. When he still didn't move, she gradually moved up more. *Please move, please move.*

Chloe was now just a few small steps away, refusing to go any farther. "C-can you let me through?" Her legs started to shake when he dipped his hand back into his pocket. Her heels made it hard for her to hold herself up.

Lucca pulled out another cigarette and flipped his lighter open. He slowly lit the end, not moving his eyes from her. He blew the smoke out, making it roll over her body. Instead of putting the lighter back in his pocket, he flicked it again and the silver Zippo shot out a flame. Lucca did one of his tricks, rolling the lighted Zippo in-between each of his fingers.

"I will if you tell me how old you are."

Wait, what?

Chloe became entranced, staring at the flame expertly passing through his fingers. She didn't know how he didn't let it burn himself.

Chloe mindlessly answered and asked her own question, captivated by the glow. "Seventeen. You?"

Lucca suddenly flipped the lighter closed. "Twenty-six."

Something told her he wasn't very happy about her answer by the look on his face.

Twenty-six. She had no clue why she'd asked how old he was.

After she'd watched him move slightly to let her pass, she really wished he would give her more room than that.

Chloe slowly walked up and turned her body to the side, keeping her eyes on him, afraid he would move when she passed through. She held her breath as she carefully started to move by him. Her face came to the middle of his chest, even in heels, and his shoulders came right above her head.

When she had successfully passed him, somehow with just mere centimeters apart, Chloe started walking as fast as she could, trying not to run back to the house.

Lucca's voice carried across the yard. "You can't run from the truth forever, darlin'."

Chloe picked her feet up faster.

Yes, I can. I've been doing it for years.

THE SOUND OF DEFEAT

Nero waited until his crew had walked out the front door before he pulled his sister to the side, asking her to take Elle to her closet to pick out something to wear to school tomorrow. He lucked out right after when Chloe told her to go on, and that she was going to leave now, too.

He watched Elle run out of the living room with his sister, loving the way she looked wearing his shirt. Nero had managed to win her back, panting and moaning underneath him. *I love the sound of defeat.*

However, he still couldn't wrap his head around the fact that he hadn't fucked her right there. She was hot and ready, yet still he had denied his body to claim her. *What the fuck is wrong with me?*

He didn't know if fucking her too early would taint her and make her think she was like all the other girls he'd fucked, or if fucking her before she learned the truth bothered him. Regardless, Nero had been given a little taste of her, and he was ready for the whole damn strawberry cake.

I really need to fucking thank Lucca. Then he remembered her lying there helpless, and he changed his mind. He understood why Lucca had done those things. Lucca had tested the water with the college kid in the diner to see if he rattled Nero. Then he broke them up, because clearly Lucca had been following them and knew he couldn't get close to her with Nero constantly around her, which all brought them to her being snatched. It was a test because Nero shouldn't have cared what happened to her. Elle turning up dead would be the best thing for his family, but instead, Nero had fought for her life, showing his cards to Lucca—his brother and his underboss. That could have turned out very badly for Elle and him. *It still could if Lucca tells Dad.*

Nero didn't think his brother would. He wanted something to gain from the whole thing, and Nero needed to figure out exactly what that was.

Nero watched Chloe put her coat on and then walked up to her. "Could I talk to you? I need to show you something."

"Um, yeah," Chloe said nervously.

Before he'd even asked, he knew she wasn't going to be comfortable with what they were going to talk about.

Nero grabbed a jacket that hung beside Chloe's. "Here, walk with me."

Nero walked towards his backdoor that she had gone out earlier.

He opened the door for her and saw her nerves had kicked in.

"Please, it's about Elle."

Chloe hesitantly walked out the door with him, and then he pulled the door to a close.

Nero started walking once he was greeted with the winter wonderland. "My mom spent months landscaping this backyard. When she was finally finished, she spent practically the whole day out here." Nero stopped to smile. "I still remember her crying when it turned cold and all her flowers would die."

"It's beautiful," Chloe whispered.

Nero kept walking through the huge yard, going toward the gazebo. "It is. My mom used to stare at the backdoor, dying to escape."

Chloe looked up at him. "Sorry, I couldn't help it."

Nero laughed. "It's okay. I'm glad someone could enjoy it again."

"I wish I could have seen it in the spring," Chloe confessed.

As Nero walked up the step and took a seat on the chair, he watched Chloe take a seat on the middle of the bench. He saw her stare out into the backyard and could see the glint in her eyes.

"Sadly, it doesn't look the same anymore. Now that she's passed away, it's not kept up the same and most of the flowers don't return."

Chloe looked back at him, the glint now gone. "I'm sorry for your loss."

Nero nodded, thanking her. It was time to move on to why he needed to talk to her, though.

"You know I like Elle, right?"

Chloe nodded. "Yes, I do."

"Then you know I need to know everyone that has ever touched her."

Chloe started wringing her hands. "W-why can't you ask Elle?"

Nero shook his head. *She won't fucking tell me.* "She won't tell me."

"I-I don't want to tell you, either."

Nero took a deep breath. "I thought you would say that."

Nero raised his hand and they heard the back door to the house open. He watched Chloe see them appear. He could tell she contemplated running away. A moment later, however, Amo and Vincent joined them in the gazebo.

Amo and Vincent sat on either side of her while Chloe held her hands tightly and tried to become as small as possible. Both made sure an inch of room separated their bodies from hers.

Vincent handed Chloe a book. Chloe swallowed as she took it, flipping to the first page.

Nero watched her flip through the pages. She had clearly never seen it before, not knowing that Elle had made it. He studied her face carefully as new pictures unfolded.

When she was on the last page and there were no more to be turned, he spoke. "Now, walk me through the pictures and tell me how she got every mark."

Chloe's eyes danced between the boys. "I-I can't. You all are n-not going to hurt me."

Nero pushed his hair back, uncertain of what to do. He'd thought it would spill out of her when she was surrounded by them. She was calling his bluff, though. *And I don't want to have to—*

"I think she needs some persuading, brother." He heard Lucca's voice from behind the gazebo and watched him walk up to join them.

Nero looked back at Chloe and saw her grip the photo album in her hands. As Lucca walked up, towering over her, Chloe slowly looked up at him and swallowed. Then Lucca gently placed his hands on the open book and started pulling. Chloe released it, letting it slide right out of her hands.

"Thanks, darlin'." Lucca placed the book on the black, small iron table meant for iced tea and beer. Then he picked up the table and dropped it down right in front of her, making her jump from the noise.

Nero watched his brother push his chair close to the table. Nero stood up, as well, pushing his in closer. He had a feeling the two had already met. *When was that?*

He looked over at Amo, who was squeezing his fists, clearly not happy with Lucca's appearance. Nero pushed his thoughts aside; he wasn't here for that. He looked down at the book before them that was still on the last page.

Lucca pulled out a cigarette. "We'll go backwards." He lit the end. "Tell him everything you know." Then he flipped the lighter closed.

Chloe watched the smoke envelope her face and then looked down at the book. "I-I-I—"

Nero jumped in. "Let's start slow. What did she tell her parents when she came home with bruises, scratches, and broken bones?"

Chloe tried to start. "A-at f-first—"

Lucca flicked his lighter on, weaving it through his fingers.

Chloe took a deep breath, staring into the flame. "At first, she tried her best to hide them by wearing lots of clothes. She told me she would slowly reveal a different mark each day to pretend it happened that day." Chloe squeezed her hands tightly together. "Then, when they got worse, she lied and told them she'd joined soccer. She got away with it because they hardly left the house since her dad was still recovering. That made it easy for her. They didn't get caught up in the details, worrying over his accident. Eventually, I think they got used to her getting hurt since she pretended to be so clumsy, so she was able to stop telling her parents she played soccer, and they just believed she was accident-prone."

Nero squeezed the bridge of his nose. That was only the beginning.

He watched her turn numb, staring blankly into the fire Lucca held in his hands. She went through the pictures, explaining what had happened and who had done it. His body turned numb with hers, his mind taking in all the information, careful not to miss a detail. He had been taken through the first half of senior year, junior year, and sophomore year. When she got to freshman year, she told him about how Sebastian had taken a fucking book to her face and her arm.

Chloe turned the page, coming to the first picture of her and Chloe together. There weren't any visible marks; however, that was when Elle's hair was the shortest and Chloe's scars the freshest. Chloe didn't say anything about the picture.

Nero watched Chloe's face turn from nothing into sadness. There was something she wasn't saying.

He went into his pocket and pulled out a picture from his billfold. "I found this behind that picture."

Chloe watched Nero toss a picture of Elle on top of the other one. She started shaking her head. "I d-don't want—"

Nero leaned forward and put his elbows on his knees. "Tell me."

"I c-can't do it. You'll hate me." Chloe couldn't stop fidgeting with her hands.

"Maybe she's had enough," Amo told him.

Lucca flipped his lighter shut with a hard snap. "She's fine."

Nero looked at Amo, unable to hide the way he felt about pushing Chloe too far. He wondered if he should let her stop and just be satisfied with everything she had given him already.

No. "Tell me." This time, he spoke a little harsher.

Lucca started back with the flicker of light. He moved it through his hands, starting and stopping the flame with a different finger from each trick he did.

Chloe moved the picture to uncover the one beneath it again. She returned to her numbness. "Cassandra started talking to me right when school started. She was popular, and I just wanted to fit in. She started saying mean things to people, and I would just sit there and listen to her. I felt bad and wanted to say something, but I didn't because I was afraid she would start picking on me."

Chloe took a deep breath. "One day, we were in the locker room and she gave me a pair of scissors. She said something to Elle about her father, and for the first time, I heard someone talk back to her. Elle started to walk away when Cassandra, Stacy, and Stephanie pinned her to the ground, hitting her head. When Cassandra asked me to hand her the scissors, I didn't want to, but Cassandra asked me if I wanted to end up like her, so I gave them to her. She was jealous of Elle's hair, so she cut it all off. That was the first time Elle and I ever met."

Nero took a breath. He was disappointed in Chloe, but he understood the pressure of high school. He had known there was a reason why Elle had short hair after so many years of not cutting it, but that didn't explain the picture of Elle clearly beaten to a pulp.

"What happened to her, Chloe?"

"C-Cassandra, Stacy, and Stephanie wanted to smoke behind the school with Sebastian during lunch. W-we met Elle on our way, and Cassandra told him she had talked back to her in the locker room. Sebastian dragged her outside and they all started kicking her and beating her." Chloe started digging her nails in her hands.

Nero started to get sick. He noticed Amo and Vincent were having a hard time, as well. He knew that wasn't all of it, though. There was something she didn't want to tell.

"Finish the story."

Chloe dug in a little more. "I-I was scared and just stood there. When they were done, they started to walk away, but Sebastian noticed I hadn't joined in. He t-t-told me...He told me I better kick her." Chloe removed her eyes from the flame and looked at the photo. "They had taken a picture of her and gave it to her later as a reminder. When I walked up to her and saw her like that, I couldn't do it. Elle saw that I wasn't going to, so she mouthed for me to kick her, and I heard her say it didn't hurt anymore." Chloe looked up at Nero. "I kicked her hard enough to make Sebastian happy so they would leave. When I looked at her eyes, she begged me to go with them, so I did. I don't know why she cared about what they would do to me if I didn't because I didn't care about her enough to stand up for her."

Nero took a long, deep breath, unable to look at Chloe any longer. He hated what she had done to Elle, but he knew Chloe had already clearly suffered. He figured her suffering was what had brought them together, yet that was a story Chloe wouldn't be able to tell.

Nero watched Lucca pick the book up and flip through the pages himself.

Lucca looked up at Chloe. "How come you were never hurt?"

"W-what?" Chloe looked back at him.

Lucca slammed the book closed. "Why did they only ever hurt Elle?"

Chloe bit her lip. "She wouldn't ever let them touch me. If-if they tried, Elle would do something to make them hit her instead."

"That's enough. You can go." Nero stood and turned his back to her, walking to the rail of the gazebo to hold him up. *She works so she can go to school and get the shit beat out of her just so Chloe doesn't get hurt.*

While Chloe solemnly stood and left the gazebo, Nero was on the verge of losing his mind. He'd found out everything he had wanted to know. Sebastian had done the most gruesome things to her over the years. *He's going to fucking die.* Cassandra and everyone else who had witnessed or done something to her were all going to get what they deserved, as well, but right now, Sebastian was his main priority. *It's taking everything in me not to fucking go out and get even right now.*

When Chloe had gone through the back door to leave, Nero turned around and saw the same battle in Amo and Vincent's eyes.

Vincent stood. "How in the fuck is she still sane or alive? Please tell me we start tonight."

Nero's hands wanted retribution, but his mind hesitated. "Go home. I'll call you if I decide to do anything."

Vincent nodded before he disappeared.

Nero watched Amo stand. He clearly wanted to say something as he stared Lucca down until he finally walked away.

"What are you going to do, brother?"

Nero looked over at Lucca. He had never been able to figure out what went through his mind. His brother was never much for words, nor did he really care about anything in his life. But tonight, he had seen something different.

Nero sat back down in the chair. "What do you think?"

Lucca flicked his lighter and stared into the flame. "I think killing is way too fucking easy."

A LOT OF MAKEUP CAKING

Elle sat on Nero's bed wondering what had happened. Everything seemed fine, the night had been great, and then Nero had told her to go upstairs with Maria.

Elle and Maria had really had a good time. She'd tried on whatever Maria had told her to and ended up with Maria giving her a couple of things. *Well, the ones that weren't too girly.*

Maria liked flowers and pink too much for Elle's taste, but Maria had a few things she had bought when she went through a phase. Elle hadn't wanted to take them, but Maria had insisted, saying she was going to give them away anyway. After looking at Maria's huge, walk-in closet that was filled to capacity, Elle hadn't felt too badly.

Then, when Nero had come into Maria's bedroom, his face had been scarier than she had ever seen it. All he said to Elle was, '*My room, now.*'

Elle could feel his fury radiating from his body as she had sat on his bed and Nero had gone into his bathroom.

Now, here Elle was, confused and worried, sitting on his bed, listening to the shower run. After a bit, she decided to use the time to call her boss and tell him why she didn't make it to work tonight, hoping to sidetrack her mind. When the call ended, she had thought he must have fallen in by how long it was taking him to take a shower, but then she heard the water turn off.

Elle was biting her nails, waiting for the door to open, and when it finally did, her heart stopped. Nero came out of the bathroom, still dripping wet. She had never seen him in anything other than dress clothes, and now he was wearing a towel low around his hips.

She watched his perfectly-toned body move toward his dresser. *I mean, perfect.* You could see every muscle under Nero's skin. They weren't bulky; his body was lean and cut. *Everything is defined; his arms, his chest, and his abs...* Elle followed a drop of water going down his abdomen, drifting down his dark skin until his towel captured it right above his...

Elle turned her head with a snap. "Don't change in here!" She had seen the towel start to drop.

"Turn your head, then."

"I am," Elle mocked him. She crossed her arms and kept her head turned; however, her gaze slowly drifted to see out of the corner of her eye. When she saw his ass, she quickly snapped them back in place, licking her lips and trying not to think of how glorious his ass had looked.

Elle felt a breeze under the covers, so she turned her head and saw Nero getting under the sheets, wearing dark boxer briefs. She tried to get up to get off the bed. *Clearly, Nero is ready for bed.*

Nero grabbed her hand. "Where do you think you're going?"

"Um, I thought I could sleep with Maria tonight."

Nero pulled her down beside him, pinning her upper body under his. "No, you're not."

How does he always do that? Elle had no idea how Nero always managed to mold her body like putty to the way he saw fit.

Elle tried to push off his unclothed chest. "Nero, I'm not sleeping with you."

"Yes, you are," Nero's voice commanded her.

Elle's body betrayed her again, giving in to Nero's demand, even though she had never slept beside a boy before. She figured he had just given her her first orgasm, therefore sleeping beside each other was a step down. *Right?*

"Then could you please change?"

"I usually sleep naked; would you prefer that?" Nero mocked her.

Elle quickly responded, "No."

She tried to ease into Nero and the bed. His anger had lessened, yet she could still tell he was mad, making her unable to relax. Minutes had passed of them lying in the silence before Elle began to really worry.

"Did I do something wrong?" Elle whispered.

Nero took a deep breath and pulled her into him closer. "No, baby, you didn't do anything wrong."

Elle released her own breath and was able to sink into him,

finally able to enjoy the warmth and feel of his body beneath her, making her own body melt next to his. Whatever it was that was bothering Nero, he didn't want to talk about it, and since he didn't, Elle would let it be.

"I had a nice time tonight, thank you." She hadn't even thanked Nero for saving her life.

Nero started moving his fingers up and down her back. "You don't have to thank me. I'm glad you had a good time."

"I did. I like your sister, hugs and all." Elle really did enjoy Maria's company. It was refreshing to find a wealthy, gorgeous girl who wasn't mean to her.

Nero laughed. "I thought you would."

Now that Nero was in a better mood, she thought she could ask a favor. "I especially liked her closet. She gave me some clothes she was throwing out, so her closet is getting pretty bare."

Nero snickered. "Yeah, right, it is. What are you getting at?"

Elle really hoped this would work for her new friend. "Well, I thought Chloe and I could go shopping with Maria."

"I see. Did she put you up to this?"

Elle sighed. "Nero, she's dying to be around girls, not her brothers. You all don't have to watch her twenty-four-seven. She's an adult." Elle didn't understand because, from what Maria had told her, she was never left alone. Someone always watched over her, and frankly, that didn't make any sense.

Nero didn't say anything until minutes later. "You all can go under one condition."

Elle didn't like the sound of that. "Okay…?"

"You let me buy you clothes, and not from fucking Goodwill or anywhere else you get worn clothes. Brand new clothes from wherever the hell my sister buys hers."

"There's nothing wrong with buying clothes from Goodwill." Elle was always judged by buying clothes from thrift shops, but the fact was, you could get hardly-worn clothes for cheap, and most of the time, stores mimicked old clothes for a ridiculous price when you could buy it right at Goodwill for nothing. She should have known Nero would judge her. *I mean, look at this house.*

Elle tried to push off Nero, but yet again, he held firm.

Nero pushed her back into his body. "I didn't mean it like that, baby. I don't care that you wear worn clothes, but I think you should have some new clothes, also. You deserve clothes that are yours and have only been yours. There's nothing wrong with buying brand new clothes, either."

Damn. Nero had completely turned that around on her. Not to mention, that was possibly the sweetest thing he had said to her.

Elle kissed his chest. "Fine."

Nero kissed the top of her head and then leaned over to his nightstand to turn the lamp off.

For once, Elle was at peace, not having to think about how she was going to survive another day at Legacy Prep. She felt safe as she started to drift off to sleep.

"Oh, and I forgot to mention; you have to spend the same amount as Maria."

THREE WEEKS LATER

Elle started gluing on the pieces of paper filled with her words to her poster board. She couldn't stop smiling, thinking about the last three weeks with Nero. Ever since the night she'd slept over at his house, her life had turned a complete one-eighty. Honestly, Elle didn't even know where to start.

Maria had become another good friend of hers and Chloe's. All three had clicked the day they first went shopping, and yes, Nero had made sure she spent the same amount of money as Maria did because he was there. Nero, Amo, and Vincent had taken them, staying in the background and just keeping an eye on them. Elle didn't understand why there was insistent monitoring of Maria, but every time Elle saw her flip her golden hair behind her shoulder, she began to understand.

Nero spending money on her didn't end there. The day after they made up, Nero told the lunch lady to take Elle's lunch out on his account. Elle had tried to protest, but the lunch lady had taken it before Elle could get a word out. She found that pretty strange that she didn't even have something to say about it, considering she was the one who had thrown away her tray. The next day, Elle thought she would be smart and not eat at all, but that really didn't work because Nero set a tray down in front of him and her.

Elle had wished the money spending had stopped there; however, when she went to the office to pay a part of her tuition she had set up on a payment plan, it was already paid. When she had confronted Nero about it, he had done what he was getting too good at, telling her she deserved everything. Then he kissed her to make her give in. Finally, he told her the last request.

He had told her to cut back her hours since she was able to keep the money. Again, she'd protested, but Nero had found a way to persuade her, saying they could spend that time together, watching all the movies she wanted. However, Nero didn't do much watching, and Elle was only able to attempt to.

Lastly, Elle and Chloe hadn't been picked on the whole time. Everyone who had ever hurt her hadn't talked, looked, or even came within five feet of her.

Elle looked up from her poster to see Stacy and Stephanie powdering their noses and under their eyes. Lately, Elle had noticed a lot of makeup caking and wearing sunglasses, and that was a hell of a lot to make it unusual. Yet, everyone kept saying a bug was going around. Elle looked at their dark, baggy eyes. *I hope I don't get it.*

Elle managed to glue on the final piece before the bell rang.

Nero waited until everyone left before he maneuvered Elle up to sit on his lap. "What are you doing tonight?"

Elle wrapped her arms around Nero's neck. "Something tells me you've made plans for me."

Nero laughed. "I might have."

"Well, are you going to tell me?"

"No, it's a surprise." Nero put his hands in Elle's hair and brought her face toward his, giving her a firm kiss.

Elle kissed him back, her tongue flicking out to trace his mouth. Her hunger had risen to new heights. Nero hadn't made a big move on her since that night three weeks ago when he had given her that orgasm, her first. He still kissed her relentlessly and touched her over her clothes, but he hadn't tried anything like he had done that night.

At first, Elle had been grateful, but every day her body burned hotter and craved for Nero to do something, anything. She didn't understand why he didn't try something since he had been persistent in the beginning. When things would heat up between them, Nero would stop, making Elle think something was wrong with her.

"Are you two done sticking your tongues down each other's throat? Because I would like to get the fuck out of here."

Elle quickly pulled away and stood up at Vincent's voice.

Nero sighed as he went to stand. "I'll remember that."

"I'm sure you will." Vincent laughed.

Elle walked out of the classroom, trying not to blush when she saw Chloe and Amo talking to each other under their breath while trying not to laugh. Elle couldn't believe the two had actually started getting along. *Well, mostly.*

She had noticed Chloe couldn't even look at the guys the day after she spent the night with Nero, but then again, she didn't even look at Elle much that day. She figured something must have happened at home that night because, every day after that, Chloe had become more and more comfortable.

Nero grabbed Elle's hand and they started walking to the student parking lot. When they finally reached Chloe's BMW , Nero opened the passenger's door and Elle got in.

"I'll call you." Nero swiftly gave her a kiss before he shut the door.

"Does he know?"

Elle looked over at Chloe's smiling face. "Know what?"

"That your birthday is tomorrow," Chloe answered.

Elle raised her eyebrow. "Did you tell him?"

Chloe laughed. "No."

"Then nope."

A WORK OF ART

Nero sat on the hood of his car, surrounded by trees and a dirt road. The sun had gone down, and Nero knew it should be any minute now.

Twenty minutes passed before headlights lit up his surroundings. He heard the door open and slam with a loud noise.

Nero walked over to the car and another sound greeted him. The sound sang to his soul. *Finally.*

"Ready, brother?" Lucca appeared beside him.

Nero looked down at his hands and made two fists. "I can't use my hands."

"I was hoping you would say that." Lucca opened the car's back door then reached in his backseat and tossed a wooden bat to Nero.

Nero walked toward the trunk and the sound grew louder. He gripped the bat in his hands. "Now, I'm ready."

Lucca opened the trunk and a crying Sebastian wailed for forgiveness.

Nero grabbed Sebastian's shirt and pulled him out of the trunk before he pushed him to the ground.

Nero stared into Sebastian's crying, pleading eyes. He had waited three weeks for this moment, planning for this all to be perfect. He had started getting even with the kids at school who had made Elle's life miserable, then the ones who had touched her. And, finally, the ones who had tortured her.

That had caused everyone who had ever hurt Elle to start to shit their pants, waiting and wondering if he was going to come for them. Sebastian had waited the longest, scared every fucking day for the last three weeks. This time, he'd told Amo and Vincent he needed to get even on his own.

"You fucking lied to me, Sebastian."

Sebastian had blackmailed the quarterback to throw the milk carton at Elle. He had felt bad afterwards and that was why he had offered to get his team to guard Elle's table. He confessed when Nero had sent out his first round of paybacks.

Sebastian went to his knees. "P-P-Please d-don—"

Nero swung the bat, crashing it against his arm. He didn't fucking care how much he begged. *He didn't give a shit when Elle begged.*

Nero took his time, slamming the bat against Sebastian's body and keeping in mind every place he had ever touched Elle. The sound of sobbing combined with the sounds of bones breaking calmed his soul.

Nero leaned down and grabbed an almost-unconscious Sebastian's face. He made sure he had broken every inch of his body but left his face untouched.

"I made you a fucking promise that you would be unrecognizable, and I keep my promises."

Nero pushed back the mass of hair from his face. As he stood, he looked over at Lucca, leaning against the car, smoking a cigarette.

"Do I finally get a turn?"

Nero walked over to him. "What are you going to do with him when you're done?"

Lucca flicked his cigarette toward Sebastian's body. "I thought I'd give him a ride to the hospital."

Nero strode back to his car, satisfied at giving him over to Lucca. Nero had just created a work of art, but Lucca, he made masterpieces.

Nero got in the car and pulled out his phone. Now that he had gotten even with everyone who'd ever hurt Elle, he could finally claim the prize he now felt deserving of.

Nero drove out onto the dirt road, smiling into the flicker of light off in the distance.

Elle watched Maria hold up a dress.

Maria shook her head. "Nope, I don't like it."

Elle laughed. "Are you planning on going somewhere?"

Nero had called and asked if she would spend the night with Maria, saying she looked like she needed some girl time. Elle, of course, had agreed and told her parents she was staying over at

Chloe's since her dad wouldn't appreciate that she was going to stay at Nero's house. Since it was a school night, too, she told them they had another project due—after all, it had worked well the first time.

Maria held up another one. "What do you think?"

Elle squished up her nose. "It's awfully pink…"

Maria put it back. "You're right."

Elle shook her head, laughing. She watched Maria flip through some more before she stopped.

Maria sighed and mumbled something under her breath, then she went to the very back of her closet and pulled out a white dress.

Elle's mouth dropped. "You own that?" The dress was plain white yet made from expensive-looking fabric. The thing that shocked Elle was it was extremely short and tight-looking.

Maria walked up to her. "Try it on."

Elle shook her head no. *There's no way I could fit into that.*

"Come on, Elle. I just want to see what it looks like on you. Please?" Maria gave Elle puppy eyes.

Ugh. "Fine, I'll attempt to fit in it." Elle snatched the dress from her.

Maria laughed and walked out of the closet to shut the door. "Oh, you can't wear your bra and panties with that dress."

What? I thought I was just trying it on. Elle threw off her clothes and, to appease Maria, she stripped all the way down. Elle stuck her legs in the dress and shimmied it up then put her arms through the straps.

She smoothed the dress down, noticing it wasn't too short. *Short enough.* However, on Maria, it would have been lucky to cover her ass. Elle wondered how in the world she'd managed to keep the dress hidden from her brothers.

"Okay, come in."

Maria opened the door a second later. "Oh, my God. It's perfect!"

Maria ran over and took Elle's hand then dragged her over to her vanity and sat her down.

Elle saw the glint in her eyes. *Oh, Lord.*

"What are you doing now?"

"Elle, I have been dying to dress a girl up. Just let me have my fun."

Elle looked at Maria's puppy-dog eyes again. There was no way she could say no, and as a result, Elle decided to be a life-size Barbie for Maria to play with.

She sat in the chair for what seemed like hours while Maria curled her hair and did her makeup. When that was finished, Maria made her put on some white, strappy heels. Elle then stood up so Maria could see her creation.

Maria clapped her hands, giggling. "He is going to love me for this."

"What?" *Who's he?*

Maria took Elle's hand and pushed her in front of the mirror for the first time—she had been careful not to let Elle see—so she could appreciate the final product.

Elle gasped at her reflection. Her hair was curled in almost-messy waves, giving her hair a lift. Her makeup was perfectly done with a bold, winged eye and pink lip gloss. *Maria couldn't resist.* The dress was it, though.

Seeing it now for the first time, the scoop neck revealed the tops of her breasts, held up nicely with the thick straps. Elle understood now why she couldn't wear anything underneath; the dress was a second skin. Although the material wasn't see-through, you could see the outlines to anything underneath it. Elle had never looked or felt this beautiful in her whole life.

"You look gorgeous, Elle," Maria complimented.

"Thanks to you and the time you spent to do so. Well, time to pull it off—"

"Wait, what time is it?" Maria looked over at the clock. "Eleven forty-five!" Maria grabbed Elle's hand and dragged her to stand in the middle of her bedroom. "Wait right here." Then Maria disappeared.

Um, okay...

Nero opened his bedroom door. "What the fuck, Maria?"

"Sorry, Nero. I needed her for something," Maria tried to calm him.

"I told you to distract her for thirty fucking minutes, not the whole damn night. We just told her you wanted her here to fucking get her here."

Maria rolled her eyes. "Yeah, yeah, yeah. Okay, you can thank me later."

"For what? Fucking stealing her from me?"

Maria started laughing, "All right, I'm leaving with Lucca. Elle's in my room." Maria started walking down the hall. "Oh, don't be mad at me for the dress. I never actually got to wear it."

What?

HOW DOES IT TASTE?

leven forty-five? Elle hadn't even realized how late it was, though she had known it was late when she had come over. *Yeah, but dang, time flew.*

Elle looked around Maria's bedroom, wondering how long she was going to take. She tried waiting right where she'd told her to, but she spun around the room, bored, until she heard the bedroom door fly open.

Elle turned back around to face the door. "Final—" Her mouth stopped forming the words when she saw Nero standing in the doorway. She thought he looked just as stunned to see her as she did him.

Nero slowly started covering the distance between them, and Elle tried to move back. She thought Nero looked too much like a wolf trying to stalk his prey right now, and she started to feel uncomfortable with the way she was dressed.

I'm going to kill Maria. "Uh-uh, what are you doing here?"

Nero stood right in front of her. "I live here, remember?"

Right. Elle wondered where Nero had gone to tonight. He looked a bit sexier than he usually did with his buttoned up shirt that was a dark gray this time. It made his emerald eyes dance and gave him a more deadly and sexy appearance. Elle licked her lips from them suddenly starting to feel dry.

Nero reached out and took her hand, pulling her toward him. "You look fucking beautiful."

Elle's heart started beating as Nero leaned down to kiss her lightly on the lips. When he pulled away, he started pulling her out of the bedroom.

"Um, where's Maria?"

"She left. Remind me later to thank her and kill her for that dress."

Left? Elle's heart began to race as he headed toward his bedroom. She suddenly felt like this whole thing might have been planned.

Nero smiled as he opened his bedroom door for her.

Elle looked into his room and saw a small table and two chairs had been placed by his balcony door. *He did this for me?*

Nero's hand came to the small of her back and he gently pushed her into the bedroom before shutting the door. Then he guided her toward the table and pulled out a seat for her. Elle stared at the pink cupcake and strawberries on the plate in front of her as Nero sat down beside her.

He reached into his pocket and grabbed the two items he had

been hiding. He placed a white candle on top of the cupcake and lit the end with a lighter.

"Happy Birthday, Elle."

Elle looked over at Nero, shocked. "How did you know?"

Nero shrugged. "Josh told me."

Should have known. The two had spent some time together and Nero had started rubbing off on Josh, who hadn't been picked on since Nero had scared those bullies that day at the bus stop.

Elle smiled as she gave Nero a quick kiss on the lips. "Thank you."

Nero smiled back at her. "You're welcome, baby."

Elle looked back at the burning candle and quickly blew it out.

"Did you make a wish?"

Elle thought about how drastically her life had changed in a matter of a month. "Yes, but I'm not going to tell, or it won't come true."

Nero picked up a strawberry off the plate. "I plan on making all your wishes come true."

"I have a lot of wishes," Elle teased.

"I think you're worth it." His expression was serious.

Elle's heart melted. She never would have thought Nero could have been the sweet type.

As she watched him put the strawberry up to his mouth and take a bite, Elle went to pick up her own strawberry, but Nero swatted her hand away. He then picked another strawberry up and put it to Elle's lips.

Elle slowly opened her mouth and took a bite. The taste was sweet and slightly sour, and she didn't know if it was the best strawberry she had ever eaten because of the taste or because Nero was feeding it to her.

He then pinched off a piece of the cupcake and put it up to her lips. Elle started to get butterflies as she opened her mouth and placed her lips over the cupcake and the tips of his fingers as she slid the morsel into her mouth.

"How does it taste, baby?"

Elle saw the heat start to rise in his body, as well. She licked her lips. "Delicious."

While Nero pinched off another piece and brought it to her, Elle looked him in his eyes as she opened her mouth for the cake. This time, she slid her lips farther down his fingers and sucked the tasty cupcake off. She watched Nero pull his fingers out and then suck a tiny piece of icing off that she hadn't caught. Elle wanted to return the favor.

"May I feed you?"

Nero smiled, pleased with her question. "Yes."

Elle's heart started to race as she pinched off her own piece. She put it to Nero's mouth, her body waiting in anticipation. She watched him grab her hand and take her whole fingers into his mouth and suck. She got chills at the sensation of his mouth over her fingers.

"How does it taste?" she asked breathlessly.

Nero held onto her hand and sucked the remaining icing off her finger greedily. "Delicious."

She felt the wetness start between her thighs as he scooped up icing onto his finger and held it to her lips. Elle couldn't pull her eyes away from him as she slid her mouth over his finger and sucked once more. She was pleased with herself when they came out clean.

As Nero scooped up another bit of icing, swiping it on her neck, Elle froze. He wrapped his hand in her hair and pulled Elle to him before he bent down and licked up the trail of icing, sucking a tiny piece of her neck into his mouth.

Elle bent her head more to the side so Nero could take more. She felt him start to kiss up her neck and to her mouth. When Nero kissed her this time, it was not light and quick; it was rough and greedy. He sucked her tongue into his mouth as his other hand went to her waist and pulled her onto his lap. Elle found herself straddling Nero and gripping his shoulders. She was just as hungry as he was. He hadn't kissed her like this in three weeks.

She felt Nero's hands move to cup her ass as he rose from the table, making Elle wrap her legs around him tighter to hold her up.

Nero placed her to stand at the foot of the bed, his hands trailing from her waist up her body slowly until he stopped at her shoulders, pulling the dress's straps down to hang off her now-bare shoulders.

Elle's stomach grew nervous, and she pulled back to stop kissing him. "Nero—"

Nero rested his head on Elle's forehead. "Elle, I have fucking waited for you. Please, baby, I can't wait any longer."

Elle could feel Nero's need and pain, aware he couldn't hold out any longer. She thought about how Nero had clearly had this all planned. *He wanted this to be special.* Elle just wanted to hear him say three words to her. Three words that she had felt the moment he bumped into her in the hallway one month ago. It just took her time to realize it.

She simply didn't want to be the one to tell him first because she was scared he would run away. Elle knew Nero didn't treat her like all the other ones in the past, and something in her just knew he loved her, too. Nero had come a long way, but saying it would be hard for him to do. Her heart loved him and her body needed him just as badly. Elle wanted to give Nero something in return for everything he had done for her.

Elle kissed his neck as she went for his shirt buttons; she had missed the feel of his chest. She kissed and licked as she kept unbuttoning his shirt. Elle glanced up into Nero's lust-filled eyes as she pushed his shirt off and onto the floor.

Nero pulled her hair back to claim her mouth again, his hands returning to her dress. Elle thought her heart was going to explode as he kissed her while pulling down her dress to expose her naked breasts, abdomen, and mound. She could see his surprise.

Nero spoke harshly, "Fuck, I didn't think there wasn't anything underneath."

When he returned to kissing her, he swiftly went to his pants and dropped them to the floor.

Elle saw how huge Nero was right before he picked her back up to lay her in the middle of the bed. *No way.*

She tried to push Nero back, her nerves returning.

Nero grabbed her hands and held them to the bed beside her head. "Do you trust me?"

Elle stared into Nero's eyes and knew she couldn't lie as much as she wanted to right now. "Yes," she whispered.

Elle tried her best not to tremble as Nero leaned his head down to her neck. He lightly kissed it, going lower and lower until she felt his breath over her right nipple, gasping when his tongue went out to lick the hard, pink tip. She arched her back to lean in closer as he laved and sucked it into his mouth. Elle squeezed Nero's hands tightly when he gently bit the tortured flesh, causing a rush of wetness to seep past her folds.

"I have waited so long to taste these pretty, pink nipples." Nero moved over to the right nipple, giving it the same attention as the other one.

He pulled his hands from hers, taking her breasts in his hands as he ventured lower to her belly, slowly and lightly kissing down while his fingers teased her nipples.

When Nero parted her thighs, her pussy glistened before him.

Elle's head fell back when his tongue thrust deep inside her, starting a rhythm over her sensitive bud. Then her hands went to his hair when he sucked her clit into his mouth.

"You even taste like fucking strawberries."

Nero slid a finger into her tight sheathe, and Elle started to feel a small wince of pain before Nero sucked her tiny bud harder. She felt another finger enter her a moment later before he started a motion inside her, steadily pumping.

Nero's thumb moved to her clit. "Baby, I'm going to try my best not to hurt you for your first time. You're so fucking tight, though."

Elle didn't understand him, the pleasure inside of her burning every inch of her body. She needed release. Her hips bucked upwards, following his rhythm, but Nero stopped and kissed back up her body, not giving her what she needed.

Elle desperately whimpered beneath him as he went to his nightstand and hurriedly slid on a condom; her body needed him to return.

She felt the tip of his length brush her entrance as he held her thighs apart and tightly to the bed, not wanting her to move.

Elle spoke between harsh breaths, "Nero, please. I need you." She tried to raise her hips up.

When he slowly started to enter her, going an inch at a time, it wasn't fast enough for her. Elle cried out, wiggling her hips, "Now, Nero!"

"Fuck, baby." Nero slid his length deeper and pushed at the thin membrane.

Elle screamed out as he tore through.

Nero quickly took her mouth with his, and his thumb went back to her pussy to find her clit, beginning to stroke.

Elle felt the pain ease away as her desire came back. She wrapped her legs around his hips and gripped his back, feeling Nero slowly start to move his hips above her, cautiously going in and out, driving her mad all over again.

She lost all sense of the world around her as Nero increased the speed and started taking his cock out more and more, only to shove deeper inside her. Elle felt the tension build in her body, growing. Her hips matched his, following his speed. She squeezed her legs tighter around his hips, wanting him to go higher inside her.

Nero pushed harder on her clit. "Do you want to come, baby?"

Elle nodded furiously and dug her nails into his back. "Yes, please."

Nero slammed his mouth down on hers, rubbing the tiny bud expertly. His hips thrust upwards at a high speed, making his balls smack at her ass.

Elle dug her nails harder into Nero when he reached a spot high within her, making her moan out in ecstasy. She held onto him tightly as she came, reaching her climax.

Nero pumped hard into her a few more times before she heard him grumble. Holding her still, she felt the jolts making her soar with his own release before Nero fell on her, exhausted but careful not to give her all his weight.

Their breaths matched each other's, both heavy and quick. When he'd regained control, he rolled away then took off the condom and threw it in the trashcan beside his bed.

Elle's breathing finally calmed when Nero moved her to lie on top of his body. She nestled into his chest, completely exhausted.

Nero started the motion of his fingers going up and down her back. "Did I hurt you?"

Elle placed a kiss on his chest. "No, it was perfect."

"Good. Next time, I'll show you how to really fuck."

TIME'S UP

lle sat up in Nero's bed, smiling as she watched his perfect ass walk to the bathroom. Her eyes went to his opened drawer on his dresser where she could see the box of condoms laying inside. Before Elle turned away from it, she noticed a picture inside, all the way in the back.

She curiously pulled the pretty picture frame out of the drawer. The picture was of four kids surrounded by a beautiful woman. She noticed a young Nero, Maria, and Leo instantly. *Aww.* The fourth child she knew had to be Lucca. Elle stared at him longer, feeling like she had seen him somewhere, but she couldn't place where. *Oh, well, he probably came into the diner one night.*

Elle went back to the beautiful woman. She had blonde hair and big, green eyes. She knew it was Nero's mother. Every time Elle would ask about Nero's family, she sensed he didn't want to talk about it; consequently, she'd dropped it, wanting to give him time to talk about it on his own.

Elle heard the bathroom door open, and her eyes went to Nero, who stood perfectly still in the doorway.

"Nero, she's beautiful." Elle watched Nero take a deep breath she swore was almost of relief and walk toward her. *Maybe he didn't know how to bring it up?*

Nero got on the bed and pulled her toward him. "She was."

Elle frowned. "What happened to her?"

Nero thought for a second before he answered. "She was murdered outside a grocery store when I was in the sixth grade."

Elle took a breath. "I'm so sorry." She knew Nero still didn't want to talk about it, so she would leave her death at that. "What was her name?"

"Melissa."

Elle caressed the woman's face through the frame. "Well, she's beautiful, and now I know how all of you turned out so good-looking." Elle laughed and then touched the young kid's face, who was the only one in the picture not smiling. She couldn't imagine how scary he was now. "Even him."

Nero forced a laugh as he took the picture frame and put it on his bedside table where it belonged. "Yeah. Lucca is... Lucca."

Elle looked up at him. "When do I get to meet him and your father?"

Nero shrugged. "Soon."

I hope so. The only one she really didn't know anything about was his father; not one thing. Elle wanted to at least know something.

"What is your father's name?"

"Dante."

Elle and Nero hung up their art projects on the classroom wall and took a step back.

"Nero, it's beautiful." Elle stared at the big drawing of Kansas City. Elle was in shock Nero could draw so well. *And with a pen!* She had also come to realize how in love Nero was with the city. Elle couldn't blame him; she was, too.

Nero pulled Elle to his side. "Not as pretty as yours."

"Nero, that's so cute. I didn't know you could draw," Vincent spoke behind them.

Amo laughed. "Yeah, it's fucking adorable."

"Don't listen to them," Chloe chimed in.

Elle leaned up and wrapped her arms around Nero's neck. "Don't listen to them. They're just jealous." She gave him a quick kiss on the lips.

"You're right, baby." Nero turned to look at the posters. "Girls love—" He paused. "Elle, could you and Chloe give us a minute? I need to talk to Amo and Vincent."

Elle curiously looked up at Nero. She never understood the boys, even after a month of being with them. "Sure, we'll wait at the wall of fame."

Elle let go of Nero and went for the door, but Vincent reached for Elle and gave her a peck on the cheek. He smiled at her wickedly.

"Happy birthday, Elle."

"Yeah, happy birthday," Amo agreed.

Elle laughed at Vincent's death wish. He always tried to push Nero's buttons, but they all knew they were just friends.

"Thanks."

Elle quickly looked back at Nero before she left, silently telling him to behave. She could tell something was bothering him, but he gave her a reassuring smile before she went out into the hall.

The art room was close to the gym and the wall of fame made of glass and sports' memorabilia throughout the years.

"So, I'm guessing Nero found out?"

Elle looked over at Chloe's smirking face. "Yeah, Josh told him."

Chloe giggled. "What are we doing for your birthday this year?"

"The same thing we always do; get fat off popcorn, cake, and ice cream, and then watch a movie."

"Good thing I already packed a bag this morning."

"Are you ever unprepared?" she joked.

I wonder what is taking him so long. In truth, hardly any time had passed, but Elle could never wait to get out of this place. Elle's eyes wandered over to look at the wall, just to give her something to do. The school's football team filled up practically the whole thing. There were so many pictures of the teams over the years. Her eyes were drawn to a particular picture of a team several years back.

The football player at the end of the line-up next to the coach was what got her attention. At first glance, she thought he was a coach because of his maturity and size, but his uniform told her otherwise.

Elle's heart started to race; she knew him. He had a slightly-younger face of one of the scariest men she had ever seen in her life. *The murder.*

Chloe noticed her unmoving stare. "What is it?" Chloe turned around and followed Elle's eyes. "Gosh, he was just as scary back then," Chloe whispered.

Huh? Elle blinked, looking at Chloe. "What did you say?"

Chloe put her finger over the glass and pointed to the player. "Lucca, Nero's brother. He is terrifying. Haven't you met him?"

Elle started to lose her breath, her chest beginning to rise and fall at a heavy speed. She wanted to grab Chloe and shake her.

"Chloe, that's Nero's brother? Y-you met him? When?"

"U-uh, after you were attacked, at Nero's house. I met him in the backyard." She quickly got out of Elle's hold. "Elle, what's wrong? You're scaring me."

"Chloe, we need to get to your car." Elle grabbed Chloe's jacket and started running. "Now!"

Fuck-Fuck-Fuck-Fuck-Fuck-Fuck. Fuck!

Nero stared at Elle's poster. She had written a poem on every page in excellent handwriting of all different sizes. Then she had glued them as a mosaic. The whole thing was white paper, filled with black words. It was cool to see which word stuck out at you. Nero had tried to read them, but Elle was embarrassed, saying they weren't any good. He had caught glimpses and read a few while she was working on them, yet he had never been able to read all of them together until now.

Nero went up to the poster and ripped off a piece. *She had seen them.*

Nero handed the paper over to Amo and then ran his hands through his hair.

Amo quickly read the paper. "Shit."

Vincent snatched it from Amo's hands. "Fuck, man. What are you going to do?"

Nero grabbed the paper from Vincent, folded it up, and put it in his pocket. "I need to meet with my father. I'll need you guys to stay with Elle. She's eighteen now, and I don't trust him not to make the call."

Nero and Vincent nodded.

"Let's go."

When Nero got to the wall, Elle and Chloe weren't there, and he started to worry.

"Where the hell are they?" *Elle said she would be right here.*

"Uh, Nero?" Vincent said quietly.

"What?" Nero turned around to look at Vincent and saw him pointing through the glass. "Fuck!"

"Chloe, could you please drive faster?"

"No, I can't, not when I don't know what we're running from," Chloe ridiculed.

Elle tried to calm her voice. "I told you; I can't tell you."

"Well then, I can't drive faster. I could get a speeding ticket."

"Your dad is the mayor, for Christ's sake; who the fuck cares!" *Shit.*

Elle saw Chloe's face and immediately wanted to take it back. She took a deep breath. "I'm sorry, Chloe."

Elle sank into the seat and just let Chloe drive the way she wanted to. *It doesn't matter; I'm dead anyway.* Elle tried not to think about Nero, but it wasn't working in the silent car. *All the fucking lies.*

Elle held her chest. She had fallen in love with Nero only for it all to be one big lie. She couldn't help thinking about all the times they'd spent together. *Yeah, like last night.*

A tear rolled down her cheek. She had given Nero a part of her she could never get back. She thought what they had shared was real, but she didn't even know who the real Nero was. The saddest part was it had been right in front of her face the whole time; she had simply been too blinded by love to see it.

Chloe passed Elle's neighbors' house, and that was when she saw a dark car in her driveway with Amo and Vincent on the hood.

Elle's nerves started to return. She had to get Chloe safely away. She was a goner anyway.

"Chloe, listen to me. As soon as I get out of the car, I need you to drive off and go straight home. Do not go anywhere."

"Elle—"

"This is not a joke. Do it!" Elle ordered her.

"O-okay." Chloe stopped the car for Elle to get out.

Elle took a deep breath before she opened the door and jumped out. "Go!" She slammed the door.

When she heard Chloe drive off, Elle contemplated running; however, they had seen that and covered the distance.

Elle held her hands up. "Chloe doesn't know anything. I never told her, I swear."

Vincent took a deep breath. "Get in the car, Elle."

Elle looked at the two people she'd thought were her friends. "Promise me you won't hurt her."

Vincent grabbed Elle's arm and tugged her to the car. "Come on, sweetheart."

Nero knocked on the door and a second later, Lucca answered. He came in to his father's home office and took a seat right in front of him.

Dante leaned back in his chair. "Time's up, son."

Nero pulled the folded piece of paper out of his pocket and threw it onto his father's desk. He watched his father read the paper and then lay it down. He could have sworn he was almost frowning.

"She saw us."

She did. Nero nodded in agreement.

Dante looked up at his son. "Congratulations, son. You finished the job."

"Well, I couldn't have done it without Amo and Vincent."

Dante gave a quick nod. "We'll plan for the Omertà."

Even though Nero hadn't spoken his vows, he wasn't going to let that stop him. "I want to get something straight first. We both know she isn't going to talk, so you're not going to kill her." Nero shrugged. "If you do, then I'll tell Maria and Leo you slit Elle's throat. You'll have no real fucking family left." Nero's eyes didn't waiver after he'd said his peace.

Dante looked over at Lucca, who was standing in the corner.

Lucca walked over and took the paper off his father's desk. "I like her."

Nero watched his father's mouth twist up into a smile.

"I think it's time I met her."

MADE MEN

Elle tried to stop her body from shivering as she walked up to Nero's house. Vincent and Amo had to push her along to even keep her feet moving. When the front door opened and she walked in, Nero appeared in the foyer. Elle turned her face away as if she had been lashed in the face. *I was.*

Nero sighed. "Follow me."

"Why not just kill me here?" Elle whispered.

Nero walked up to her and reached out, but Elle jumped back. *Don't touch me.*

Nero ran his hands through his hair. "Elle, no one is going to hurt you; I promise."

Elle held up her hands. "Don't."

She had heard his deep voice make the commitment to her,

making her body respond, believing he was telling the truth, but Elle knew better now. Her body would have to catch up later.

This time, Nero slowly reached out and pulled Elle along. He took her to two huge, wooden doors she had never been through before and turned the doorknob. She tried to keep the bile down in her stomach as he pushed open the door until a smoke-filled room greeted her.

Elle looked past the smoke to see an immaculate man with jet-black hair, wearing a full suit. *Oh, shit!*

For some reason, Elle had never thought she would be meeting him. *Wait, why is he here?*

Nero pulled her inside and shut the door. "Elle, this is my father—"

"The boss," she whispered.

Dante smiled. "Nero, let me talk to her alone."

Elle swallowed as Nero gave her a squeeze before he left.

Dante exhaled, blowing more smoke into the room. "Sit down, Elle."

Elle's body obeyed his command. When she sat down and looked at his cold, ice-blue eyes, she never understood how she hadn't seen it before. They all sounded, looked, and acted alike. The only difference was, with age, they all got fucking scarier.

"There's no need to be afraid; I'm not going to hurt you."

Elle looked back up from her shaking hands. "You're not?"

"No. My family has made it clear not to touch you."

They have? Elle took a breath in an attempt to relax. It worked. *Sorta.*

"Nero gave me this." Dante handed her a piece of paper.

Elle took it and saw the piece of paper that had once been on her poster...

Made Men

I see four made men standing, I shall not tell.
The Boss.
The Terrifying.
The Scary.
The Paranoid.

I see three made men standing, I shall not tell.
The Boss.
The Terrifying.
The Scary.

I shall not ever tell.

Dante leaned back in his chair and took a hit. "It's very good. I'm just curious as to why you think the man I killed was made?"

Elle curiously looked back at him. "When I was going to work, I passed him and another guy. He looked scared as the other guy told him the big boss gave him a job, and he didn't have a choice."

Elle saw something flicker across his face. *He didn't know.*

"Unfortunately, I wasn't able to question him, so thank you. In return, understand I'm letting you live, regardless of what my sons think.

So, I'm hoping this is the only and last poem you write about me."

Who? Nero and Leo? Elle tried to clear her throat so her voice wouldn't sound so terrified when she spoke. "Yes, I swear. I write so I can get things off my chest; that's the only reason why I wrote it."

She watched him actually give a small smile at her response.

"My wife used to garden; that was how she dealt with things." He put out his cigar. "Did Nero ever tell you about her death?"

"He just told me she was murdered outside a grocery store."

Dante leaned forward. "Nero had gotten sick, so she had gone to the store to pick up some medicine and soup. I needed all of my good men, which unfortunately hadn't left her guarded well. What I'm trying to say here is that Nero feels responsible for her death, but we both know it would have happened anywhere. I choose *the family* over my family, and that is something I have to live with every day."

Elle couldn't imagine how they felt. Her dad's accident had been hard enough to deal with; she couldn't imagine if she'd lost him.

"Elle, you're smart enough to know that you and Nero could never work out because, ultimately, Nero is not going to stay faithful to you. I gave him a job, to do whatever it took to find out what you knew. The first day on the job, he brought a girl home and I told him he had to stop fucking around until it was done."

Don't do it, Elle. Despite how badly those words stung and how her heart ached, Elle kept it together. She didn't want him to see her cry.

"It won't matter if he cheats on you or not; Nero finished the job and he is becoming a part of the family officially. It's something he has wanted ever since he was a kid. You can't stay faithful to both families. I found that out. You don't deserve to end up like my dead wife."

Elle solemnly nodded. She was in desperate need to get out of here. *I seriously have to get out of this house.*

"All right. It was nice to finally meet you, Elle." Dante held out his hand.

Elle stood and shook it. *I can't say the same.*

Dante continued to shake her hand. "I'm a man of my word; no harm will come to you."

"Thank you." Elle finally went for the door with the walls closing in on her.

When she turned the knob, he spoke again. "For your sake, I hope I never have to meet you again."

Elle opened the door and went through, unable to stay in there a moment longer. It was everything Elle could do not to run down the hall and out the front door. It was hard for her to even stand up straight.

She heard a door fly open and then was dragged inside and pushed up against a wall. She looked up and saw Nero.

"Get off—" She couldn't even get all the words out before Nero slammed his mouth down on hers. Elle's lips moved with his.

No! Elle stopped kissing him and tried to break her mouth free. "Stop it."

Nero took her mouth again while his hand tangled in her hair.

Elle's tears broke free. "Please," she managed to get past his tormented kissing.

Nero pulled his mouth from hers. "I'm sorry, baby. I didn't think you saw them. I didn't want you to find out that way."

"Everything has been a lie, Nero."

Nero swept her tears off her face. "No, it's not."

Elle looked past her tears and into Nero's emerald eyes. "So, when we were in the supply closet and I asked you why now, that wasn't a fucking lie?"

When Nero didn't respond, she had her answer.

"You were forced to be with me, and it was so bad for you, you fucked Stacy the first night." Elle squeezed her eyes shut. "In the same bed you fucked every other girl and you fucked me. I gave you something I can never get back." Elle opened her eyes to look Nero in the face so he could witness what he did. "Then you made me fall in love with you, and that's why I hate you the most."

With one fell swoop, Elle's once-mended heart crumbled into tiny particles, unable to be repaired. Her mind, body, and soul knew Nero was her one true love—the thing inside her she couldn't ever describe. She knew, however, even though he was her true love, that didn't make her his.

Nero grabbed her face in his hands. "Don't do this. Baby, I—"

"Let me go. Please, Nero, let me go." Her eyes created new tears to take the place of the ones he wiped away. Elle's eyes pleaded to him. *Let me go.* She saw the war take place behind his eyes before he finally did.

Nero reached into his pocket and pulled out a small black box wrapped in a pink silk ribbon. "I was going to give this to you tonight." Nero grabbed her hand and placed it in her palm.

Elle shook her head. "I don't want it."

Nero's voice turned dark. "Take it."

Elle held onto the box just so she could get away from him before she changed her mind.

As Nero took a step back, she was able to open the door. Elle held the doorknob in her shaky hand, taking one last look at Nero. Then she pulled the door closed.

Elle finished going down the hall, barely able to hold her own weight. When she got to the foyer, she saw Amo and Vincent nervously waiting.

Elle tried to quickly wipe away her tears. "Vincent, can you give me a ride?"

"Sure, sweetheart." Vincent walked to the front door and opened it for her.

Elle stopped at the small table beside the door that used to only hold flowers; now, it was filled with pictures in pretty frames of Nero's whole family. She placed the box Nero had given her on the table and went out the front door.

Dante sat back in his oversized leather chair, frowning. *I just saved her fucking life.*

Dante understood why his family had become infatuated with her. Truthfully, he had known they would the moment he watched the tape of her running out from behind the garbage can.

I did her and Nero both a favor. Dante had learned his lesson years ago not to get involved with women besides fucking. He thought his son wouldn't love a woman at least for a few more years, but he should have known Nero was a chip off the old block.

He heard the door knock for a split-second and watched Lucca and Sal enter.

"The girl said she passed him on the way to work. Heard him and another guy talking about how the boss gave him a job."

The guy had come into his hotel, sketchy-looking as fuck. In this business, you just know when someone is up to no good. They were patting him down when he tried to pull out his piece. Thankfully, it had all happened by the alleyway door, and they had been successful in taking care of the problem. *We thought.*

Lucca crossed his arms and leaned against the wall. "There's only two families in this city."

"Think they are trying to take back control?" Sal asked.

The Caruso and the Luciano family used to share the city before Dante's time. Both families had an understanding, but over time, a war had broken out between the two; the Caruso's had won, taking control of the city and giving the Luciano's a small piece.

"Possibly. Let's keep this between us for now. They don't think we know anything, so we all need to keep this quiet and look into this ourselves. I don't need a war on my fucking hands unless they ask for it."

Lucca and Sal nodded in agreement.

Dante pinched the bridge of his nose. "I've been hearing whispers of a fucking mole."

"What do we know?" Lucca asked.

"Not much. All I know is they're doing it right this time. We're not going to fucking suspect him for a while, years maybe."

"All right, we'll look into it." Lucca nodded.

Dante decided to tell them what they had been wondering the moment they walked in the door. "We let the girl live; for now, anyway."

payments. Today, she was going to pay them a month in advance. That way, she wouldn't feel any pressure swinging back into working every night again.

Elle reached the lunch lady and handed her the cash. "1089."

The lady handed back her cash. "You're already paid up for the rest of the semester."

What did she just say?

"Excuse me?"

"You don't have to bring lunch money anymore. Next."

Elle dropped her mouth and slowly walked away. She quickly shut it when she passed Nero's new table. It was the same one they had sat at when they had broken up before.

She quickly took her seat at the table in the corner and so did Chloe.

Chloe leaned over the table. "When has your lunch account ever been positive?"

"Never." Elle pushed the tray away. "I don't even want to eat it, Chloe." *Not if he paid for it.*

"No, that's free food. You better eat it." Chloe sighed. "Elle, are you ever going to tell me what happened?"

Elle shook her head, staring at her food. She felt too bad to be hungry anyway.

"Elle, tell me something. They were my friends, too, you know."

Elle looked up at Chloe. She had been starting to really like them, and she had actually grown comfortable around them.

She's right. "Remember how we caught him at Poison with another girl?"

Chloe nodded.

Elle sighed. "Well, this time I caught him in an even bigger lie. He played me the whole time, Chloe. They all did."

She was thankful when Chloe decided to leave it at that. Chloe knew when Elle kept a secret, and especially from her, it had to be bad.

Through lunch, Elle forced herself not to look at their table no matter what. When they went to go throw their trays away, Elle put her hands in her pocket and felt the cash that had been meant for her lunch money. *Wait.*

Elle darted out of the lunchroom in a split-second.

Chloe was hardly able to catch up with her. "Elle, where are you going?"

"The office."

Elle hurriedly made it to the office and threw open the door. She went straight to the front desk.

"I need to pay my bill."

"Okay, what's your name again?" a woman with a tight, brown bun and glasses asked.

Really, you can't remember my name one time after all these years? "Elle Buchanan." When it came out hasty, she watched the woman stop to glare at her.

She clicked her mouse a few times, and Elle saw her face become shocked.

"You have a zero balance."

Zero! He didn't even pay the fucking bill due. No, he paid the whole thing!

"I didn't pay it. Take it off!" Elle started pulling all the money she had out of her pocket and throwing it on the desk.

"I can't do that—"

"Take it off!" Elle's eyes began to water all over again.

For the first time in Elle's life, Chloe grabbed her arms. "Elle, it's okay. It's all going to be okay."

MARCH

APRIL

MAY

THE SCARIEST PLACE ON EARTH

Now *that it was officially* June, the weather had turned into a hot summer in the city. Elle walked down the hall, looking at all the shorts, skirts, and dresses. She still wore the same things she had been wearing the past few months, and that was jeans and a three-dollar shirt from her favorite place on earth. She had grown to understand Chloe's love for black, especially the super-faded, old black t-shirts with some heavy metal band she could barely read since the letters were peeled off.

Since her freak-out in the office, Elle had learned to flip her switch. Despite Nero paying off her tuition, Elle had worked every night to keep busy. When she went to bed at night, she would cry herself to sleep, having to flip over her pillow from the pool she created. Then, as soon as she got out of bed in the morning, she would shut down and become a zombie. Nothing would make her happy and nothing would make her sad. Then it would start all over again as soon as her face hit the pillow.

Every day, she would cry herself to sleep less and less until the zombie filled her whole. Almost all of her. Her thoughts were now hard to come by. It was better for her not to think at all; otherwise, she would have lost her mind, thinking about Nero.

She trained herself not to look at him, and eventually he got the memo and didn't come near her anymore. What's more, she no longer felt his stares at the back of her head. Nero didn't have to follow her any longer; no one even talked to her besides Chloe.

When she heard about Sebastian being in critical condition and having the whole right side of his face burned off, she had pieced it all together. She realized no one had gotten a fucking cold. Nero had kept his promise of watching everyone who had ever hurt her scream in pain. Unfortunately, the latter—of her screaming his name—had also come true.

Elle couldn't believe how she hadn't seen how terrible they all were. They clearly all killed for a living. She made sure she and Chloe stayed away from all of them, including Maria.

Ultimately, Elle did feel bad for not talking to Maria, though. She couldn't help who her family was, yet Elle knew if she and Maria stayed friends, that gave an opportunity for Nero.

Elle had wished the past few months would fly by, but unfortunately, they were the slowest of her entire life. The graduating senior activities only made it that much slower and that much more irritating. She had to listen to all the chattering about who was taking who to prom. Yes, she had heard several girls ask Nero, and yes, she and Chloe hadn't attended. It wasn't like they would have gone if she and Nero were still together. Chloe wouldn't have been able to handle it, and Elle would have never gone without her. Then there was this other thing of her being absolutely miserable at school for the past four years.

Elle was closer than ever to leaving; only two more weeks stood in front of her freedom. She and Chloe both were going to attend Stanford in the fall, and they could finally move on with their lives.

Brring.

Elle didn't even realize English class had started, and now it was already over. She picked up her satchel and headed for the door.

"Elle, could I speak to you?" she heard Mr. Evans speak behind her at his desk.

Elle nodded for Chloe to go on to class then she turned around and went to Mr. Evans' desk.

"Yes?"

She noticed a worried look in his eye.

"I have finished grading the final essays, and I would like you to take a look at yours early."

"Okay." The final essay was actually a redo of the first one he had assigned to the class, a five-hundred-word essay on who you love the most. This time, he had asked for it to be a five-to-seven-page paper. Basically, he wanted us to see our own growth and how our feelings could possibly change toward a person.

Mr. Evans held a huge packet of paper in his hands. "I would like to say I'm sorry about your father. That must have been hard. I can tell you really love him."

Elle held out her hand. "Thank you."

Mr. Evans placed the big stack of paper in her hands. She hadn't remembered it being so long.

"You know, sometimes I accidentally staple students' papers together." He let go of the papers. "You can read it in here. I'll need it back. I don't want the students to think I'm playing favorites by letting you see your grade first."

Elle stared at Mr. Evans before she turned to take a seat.

After she saw a big red "A" at the top, Elle flipped through the pages until she got to a paper she clearly hadn't written with Nero's name at the top of the paper. She quickly shut her eyes.

Elle took a deep breath and made sure her off switch was shut tight before she opened her eyes and started reading.

Nero's paper began of him talking about his mother, of how much he had loved her and still did. He talked about how he had never been the same after her death. Elle stopped reading at the next sentence.

She bit her lip, and then she started reading once more.

At the beginning of the semester, when you asked who I loved the most, an image of my mother popped in my head. When you asked me who I loved the most for the second time, it wasn't an image of my mother. Instead, it was replaced by an image of a strawberry blonde with big, blue eyes.

It took me a long time to figure out the exact moment I fell in love with her, partly because I denied that I did until it was too late.

I fucked up so badly and did so many things wrong, to the point of no return, so I let her go. The selfless part inside of me wants to say I did the right thing, and the selfish part of me thinks I made the biggest mistake of my life. I guess the selfless side won out because, every time I look at her and see what I did, I realize I don't deserve her.

I was never supposed to fall in love with her, but that was the best mistake of my life. I will always love her; I have ever since I purposely bumped into her in the hallway.

Elle stared at the big red "A+" at the bottom of the paper. She closed her eyes and held the switch down perfectly in her mind. After a moment, Elle was able to open her eyes.

She stood and went back to Mr. Evans, putting the paper on his desk. Then, Elle went to walk away.

"You know, I stand in front of the classroom every day, and all I see is you with your nose in your books and your papers."

Elle turned around. "Isn't that what I'm supposed to do?"

"Yes, but you don't get to see him."

Elle looked down at the ground. "Why are you doing this?"

"I know you've had it pretty shitty in here, Elle. I'd hate to see it just as shitty out there."

Elle looked back up at Mr. Evans and nodded. She headed out the classroom door and started walking to her next one.

She continued the day and couldn't help picturing what Nero had written in her mind. The light switch in her head started to flicker, wanting to come on.

When the lunch bell rang, she knew she would have to see Nero, and seeing him right now was something she wasn't going to be able to take until she had control. She wanted to think this out, sleep on it and decide if she wanted to go down that long, hard road again.

Yes.

No.

They got halfway to the cafeteria before Elle couldn't go any farther. "I need to go to the bathroom."

"Uh, Elle, are you sure?" Chloe asked her.

"Yes." Elle and Chloe hadn't gone to the bathroom at school in years. They would hold it in no matter what because the scariest place on Earth was the girls' bathroom.

Elle practically ran in and went straight to the sinks. She ran the cold water and stuck her hands under.

Chloe stayed right by the door. "Are you okay?"

Elle didn't answer; instead, she leaned her head down and started splashing water on her face.

A stall flew open.

Elle's head was shoved hard into the sink, the faucet hitting the top of her head. Elle's hair was pulled back and she stood, looking in the mirror to see Cassandra standing behind her.

"Chloe, run!" Elle screamed.

Elle's head started to throb, but her adrenaline kicked in. She grabbed for the hand behind her head and started to dig her nails in. Her other hand went for Cassandra's hair, and she started to pull as hard as she could. When she heard Cassandra scream, she used all her body weight to shove Cassandra from behind, knocking herself loose.

Elle flew around and immediately felt dizzy. She wasn't able to move fast enough before Cassandra ran forward and jammed her into the sink, making Elle fall to the ground.

Cassandra stood over her, just like she had years ago. "Nero is not here to protect you now." She rammed her foot back and kicked her in the stomach.

Elle tried to fight her eyes from closing.

"He dumped your ass because you are fucking nothing but a waitress." She rammed her foot back into her stomach.

She felt the puddle of blood soak under her face just as her tears on the pillow had done.

"This is for Sebastian."

Light switch off.

Chloe's hands landed on the bathroom door before she swung it open. Her legs ran as fast as she could with the image of Elle's face in her mind. Chloe's brain couldn't think, yet her body knew what to do.

In what felt like a split-second, she was in the cafeteria, heading straight for the other side of the room to the table that held the only people in this whole entire school who would help.

Chloe hadn't spoken a word to any of them in months, let alone the one who clearly had destroyed her best friend, but that didn't matter anymore.

"Nero!"

The whole table stood at her words, and Nero's worried face looked her in the eyes. When she saw his eyes—the visible pain and worry—she wondered whom had ended up destroying whom.

"Elle. Bathroom," she got out between short breaths.

Nero flew out of the cafeteria and they all followed behind. He ran down the hallway until he pushed through the girls' bathroom door with them all following.

When Chloe saw the pool of blood and Elle lying helpless on the floor, she didn't know if she would survive this time, or if she even wanted to. She leaned back up against the wall to steady herself. The whole thing played slowly before her. *No, Elle.*

Nero fell to his knees beside Elle's limp body. "Elle?"

Chloe covered her ears when Vincent started kicking the stalls in, yelling obscenities and looking for the person who had done it. She started sliding down the wall, her legs unable to hold her body while Leo took out his phone and dialed 9-1-1.

Nero rubbed Elle's hair out of her face. "It's going to be okay. I'm here, baby," he crooned to her.

Chloe finally made it to the floor and gripped her legs to her body. *Why couldn't I help her? Why did I leave her?* She heard Amo's voice trying to comfort her. *Why do I always just stand and watch?*

Vincent came to stand over Nero and Elle. "No one is fucking in here."

Nero didn't take his eyes off Elle, still rubbing her head. "Tell me who did it."

Chloe squeezed her body tighter. *Why can't I cry for her? What's wrong with me?*

Nero turned to look at Chloe. "Fucking tell me!"

Do something right! "Cassandra," she whispered.

"Amo, make sure she fucking understands." Nero went back to crooning to Elle.

Her view became blocked by Amo's body as he sat down in front of her. She now stared at his face, yet she was seeing past it at the same time.

"Chloe, tell them you saw nothing. You don't know who did it," Amo spoke to her.

I saw nothing. I don't know who did it. I saw nothing. I don't know who did it. I was in a car wreck; that's all I know. I was in a car wreck; no one hurt me...

BEEP... BEEP... BEEP...

Nero sat in the waiting room with his crew and Chloe, waiting to hear from the doctor. *Not like they're going to tell us shit. We're not family.*

The last few months had been pure torture on him. That night, now months ago, he had talked to his father, yelling at him because he had known his dad had said something to her. In response, he had reminded Nero of what had happened to his mother, asked him if he wanted the same fate for Elle. So, Nero had let her go for good.

At first, he'd stayed close by her, something in him secretly hoping she'd give in and talk to him and it would make him change his mind. Then, when she'd made it a point of ignoring him, not even looking at him, avoiding his face, he had backed off, giving her the space she needed because he couldn't take her not being able to even look at him.

Nero had watched her from afar at that point. She had kept

working and adding hours on, despite him paying for her school. He had spent every fucking night the past few months following her to work, watching her from his car and then following her back home to make sure she made it there safely.

The worst part of it all was watching her turn into someone else. She didn't look or act the same, and it was all because of him. *I fucked her up.* He knew it was all on him.

Elle wasn't alone, though; Nero had changed, too. He couldn't sleep without seeing her, so it was better not to sleep at all. Nothing tasted good to him besides fucking strawberries, and eating fucking strawberries was painful. Before Elle, he had fucked every girl who looked his way; now, he couldn't even look at them because it wasn't the girl he wanted to look at. He had several offers to go to prom, turning them all down. It had gotten so ridiculous that, when a girl came up to him, he just waved them away with his hand.

His balls officially hated his guts. His dick had been inside so many girls, and then, when his dick had finally gone inside Elle, there was no comparison. He couldn't even try to fuck someone else. *It wouldn't have done shit.* Nero had to take a freezing-cold shower, one right after another, to ease the pain in his groin.

Now, after seeing Elle helpless on the bathroom floor, none of it mattered anymore. He didn't think Elle was better off without him any longer, and he wasn't his father—he would protect Elle above anything else from now on. *Not even the family will come before her.* Nero was now going to take what was his, whether she wanted him to or not.

Nero saw Elle's parents and brother come in, asking to see her.

The nurses told them to remain in the waiting room for the doctor.

He watched them come in. Her mother had tears flowing from her eyes and so did Josh.

Nero stared at her father as he rolled in.

"What happened?" Elle's father asked Chloe.

Nero stood. "We need to talk, alone."

"I didn't ask—"

"Now," Nero said coldly, making the waiting room go silent.

He walked out and down the hall to a quiet part of the hospital, her father following behind.

"What makes you think I want to talk to you? You were the worst thing to ever happen to my daughter," Elle's father spat at him.

Nero flexed his jaw. "What makes you think I want to fucking talk to a father who doesn't give a shit enough to see his daughter is getting the shit beat out of her at school?"

"What? She is?" Concern showed on his face.

Nero stood right above him, looking down at him. "Maybe if you lay off the pain pills and fucking got over the fact that you can't walk anymore, you would have seen. But I know, deep down, you knew, and don't tell me you didn't."

Elle's father looked down. "No, I—"

"I don't want to fucking hear it. When they look her over, I guarantee they're going to see past injuries, and there's no telling how many they will find. I suggest you talk to the doctors alone, unless you want her mother finding out."

He nodded in understanding. "What are you doing here? If

you think you and my daughter are getting back together, you're mistaken. I know all about the Caruso family; I hear the rumors. I will do whatever it takes to keep her from you. I think we both know you've done enough already."

"I know I fucked up. That's the difference between you and me." Nero squatted down so he could clearly get his message through. "She will go to college here now. She will live with me now. Elle is mine now. You try to keep her from me, I will tell Elle the truth about your little forklift accident rollover. About how you were drunk while operating machinery." Nero saw the surprise in his face. "Yeah, see, I have friends in this city, and if you don't care that I'll tell her the truth, then I'll have them kill you. That way, I can still look Elle in the face every morning. Are we clear?"

Elle's father took a minute before he nodded.

Nero rose back up. "Good. Now understand, I know you're still her father and I'm not going to come between Elle and her family, so you and I might as well start to get along." Nero held out his hand.

Elle's father stared at Nero's hand before he finally shook it. "Elle better not get hurt again because of you."

"She won't," Nero said matter-of-factly. He went to walk off before he remembered to add something. "Oh, and Josh, he started to get picked on while on the bus. I handled it, but you better not turn your head the other way again. You do, and I'm sure Elle won't mind Josh living with us for a while."

Satisfied, Nero finally walked off.

Beep... Beep... Beep...

Elle heard the annoying noise and wondered what it was along with the sterile, old smell in her nose. She lazily opened her eyes, but only one managed to actually open. She could see a fluorescent, white room and her father in the corner, sleeping in his wheelchair. Elle realized she was in the hospital.

What happened? Elle couldn't remember. The last thing she did remember doing was splashing some water on her face.

She felt the soreness of her belly and the throbbing in her head, along with her clearly-swollen eye. She closed her eyes to try to remember what possibly could have happened. *Sink. . .? I was rammed into the sink.*

Elle looked back at her father. "Dad?" Her voice was hoarse.

She watched him quickly wake up and roll to her bed.

"Elle, you're awake. How do you feel?"

"Sore. How long have I been asleep?" Elle didn't even want to ask what had happened. She at least knew someone at school had tried to hurt her. *Tried? They did.*

"A day." He took his hand in hers. "Why didn't you tell us, Elle?"

Elle tried to smile. "Tell you what?"

Her father squeezed her hand. "Elle, I know. You don't have to pretend. The doctor showed me the scans and x-rays. Luckily, I'm in a wheelchair; otherwise, I think they would have thought I was hitting you all these years. Don't worry; your mom just thinks you pissed someone off."

Elle looked away from her father. "It started right after your accident. I didn't want to add more to your plate. Then, I'd kept it to myself for so long I didn't know how to tell you."

He squeezed her hand tighter. "I'm sorry I didn't notice. I should have cared enough to see it."

Elle looked back at him. "It's not your fault. I was a good liar, and I should have told you the truth."

"No, Elle, it's on me."

Elle smiled at her father. "I love you."

"I love you, too, Elle-bell." He cleared his throat. "You have someone out there who has been waiting to see you."

"Chloe. Is she all right?" Elle hoped Chloe had made it out okay.

"She's fine. She's at school right now. Nero's here. He hasn't left since you got here."

Elle's eyes drifted down to the bed. "Oh. Tell him I'm fine, and he can go home."

"You don't want to see him?" he asked curiously.

Elle shook her head.

"He's been out there a long time, Elle."

"I didn't think you liked him very much." She watched her father think a moment before he spoke.

"I didn't, and I still don't, but when the hospital asked me if you had insurance, and I told them no, they asked me to fill out some paperwork to figure out a payment method. After I filled it out and took it up to the desk, they told me never mind, that it was already taken care of. Anyway, what I'm trying to say is, I don't know what kind of care they would be giving you right now if it wasn't for him, and now I know he wants you taken care of." Her father cleared his throat again. "Now, do you still not want to see him?"

Elle shook her head again, afraid if she talked she would end up crying.

"Okay, I'll go tell the nurses you woke up." He gave her hand another squeeze before he rolled off.

Elle slammed her eye shut when her father left the room. Her switch was now broken and she could feel again. *It still hurts.*

Elle didn't want him to see her like this, broken. *I don't want him to be with me just because I'm broken.*

Elle thought about the paper Nero had written, still not knowing how to feel about it. *He still lied to me. His father's a killer. They're all killers. And Nero's in the fucking mafia.*

Elle took a deep breath. *No, stay away from him.*

The doctor came in to examine her, telling her she had a scalp laceration and another concussion, meaning she had gotten a few more stitches to add to her collection. She had taken a kick to the eye, but it would heal; she just got a pretty, black eye to match her stitches. Lastly, she had some stomach bruising, but again, the doctor said it would all heal. She was extremely lucky not to have broken anything or have a serious injury. They told her they would keep her in the ICU for the night to monitor her since she had been unconscious for a little over twenty-four hours, and then she would be moved to a regular room until she was discharged. *Thank God.*

THE BOOGIEMAN

Elle was sleeping when she felt the bed sink in beside her. She slowly opened her one good eye and saw the silhouette of a man she had never met before. When her eye adjusted to the now-dim hospital lights, she focused on his face. *Him!*

Elle opened her mouth to scream, but his hand covered it.

"Shh, I'm not going to hurt you." His voice was deep and non-emotional.

Elle took a breath and even though her hair stood up, terrified at looking at his blue-green eyes, she nodded.

He slowly uncovered her mouth. "I'm Nero's brother, Lucca. It's good to meet you, finally."

Elle swallowed the lump in her throat. "How did you get in here?" It was the middle of the night, and only authorized friends and family could even come back to see her during visiting hours.

"Really? That hurts my feelings."

What feelings? Elle knew it was a dumb question; the guy clearly went wherever he pleased. She doubted it was even a challenge for him.

She sat up in bed, not liking the feeling of him looking so far down at her. "What do you want?"

Lucca shrugged. "To talk."

Elle felt like he was sitting too close to her body on the small bed. It was hard to be almost at eye-level with him; however, she didn't want to show him how scared she actually was of him. Besides, there was something she had needed to talk to him about, as well.

"You don't strike me as the talking type."

It was somehow possible for his eyes to turn even more deadly. "I am when it concerns my brother. Did you know he's been sitting out there the entire time?"

Elle blinked her eyes a couple of times. "He's still out there? I told my father to tell him I was fine and to go."

Lucca put his arm on the other side of her hip and leaned toward her, making Elle lean back from his cold face. "So, you knew he's been sitting out there, waiting for your fucking permission?"

Elle was scared shitless; she had to admit it, being inches from his face. She swallowed again and nodded her head.

"Did you know he spent a whole damn month tracking down every person who laid a finger on you? The day before your birthday, he was finally able to take a baseball bat to Sebastian, and then I bet he finally allowed himself to fuck you. He wanted to deserve you. Did you ever think about how you got here? He found you fucking lying on the bathroom floor, and by looking at you right now, I don't even want to know the last image of you he had in his head." Lucca leaned in an inch closer. "So, I think the least you could fucking do is let him see you."

I didn't know. Elle shook her head no. "For three and a half years, I was hit around. He didn't save me. For three and a half years, seeing me every day, he didn't want me. The only reason he talked to me was because your father murdered someone, and he sicced him on me. I had been going crazy, wondering when someone would come and kill me, and Nero was right there the entire time, deciding whether I lived or died. So, fucking excuse me if I don't want to see him." Elle held onto his eyes, no matter how hard it was.

Lucca's mouth turned into a smile. "I knew I liked you." Lucca backed away from her but didn't remove his hand. "You weren't going to ever die in the first place. I wasn't going to let my father touch you, and deep down, he wasn't ever going to touch you anyway."

You? "What?"

"The moment I saw you, I knew he would fall in love with you. Do you know why?"

Elle slowly shook her head.

"You remind him of our mother. You remind us all of her. You have her blonde hair, except yours has some pink in it. You have the big, curious eyes. You're smart, and most of all, you're strong. Our mother could handle the fact that she was married to the mafia, not to mention the head of the family. It takes a lot of fucking guts to deal with a made man, and you can handle it, no matter how high up the ladder Nero goes."

"It doesn't mat—"

Lucca shut her up with one look. "Nero took her death the hardest. He blamed himself—still blames himself. It was as if he fucking shot her himself. Then you come along and it happens all over again. He blames himself for every person who ever hurt you. He blames himself right now that you're here in the hospital. And ever since you walked out on him, he acts like he fucking killed you. Do you want Nero to take on something like that all over again? If you don't get over the fact that Nero didn't know how to tell you the guy you witnessed being killed was murdered by his fucking family, then you leave him just like Mom did."

Elle turned away from Lucca, not able to look at him anymore. What he had told her made her feel incredibly small.

Lucca grabbed her chin to make her look at him again. "Nero better see you by tomorrow night. Don't make me fucking come to you in the middle of the night again. Do you understand?"

Elle gently nodded. "Yes."

Lucca dropped his hand from her chin. "Good."

Elle knew he was about to leave, so she quickly spoke the words before the sane part of her thought against it. "Chloe told me she talked to you."

She swore she saw a hint of emotion when she'd said her name. Not even when he'd spoken of Nero or his mother had he shown an ounce of emotion, regardless that he had come here for Nero.

"So?"

She could hear the slight change in his voice, as well. *I don't think so.*

"So, stay away from her." Elle could fight anyone off for Chloe, even the boogieman in her fucking bed right now.

Lucca leaned back toward Elle, again right in her face. "Do you know who you're talking to right now, darlin'? I have killed men and women after torturing them for hours. I am the underboss of the Caruso family, and one day, I will own this city."

Elle kept her hold, no matter how bad her skin crawled. "I-I don't care who you are. Leave her alone." *The last thing she needs is a man like him.*

Lucca smiled. "I know you've protected her, and that you couldn't leave her to fend for herself at school. Tell me what really happened to her that made you risk your life every day just so no one would touch her."

I will never tell. This time, Elle moved her face closer to his. "If you hurt her, I will kill *you.*"

Lucca quickly grabbed her face and rubbed her jaw. "You're lucky I owe you." He dropped his hand just as quickly and stood. "Remember, darlin', you have till tomorrow night."

Elle watched him disappear into the shadows before her eyes— well, eye. His ice-cold voice ran through her head, '*I owe you.*' Elle's body shivered; as a result, she lay back down and pulled the cover up to her head. *For what?*

The next day, Elle had a full day. They had moved her out of ICU to a room on the fourth floor where it was much quieter, and the room was a thousand times bigger. They'd said she was looking good. She was eating well, walking well, talking well, and going to the bathroom on her own. She was still sore, but that was to be expected. The doctors told her they wanted her to stay one more night, and then she would be free to go.

Now that she was out of ICU, everyone could finally visit her freely. She had immediately told her father to tell Nero she still didn't want to see him, and to her surprise, he'd respected her wishes.

Everyone had come to visit her; Chloe, Amo, Vincent, Leo, and even Maria along with her own family. She officially had a stockpile of flowers and cards, and in return, Elle had apologized to the ones she hadn't talked to in months for disowning them because of Nero. *Even though they helped conceal the truth.*

When it had started to get dark, she told her family to go on home and she just wanted some rest like the night before. Elle couldn't rest, though; she simply sat in bed, staring at the blank TV screen.

Elle heard a quick knock on the door and the nurse came in.

"Just making my rounds for the night before I head out. How are you doing?" She walked over to check the readings on the machines.

Elle gave her a half-smile. "I'm fine, thank you."

"All right, honey. Is there anything I can get you?"

Elle looked out her window, seeing the just-now-darkened sky. She took a deep breath. "Is he still out there?"

The nurse smiled at her. "You mean the one who's been out

there all day, real handsome?" She patted her hand. "He is."

Elle swallowed, her throat suddenly dry. "Can you tell him...?" She trailed off.

The nurse gave a squeeze to her hand. "I'll get him for you."

Elle continued to stare out the window as the minutes passed. She could barely hear the door open and the footsteps coming to her bed.

"Elle, will you look at me?"

She couldn't remember the last time she had heard his voice, the last time he had spoken her name. His voice still sang to her and stilled her soul, even after all that time.

Elle slowly turned her head so he could look at her. She heard his soft gasp then his small, contained growl. Then she did something she had trained herself not to do. For the first time in months, Elle gradually lifted her eyes to look at him. Even though she could only see well out of one eye, she noticed Nero's changes.

His hair was long, his face scruffy, and dark circles under his eyes conveyed there was no telling the last time he had slept. She had never seen Nero any less than immaculate, yet right now, he looked as if he was wearing the same clothes he had worn when she had gotten here.

Elle suddenly didn't feel good after seeing what Nero looked like. *I did that to him.* She now understood why Lucca had come to see her.

She watched Nero sit on the edge of her bed and she scooted over, afraid to touch him.

Nero sighed. "Elle, I'm—"

Elle quickly stopped him, speaking over top of him. "Why

don't you go home and get some rest? I'm being discharged in the morning. We can talk after we've both been home and had the chance to clean up."

Nero shook his head. "I'm not leaving you."

"Mr. Evans let me read your essay," Elle whispered abruptly.

Nero didn't respond.

"Please, go home and get some rest, then I promise we'll talk." Elle looked into his pain-filled eyes. "For me, Nero."

Nero pushed back his long hair only for it to go back where it had been. "Okay." Nero stood back up and looked at her damage. "Do you know who did it?" His voice had gone deadly.

Lie. "No, I don't remember anything."

Nero flexed his jaw. "All right. I'll see you tomorrow."

"Bye," she quietly said as he walked out of the room.

Elle laid her head back on the bed, thankful she didn't have to look at Nero any longer. She hated herself right now for how he looked. It was too painful for her to see the toll she had put on him. Elle knew she didn't look so hot right now, but that was different. She could always deal with seeing herself hurt, but seeing someone else hurt and knowing she'd caused it was too much for her. Especially someone she…

Elle shook her head, realizing she had lied to him, even after she had gotten mad at Nero for all his lies. The truth was, she had remembered what happened, but Elle didn't want Nero to know, too afraid he'd kill her.

It was Cassandra.

ROLL OUT THE
GOLDEN CARPET

"**J**ust *sign here, and then* you're free to go."

Elle signed the paper on the dotted line. *Where are my parents?* She looked at her nurse, holding a bag. "M-my ride's not here yet."

"Yes it is, honey. He's waiting out front. Now, let's get you dressed."

Elle figured her mother hadn't wanted to leave Dad alone long in the car, so she slowly got up and the nurse helped her change into a pair of her sweats and a t-shirt from home. Elle sat down in the waiting wheelchair. *Ugh, I can finally go home.* Needless to say, Elle was sick of hospital food, the constant monitoring, and the horribly-uncomfortable beds.

The nurse walked her down the hallway, into the elevator, and to the sliding doors. When the doors opened, Elle was greeted with a black Cadillac and dark-tinted windows. A brand-new Nero was there, leaning up against his car. *Nero?*

Nero opened the passenger's door.

Elle wanted to say something to the nurse. She looked around. *Crap, but then who would take me home?* The nurse parked the wheelchair; however, Elle didn't go to stand, still in awe of how in the world she was in the situation.

When the nurse didn't go to move her because Nero was there, Elle had no choice other than to stand. She shakily stood up and felt Nero's arms go around her waist. She looked up at him, wanting to protest, but that only made her body melt more into his. She saw the flash of need fill his eyes at the instant touch. Elle's body remembered the night she and Nero shared, which felt like years ago. She wished she had never experienced the true pleasure because, if you never experienced it, then you never knew what you were missing.

Nero sat her down in the car, and she felt him linger on letting her go. He even buckled her seat belt, and all Elle could do was stare inches away from his refreshed face.

Nero had gotten his hair cut back to the shorter length she loved on him. He had even shaven his face, revealing his perfectly-tan skin and square jaw. His eyes were still slightly dark under them, but she figured one night of sleep wasn't going to remedy them immediately. The scent of clean, fresh, hot male enveloped her, and it smelled just like she remembered. His clothes were also perfectly new and crisp.

When Nero finally shut her door and went around the car, she slammed her eyes shut. *Dammit, dammit, dammit!* She tried to think about anything except his face and scent as she held her legs tightly closed.

Nero slid in the car and put the car in drive, pulling out.

"Why were you the one to pick me up?" Elle finally asked.

Nero shrugged. "Because I went over to your parents' house to get you some things and told them I would."

Elle's mouth dropped open. *My parents' house!* "What the hell? You pay for my medical bills and they roll out the golden carpet!"

Nero smiled, flashing his teeth at her.

Elle crossed her arms. "Nero, you can't just pay for my lunch, school, and hospital bills to fix what happened between us. I don't care about how much money you have!"

Nero gripped the steering wheel. "I know you don't give a shit about how much money I have. Besides, I didn't pay for everything to make up for what I did, Elle. I did it to make your life easier, and what do you do? You fucking go pick up even more hours than you started school out with."

Elle darted her face to look at him. "How did you know that?"

"Do you really think I would let you go to work alone after what happened to you?"

"You've been following me this entire time?" Elle whispered.

"Every fucking day," Nero gritted out.

Oh, my God. Elle blinked, remaining in shock at Nero's actions. If Elle hadn't been such a zombie these past few months, she would have noticed and maybe...

Elle watched Nero drive past the road to go to her house. "You missed the turn."

"No, I didn't," Nero said matter-of-factly.

"Well, then where are we going?" Elle didn't understand. She wasn't in good shape to go anywhere.

"Home."

What is he thinking? "Nero, I'm not going anywhere with you. Especially not your house where you fucked countless girls only to fuck me right there, too. And there's no telling the girls you've fucked these past few months."

Nero flexed his jaw and gripped the steering wheel without saying a word.

Elle felt bad as soon as she said it, even if it was the truth. She could feel his anger beside her, his pain. She closed her eyes and rested her head on the door, wishing her off switch would come back. She also wished her heart hadn't been stolen from her. Elle suffered from a big wound right in her chest, and no matter how sore her body was, none of it hurt as much as that.

When Nero didn't go in the direction of his house, Elle asked him over and over where he was going, but he never said a word. Elle really began to worry when Nero parked out front of the Kansas City Casino Hotel, right next to her work. That was where Nero's family had come from when they'd killed the man.

She watched Nero walk to her door and open it. Elle didn't want to go in, but Nero leaned over, swooped her out of the car and slowly put her to her feet.

"N-Nero, why are we here?" Elle tried to get out.

Nero grabbed her around her waist to hold her up. "It's okay, Elle. You know I'm not going to hurt you."

Elle took a deep breath and put her weight into Nero, letting him walk her inside. When he opened the door, her head felt like it was going to explode from all the noise of the machines and the change swishing around. She had to close her eyes and let Nero guide her. Nero walked her to an escalator and held her to him to steady her. She couldn't take the pain anymore; therefore, she put her head into Nero's chest, wanting it to go away.

Nero leaned down to whisper in her ear, "I'm sorry, baby. I should have brought you in the back."

At the top, Nero quickly swept her off the escalator. Up here, it wasn't so loud, and she was able to open her eyes. She saw a security guard wave Nero past the crowd, and then they headed toward some elevators. Nero led her onto an elevator and went to press a button when a crowd of people joined on. He pulled her toward him again.

Elle put her face back in Nero's chest, not wanting to see the looks people were giving her. She thought the elevator ride was the longest one of her life as it kept stopping and starting, making her sick.

She felt one of Nero's hands leave her for a moment before it returned and started soothing her.

This time, when the elevator went up, it didn't stop for quite a bit. When she heard the elevator door open, Nero moved for her to walk again. That's when Elle noticed the button lit, indicating they were on the top floor.

Nero took a right and led her down a long hallway until he

reached the last door on the left. He pulled out a key and slid it through the slot like a credit card before opening the door.

Elle walked through the door Nero held open for her and her mouth dropped open. It was a loft. The downstairs had a big, flat-screen TV, a leather sofa, and a huge kitchen and dining room all connected. Everything was black and white, and everything was brand new and modern. Elle still couldn't pick her mouth off the floor when she saw the view. It was a corner suite with floor-to-ceiling views.

Nero took her hand and led her up the steps where she saw a huge black and white bed low to the floor. The windows had carried up behind the bed, making the city the backdrop.

"Where are we?" She was in complete awe, never having seen anything like this even in a magazine.

Nero couldn't take his eyes off Elle's amazed face. "Home."

Elle, shocked, turned to look at him. "You live here now? How?"

"My father owns the hotel, and he's been saving this room for me since I could remember. I got to design it a few months ago, and it was just finished last week. Do you like it?"

"Yes, it's beautiful." Elle looked down at the black, hardwood floors. "Was he waiting to give it to you when you joined the family business?"

Nero sighed and walked toward her. Taking her hand again, he brought her to a door and opened it.

Elle saw a huge, walk-in closet just as big as Maria's—*wait.*

"Are those my clothes?"

Nero took Elle's chin in his hand. "Yes. I've been telling you this is your home now."

What in the hell? "Did my parents approve of this? How in the world did they agree to this?"

"I told them you needed to be monitored, and I could provide that. I have a doctor on call who will check on you. Baby, you hit your head pretty hard this time. You clearly just had a headache, and if they get worse, that's not good."

Elle moved away from Nero, all of this too much, too fast for her to handle. She felt a little betrayed by her parents and by Nero for not even asking her if that was what she wanted. *He's acting like I don't* have *a choice.*

"I need to take a shower." *Then I'm calling someone and I'm leaving.* Elle would leave now if she didn't feel so gross. She still felt the hospital all over her.

Nero nodded his head. "The bathroom is over there." He pointed to the only other door up here.

Elle looked through the closet rack, trying to find something comfortable for her to wear; *nothing.* She noticed some of her clothes were not here, mostly just the ratty ones. Elle decided to look through the drawers of a big chest in the closet and saw a bunch of lingerie with tags still on them. *What the fuck?*

She looked at the sizes and saw they were all correct for her. *You have got to be shitting me.*

Elle went through the rest of the drawers, hoping she would find something comfortable to wear, but the only thing comfortable-looking were Nero's t-shirts. *Fuck!*

Elle went back to the rack and snatched down a pair of jeans and a sweater. Before she left the closet, she saw a white dress hanging up. When she realized what dress it was, she wanted to stomp on it.

Elle came out of the closet with just her sweater and jeans. When she saw Nero sitting on the bed smiling, she stomped off into the bathroom where she slammed the door shut.

Fuck you!

WASH ME

Elle rested her head on the bathroom door, trying not to cry. She was feeling far too overwhelmed; just days ago, she had felt nothing, and now she could feel everything again. All these different emotions were hitting her full-force from reading Nero's letter, being in the hospital, and then talking to Nero again.

Elle's tears started to flow as she silently cried in the bathroom. When she turned around, the bathroom was just as gorgeous and modern as the rest of the apartment. It was floor-to-ceiling black and white tile, a huge walk-in shower, double sinks, and a bathtub that looked like a huge bowl.

She tried to muffle her tears as she began attempting to pull her shirt off. A moment later, she felt Nero's hands at her shirt.

"Get out!" she yelled at him through her crying.

"Let me help you, baby," he murmured to her as he pulled the shirt over her head.

Elle quickly covered her exposed breasts and began to shake. "P-Please g-go." *Please, please, please.* Elle knew she wasn't strong enough to fight him.

Nero saw the huge blue and black marks on her stomach. "No." His hands returned to her body and pulled down her sweatpants and panties. "I am not fucking leaving you again."

It was too hard for Elle to stifle her crying anymore, so she merely let it out. "You hurt me, Nero."

He pulled her to his body. "I know I did, and I'm sorry. I am so fucking sorry, Elle, for everything. I'm sorry I didn't notice you for all those years, and that I didn't say anything when they picked on you. I should have told you about my family, no matter how afraid I was to lose you, because I lost you anyway." Nero made Elle look up at him. "I shouldn't have let you go and left you alone for all those months, and I'm sorry I wasn't there to protect you."

Elle blinked back her new tears. "I'm sorry I didn't see you hurt—"

"Shh, baby. You have nothing to be sorry for." Nero wiped the tears off her face and then took her towards the shower. He quickly turned it on and checked the temperature before he led Elle to walk in.

Elle continued to hold her body while standing still under the water as she watched Nero pull off his clothes. *I knew I wasn't going to be able to fight him off.* Truthfully, she didn't want to anymore. She needed Nero because without him, she was nothing.

Elle backed up as Nero entered the shower, standing there as he took a loofa hanging from the wall and poured some soap on it. She grew nervous when he pulled her towards him to stand in front of her. He pushed at her hands to make her drop them from her body before he touched the soapy loofa to her skin and began washing.

Elle's breath caught in her throat as Nero rubbed the loofa over her breasts. Then, when he lightly swiped down her abdomen, Elle's stomach clenched as he ventured lower.

"Open," Nero commanded.

Elle quickly spread her legs at Nero's harsh word and got the pleasurable feeling back from doing as he asked. When the loofa went between her legs, Elle bit her bottom lip to avoid moaning. It had been a long time since she had been touched there, and she'd felt more of Nero's hand than the loofa.

After what seemed like an eternity to her, Nero turned her around and washed her back. Elle saw the shampoo and grabbed it so she could wash her hair; it was the same shampoo at her house that she'd used for years, the kind with the berry scent. Elle smiled as she poured some on her hand and started rubbing it into her hair. *He thought of everything.*

Nero put Elle under the water and began rinsing her off, massaging his hands into her scalp. Elle thought she was going to draw blood from her lip by the time this was over, but before she knew it, she was all rinsed off.

Nero grabbed another loofa, pouring on some soap before handing it to her. "Wash me."

Elle slowly took the loofa out of his hands and touched it to his chest. She began making circle movements over his body. She went from his chest down his arms and back to his chest, going lower to his abdomen.

Elle bit her lip again as she saw how hard his dick was. She ran the loofa down over his cock and balls and heard the deep groan out of Nero. She looked up at him, seeing the pain he was in. She had known he had to be in pain just by looking at how hard he was, though.

Elle went to run the loofa over his cock again except this time, her hand wrapped around his length.

Nero swiftly grabbed her wrist and kept her hand from moving. "Don't. You're still sore, and I'm on the verge of fucking you already."

Elle looked back up at him curiously. "Is that why you haven't kissed me yet?"

"Yes," Nero gritted out.

The feeling of butterflies returned after being missing for months. Elle leaned forward and kissed Nero's chest.

"Kiss me." Elle looked up at him, and he planted his mouth on hers.

Elle hungrily kissed him back and squeezed her hand that was still over Nero's cock, making him drop his hand. She took the opportunity and slid her hand down his length. She saw his eyes change to the wolf she remembered before watching him quickly leave the shower.

Elle frowned. She didn't want him to leave her, but he was back before she could protest, seeing he had left to get a condom out of the bathroom drawer. When she looked at his face, she again saw his torment.

Nero pushed her up against the back shower wall with his body but stopped himself before he touched her.

"Baby, I don't want to hurt you." His hunger and conscience were fighting against each other.

Elle didn't care how sore her body felt, or how badly Nero could hurt her by how hungry he must have been.

She leaned towards his chest and said, "I trust you," before her tongue licked over his nipple.

In one quick motion, Nero had her legs wrapped around him and her back up against the wall, causing Elle to gasp and grab onto his shoulders. She could feel him press against her entrance, making the shower water not the only thing that slickened her flesh.

Nero took deep breaths, trying to calm his shaking. "Did I hurt you?"

Elle shook her head, staring into his emerald gaze.

"You're the only girl I have looked at these past few months and imagined my dick sliding into. I haven't fucked since the night I fucked you, Elle, and you're the last one I will ever fuck. Tonight will be the first night anyone has slept in that bed and in this place. I couldn't sleep here until you were in the bed beside me where you fucking belong."

Holding her with one arm around her waist, he slowly slid her down onto his dick. Elle's head fell forward onto his shoulder as a whimper escaped her throat. Then Nero began to pump high inside her slick pussy.

"Everything I wrote in that paper was true." Nero's hips quickly thrust back and forth, faster and faster, driving him in deeper and deeper.

Elle's heart started to return to her at Nero's words and actions. The first time they had been together, Nero had been tender and sweet. Now, Elle felt like she was stuck in the middle between pleasure and pain because Nero was fucking her hard, rough, and fast all at the same time while holding her gently against the wall. She knew he was doing twice the work by not letting her move her hips, afraid she would get hurt.

She could feel the water beating down his back and on her legs and arms, making it all the more erotic. Elle knew she wasn't going to be able to last long, the build in her pussy growing strong from Nero fucking her so fast. She dug her nails deep down into his flesh as her legs squeezed him tighter to her.

Nero took his hand off her ass and grabbed her face to look at him. "I love you, baby. I fucking love you more than anything."

Elle started shuddering and crying out as Nero somehow drove into her harder. Her body began to convulse as the climax rocketed through her. She clung to him as he reached his own peak, bringing a few more short bursts to her body.

"I love you, too," Elle whispered as she went through the aftershocks. Her heart had fully returned.

Nero claimed Elle's lips, driving his tongue deep into her mouth, tasting her sweetness once more. He pulled his cock out from inside of her but held her to him as he turned the water off and got out of the shower. Then he placed Elle against the sink.

Elle braced herself, unable to stop from shaking. She didn't know if it was the after effects from the fucking or from being cold from the shower. Elle shivered again. *Both.*

She watched him pull off his condom then throw it in the trashcan before he grabbed a towel. After Nero quickly dried Elle off before himself, he lifted her back into his arms and carried her to the bedroom where he lowered her down onto the bed.

Elle expected him to lie down with her, but instead, he went to the nightstand and pulled out the small, black box wrapped in the pink silk ribbon she had left behind months ago.

Nero lay down on the bed, grabbing Elle to lie beside him. He pulled the covers around them both and snugly wrapped Elle. Then he handed her the box for the second time.

Elle just stared at it. "You kept it?"

"Of course I did. Open it."

She pulled the silk ribbon and it fluttered away. She then opened the box, revealing a rose gold chain and strawberry charm. "Nero, it's beautiful."

He took the box from her then pulled out the necklace. "I had planned to give it to you that night and tell you I loved you. That was the last gift I wanted you to get on your birthday."

Elle's heart ached for all the time they had lost together and the months they had been miserable. She sat up so Nero could finally put the necklace on her. Then Elle touched the necklace that hung from her neck and turned around to kiss Nero hard on the lips. "Thank you."

Nero lay back down and held Elle to his chest. "I love you, Elle."

Elle smiled against his chest. "I love you, too, Nero."

Elle had dreamed about lying next to Nero. She had missed the feeling of him naked and beside her. When his hand started soothing her back, she melted into him, her lashes falling to rest on her cheeks. Nero turned out the light and kissed her on top of her head.

"Get some rest, baby."

For the first time in what felt like forever, Elle fell fast asleep, without tears.

Elle started to wake when she felt the covers removed from her body. The air whipped at her skin, making her curl into a ball. She suddenly felt fingers circle her ankle and Elle opened her eyes.

She was disoriented at first, looking at the night city through huge windows. *Where am I?*

She was then slowly pulled down the bed, and Elle fully woke. Scared, she looked to see who had her and found Nero on his knees on the floor at the foot of the bed. Looking at his dark face, her mind came back and she remembered where she was and what had happened, bringing a smile to her lips.

"Nero, what are you doing?" she asked sleepily.

Nero pulled her all the way to the end, making the bottom of her legs fall off the bed.

She now knew why Nero made everything black and white in the apartment. The city lights came in through the windows, giving the room plenty of color. The colors danced off his face, and now that she was closer, she saw he had a look in his eyes that somewhat excited her and scared her shitless at the same time. She quit breathing when Nero rose a little higher and bent his head down.

Nero started placing tender kisses over her belly, kissing every inch of her bruised stomach. "Baby, tell me who it was."

Elle looked down into Nero's eyes, now understanding the scary look. Her stomach lurched at what Nero might do to Cassandra. *Might? No, for sure.*

Elle shook her head. "I don't know."

Wrong answer. She saw the something terrifying flash in his eyes.

Nero shot out, grabbed Elle's legs and brought her closer to him. He spread her legs farther apart then his face disappeared between her thighs.

Elle threw her head back as Nero's tongue ran along her slit. She gasped when his tongue finally dipped inside and he laved at the tiny bud. She felt his hand travel up to her breast and squeeze it, making it become tender. He pinched her nipple as he plunged inside her opening with his tongue. Elle reached for his head, taking his hair in her hands.

Nero used his free hand and started rubbing her clit with his thumb while he began fucking her with his tongue.

Elle groaned and gripped him to her tighter when Nero pinched her clit. She lifted her hips off the bed and started panting, ready to come.

"Do you want to come?" Nero asked her through his fucking.

"Yes! Yes!" Elle screamed.

His voice turned dark. "Then tell me who it was."

Elle shook her head angrily. "I don't know!"

Nero moved his tongue over her clit as he slid his fingers deep inside her. His fingers started pumping in and out of her slick pussy.

Elle was more than ready to come, but Nero wouldn't hit the spot to throw her over the edge.

"Nero, please," she whimpered.

Nero bit her clit between his teeth and twisted her nipple. "Tell me," he ordered angrily.

"I told you! I don't know!" Elle wailed. She tried to move her hips so she could get him to reach the spot she desperately needed.

Nero threw her legs over his shoulder and sucked her clit into his mouth. He surged deep, in and out of her pussy, with his fingers.

Elle was on the verge of tears. Nero would bring her right to the edge, only to take a step back. Then he would do it all over again. She moved her head from side to side, begging him to let her come. However, each time she told him 'I don't know,' he only brought her closer to the edge, not giving her release. She lost count of how many times he had done it to her and had no idea how long it had gone on.

Elle tried to move away, unable to take the torture any longer, but Nero held her still.

"Nero, please stop. Please." Elle started to cry.

"Who. Fucking. Did. It?" Nero ground out.

I can't do it. "I don't know, Nero," she cried. "I don't know."

Nero growled and drove his fingers hard into her wet pussy. Elle screamed louder than she ever had when Nero finally hit the spot that had been in agony from the torture. She was finally able to reach her climax, and this time, when she experienced it, she was knocked senseless from the rocketing that overtook her body.

"Why couldn't you fucking tell me, Elle? I know you're lying to me!" he screamed at her as he rose to his feet.

Elle looked up at him through her wet eyes and started shaking. *I can't.*

Nero took a deep breath and buttoned up his shirt. "I know it was Cassandra, Elle."

Elle's eyes widened. *He knew? How?*

"Chloe told me. She was who told me about everyone who had ever touched you. I found the fucking picture of you almost beaten to death behind the other picture in your photo album." Nero buttoned the last button with his shaking hands.

What? Chloe? Elle saw Nero turn to go down the steps. *No!*

Elle jumped off the bed and stood in front of Nero, hanging her head down. "I-I'm sorry. Don't go."

Nero stared at her before he moved to pass her, but Elle reached out and quickly wrapped her arms around Nero's waist.

"D-Don't go. P-p-please, Nero."

As Nero grabbed Elle's arms and tried to pull her off him, Elle gripped him tighter.

He will kill her. "No, I'll do anything. I won't lie to you again. I promise."

"Elle, she has to hurt for what she did." His voice was like ice.

"Please!" Elle moved down his body and went to her knees. She went for his pants and started unbuttoning them with her trembling hands. When his cock flung out, Elle leaned in.

"No!" Nero stopped Elle's head from coming any closer, groaning as she looked up at him through her wet lashes.

"Please, don't kill her," Elle cried, gripping his legs. "Don't leave me, Nero."

Nero pulled Elle's death grip from his body. "Stay here. Don't think about leaving. You can't; there's a guard by the elevator." Then he dropped his hands from her and zipped himself back in.

Elle's head fell to the floor. She softly cried, not able to breathe as Nero walked away from her.

Please, God, please.

THE REAL NERO

Nero was sitting in a chair in a pitch-black room, thinking about the way Elle felt. It had been so long since he had touched her, held her, kissed her. *Never again.* Nero wasn't ever going to let that separation happen again.

He didn't like what he had done to Elle, but the fact was she never told him anything, and he was determined she wasn't going to keep things from him anymore.

She will learn. Nero was going to teach her how things were going to be different now. Nero was now a family man, and he was a rough lover, but he knew he would have a lifetime to coach her.

He heard the rustling of keys, watching the door open through the shadows. Then the light flipped on the next instant.

Cassandra stood still when she saw Nero sitting in her living room on the chair that faced the door. "H-how did—"

Nero smiled. "I walked through the front door."

"M-mom! Dad!" Cassandra screamed, unmoving.

Nero laughed as she screamed. "They're not here."

Cassandra's eyes started to water. "What did you do with them?"

Nero shrugged. "Nothing. They just had a little emergency at the hospital with Sebastian." He was telling the truth. Sebastian was still recovering, trying to walk again and healing his third-degree burns. Nero hadn't seen Sebastian in a while, and he had decided to check on his progress. *He just might have taken a few steps back.*

"What d-did you do to him?" A tear fell down her cheek.

Good.

Nero stood from the chair and walked towards her. "Nothing more than what you did to Elle."

Cassandra still didn't move as Nero stood right in front of her.

"Don't hurt—" She started to cry.

Nero grabbed Cassandra, turned her around, and shoved her up against the wall. He heard her nose break. "You should have fucking thought of that before you beat the shit out of Elle." As he let Cassandra go, she fell to the floor, bawling.

Nero held up his hands and made a fist. "Now, Elle gets upset when she sees my hands are hurt, and we can't have that. She also begged me for me not to kill you, which I will never fucking understand. So, I think it's only fair if you hurt the way Elle was hurt."

"You can come out now." Nero walked back to the chair.

I'm about to enjoy *the fucking show.*

Cassandra's face lifted and turned towards the clicking of heels.

She watched a tall blonde appear, wearing a light-pink, airy dress. Her eyes fell to the expensive, tall, nude pumps.

She stared up at her when she reached her.

The blonde sweetly smiled. "Hello, I'm Maria."

Cassandra began to crawl away on her hands and knees.

Maria snickered and put her heel over Cassandra's hand. "Honey, there's nowhere for you to hide."

Nero laughed as he heard the high-pitched scream come from Cassandra. He watched the best show of his fucking life play before his eyes. He had known Maria would show no mercy, and the begging and pleading was what he lived for.

When he watched Maria smooth down her hair and dress, he stood to join her.

Maria looked down at her once-gorgeous pumps. "You owe me a new pair of Christian Louboutin's."

Nero laughed. "Best money I'll ever spend."

Maria kissed Nero's cheek. "I'll send you the link." Then she left the house with the click of her heels.

Nero returned his eyes to the mess on the floor. *She was good.*

Maria had given Cassandra a whole makeover, right down to a nice haircut.

Nero leaned down beside Cassandra to make sure she heard him well. "So, you know the drill, right?" He waited for her to answer, but she wasn't able to. "Oh, that's okay; I'll remind you. My father owns your father, and I'd hate to see you poor and cold out on the street. Let's face it, babe; you can get plastic surgery to fix that face of yours and your popped implant, but we know you're not the working type." Nero grabbed and pulled hard on the little bit of hair left on her head. "I'll kill you and every motherfucker with the last name Ross in this fucking city if you come near Elle again."

Nero stood to his feet and headed for the door. "Go get yourself cleaned up, babe. Mommy and Daddy should be here any minute."

Elle was in a tight ball under the covers. She couldn't sleep. Nero had been gone for hours. She hadn't even moved when she crawled back in bed after Nero had left her.

She practically jumped out of bed when she heard the door downstairs open. When the light footsteps reached the stairs, Elle grew nervous and started breathing heavily from her heart racing. She didn't even move when she felt his presence standing at the foot of the bed.

"I know you're awake," his dark voice spoke.

Elle swallowed as she sat up in the bed and held the covers around her breasts. She stared up at him, and for the first time, she believed she saw Nero for who he really was. *A made man.*

Nero held Elle's eyes, making her see. "I will fight. I will torture. And I will kill in my line of work. I knew I would join the mob ever since I could remember, and you have to accept that because I am not giving you an option. It's a part of me, just how you're a part of me, but nothing—nothing—will ever come before you.

"No one will ever fucking touch what's mine and not pay for it. That's why she had to be dealt with." Nero raised his hand when Elle looked like she was about to cry again. "I did not fucking kill her, but I promise you she wishes she was dead. However, I am *not* going to find you lying on the bathroom floor again, so the next person will not be so lucky. If anyone ever lays a hand on you, I will fucking kill them, and no amount of begging or crying will stop me. If you pull that shit again, I will torture the fucker twice as long. Do you understand me?"

Elle's body tingled as he spoke. She wanted to be afraid, but instead, her body grew taut at every word. Elle slowly nodded her head, staring into his emerald eyes.

"Come here," Nero's deep voice commanded her.

Elle leaned forward, going to her hands. She knew this was what he'd wanted, what he had been waiting for by the expression on his face. She didn't pull her eyes away as she crawled towards him, taking her time in order to savor the enjoyment on his face.

Elle stared up at the real Nero through her lashes as she sat before him on her knees. She understood why Nero had a bed so low, and knowing she was about to enjoy this as much as he was, her knees would thank him every day. *Maybe more.* Elle squeezed her thighs together in anticipation, her hands wanting desperately to go to his pants.

Elle gasped when Nero reached out and held her chin firmly. "What do you want?"

Elle licked her lips. "Can I suck your dick?"

Nero gripped her chin tighter. "Are you ever going to lie to me again?"

"No," Elle answered right away.

"No, what?"

"No, I will never lie to you again. I promise." Elle's eyes showed him she was telling him the truth.

Nero dropped his hand from her chin. "Good. Now, tell me what you want."

Elle wiggled closer to him. "Please, may I suck your dick?" she begged.

"Yes, baby," Nero groaned.

Elle quickly reached for his pants and unbuttoned them with shaky hands. His cock flung out faster this time, being a lot harder. Elle's hand quickly covered his thickness, and she wrapped her mouth around his head. She teased his tip with her tongue before looking up at his tortured face. She sucked him deep into her mouth and slid it back out. When Nero grabbed her hair, she obeyed his unspoken command, sucking on him harder as her hands went to play with his balls.

"Deeper," Nero gritted out as he pushed her down farther.

Elle quickly learned how Nero wanted to be sucked. She took him deep into her mouth and let his tip slide into the back of her throat. A deep noise escaped from Nero's throat, and Elle sucked him farther back as she squeezed his balls. Over and over, Elle devoured him until Nero held her head still as he came, making Elle take everything he had as he jerked in her mouth.

"Fuck, baby. I knew you would be good, but damn."

Elle smiled up at him, pleased with herself.

Nero went to the bed and grabbed Elle for a hard kiss. He then flipped her over, back on her hands and knees and pushed her ass high into the air.

"This is the last box of condoms I will buy. The doctor will come to see you to get on the pill tomorrow." Nero went to his nightstand and slid on a condom.

Elle bit her lip when his dick ran along her entrance. She pushed her ass back at him.

"Oh fuck yes," she moaned. "Please."

In one swift movement, Nero went deep inside her, fucking her somehow harder and faster than he had earlier as he gripped her hips. Elle screamed and pushed back at him, glad Nero let her join in.

She didn't last long; the sound and feeling of his balls slapping against her sent her over the edge. Nero held her up to reach his own climax and Elle lay limp in his arms, feeling his jolts deep inside her.

It took a few minutes before Nero could recover. When he did, he went back to the head of the bed then pulled Elle into him. His hand started soothing her back, just like he always did, before he spoke.

"You stayed at Legacy Prep because of Chloe, didn't you?"

"Yes." Elle knew she'd never told Nero much of anything the month they were together, but she wasn't going to be able to keep everything from Nero from now on. *I will keep secrets that aren't mine to tell, though.*

"Why? She was originally with them when they did those things to you."

Elle took a deep breath. "The day I came back to school, after I was beaten, was the day Chloe returned back to school with her scars. I thought I looked bad, but Chloe... I could tell she was traumatized. I knew she went through something much worse than what I did. I heard them calling her 'freak', and I just lost it."

Nero's fingers continued the motion. "What happened to her?"

I can't tell you. Elle didn't say anything.

"She wasn't in a car wreck, was she?" Nero tried again.

Elle could at least answer that for him. "No, she wasn't."

HAPPILY EVER AFTER

Elle and Nero had returned to school for the last week, and it was the best week of her life. Nero made her quit the diner and put in an application to the local University for her. He assured her that, even though it was late, there was no way they wouldn't accept her with her 4.0 GPA. He also told her if it took more than two days to do so, he would make a trip down to the admission office. She was now one day away from graduating, and Nero had somehow managed to talk her and Chloe into walking across the stage to take their diplomas.

Elle pinched herself every day, wondering if it was all real. Her last first day of school had ended up being the worst day of her life. *Or so I thought.* She now realized it had turned out to be the best day in her existence because, if she had never witnessed the murder, then Nero would have never been forced to talk to her in the first place. *I would have never gotten my happily ever after.*

Brring.

For the first time ever, that was music to her ears. *I am free. Free at last.*

Nero and Elle smiled at each other as everyone ran out of the art room, screaming. Nero stood and took Elle's hand, helping her stand up.

"Where are we going?" Elle laughed as he started dragging her.

Nero led her towards the back of the room and opened the art supply closet before pushing her in. "It's the last time I'll get this chance, and I have been fantasizing about this ever since I brought you in here the first time."

Elle tried to stop Nero from closing the door. "Nero, we can't—"

Nero shoved her back against the door and planted his mouth on hers. She lost all sense as Nero thrust his tongue deep in her mouth. She opened wider for him and rose to her toes.

Nero began unbuttoning her red and white plaid shirt. He pulled it down her shoulders, making it drop to the floor. His eyes then fell down her body to her pink, lacey, push-up bra and blue jean shorts.

Elle's chest began to rise and fall heavily as she looked up at her hungry wolf's emerald gaze. *I fucking love him.*

Nero's gaze returned to her big, blue eyes. "Pick it up."

87245800R00222

Made in the USA
Lexington, KY
21 April 2018